The Forlorn Trail

Printed in the United States of America

First Printing, 2023

ISBN 979-8-9859095-2-4 *(paperback)*

ISBN 979-8-9859095-3-1 *(ebook)*

Auberdine Publishing

2519 S Shields Street

Suite 1K #612

Fort Collins, CO 80526

The Forlorn Trail

Jacob C. Sadler

Auberdine Publishing – Fort Collins, Colorado

Dedication

To Madelyn. You have always been so supportive of my manic creativity. Whether it is taking the dog out in the morning so that I have 30 more minutes of writing before work, or bringing me coffee on Saturday editing binges, I promise you the little things are noticed. And the big things, too.

You edit everything, no matter if it is just a sentence or the entire book. Without you, I imagine my writing would mostly be a compilation of bloopers. I am still so glad you caught that one doctor—with no hands—clapping.

To any aspiring authors, get yourself a significant other like the one I have. Because you may write great books, you may even sell a few—but you will be a failure without someone like her.

Chapter 1

"Belford was a frontier town at the farthest edge of the known West. Notable for being the birthplace of Jessie J. Bingham, renowned explorer and naturalist, the small town was mostly known for its cactus farms. Before the Flowers Affair, few people could even find the settlement on a map. Now, of course, every child in the country can tell you that Belford was the beginning of a grand adventure."

– The Ballad of Jessie Bingham, 3rd Edition.

Jessie's lips cracked as he walked down the dusty road. He passed a group of sun-kissed folk, all hiding behind wide-brimmed hats. He walked alongside adobe walls pocked by succulents. He smelled the produce at the market. The region's staple crops—cactus, pigweed, and tepary beans—made him sigh.

Going into Belford always reminded him of his wife. For that, he loved and hated the town. He stared down the thoroughfare, enchanted by ghostly nostalgia. The streets and stores had been the stage for so many stories. Now, Belford was like a cheap play Jessie could not stop attending. He looked at the saloon, Porfirio's house, and the market. He could set up the actors with his mind, put a young man with flowers by the working house, place a beautiful girl holding his hand... But they would never say any new lines. *That story is over.*

All he had left of his wife was a faint scent on her clothes, a wedding band hidden in his lockbox, and their children. Yet like the smell on her clothes and the color of her ring, the children were fading. He could not lose them, too. He would not.

Jessie entered Don Marcos' drugstore. His senses were assaulted by a mixture of unnatural smells and mercurial remedies. The doctor saw him enter and began processing the usual order.

While he did, Jessie looked out the window. People were dressed in their best clothes, all thinking soon they would be the sons, daughters, and wives of rich men. Everyone talked of gold now.

The doctor saw him staring and commented on the gossip, "Bout time we went past the Forlorn Hills."

"Past the Hills is savage country," Jessie responded. He mistrusted small talk from businessmen.

"Ain't no savages no more," Marcos claimed. "Tlacon done disappeared. Kuahtec, too. Army done struck a nerve, I'd a reckon." Like the rest of the town, he did not care to know the reason behind the sudden vanishing of two violent tribes. Like the 6th cavalry that had pursued the nomads across the plains, Marcos was more than content to forget the natives. Gold was better gossip, anyhow. Better for business.

Jessie, however, was not referring to those natives. The Tlacon were familiar enough now. They used the same trading posts. The Kuahtec practically taught his father how to farm, and Belford by extension. "I doubt the Lugal will take kindly to looters in their lands."

"The Lugal are a myth, Mr. Bingham. Besides, Collin Flowers ain't gone very far. He's just west-a-ways panning in a stream." He smiled wolfishly, "I reckon that'll be five dollars and forty-nine cents."

Jessie looked at the tiny tinctures and then at Don Marcos. He was not surprised he had raised the price again, but *that* was almost unpayable. "That's a full dollar higher than last month."

"Indeed." Doctor Marcos picked some pigweed out of his teeth and flicked it onto the floor. "But as the only qualified sawbones hereabouts, I'd wager my price remains competitive." A rotten grin flashed on his face.

"You're a doctor," Jessie asserted, as if the grimy swindler cared about the honor of the profession.

"I am a businessman," Marcos said without the slightest shame. "You want to be cheap?" He wiped his dirty hands on his apron; they remained filthy when he motioned at the door. "Try death. It's a free remedy for all ailments."

"My children," Jessie paused and pocketed his fists. "Will be your customers their entire lives."

Don shrugged. "Which may or may not be very long."

Jessie Bingham bit his lip and wrinkled his nose. His children could not afford to go without.

"Especially with a dallying daddy," Don stared at him.

Jessie formed an insult, chewed on it, and then spat it onto the floor. Five dollars and forty-nine cents flew onto the counter. Two dozen minuscule tinctures clanked in his coat pocket as he stormed out of the Donaciano's Drugstore. He stared down the main street for a moment, wiping his brow several times of a stubborn glare. Jessie breathed the morning air and jogged down the porch steps. He had more to do that day than nurse his pride.

Jessie drank from his waterskin, rationing every swig. He wiped his mouth and rubbed his eyes. When he reopened them, Sheriff Biggs was walking toward him. "Mister Bingham, if y'could spare a moment."

Jessie pivoted, "Bout all I *can* spare these days."

Crawford Biggs responded to Jessie's self-pity with a polite frown. The sheriff was the mayor's ideal instrument and was played often. Whenever he entered a room, fear of the mayor entered with him. Lately, he had developed his own, weighty reputation. The sheriff inquired, "See or hear anything abnormal on y'land these last few nights?"

Jessie shook his head, "Not at all."

Biggs glanced at the Forlorn Hills. "Hmm." He rubbed his chin with apprehension. "Your family is closest to the Hills..."

"This ain't related to why you hired another deputy, is it?"

The sheriff was a careful man. He said nothing.

Jessie forced small talk, hoping to glean more about the topic. "I hear the 6th cavalry is bored to all hell with no natives to fight. Ashwood's a glorified brothel now."

Sheriff Biggs had no interest in talking about the vanished natives. *That* was old gossip. There was only one thing the town cared to talk about now. "Collin been minin' quite a long while..." He changed the subject, "How's the yield lookin' this season?"

Jessie politely frowned. He did not wish to describe the full extent of his family's ruin, least of all to one of the mayor's men.

The sheriff found his answer from the silence. "You put an ad in Mr. Pacheco's paper f'some hands?"

Jessie turned, "I'm currently fixin' to do just that. Hopefully, Collin Flowers don' come back with too much gold, or ain't nobody gonna bother farming."

"If he come back at all," Sheriff Biggs scowled at the hills.

Jessie quoted some gossip he had overheard that morning, "Collin Flowers say, what... The gold's probably only a skip down the other side of the hill?"

"Skippin' down a mountain seems awfully dangerous." The sheriff tapped his belt and tipped his hat. "You take care of those youngins."

"I'll do my best," Jessie said. *If that damn Don Marcos will let me...* Thinking about the doctor boiled his blood. He found himself thinking. *How can a man function so well as a parasite?* After another bout of anger, Jessie dragged a hand down his face. He tried to give the doctor some grace. *He was probably born poor and struggled all his life. Hoarding wealth like a dragon is his way of soothing a shattered psyche.* Humanizing the bastard made Jessie feel somewhat better and he continued to the newspaper office.

Porfirio's door was locked. Jessie peered into the window. Whiskey bottles leaned against the immobile printing press. Ever since his family left him, the newspaperman's addiction had only worsened. Jessie sighed and went to the saloon.

As ever, the wet-room was loud with day drinking, gambling, and whoring. Jessie regarded the room. Mr. Willows had taken a great loan from the mayor to renovate the saloon and now, it looked positively proper. All the comforts of the East had been imported. Whores lounged in cushioned couches. Drunks braced themselves on artisanal wallpaper. A new piano was being played by a man too inebriated to pick his nose, let alone make music. The O'Siah boys and some Wagoner girls were playing cards on finely carved tables, celebrating a successful spring harvest.

On the other side of the saloon, Solomon Rodgers leaned in and tried to steal a kiss from Cleona Flowers. She swatted him away and giggled, "Not until my father come back. He ain't let you propose, yet."

Kate Flowers towed her daughter away. She whispered loudly, "Not that he'd permit an itinerant-a marry ya, once we're gilded an' such."

Jessie snorted. Nobody had ever crossed the Western Basin. Not even the nomadic Tlacon. All who tried either vanished or came back cracked. Still, it was hard not to be tempted by imagination. *A pocketful of gold would keep Elijah and Ethel healthy for years...* Jessie blinked away the gleam from his eyes. He could not provide for his family if he were killed by a Lugal, or worse.

The barkeep, Willie Willows, was cleaning a glass while listening to Crawford Biggs. Most towns had accountants, debt collectors, and bounty hunters. Belford had Biggs. The sheriff was presently twirling a spoon around his glass. Though he seemed calm, Mr. Willows was swaying as if drunk. The saloon proprietor was not making eye contact and even rolled his eyes when the sheriff mentioned something about, "The mayor's business."

Meanwhile, Jessie's elusive newspaperman was playing cards with the town madame. He was rubbing his white mustache, curling one side around his finger. He then pointed at Veola, "I've never met a woman as lucky as you."

The madame grunted a laugh and counted her earnings.

"Might be," Porfirio swayed. His whiskey bottle sloshed. "I've never met a woman as deceptive as you."

Veola did not bother to look up.

Jessie pulled a chair to the table and sat, "Mornin' everyone." He tipped his hat at Veola Rosalee, turning to Porfirio before she could look him in the eye. "I missed your paper this morning."

Porfirio Pacheco swallowed a burp. "Nothin' to write 'bout now but drought," He glared at Veola. "And cheats."

Jessie tried to play the diplomat, smiling at Madame Rosalee and declaring, "Nonsense. Why, you could write 'bout the imminent return of Collin Flowers?"

As Porfirio began deriding such content as drivel for drugged masses, Jessie turned his attention to Veola. "Miss Rosalee, if I may..."

Veola finished counting her earnings, lowered her chin, and smirked. Her eyes peeked out from above her spectacles. "If I may," she mocked. "You know I loathe formality."

Jessie licked the inside of his bottom lip and swallowed. He pointed, "You'd count as well behind a teller's booth than at a dealer's table." He added a quick addendum, "Meanin' no implication."

Veola stood, sweeping the earnings into her brassiere. "Meaning no implication." She wiggled her fingers in a wave, "Thank you for your patronage, Pacheco." She put a hand on Jessie's shoulder, "Come by for tea whenever you want, sugar."

Jessie looked at his lap, "Go on and make someone a sinner." His eyes drifted to the exit when the madame strutted out; he rolled his neck as if he were only stretching.

Porfirio twirled his mustache. He filled his glass with more whiskey. "Glendolyn been at rest a year, Jessie. No need to feel guilty for havin' needs." He took a swig, "Though there are finer vintages than that succubus."

Jessie's thumb probed his ring finger, gliding over his wedding band. He sighed and redirected the conversation, taking the old newspaperman's whiskey and replacing it with a glass of water.

Porfirio snatched back the glass, "Oh leave a man to his vice, you hypocrite."

Jessie held his tongue and his gaze.

Porfirio squinted and waved his finger, "Stop that, you." He swiped the whiskey back and donned his shiny, white hat. "With your piercing eyes."

Jessie chuckled, releasing a gust of air out his nostrils. He smiled, but he clearly could not wash away a look of concern.

"There it is. That damn empathy." The old man clenched his jaw while his tongue roamed the inside of his cheek. "I swear, Jessie Bingham. I'd hit you if it weren't like hittin' my damned self."

Jessie scratched his head and smiled. He stood up, patted Porfirio's back, and took back the whiskey. He set it on another table, sat beside his friend, and folded his hands. "Think you could put an ad in your next issue for me?"

"Needin' some hands?" Mr. Pacheco intuited.

"Nobody can say alcohol dulls *your* senses," Jessie affirmed. He gave Porfirio the specifics for the advertisement.

"Second page, one position... Free of charge," the newspaperman wrote on his notepad. He tapped his pen on the paper, "I'll need to include your rate."

As always, Jessie told the truth.

"That's hardly a livin' wage," Porfirio frowned.

Jessie placed his folded hands on his stomach and smiled at a group of children playing in the street. "Any higher and I wager my children won't be livin'." He rubbed his hands on his lap. "Damn Don Marcos..."

Porfirio eyed his notepad and then looked at Jessie. He stretched his lower jaw to the right, saying nothing. It was the mannerism of a man who wished to be of more help.

"Any word from your daughter?" Jessie asked, wishing to talk about someone else's problems.

The newspaperman glanced at the post office.

"People get so busy living their lives," Jessie was quick to say.

Porfirio nodded. His hand mechanically reached across the table and cupped the air. Noticing the movement, the drinker coiled his fingers and then scratched his nose. "Flowers and his men probably found gold by now."

"Maybe," Jessie replied. He was not keen to believe in fables. Especially not when told by greedy men like Collin.

Porfirio leaned in his chair and stared at the foreboding mountains of the West. "You'd think after five generations of Pachecos, one of us would have crossed those Hills."

Jessie shrugged. It was his way of continuing the conversation without having to put in too much effort. He added, "They'd still have to contend with the Lugals."

It was Porfirio's turn to shrug. "Probably would-a ended up like them cracked wagoneers in the sanitoriums."

Jessie said sardonically, "Or, they reached the Final Ocean, created a paradise for the common man, and lived happily ever after."

Porfirio snorted with amusement. The gesture quickly turned dour. He folded his arms and stared emptily into his full cup.

"Sorry," Jessie apologized, not knowing what he said exactly.

Porfirio's chin rose with a glimmer of pride. "If a man's responsible for how the world interprets his word, we'd all best be hanged."

"All the same," Jessie continued, looking at Mr. Pacheco's white hat. It looked like the fin of a shark. "Nobody thinks you less of a man for your family leavin' you." *You don't have to run the paper all alone,* he wanted to say. *You're killing yourself.*

Porfirio's lip curled upwards and he looked at Jessie sternly. "Nobody thinks *you* less a man if you cannot work your land. Flash flood coulda happened to anyone." He interrupted Jessie's remark about a farmhand, "I know, I know. I will put an advertisement in the next issue." He stifled a belch and muttered, "The hands we are dealt, huh?"

"Hm?" Jessie asked. He had not heard Mr. Pacheco over the clamor at the counter. *Barkeep Willows is getting mighty angry,* Jessie noted.

Porfirio did not answer directly. Instead, he complained, "I spent my youth raising children... And not-a-one care to help me grow old."

Jessie scratched his nose and cleared his throat. Both men knew it was a mannerism of a man who had something to say. Neither spoke; each preferring to nod and smile. The conversation shifted to innocent questions about Jessie's family. They talked about the twins and their growth spurts. They discussed their obsession with storytime."

"I can't get 'em to bed 'fore midnight. 'Specially if Eli demands history. Boy loves a true story." He widened his eyes and turned his cheek as if his son's imagination was paramount gossip. "Why, Elijah is convinced that there is a giant on our land. Says he saw one come down the mountain this morning."

Porfirio laughed. Jessie continued, nodding heroically. "He and Ethel are leading an excursion to find it soon."

Porfirio swayed with amusement, pointing a finger, "If that happens, they can take this dusty corpse with them. I've got one last adventure in me."

Jessie was about to scold Porfirio for calling himself a corpse. An uproar across the saloon silenced him.

"Damn the mayor!" Mr. Willows yelled from behind his bar. He wiped his hands and threw down a wet rag. "Her father woulda given me more time!

"Calloway ain't mayor," Sheriff Biggs declared. He shrugged, "Not anymore."

Porfirio gripped his pen and whispered, "Finally. Some news. I was 'bout to shoot myself just to have somethin' to write about."

Jessie did not laugh. Sheriff Biggs was mean like the sun was hot; that was just his nature.

"Now," Crawford Biggs said with relish. "I got clearance to collect y'debt any way I see fit."

Most conversations began to fizzle as more and more of the saloon paid attention to the two men.

The barkeep removed his apron and placed a serrated knife on the counter. "Go on, then. Try me. I ain't gonna pay a con artist. Least of all a blind one."

"Now let's not be silly," Crawford pouted, tapping the pouch of coins protruding from his belt. "This is just the price of civilization. Or is you a savage?"

"Only savages I know 'bout come from the Big House these days," the barkeep declared defiantly. "You ain't nothin' but a rabid dog servin' that—"

The saloon doors creaked open. The barkeep's eyes widened. Those who did not want to seem complicit in Willows' comments coughed. Porfirio wrote furiously.

Two quiet steps carried a resonant message. A long, relaxed breath made a few spines tingle. All the saloon sat at attention. The mayor strode into view, escorted by a shadow as tall as the air was dry. Although none could see the mayor's gaze behind her wide-brimmed hat, all knew it languished on Mr. Willows.

Half-chewed meals were quickly swallowed. Even those who most wished to mind their business now paid undivided attention. All watched the mayor. Pity for the barkeep was palpable.

Silence echoed. Only creaking chairs could find a voice.

Jessie glanced at the mayor and then at Biggs. The sheriff had sunk into a corner, watching the scene smugly. Meanwhile, Mayor Thorne remained at the entrance, leaning lazily on her walking stick. Just as the silence started to grow into deafening tension, Mr. Willows took a sharp breath. He prepared to speak his case.

The mayor rolled her long fingernails across her cane. *Tap. Tap. Tap. Tap.*

Willows' windpipe zipped shut. He raised his arms and unsteadily poured a drink. "Same as usual, Mayor?" He pushed his white flag forward.

Mayor Thorne did not answer the barkeep. Instead, pale, foggy eyes met the townspeople's. Not one person in the saloon was spared that stare. Leaking pupils tested all in the room. Everyone bowed their heads or averted their gaze. All the while, fingers tapped on the walking stick. *Tap. Tap. Tap. Tap.* Finally, the mayor looked at Jessie.

Common sense told him to look away. Mayor Thorne may be going blind, but her regard was something to respect. Yet, when Jessie's eyes met those hiding behind the hat, he remembered the kind-hearted woman who once could see. Despite her reputation, her deeds, and her nearby muscle—Jessie frowned at her.

The mayor's cheek twitched. She resumed her confrontation with the barkeep. She walked up to the bar, lifted her walking stick, and pushed the drink off the counter. Willows winced as the glass shattered at his feet.

Willows wavered, "I was just telling Mr. Biggs how much I resp—"

Thorne's knuckles tensed and whitened around the walking stick. They cracked audibly.

"That's not right. I've been so forgetful these days. I was actually saying—"

The mayor bit her lip and raised her brow expectantly. She cocked her head inquisitively.

"That, I," sweat leaked down his forehead. He clamored for a washcloth and wiped his brow. "I don't have the payment. But I can have it next week."

Thorne waited silently.

"O-or, I could give you half right now and...?" His bargain faded as the mayor continued her unrelenting stare.

Finally, Mr. Willows knelt below the counter. Keys clanged. A lockbox whined open and slammed shut. Shaky hands placed a stack of bills on the counter. "That's all of it."

The mayor smiled and pursed her lips, "Why don't you hold onto it? I would not want to extort. Mr. Biggs will stop by next week to *appreciate* my investment." At that, the mayor turned. Her slow steps caused the creaky floorboards to groan. Her clanking cane made the second-floor rain down dust. She left the saloon without another word.

Jessie got up. "I need to give the twins their tinctures." He tipped his hat. "I've had my fill of civilization."

"M'yes," Porfirio nodded, scribbling down the last of his notes. "A town is a wild environment for the undomesticated sort."

Jessie smirked, "How long you been sittin' on that line?"

Porfirio's eyes rolled up to his forehead. "Bout six months, I'd say."

Jessie patted the old man's shoulder and departed, "I like it. Could even be first page material, if you stopped using so many big words."

Porfirio took back his whiskey bottle and slunk into his seat, "Big words are all little men have anymore."

Jessie did not respond to that. He left the saloon annoyed by Pacheco's pessimism. *His children left him to lead their lives. At least he had a chance to say goodbye.* His thumb mechanically checked if his wedding ring was still on. When he felt the calming metal, he looked at the sky. He wondered where his wife would be among the stars that night. He smiled as a new moon rose.

Jessie strolled out of Belford. Perhaps it was because he was beginning to feel old himself, or perhaps he was simply used to breezing past on horseback—but on that evening walk, he found himself in awe of the town's age. No coat of paint could conceal the lichen's senior claims to every home. Even the grey-haired looked young beside the mighty junipers with their twisting trunks and bristly beards. Beside the junipers wove a cracked cobble road, winding through town like a wrinkled smile.

Belford may have been a young town, but the land was ancient. Jessie strode past the prehistoric cemetery, erected by the ancients of Copper Valley. Not even the Kuahtec could read those stones. He felt the depth of the land's roots as he read inscriptions of names he could not pronounce. He felt small next to the cryptic stones that covered the countryside, carved in languages known only to the past.

Even the native fish seemed ancient. The silt catchers along the shore floated as if already dead, hardly moving as they gulped the dirty discharge of the Copper River. They swam without hurry or worry, long ago losing their vision in the silty waters of the stream.

Yet there were animals in the water that swam with haste, hunters and scavengers. Coyotes howled across the bank. Birds hopped through the mud. Lines of ants marched toward some destination. Jessie followed their trail and found the washed-up bodies of several animals. *Floods got 'em*, he thought. As Jessie walked down the path, the setting sun cast a red light upon the carrion. Crimson stained the bodies. Flayed strips of leather floated past. Jessie cupped his hands over his eyes, shading his view.

Jessie gasped. Those bodies were two-legged. He jogged toward the corpses, counting their number. He did not recall how many men bought into Flowers' fable, nor could he tell from the mangled faces who the men were. Yet, Jessie's suspicions were soon confirmed. Ants and other insects swarmed the body of Collin Flowers.

Jessie swatted at the pests and knelt by the riverside. Rigor mortis had turned the man's flesh to stone. He studied the scene.

The bodies are badly beaten. Must have washed down from the Hills. He approached a body. The hands were lashed as if from a whip. Yet, the hands were unyielding. The corpse would not let go of its belongings, even while birds pecked at its flesh. Worst of all, the gaping mouth was empty. The teeth were broken into fragments and the tongue... Jessie shuddered. The tongue was staked to its forehead.

Jessie walked from corpse to corpse. All the miners' bodies were similarly disfigured. All save one. The corpse of Collin Flowers was pristine, without bruises or blood stains. The would-be miner did not look dead at all.

Jessie eyed the pathway home and then knelt beside the body. He took Collin Flowers' bag and peeked inside. He had not expected to see any golden flecks or nuggets, and so was unsurprised by the dull rocks in the pouch. Jessie probed the rocks, sweeping his fingers against the surprisingly polished stones.

Collin gasped.

Jessie lurched away, screaming, "Host on High!"

Flowers' chest rose and then collapsed. The body sank beneath the current.

Jessie stared at the body suspiciously before concluding, "Just a death gasp." He turned his attention to the miner's haul. He stared at the dull objects and rubbed his fingers against the ore. It felt smooth as skin but very strong. He opened the lip of the bag to get a better look.

Dusken sunlight shot into the satchel and suddenly, the stones began to vibrate and glow blue. Jessie gazed with terrified curiosity, listening to the cricket-like chattering of the stones. The vibration grew and grew until the deafening clattering began to frighten him. Jessie closed the lip of the bag and pushed it away.

The glow diminished and the satchel went silent. The sun's rays retreated behind the Forlorn Hills Jessie looked to his left and right as if the pinyon wood was eavesdropping. Despite feeling that he should toss the glowing rocks into the brush, he reached inside and pulled out a finely polished sphere. *Collin has come home and not with gold.* He pocketed the shimmering stone and doubled back to inform the law.

Chapter 2

—o—

"Collin Flowers and his gang of unfortunates have been found washed up along the banks of the Copper River. All-a-one were undergoing the cooling process. Mayor Thorne forbids any travel west until the sheriff's investigation is concluded."

–The Belford Inquirer

Jessie gazed at the mysterious stone. He tapped the silky sphere, smoother than any river pebble. He foolishly expected the rock to glow as it had when he had first touched it. But ever since Jessie brought the relic home, it had remained stubbornly inert.

Like a rock, Jessie's impatience and reasoning began to say.

He rubbed his fingers along the corners of the stone, feeling the polished black edges. He wondered what smith created the odd jewel, nature or man? Jessie leaned forward and pressed his chin onto the table, staring at the stone from its own level. He whispered, careful not to wake the twins in the other room, "What are you?"

If you would just shimmer again... He maneuvered the black stone. Jessie followed the sun's rays as they pierced into the room. White light entered the dark orb and split into a rainbow. With a turn of his wrist, the colors of the rainbow would widen or withdraw. Jessie had never seen a metal so lustrous. Gold was mud in comparison.

Jessie tapped the jewel again. He smirked at what must have been a ridiculous sight of a man knocking politely on a rock. He leaned in his chair and chewed on his cheek. "But you are no simple stone..."

He gazed out the window, squinting at the morning rays. The sun was rising over the Forlorn Hills. Whether or not Collin Flowers had found gold did not much matter now, Jessie was sure of that. *What had he seen on the other side of the mountains?*

He recalled stories of a people so old and wild, even other natives called *them* savages. Jessie turned and eyed the large map displayed across the wall. There was Belford along the Copper River, Ashwood, Silverfork, and Montgomery Mill—all along the eastern edge of the Forlorn Hills. The Copper River, the Pinyon woodlands, and the various trading points were all displayed in detail on the map. But the western side of the mountains was blank. None crossed the Forlorn Hills. Most westbound wagoneers had the sense to avoid the vast basin altogether, going around for miles. Jessie stared at the blank void on his map.

It was said only the Lugal lived in the basin west of the Hills. But the Lugal were notoriously mythical, bordering on fantastical. They were so legendary, even the wandering tribes feared them. But as far as Jessie could tell, the only folk who had actually seen them were librarians, catching glimpses only in old explorers' tomes. Jessie studied the blank part of the map. He remembered his father's response when he had asked about the land beyond the hills. Laurent Bingham had chuckled, *'The Lugal are the grand savages, the culmination of a hundred years of conquest. Every explorer, conqueror, and liar from the last century has contributed to their legend. The Lugal are a simple myth made to keep city folk entertained when the comforts of civilization took all challenge from their lives.'*

His father never tested his theory, though. Laurent remained comfortably in his cushioned chair, telling young Jessie secondhand stories of a people he did not believe in.

Jessie had liked the stories growing up. Belford was a simple farming town with an ordinary history. There were cheats, murders, and intrigues—but nothing otherworldly to stimulate a young imagination. Laurent Bingham's voice came back to him again, *'We're a young country. We got no myths but the ones we make for ourselves. We may have been founded in the east, but it shall be in the west where our genesis springs.'*

Now, with such a stone as was on his breakfast table, Jessie wondered what fable he found himself in. There were so many questions and so little time to ponder before the twins woke... *Why was the Flowers gang killed? Who killed them?*

"Daddy, I feel woozy..."

Damn it, Jessie winced. His project would have to wait.

He turned around and smiled at his daughter, and then at his groggy son. "That's no good!" He went to the counter and fixed them each some garter pemmican. He brought them their breakfast and had them each sit at the table. "Munch my munchkins."

"I'm not hungry," Elijah complained. "I'm tired of pemmi."

Ethel seconded her brother. "Can we just get our medicine and go play?"

"You can play," Elijah yawned. "Daddy and me gots a lots of work."

"*Daddy and I have a lot* of work," Jessie corrected his son, handing him and his sister their tinctures.

"Why's it matter?" Elijah asked, wincing slightly from the taste of the tincture. "We're just farmers."

School starts early today, he decided. Jessie sat across from the children and said in the tone he reserved for when they played a game. "Fix your hands flat on the table, so I can see your palms."

Elijah and Ethel did so, smirking.

"Fantastic!" Jessie peered at his own palms. "See those bumps?"

Elijah nodded. Ethel began scratching them.

"Those are called callouses. We get them from working hard with our hands. Most learned folk don't get them."

Elijah looked at his father proudly, "But we work hard, don't we?"

"We sure do. See, these callouses help us grasp hard things. They make toilin' easier. But we have our brains to train, too."

Ethel, who had been busy picking off her callouses, suddenly paid more attention. "But we're farmers. We don't got the money to get educated."

Jessie scratched the top of his ear. He reassured her (and himself), "A paid education is paper. And it ain't proper, no-how. Real education comes from all around; we just got-ta notice it."

Elijah bit his lip, deep in thought. "But we don't have the time to read books. The farm is either soaked out or dryin' up."

He's got my green eyes, my blonde hair. Now he's getting my anxiety, too. Jessie folded his hands and bit his tongue. "I wager the answer to the drought is in a dusty old book... Point is, just because we farm doesn't mean we should be ignorant. Like callouses help us grasp hard things, an education helps us grasp hard ideas." He pointed a fork of pemmican at his children, "Like the drought."

Elijah was silent. Taking a cue from his father, he reluctantly bit into his breakfast. The mixture of smoked snake meat, pigweed seed, and pinyon nuts was the Bingham family staple. It was easy to acquire and required very little water. Unfortunately, the three of them were all quite tired of it.

"Did mama have an education?" Ethel asked.

"Not a formal one, no." *But she had your curly, blonde locks. And those dimples.* He added, "But she knew the stars like she was born among them. Knew every constellation, when a star would pass to the other side of heaven..." Jessie groped his wedding ring. "And my, oh my. She could make even pemmican taste good." He looked at the roof with a deep breath. *I should clean the graveyard today...*

His eyes drifted back to the table. Elijah chewed a particularly fibrous mouthful. Ethel put a handful into her pockets.

Jessie licked his lips, placed his hands on his lap, and rose. "Who wants dessert?"

The Bingham clan was out of the cabin in record time. With his twins in tow, he began instruction. He quizzed his son, gesturing at a collection of green and yellow circles growing on a large boulder, "Eli, what is that?"

"Lichen," he answered.

"Good..." Jessie knelt beside the tiny forest of fungi and algae. "Why is it growing on the north side only?"

"It don't like the sun."

"It does not," Jessie smiled. "With a little bit of mathematics I will teach you when you are older, we can use the lichen to find out how old things are. Rocks, tombs. Anything."

Elijah wanted to learn the math at that moment, despite not knowing how to add or subtract. Ethel could not be bothered. So, Jessie continued the hike. He said as he searched his pockets, "Do either of you know where honey comes from?"

They gleefully shouted, "Bees!"

"That's right," Jessie beamed. He removed his fire starter. "Problem is. Where to go to find the honey?" He frowned at his children. Just as they were about to ask him more questions, he raised his finger and then put it into his mouth. He whistled three separate notes.

A little bird hopped from the branches. It tilted its head at the trio and then fluttered to the ground. After a preliminary investigation of its accomplices, the bird flew back to the branches and replied with the same three notes. Then, it glided to the next tree in the path.

Jessie saw Ethel's amazement and patted her back, "It's a honeyguide, baby girl. It will lead us to a beehive."

"Woah," was all Elijah could say.

Jessie ruffled his son's hair, "Don't worry so much about the drought. We may have lost a good crop this year. We may be behind on our deliveries to the Big House. But a learned person always has a way to food."

They followed the honeyguide for half a mile until they came upon the banks of the Copper River. The silty stream was a bit higher than usual, owing to the spring melts. Their guide flew over to the other side effortlessly. It waited with a cocked head for his accomplices.

Ethel groaned, "The stones are wet, daddy!"

"Not all of them," Elijah said confidently. He hopped from one to the next. About halfway across the river, though, he slipped and fell backward. Luckily, his father was behind and caught him. Elijah readjusted his backpack and kicked the stone. "Stupid rock."

Jessie laughed. "Don't get mad at the stepping stone for being wet. Just go to the next stone!" He nudged his boy forward.

The honeyguide did not wait for them to cross. Once they were back on the trail, they had to jog to keep up. After several minutes of chasing their guide, they found it perched expectantly above them. It tilted its head back and forth and then hopped toward a nearby pinyon. Many bees swarmed above it.

"Now, my little dears," Jessie raised his fire starter and his brow mischievously, "Which of you can make me a fire..?"

Smoke found its way into the hive; the hive found its way to the ground. The honeyguide took its payment promptly, picking at the wax while the bees were most docile. Meanwhile, the Bingham family collected as much honey as their mouths and jars allowed. Full bellies made their way back to the cabin. After the initial sugar rush, Ethel and Elijah fell promptly to sleep.

All according to plan, Jessie thought to himself. The sun had not yet reached the top of the sky, giving him more than enough time to do his work. He had much travail before the twins woke, which could be in moments or in hours. After a minute of rest for himself, he gathered his brushes, washcloths, and a bucket of water.

Jessie paused at the door. He glanced at the dining table, where the mysterious stone had remained all morning. He set down his supplies and investigated once more. He touched the surface and recoiled. Despite being bathed in the sun's rays for hours—the stone was cold.

Jessie lost himself in the jewel. He forgot about his work as he stared at the reflection upon the glassy surface. The glossy silhouette shimmered slightly, even when Jessie was still. He was so engrossed, he did not hear Veola Rosalee enter the cabin.

"Well hello, stranger," she whispered.

Jessie jumped. "Host on High!"

"Ooh, I love an archaic swear," she chuckled. The madame swayed as she approached. She put a hand on his shoulder and, seeing the stone, was taken aback. "That one of those *things* Collin Flowers found?"

"Not as interesting as gold, I am afraid," he lied.

Veola went to the stove and lit a fire under the kettle. With a tone reserved for those who witness disaster only from the paper, she remarked, "What a tragedy."

"Indeed," Jessie sniffled.

"I hear Kate Flowers won' let that Rodgers boy marry her daughter now. It caused quite the clamor."

Jessie heard her words belatedly, registering them long after she had spoken. When he turned to reply, his eyes remained on the gemstone.

Veola pointed out, "You seem busy. Should I go?"

"I am busy," Jessie snorted in agreement. "Between the fields, the drought..."

Veola Rosalee shook her head. With her lips pressed, she soothed, "I know. I know." The madame sat beside Jessie and began touching him.

"No," he said sternly. "Not here." Jessie checked if his wedding ring had fallen off his finger. "Not anywhere, for that matter. I told you, I don't want that."

Veola froze, her stare calculating. "What do you want, Mr. Bingham?"

Jessie glanced at the floor and then at the madame. "You know me, Veola," he smiled weakly, "I love women." He stared apathetically at her breasts before meeting her gaze, "But lately, I've found I enjoy their company more than their bodies."

She raised her brow and snorted. She shook her head and returned to the stove. Veola did not speak for a moment; instead, she interrupted the kettle just before it started shrieking. She poured them each a cup of tea. With a hand on her hip, she asked, "When did you become such a gentleman?"

Jessie grinned, though he was not amused. Whenever Veola Rosalee came around, he feared what his wife might have said. Jessie sipped his tea in silence.

"I take it you've got some tasks to accomplish?" Veola inquired. She flicked her grey hair behind her shoulder and eyed the walls with a carpenter's fascination.

Jessie nodded.

Veola shooed him, "Go on then. You're the worst type of company when you got some chore on the mind."

Jessie took his leave. He could see her hands folding over her chin. He had insulted her. Struggling to form an apology, he merely said, "There is honey in the cupboard."

Jessie strode out the door with his throat tightened. Once he visited Glendolyn's stone, he would feel more at ease around Madame Rosalee. He made his way to the Bingham graveyard, passing the only part of his acreage which still could be irrigated. The hardiest of his family's crops grew there, most of which were named after pigs, as in abundant times only livestock ate them. Now, all the parched people of Copper Valley made pigweed dough, boiled hog potatoes, and ate sow-thistle salads.

Jessie passed through a wrought iron gate and was greeted by his father's mighty tombstone. When Jessie turned sixteen, he had quarried the stone for his father, replacing the inadequate, wooden stake. The monument had been Jessie's way of declaring he was a man. Unfortunately, he had been overzealous then and had chiseled '*Laurent Bingham*' too deeply. Now, lichen liked to squat in the shaded caverns of Laurent.

He cleaned the inscription and was reminded of a conversation between him and his father, when Jessie was Elijah's age.

'*There'll be a time when squash don' grow. When corn don' grow. When wheat ain't found nowhere but in your dreams. You mark my words, Jessie boy—this drought won't let up. See them mountains? The Forlorn Hills been getting' taller, stealin' all our water.*'

He had interrupted, always trying to appear clever for his father, '*The mountain has senior water rights.*'

'*One might say,*' Laurent added, bemused. '*I will not be around forever, and neither'll be our senior claims.*'

Jessie had not understood death at that point, but he could tell his father was sick.

'*Mayor Thorne thinks he can just come from his pampered city and dole out water rights, but they can't dole out rain. This the west. Oh sure, Calloway tried with his dam... It don' matter. We humble folk don' need be taken away by big plans.*" He knelt before his child and told Jessie, "*This spring, we'll not be pullin' weeds.*'

Jessie looked back at his field of weeds. The acreage brought a mix of nostalgia and pride. The other farmers in town called the guild of crops a "Bingham Field" and most had adapted to his father's ways. A few farmers, like the Rodgers clan, had stuck to growing oranges and alfalfa. They were itinerant hands now.

Jessie wished his father had been alive for his children. *You would have taught the twins so much more than I ever will.* He bowed his head and moved to his mother's gravestone. He cleaned it off easily. His father had made the stone; lichen did not like to grow there.

Jessie walked to the next stones, all belonging to Jessie's unborn siblings. Those graves were made of crude rock without any marking, save for the lichen. The blotches on those stones helped to identify his siblings. Plus, the stones with the largest lichen were the oldest, allowing Jessie to remember his unnamed sibling's ages.

Finally, he came to his wife's grave. Glendolyn Bingham's headstone was the most glorious of them all. The stone was carved in the shape of a whale's fluke, in honor of his wife's dream of one day going all the way west—to the Final Ocean. She had never gotten the chance, but Jessie liked to think she swam with mighty whales somewhere in the stars.

Jessie knelt before his wife's stone and began scrubbing the dirt off her base. He pulled the clovers growing around her foundation. He left the columbines; his wife liked those. He paid particular attention to the shaded folds around the fluke, knowing wasps liked to nest there. He went to the other side of the stone and scowled at a blackened spot. He tried to scratch it off to no avail. He took his washcloth and gave it a thorough lathering of water. Nothing. Jessie began questioning if the blemish had always been there. *No, no. It was perfect.* Jessie began scrubbing profusely, spilling his sweat and his cleansing water.

"Damn it all!" He slammed his fist against the marking. The blemish, as well as a portion of his wife's grave, broke off. Jessie froze. He blinked at his wife's memorial, his mouth agape. "No, no, NO!" He scrambled to put the fallen fragment back together.

"Daddy, are you gonna tell us more of that story tonight?"

Jessie ignored the question. He put the broken piece back in place. Without any way to glue it, he only grew more irritated. He cradled the stone and tried to think of a fix for his mistake. Just as he was concocting a list of ingredients to create an adhesive, Ethel asked her question again.

"Are you gonna tell us that story, daddy?"

Jessie hurled the stone to the ground, "Yes, of course. Ethel, baby—go back inside."

Ethel asked, nervously, "What'ya doing?"

Well, I am dealing with the emotional consequences of neglecting my marriage and am currently knee-deep in a personal crisis. Jessie swallowed, immediately fatigued by the conversation. "Working."

"On what?" Elijah jogged up. "Can we help?"

"Go back inside, both of you," Jessie said, his body shaking. He was suddenly very, very tired. He never communicated well when he was tired and did his best to avoid more conversation. He stared morosely at his wife's stone.

"Veola won' let us play," Ethel persisted. "She said you need"

"She does not know what I need, sweet girl." Jessie breathed sharply and enunciated each word, "Go inside."

Ethel lingered, giving him a nasty look. However, she eventually did as she was asked and stomped away. Elijah, however, was as persistent as his mother. "I checked on the hog potatoes. I think they are—"

"Elijah!" Jessie shot to his feet, "Will I have to pass into the next life for you to finally follow a simple instruction?"

Fear. Dejection. The little boy's eyes welled.

Jessie closed his eyes, unable to see his son cry. "Listen," he tried to apologize, "I did not mean to shout." He opened his eyes and walked toward his son. Like a mouse, Elijah skittered away.

Jessie felt the natural shame of a failed father. He swallowed and looked back at his wife's grave. Her memorial was still resplendent, despite the slight fracture. He bowed his head, feeling the rightful shame of a poor partner. He kicked the fragment into the neighboring field. As was becoming Jessie's tradition, his anger began to mutate into a new sensation. His fists became limp balls of insecure flesh. Jessie trudged past his crops, head bowed. He thought about what he would say to the children, how he might twist his ineptitude, his stubbornness, and his anger into a beneficial education.

At the door to the cabin, Veola Rosalee was waiting with a tapping foot. "I had them eat their supper, but they wasn't keen on talking."

"Thank you," Jessie managed. "I uh, I am going to talk with them."

"I'm not going to be their mother," Veola folded her arms.

Jessie swallowed, wiggling his wedding ring. "So you won't watch them tomorrow?"

Veola squinted, "I'm a whore, Jessie Bingham. Not a nanny." She glided forward, her dress swaying in the wind. She put one hand on Jessie's chest and another below the waist. "I have a whore's needs."

Jessie bit his cheek, feeling too much like a father to be much of a lover. He reached into his back pocket and paid her for her trouble. "I told you, Veola. I need time to mourn."

The madame stowed the money in her brassiere, "It's been a year, Mr. Bingham." She turned and walked proudly back to town.

Jessie took the formal tone as a warning. He would have to give Veola more, and soon. He looked at his feet. Then, he stared at the door, preparing an opening statement for his children. He took the doorknob and stepped cautiously inside. The candlelight was dim and his children were sitting on the floor, staring at the dark gem. Fighting his urge to scold them and swipe the stone, he joined their circle.

"It is pretty weird, huh?" he asked Elijah.

The boy nodded. He did not look at his father.

"Are you mad at me?" Jessie asked, seeing if his son would articulate his emotions.

Elijah shook his head, eyes fixed on the gem.

A lie is most harmful to oneself, Jessie might have said. He put a hand on Elijah's back, shifting eye contact from him to Ethel, "Something was wrong with mama's stone and I could not fix it. I took out my frustration on the both of you because I felt helpless."

Elijah looked at his father, "What's wrong with mama's stone? Can I help?"

Jessie patted his son's back and shrugged. "Maybe. It isn't important." He gestured for the children to scoot closer. Ethel did so immediately, just as forgiving as her father. Elijah, just as stubborn as his mother, took a moment.

"I do not mean to excuse my behavior," Jessie continued. "When I explain why I get angry, I just want you both to understand my perspective. That's important in life, to understand someone's point of view. It helps avoid a lot of nastiness." *It would have helped my marriage,* he might have said, if the twins were older.

"I forgive you, daddy," Ethel said, resting her head on her father's lap. She was always eager to remain her father's baby girl. Indeed, she probably would still be wetting the bed were it not for her brother's eagerness to grow up.

Elijah muttered, "Yeah. Me too."

Jessie breathed easier, "I am not asking you to never get angry." He smirked, "We all know I do not have that power. All I ask of you two is that you be aware of *why* you are angry. We cannot always control our emotions, but we can learn from our more uncontrolled moments."

The children were silent for a single second before, as was typical, their forgiveness and their energy combined. Ethel rubbed her head on his leg, "So will you finish the story, now?"

Jessie nodded. "I should never have started it in the first place!" He meant what he said, too. The children were far too young for tales of the Trail. *Your mother would never approve.* He acted as if he could not remember where they left off. He picked up the mysterious stone and began tossing it from one hand to the next, "It was an old story I think."

Ethel giggled and Elijah got to his feet, bouncing happily. He pointed, "You know what it was!"

"Hm," Jessie frowned, "Was it the tale of old Nathaniel B. Thorne?"

"Noooo," the twins shook their heads.

"Oh, of course! We were following the histories of Montez Pacheco. The Kuahtec raids, I believe?"

"Nooo!" they shrieked.

"You're right, you're right," Jessie at last ceded. "We were talking about the Forlorn Trail."

The twins squealed so loudly, they did not hear the black stone in Jessie's hand. Like bees trapped in a lightless hive, the gem buzzed. Jessie's heart raced as the polished gem surged. Forgetting his words, he simply stared at the stone. It seemed that despite the dim room, many lights were bouncing within the artifact. "Where did we leave off?"

Elijah recounted hastily, "The wagon trains went missing. Nobody knew if they reached the Final Ocean."

Ethel joined in, "Then, Dan Bandelier and his outfit robbed Silverfork!"

Jessie smirked. He had left them on a cliffhanger. He set the stone down and began where he left off:

"Well, there had been a few disappearances in the Western Basin, but the danger of the Hills was not common knowledge then." Jessie continued. "So, when Bandelier robbed the bank at Silverfork, he didn't think twice about goin' west. He and his outfit crossed the Forlorn Hills with the law close behind."

"The sheriff at Silverfork, Clyde Wheatridge, was a smarter man than most. Porfirio's father liked him, at least." Jessie briefly lost track of where he was in the story. "Ah, anyways. Sheriff Wheatridge would not follow Bandelier down the western slopes of the Hills. He told his deputies to hole up near all the passes."

"And did they catch Bandelier?"

Jessie nodded. "Dan Bandelier was found crawling the streets of Silverfork two days later. When the sheriff brought him in, the quickest con west of Ashwood couldn't remember his own name."

"But he had provisions!" Ethel blurted. "The finest outfit of outlaws since Kimmy Vanheidt."

"He did," Jessie ceded. "And are you quoting Mr. Pacheco, little lady?"

Ethel grinned. "Maybe."

Elijah was puzzled and asked in a breathy voice, "What happened to him?"

"Nobody knows," Jessie said. "Porfirio would go up to Greenview Sanitorium and interview him from time to time. He said he was a fine, peaceful fella—more like an old dog than a rabid outlaw."

"Now, most people thought Dan Bandelier got what was comin' to him. Thought his madness was divine. Even still, most people were wisenin' up. Rumor was growin' that there was a danger beyond the Hills. Folks started preferrin' the longer way West. But a few still dared the Trail. And a few came crawling back, cracked."

"Now," Jessie began, repositioning so that the sphere rested between his legs. "When I was very young, a woman approached your grandfather. She wanted to pay him a small fortune to lead her to the Final Ocean. Your grandfather almost went. But when she demanded they use the Forlorn Trail, he refused."

"That's lucky," Ethel remarked.

"Very lucky. Because that woman was Catalina Romero."

The twins gasped. Ethel whispered, "That old lady that never leaves her house?"

"The very same," Jessie replied. "She and her family eventually found another person to guide them, but..." Jessie did not want to tell too violent a story tonight. *They are too young for this part.*

"But *what?*" Ethel pressed.

Jessie skipped the gruesome portion of the story. "Only Catalina and her infant boy returned."

"But how come she didn't come back cracked?"

"Be nice, Ethel," Jessie chided. He admitted, "All of Belford asked that same question. Some, like Julila Thorne, thought she *was* cracked. Others, like my daddy, thought she was still sharp."

"But how come she ain't went mad?" Elijah asked indelicately.

"She's never said. But unlike all the others, she remembered her name." The awestruck eyes of his children made Jessie feel guilty. Catalina had been viewed like a freakshow oddity ever since returning. "Don't ever mention the story around her. Understood?"

"Well, she never leaves her house," his daughter grinned.

"Ethel," Jessie warned her.

"Fine," she agreed. Her face scrunched into a serious pose, "Has anyone made it to the end of the Forlorn Trail?"

Jessie paused for effect. "A man by the name of Clanton Jones may have gotten the farthest."

"Did he come back crazy, too?"

"Nope. Didn't come back at all."

"How do we know he got the farthest?"

"Because they found his sketchbook, just layin' on a rock in the southern ranges."

Ethel was skeptical, "Maybe he didn't go west at all. Just left that journal there and made it seem like he had."

"That's what the Thorne thought, too." Jessie sighed. He remembered that day vividly. "Everyone was quick to dismiss the notebook as a ruse, but then old Catalina Romero came out of her house, looked at the pages, and knew it was authentic."

Silence from the children. Finally, Elijah interrogated, "How did she know they was real?"

Jessie remembered the day. "The Thorne and their lackeys were inclined to ignore the sketchbook, but Porfirio Pacheco had a hunch it was genuine. He knocked and knocked on Catalina's door until she stormed out, swiped the journal, and peered at the pages."

The woman's eyes had haunted everyone who saw them that day. Jessie still remembered how they seemed to retreat deep into her skull, hollowing the sockets. "Just from looking at Catalina's face, everyone knew the journal was genuine."

Jessie looked at his children, who were not nearly as frightened as he had been that day. He debated not telling them the rest of the tale. They seemed so unaffected by the story, though—he figured they would not let him sleep if he ended the story there. He sighed and began fidgeting with the black sphere. "She looked at one page for a long while, shaking her head. She peered at us all, a market square full of wondering eyes." He stopped to catch his breath. He felt the same sorrow for the old woman now as he had that day, "She broke into tears and ran off. She threw the sketchbook into the crowd."

Jessie stared at the shimmering core of the spherical jewel. He gazed at the faint glow, as if telling the glittering core, "I was the one who caught the journal. I saw what Catalina saw."

"What did Clanton Jones draw?" Elijah whispered.

"That page was not a drawing. It was a single sentence, written over and over until it was barely legible." The entire experience that day haunted Jessie well into adulthood and he felt conflicted about continuing. Yet, he found himself incapable of staying silent.

Just as Jessie opened his mouth, he felt his veins swell. Blood surged to his brain like floodwaters gorging the banks of a mountain stream. His chest tingled, his hair stood up. He spoke, but the voice was not his own:

> *"There is light the eye cannot see*
> *Sounds the ear does not hear*
> *Horrors man cannot fear*
> *What do gods see in the mirror?"*

"Woah," Elijah gasped. "How did you do that voice?"

Jessie blinked, first at his children and then at the stone. The blood in his brain settled back to the rest of his body. His hair fell flat. Without thinking, he leapt to his feet, grabbed a blanket, and threw it atop the sorcerous stone.

"Time for bed," he commanded.

Chapter 3

——◦——

"Miners found strange, glowing ore west of the Hills. Why do they glow, what is their purpose, and what might be their market value? This humble reporter has several theories regarding these great riddles of our time, all of which have been categorically dismissed by Mayor Thorne. For those with kin newly retired, Mr. Craw of Craw's Cradles is offering discount coffins of the finest pine."

– The Belford Inquirer

Jessie slept in his children's bedroom that night. Luckily, neither child seemed to think anything about the foreign voice which had burglarized his words. Indeed, they thought sleeping at their door was his way of playing a game.

"Just a game," he had lied. "That's right." He fell asleep wondering about the existence of witchcraft, or whether his mind was simply going to seed.

That morning, the most interesting conversation topic was whether they could have a dog. Jessie was glad the children did not share his unease. That did not mean he would finally say yes, though. "Just because you keep asking does not mean my answer will change, Ethel."

"But, why not? The McLeary have five dogs!"

"The McLeary can feed five dogs," Jessie responded. He found it hard to dismiss his children with a stern 'no.' He liked dogs. He just did not like burying them. "Dogs are a lot of hard work."

"We will take care of it," Elijah argued.

Will you dig its grave? Jessie nearly asked. He thought better at the last minute and instead said, "I'll think about it. If the autumn harvest is better than the spring."

After a series of 'yippee' and 'woohoo', the children were ready to take their tinctures. Jessie went to the medicine cupboard. He opened the cabinet and to his horror, all the tinctures had somehow fallen from their shelf. The golden contents were a quickly drying puddle.

"Oh no," Jessie groaned. Elijah asked what was wrong, but he did not have the heart to tell him. The little boy was too much of a worrier. "Nothing, I miscounted your medicine is all. Seems we'll have to make our trip to town a little earlier."

He doubled back to the breakfast table, put a hand in Ethel's pockets, and put her pilfered pieces of pemmican back on her plate. "Eat."

He went to his bedroom and opened the lockbox under his bed. He laid out writs of ownership, bills of sale, and his wife's wedding ring. He stared at the pile morosely. Which portion of his children's future would he sell today? His eyes lingered on Glendolyn's ring. His back spasmed.

Jessie dug to the bottom of the lockbox. He took out the fragment of her wedding dress and pressed it into his face. He inhaled slowly. *Her scent is almost gone, now.* He exhaled and delicately placed the cloth back at the bottom of the lockbox, where it might be spared from time a little longer. He then returned Glendolyn's ring, burying it below all the things a robber would hopefully prioritize. Then, he chose his sacrifice. Jessie swiped the deed to the southwestern parcel.

He rejoined his children. The twins were standing at the doorway, sunhats on and waiting. Elijah was holding the reins of the family horse. He said proudly, "I got Genie ready!"

Jessie hoisted his children up onto the specially fashioned saddle. He glanced at the dusty conestoga. The wagon had enough room for the three of them *and* a harvest. But Jessie had sold their last draft horse. Genie could not pull the wagon by herself. He cleared his throat. "Have you apologized to Genevieve for your recent growth spurts?"

"Sorry, Genie."

Jessie brought himself up, taking the reins and making sure Ethel was holding on to her father before they began. When he felt her hands lock around him, he asked Elijah if he was holding onto his sister.

"Yes," he groaned. "You don' have to ask."

"But I always will." He took his hat from the rack and as Genevieve turned, he pulled the cabin door closed.

The road to town was quiet. The only chatter came from nesting birds. The only pedestrians were two charging chipmunks; the only loiterer was a snoozing snake with a chipmunk-shaped belly. Despite the quiet, the journey was not uneventful. Ethel and Elijah were both nauseated by the ride, forcing frequent stops to quell their stomachs. By the time they arrived in Belford, Ethel had succeeded in keeping her breakfast down; Elijah had succumbed.

Veola met them at her brothel. One of the madame's employees hitched Genevieve while Veola took them through an adjacent alley. They entered her room from a separate entrance and climbed several stairs until they reached Veola's lofty room. There, she gave each twin a sugary snack. When the woman smelled Elijah's breath, Jessie told her, "We did not have any medicine today."

The old woman scowled, "I thought you bought a fortnight's supply?"

"I thought so, too. I'm fixin' to head to Donaciano's."

Veola breathed deeply, putting her hands on her hips. "And I am left alone again with them."

Jessie was cornered by three pairs of unhappy eyes. Elijah was trembling—no doubt from his nausea, Ethel was picking a scab—no doubt from her nerves. Veola looked at the children, rolled her eyes, and told Elijah to take a bath. "And Ethel, don't you dare leave another scab on my floor."

Jessie thanked the madame profusely, taking her hands and telling her, "You are wonderful, Veola. I'll make a day for us, just us. I promise."

Veola turned a wrinkled nose from Ethel and looked Jessie up and down. She readjusted her cleavage and said, "You best decide where your priorities are, Mr. Bingham. Even old ladies have needs."

"You aren't old," Jessie approached. "You're ripened."

"Farmin' metaphors don' make a woman feel appreciated," Veola turned. "I ain't cleanin' vomit today. You just get on."

Jessie left the loft knowing he would have to make a few concessions to the madame. He departed the claustrophobic alley thinking of all the ways he could please the madame without *pleasing* her.

The thought of sex at all, with any woman, revolted him. *Besides,* he thought, *the last time I slept with her, Glendolyn got sick.* Jessie wiped his face and steered his anxiety. Dwelling on his failures as a husband would only interfere with his success as a father. If Veola wanted sex, so be it. He needed to keep Glendolyn's children safe, one way or another. He was quickly approaching the age his father was when he fell ill. Jessie nodded, *They'll need a home if they lose me.* He turned onto the main street in a hurry. A gust of wind blew hot sand into his nostrils, forcing a sneeze.

He pressed a finger one by one to each nostril and blew his snot. He wiped his nose and stared at the end of the road.

The Big House—officially the mayoral offices—had been the residence of the Thorne family for almost a century. From Calloway the Fifth to Mary Anne, Belford had 'elected' four Thorne Mayors, all serving life sentences in that prison of power. Belford had practically become a family fief and the Big House was Thorne Castle.

Jessie jogged up the pretentiously steep steps. He pushed open a silver-laced doorway, sourced back east where trees were tall and mining was easy. The great doors parted down the middle, groaning against the echoing floor. The dark foyer greeted Jessie with silence.

"Hello," Jessie said after a minute. Usually, there was some servile man-beast at the entrance, ready to toy with him like a cat playing with a mouse. Now, however, there was nobody. The only other folk in that foyer were portraits of the ruling family. Jessie sniffled loudly, attempting to attract someone's attention. When nobody came to fetch him, he wandered toward the portraits.

Calloway the Fifth. Jessie's father never liked him. The patriarch of the Thorne had left his iron sludgeries out east to monopolize the water business. He had tried to dam the Copper River, only for it to flood and drown his younger brother.

Jezebelle Thorne. The smallest of the portraits, Jezebelle was Calloway's first cousin. Jessie shook his head, disgusted with how wealth broke down the barriers of smart breeding. Jezebelle never provided children and one day, mysteriously died.

Julila Thorne. Jezebelle's sister married Calloway the same year Jezebelle died. She gave birth to two inbred children.

Montgomery Belford Thorne. Jessie could not stop a snarl from appearing on his face. Of all the mayors, he was the worst. He let gangs lodge in the Big House and rewrote the law like it was always a rough draft. He was plain mean. When he died, many suspected his sister, Mary Anne, of foul play. Nobody cared enough about Montgomery to investigate.

"Whatchyu want?" Came a voice from behind.

Startled, Jessie turned. A short man glared at him. Jessie responded, "I have business with the mayor."

"She busy."

Jessie smiled, "Would you just tell her that J—"

"Busy," he repeated as if it were only one of a dozen words he knew.

Jessie licked his top lip like a rattler. His eyes darted down a corridor. The man stepped to his right, blocking the view. Jessie narrowed his gaze, nodding. "Alright, fine." He turned to take his leave.

Just then, a door swung open. Out came an old woman, tears in her eyes but pride in her stride. Catalina Romero stormed down the darkened hallway, pointing into the void, "You bringin' the devil, Thorne. After what happened to Valentina, I'd think you'd be wiser!" She brushed past the servant but stopped to give Jessie a pitiful look. "That witch ain't worth your time, Bingham." With a "Hmph," she left the Big House.

Mayor Thorne followed behind, slowly. Just as the great wooden doors of the mayor's abode crashed to a close, a cane clanged in the corridor. The mayor's voice preceded her, "Jeremiah Horn, did I not make myself clear?"

The servant responded, "No meetings today."

Step by step came the mayor. Every footfall straightened the stout man's posture. Every rasping breath made the servant more statuesque. Bloodshot eyes fixated on the poor Mr. Horn.

The man bowed his head and begged, "I can take him away?"

"Clearly you cannot," The mayor replied, popping her lips. "*She* took up half my morning with her... anxieties." She squinted like a viper, "If I have to talk to one more grieving parent or silly widow, I will hang you."

Horn stiffened.

After a pause, she clicked her tongue and pointed her cane. The servant scurried away, closing the door behind him hastily.

Mary Anne Thorne stared at him, letting the puss in her pupils leak down her cheeks like pestilent tears. Finally, she spoke. "Jessie J. Bingham."

"Mayor."

Mary Anne clasped her hands around the tip of her cane, leaning on it. "This is the second time this year."

Jessie rubbed the claim in his back pocket, feeling naked before the mayor. He sucked in his bottom lip, took off his hat, and pointed it down the dark corridor. "Shall we?"

The mayor responded with a twitch of her brow. "M'yes. After Romero's visit, I need a simple transaction."

"What did Ms. Romero want?" Jessie presumed to ask.

"There is some proverb about cats and the curious," the mayor alluded. "I cannot quite remember it."

"Right," Jessie immediately replied. "Sorry."

Despite chastising him, the mayor broke from her usual brevity. "Catalina Romero has gone mad. Savages butchered her family on the Forlorn Trail, if you remember."

"You know I remember," Jessie remarked. *Valentina was your only friend.*

Mary Anne ignored the comment. She guided him through the Big House, passing many large ballrooms, meeting halls, and libraries. Cobwebs coated the doorknobs, dust covered the darkened rooms, and the musk of aging furniture wafted through the air. "And now, to lose her son in the Flowers Affair. Simply, a coat of varnish on an already tortured life."

At last, at the end of the hall, they came to the mayor's office. Unlike her father, her mother, or her brother—Mary Anne never utilized extravagant halls or sitting rooms. Instead, she conducted all her business in the smallest room of the Big House: a closet. Although most found it odd that the mayor worked in a glorified cupboard, nobody dared gossip about the fact.

The mayor sat, eyes full of impatience. Jessie took out the deed, placed it on her desk, and took a seat opposite her. She combed her fingers through her thin air. Many strands of blondes, browns, and even a few greys floated off her scalp. Mary Anne Thorne donned a pair of heavy-looking spectacles and began combing the fine print.

Jessie looked around the room; the mayor's office was no bigger than his root cellar, yet the walls were completely masked in decorations. Paintings were placed intermittently, awards dotted some spots, and a few tapestries were draped from the surprisingly high ceiling. However, the most important and most prominent form of wall art came in newspaper clippings.

Most of the newspaper clippings focused on individuals—all of whom were at one time enemies of the Thorne. Criminals, bandits, upstarts, political opponents, labor workers, angry mothers—all were represented in cautionary tales. Foreclosures, unfortunate fires, random accidents...

This was the mayor's town and all who met with her knew it.

Jessie had been into the office before and was not overly disturbed by the flagrant display. What he was distracted by, however, was a black stone lying atop the mayor's desk. This was a new addition to Mary Anne's office and one Jessie did not think was a fear tactic. *I wonder what she's learned about the relics.* He moved his head slightly, watching the shimmering rainbow within the darkness. His legs began to bounce; he fidgeted in his pockets.

Mayor Thorne crumpled the parchment. "Why are you selling your land, piece by piece?" She allowed several seconds of silence. "I am a busy woman, Mr. Bingham. I would caution against long pauses, deep breaths, and stuttering."

Jessie nodded, "Sorry, ma'am. Yes, this is the second parcel."

The mayor's face contorted as her jaw slowly swiveled from left to right. "Redundancy is ill-advised."

"Need a little extra income."

"On account of that spring flood?"

Jessie hesitated for half a second before nodding. That amount of delay was enough for his lie to be noted and decoded. Mary Anne declared without any doubt, "Seems your children are growing more and more expensive."

"And my land less and less profitable," Jessie found himself saying.

"Why should I be interested in unprofitable land, Mr. Bingham?"

A sliver of air escaped his throat. He cleared his throat, "Well, ma'am. You're interested in all land."

The mayor grunted a laugh and looked to her side. When her gaze settled back on Jessie, she was smirking. Her body swayed bemusedly while she spoke. "And how does that make you feel, Mr. Bingham? Do you think I'm a filthy monopolist? A swindler?"

Jessie gambled, toying with his wedding ring as he answered. "I think our country was founded on a healthy mistrust toward government."

Another laugh, this time more of a snort. Mary Anne looked around at her family's edicts and her own personal, political trophies. "Careful with that wit, Jessie Bingham. This wall doesn't have space for you."

Jessie did not respond. How could he? There was always a level of conniving in the Big House. Calloway was the king of conquest, after all. But this woman... Mary Anne was a different mayor than them all. She was so very calm. Jessie never knew whether the mayor was plotting benevolence, malevolence, or her unique mix of the two.

The mayor remarked, "Donaciano Marcos is renovating his drugstore."

"He is."

"Medicine is a fine profession. But not ornate."

Jessie met her throbbing stare, gazing at the irritated pimples that coated the bags under her eyes. It was hard to believe she was only five years his elder. He glanced at her cane. "That is true."

"Anything you want to say about that?" After her question, her mouth remained slightly open, her eyes unblinking and hungry.

"No ma'am," Jessie said. He disliked Donaciano but he disliked violence more.

The puss-coated eyes turned from Jessie and stared at a blank space on her wall. "I will pay market value for the parcel."

"Thank you, ma'am," he said, bowing his head.

"Yes," the mayor replied, giving him dozens of sleek bills.

"Bank's closed today," Jessie remarked. Donaciano could not make change for such large denominations.

"It is."

Jessie blinked. "Right." Feeling he was dismissed, he put on his hat and turned to leave.

"And Mr. Bingham?"

"Yes, ma'am?"

"When you found Collin Flowers, did you notice anything strange at the scene? Besides the tongues staked their heads, of course... Anything you did not tell the sheriff?"

Jessie turned. The mayor was now staring at her desk. The obsidian lamp ensnared both their eyes. The colors within the sphere danced. He blinked, unable to look at the stone without hearing the voice from last night. "This about Ms. Romero?"

"That old fool?" The mayor made a weak attempt at chuckling. "She lost everything when the savages sacked her wagon." She clicked her tongue. "Losing her son in the Flowers Affair broke her mind, I reckon... Now, anything else you want to tell me?"

Jessie broke the stone's captivating spell and looked at his feet. "No, ma'am." He thought the mayor would catch his lie. Perhaps she did.

"Pity," was all she muttered. "Send my well-wishes to your babies."

"I will, ma'am." Jessie practically bowed. "Thank you, kindly." He did not linger in the Big House. He left the confined closet and the cobwebbed corridors. He bolted past the mighty door with a mix of breathless nervousness and giddy excitement. He could pay for his children's medicine. Today, he did not have to compromise pragmatism and paternalism. He could be a father. He rubbed the pristine bills in his hands proudly.

Jessie pocketed the money and stared down the sweltering street. Heatwaves like wisps floated from the road. Men in tall hats hid from the sun in their personal shadows. Women like prairie dogs darted from one store to the next, their arms full of supplies. Jessie noticed himself smiling at the scene. *How easy it is to appreciate the moment with a little money...*

"Mr. Jessie Bingham," Porfirio called from across the road. "Have you come in-ta town just to see poor ol' me?"

Jessie flashed a less-than-genuine smile. He could almost smell the liquor on the man's breath. "Afternoon, Porfirio."

"Indeed it is," said the newspaperman, now distributing a paper to the doorstep of the newly widowed Kate Flowers.

"That tomorrow's edition?"

"Yep," Mr. Pacheco replied, "Had-ta hire a new errand boy to keep the crofters like y'self informed. News writes itself now-a-times."

Jessie glanced at the adobe walls nervously. "I'd wager it does." *But we do not have to insult poor Kate and Cleona by gossiping at their doorstep.*

"Ah well," Porfirio declared, quite intuitively, "Best not dally on the doorstep a-the despairing."

"My thought exactly," Jessie remarked.

They walked down the road together, Porfirio pulling his newspaper cart Kuahtec-style. Two pinyon poles rested on his shoulders, two wrinkled hands wrapped around the wood, and two creaking wheels rolled along.

"I wish I had been on that expedition."

"No you don't," Jessie remarked coolly.

Porfirio paused, stared into Jessie's eyes, and laughed, "No, you're right. There weren't no glory in their deaths."

Jessie found himself unable to respond. They lived, at least superficially, in modern times. Most folk were literate, or at least pretended to be. Most people were raised with manners, or so they claimed. Indeed, the common view of learned folk was that the world had reached the end of civilization. Education had followed its natural course and culture had reached the pinnacle. Yet, here was Porfirio Pacheco talking about glory as if he were a castle-aged warrior.

"What-dya-say?" Pacheco slurred.

"Hm?" Jessie asked. He had not been listening particularly well.

"Bout comin' in for a drink?"

"Oh," Jessie nodded. "Sure."

They entered the oldest home in Belford. The Pachecos had lived in Copper Valley back when Tlacon were princes of the plains and Kuahtec ruled the river. More than a few thought they might be native themselves.

Porfirio lowered a large lever; the printing press began chomping and chewing fragments of stories. The newspaperman poured himself a shot as Jessie explored the office. Porfirio's workplace looked like it was perpetually ransacked. The various papers, bottles of ink, and miscellaneous curiosities that littered the floor reminded Jessie of the mayor's office.

Porfirio handed Jessie a glass of water and downed his agave spirit in one gulp. "How'd they die? The miners. Sheriff won' spare me a syllable. Couldn't even get a peek at the bodies. Had 'em all buried before some of the families even knew it!"

"Fine," Jessie leaned in, "I will tell you. If you swear to hold the information for three days. That way I don' step on anyone's business."

"I swear on my family's life."

"Swear on your printing press."

"Now wait-ya just a moment!"

"Swear it."

Porfirio flashed his teeth in a grinding wince. "I swear on her."

They each took a seat. Jessie leaned forward and whispered, "I don' know how they died, bu—"

"Ya see any sign of a shootout?" He pursed his lips and squinted at the ceiling, "A bit of a fusillade? What about arrows? Have the Tlacon and Kuahtec returned?"

"No arrows. Didn't see any sign of a shooting, either. Not clearly, at any rate. But the strange thing—what I gamble Biggs wants to keep hidden—was the faces."

Porfirio licked his lips and found a piece of crumpled paper.

Jessie's voice cracked, "Their tongues were cut out and staked to their heads."

Porfirio's eyes widened. He belched as he wrote, "A clear metaphor." He burped again, "Juicy."

"But not Collin Flowers."

Porfirio put down his pen. "What-dya mean, '*Not Collin Flowers.*' He was not so, uhm, ritualistically ended?"

Jessie suddenly felt a chill, "Were it not for the rigor mortis, I'da said he were alive." So distracted by the miner's stones, he had not given much thought to the miners themselves. "Perhaps there was strife?"

"Yes, a greedy sorta sickness," Porfirio's head bobbed as he wrote. "The Tlacon and Kuahtec been gone for months. If savages was the ones that murdered Flowers, I'll get sober." He placed his pen calmly on the paper. "There's a mystery here..." Suddenly, his body convulsed and he threw the objects into a pile of trash. He bolted to his feet. "Damn these bones."

Jessie jumped up. He watched the drunken writer with some apprehension. He debated taking his leave.

Porfirio marched toward the bottle of spirits and drank from it directly. He groaned, wiping his face as the stinking drink spilled down his chin. "If I was just a little younger, this story could have been my greatest work."

"It cannot, still?"

The newspaperman flashed a defeated smile. "Old age makes you a scavenger... And I am a scavenger, Jessie boy. Real stories is hunted."

Jessie put his hand on Porfirio's prized printing press. "I'll be straight with you, Porfirio." He paused to produce the correct combination of words, a concoction that would make Porfirio reflect but keep him from throwing something else. Slowly, he began, "There are no rewards for 'world's most cynical man.' If you made half as many happy sentences as you make unhappy ones, the whole country might think you the most charming of thinkers."

"I ought-ta argue."

Jessie took it as a slight victory that he did not. However, Porfirio did not seem interested in speaking at all. He looked around the room, at his hands, and then at Jessie. He smiled, tipped his hat, and began unjamming the printing press. His symphony of swearing was unhelpful in dislodging those rusted joints.

Jessie left the newspaperman to his toil. He crossed the street and made his way to Donaciano's drugstore. Crawford Biggs was standing at the entrance, curling his fingers and cracking his knuckles. It seemed to Jessie, the sheriff was waiting for him.

"Those youngins sure is expensive."

"All good things are," Jessie replied.

"Ain't that true," the sheriff smiled. "Well, I best be moseying." He tipped his hat and strolled away. A group of men exited Donaciano's drugstore, led by a shirtless giant with blood on his chest. The sheriff said to the man, "Alright, Rosco. Off to Mr. Willows."

Jessie stepped out of the men's way. These were the sheriff's deputies and most were recent arrivals to Belford. Jessie did not know any of their names, as he only saw them when the mayor was stirring up trouble.

Jessie hesitantly entered Donaciano's and said, "The usual."

The doctor did not lower his chin. He did not smugly stare past his spectacles. Indeed, the doctor was nowhere to be seen.

"Don Marcos?"

Two curtains parted and the doctor shambled into view. He was cradling his hand. His knuckles were blackened. His fingertips curled into hooks. He said nothing as he slowly fumbled with his wares. The doctor gathered several tinctures, groaning as he moved. He slid them gently into a bag and pushed it across the counter.

Jessie gaped, "Are you alright?"

The doctor growled, "Shut up."

Jessie's face flickered as the pity left it. "How much?"

"On the house."

"Surely, not yours?"

Doctor Marcos snarled, "Surely not." He pulled a crumpled paper from his pocket and tossed it at Jessie.

He recognized the document immediately— a claim to a small parcel. *She asked about the doctor...* His eyes widened. *Biggs loitering outside was no accident.* The mayor had paid him market price for a parcel she had not bought. He glanced at the doctor's maimed hand. *Mary Anne, what have you done?* At once, Jessie felt the characteristic guilt that had plagued him for over a year. Jessie felt the need to apologize to the filthy doctor. However, the doctor interrupted his sympathy.

"Now get outta my store."

The guilt left him. Jessie departed without a word. He walked into the main street and looked at the Big House. He squinted, seeing a figure standing upon those imposing sandstone steps. Then, he blinked at his bag of medicine. Not only was there the usual amount—there was double.

He looked back at the Big House. The figure was gone. Jessie cleared his throat, blinked, and acted as calmly as he could. With only the slightest skip in his step, he went to collect his children.

Chapter 4

◆

"Sheriff's investigation concludes savages were to blame for the Belford Butchery. As a humble connoisseur of the highest proof, this reporter requires further evidence to believe savages—who recently disappeared themselves—have committed murder in Belford. Indeed, to murder without pilfering an ounce of the miner's haul!"

– The Belford Inquirer

Jessie skimmed the rest of the newspaper. *He knows better than to question the Big House in print. He's one unfavorable story away from being a story himself.* He exhaled a gust of anxious air.

"You can't be mayor," Elijah told his sister. "You have to be a Thorne for that."

"That's not true," Ethel said confidently. "It is a position. It's uh, uh."

"Elected," Jessie chimed in.

"Yeah," Ethel declared proudly. "That means if I convince enough people, I get to be mayor."

"Good luck," Elijah scoffed. "Thorne won't let nobody step on her. She's a bi—" Elijah ballooned his cheeks and stared frightfully at his father.

Jessie put down the paper and gazed back at his son. Five seconds of fear and shame was a sufficient punishment for nearly swearing. "Good catch." He stood up from his chair, "But don't be so dismissive of your sister. Or the mayor, for that matter."

Elijah joined his father at the doorway where they strapped on knee-high boots. "But, daddy. She gots a reputation for a reason. She got all this money."

"Having money does not make you a bad person."

"But we don't got nothing!"

"We have a lot more than you know," Jessie told him. "Biggs, Marcos, Thorne... They ain't bad people. They've just been given bad parts to play in a lot of people's stories."

Elijah stared at his father in disbelief. He shook his head and proudly stated, "You're wrong."

Jessie laughed, "Could be I am." He ruffled his son's hair. "You're still going to make a gift basket for Mr. Marcos."

"Why, though?" Elijah's face scrunched up with indignation. "He was abusin' you."

"Sure was," Jessie agreed.

"Don't mean he deserved to get beat," Ethel said, cocking an eye as children do when they are awaiting praise.

"That's exactly right, Ethel," Jessie beamed.

Elijah's little lips trembled with countless choice words. He settled on one of his father's favorites, "That dumb bastard don't deserve nothin'."

I know that, Jessie wanted to say. *But your grandfather would turn in his grave if he heard us say so.* He massaged his brow. Laurent Bingham had never let poor behavior influence his own. And for that, he made friends with everyone. Even the Kuahtec loved his father.

Ethel chimed in, "Was mama always so forgiving?"

Jessie could not contain himself. The mention of their mother threw him over the edge. The insecurities he would rather not acknowledge manifested as irritation. He dragged his hands down his face and muttered bitterly, "Course she wasn't. That's why we were always figh—" He blinked at the twins. He absorbed the shock on their faces, formed an apology, and failed to say it. "Grab the basket, Ethel."

Elijah glared, intent on finding something more to argue about. Ethel changed the conversation before her brother could say some new swear he had learned. "Is Ms. Rosalee coming today?" There was a hint of trepidation in her voice.

She needs a break from watching you. "Veola said you two were growing close, that she was teaching you all sorts of crafts."

Ethel nodded hesitantly.

Jessie frowned, feeling he could please nobody. "Veola is working. Y'all will have to behave while I am in town."

"Is she our new ma?" Elijah asked. Though he was doing his best to sound stoic, the worry in his voice was unmistakable.

Jessie swallowed. He looked at his ring, "No, Ms. Rosalee is not your mother." He cleared his throat and opened the door. He pointed, "Your mama is just outside, waiting for you always."

"Where?" Ethel hurried to the door, staring hopefully.

"He doesn't mean it," Elijah muttered.

"Hey," Jessie said sternly. "Hey, look at me, Elijah." Jessie recalled what his father had once said to him when his own mother had passed away. "Your mama is in the stars."

Jessie had never really believed his father when he said such things. At best, he thought it was a comforting lie. His father's version of a pewside parable. Then, Glendolyn died. Suddenly, a woman living in the stars seemed not only possible—but necessary.

"How's she in the stars?" Ethel asked, curiously.

Jessie got to a knee and invoked the most powerful response of all, one which no child dared question. "Magic."

That proved a suitable answer for the twins. Elijah asked, "Did mama know magic?"

Jessie smiled, "In her way. She was always adventuring. Woulda made it to the Final Ocean one day... Were it not for me distractin' her."

"She musta loved the farm," Ethel said. "We adventure every day!"

Jessie nodded, glad the children had no memories of their parents' countless fights over the farm. "I guess we do, huh?" He recounted, "Though, mama loved unfamiliar things, mysteries and such. She always wanted to see the things she read about in a book. She was always talkin' about the ocean, the whales."

Elijah questioned, "Have you seen the ocean?"

"No," Jessie answered. He looked outside at the blue sky, imagining that the sea looked something like that. "Maybe we will all take a trip one day." He finished strapping on his boots, "Let's get this gift basket ready."

They combed their cabinets and cupboards; they fetched treats from the fields and the forest. Then, when the basket was brimming with agave spirit, gin, honeyed pinyon nuts, prickly cactus jam, and a fresh pigweed salad—the three stepped back to admire their work. "Now that's a *"thank ye', kindly"* if I've ever seen one."

Elijah mimicked his father, humming, "Mmmhm."

"So..." Ethel folded her hands behind her back, crossed her legs, and traced shapes on the floor with her big toe. "When you uh, when you are in town, you c-could look for a puppy?"

Jessie chuckled. She was not going to let a single day go by without asking. "I will be keeping my eyes open." He picked her up, "Now, what are you two going to do while I am gone?" He placed her on his comfy chair, with its sinking cushions and oversized armrests.

Elijah said, "We're gonna work the cactus mounds and make sure them grasshoppers ain't eatin' the pigweed."

Ethel pouted, "I thought we was gonna skip stones!"

Elijah widened his eyes. He signaled her with a flick of his head.

Jessie laughed, "I'm not workin' today. Why should you two?"

Elijah bowed his head, ashamed, "Because we gots to pull our weight."

Jessie frowned. He had felt like such a good father only days ago. Now, without rain or steady income, he felt like the same beggar. For the twins' sake, he smiled widely. "Hey, you." He charged his giggling son and picked him up. "See? You aren't much weight at all." He put Elijah next to Ethel and said, "Now. If you are going to skip stones, what are my rules?"

"Watch for critters before you skip," declared his daughter.

"Don't climb on boulders," said his son.

"Why's that?" Jessie inquired.

Elijah was quick, "Because rattlers nap between the rocks."

"Good," Jessie lifted his head and asked Ethel. "And, baby girl—how do we announce ourselves to our slithering friends?"

"Stomp so they can hear us."

Jessie smiled, eyed the door, and raised his eyebrows. "Have fun."

The twins charged outside. Jessie listened to the sweet sounds of their carefree laughter until, finally, he was left with his thoughts. He gazed at the gift basket, dreading giving that pustule of a man anything nice. Still, he had to do what was good for his children. *Marcos did not deserve the sheriff,* the better part of his character argued.

The worst part of his character was rather tickled by Marcos' misfortune.

Jessie cleared his throat. He would bring the gift basket and be done with it. First, though, he needed to be sure the twins would not get into trouble. He knew the children hiked with care. He had taught them that. He knew they could avoid a rattler; he had made sure of it. He knew they could skip stones without injury. Speaking stones were another matter entirely.

Jessie went to his bedroom and took the polished jewel from his dresser. He could not have it so accessible, especially if he were gone. It would have to go in the lockbox. He got as far as unlocking the contents and lowering the artifact. Then, sunlight hit the center of the stone. A glinting rainbow began to dance in the void. It seemed almost feminine in shape, with hips moving left and right to entice Jessie's animal eyes.

His hands trembled, wanting to explore the stone. He began probing the smooth edges. Then, he tapped the dancing core; only, the colors seemed beyond his reach, as if behind a thick window. He waited, breathlessly. The stone remained inert, save the glittering core which taunted him with its movement. "Oh, to hell with your games," he finally gave up.

"Just a toy, that's what you are. Something from out east meant to impress rich children." Jessie rubbed his eyes, sighed, and grabbed the door. His hand gripped the metal knob and as it did, the hair on Jessie's head stood tall. A gust blew through the room, shutting the door.

Jessie blinked. *There are no windows open.* He glanced at the spherical relic. He had forgotten to put it away.

Outside, the birds were squawking. Jessie recognized those calls, hearing them many times on a game trail. There was a predator. Jessie turned, gazing suspiciously at the motionless room. He approached the window and peered outside. The crows cawed from their perches. No hawk was circling ahead, no puma prowled below. Indeed, the birds neither looked at the ground nor the sky. They stared at the cabin, directly at him.

Jessie walked casually, inconspicuously, to his side of the bed. He slowly hoisted an antiquated weapon off its wall mount. More a glorified arquebus with updated engineering, the family rifle gave Jessie confidence. He raised his voice at the intruder—

His voice was not his own. Nor were his words. A being spoke in a language Jessie did not know but could comprehend fluently. "Common eyes cannot see the vision of Ur."

Jessie squirmed, trying to force the voice out. Not only his mouth had been commandeered. His entire body seemed to jolt without his consent. His toes tingled as if asleep. His fingers coiled around strange objects he was not touching. His mouth opened and the voice recited:

> *"Clay dries when overworked*
> *The mind hardens when overtaught*
> *Hands of the sculptor soon ruin the sculpture*
> *The rope snaps when over-taut"*

Then, as suddenly as the sorcery started, it stopped. Jessie felt his body relax. His spine loosened; the sensations gripping him faded. He brushed his hands against his pants, relieved to feel only fabric. He listened to the birds, now carelessly chirping.

The threat was gone.

Jessie removed the sphere from his pocket and hid it in his wife's jewelry box. He locked it, checked that it was locked, and kicked it deep under the bed. He left the room with sweat leaking from his hand onto the rifle. He swiped the gift basket and jogged out of the cabin. His mind was enthralled by thought. He did not note his actions nor his surroundings for some time, contemplating the events with a mix of depressive dread and childish curiosity.

When his mind rejoined his body, Genevieve was taking him to Belford. Dull aches came from his knuckles. He looked at his hands—one was coiled and trembling around the reins. The other was stiff and sweaty, glued to his rifle.

He swallowed, looking at the graveyard which lined the perimeter of town. Once, the prehistoric cemetery had fascinated him. It still did, but for different and more haunting reasons. Now, the tombs carved in foreign script made him shiver. Jessie could not tear his eyes away from the symbols on the graves, wondering if *that* was the language he had just spoken. The tombs mocked him with resigned silence, revealing no secrets.

The mythical Lugal captivated him. He pondered the fate of Collin Flowers and what role the Lugal might have played. Could Collin have drawn their ire, or did their doom lay latent in the stones?

Jessie was sure he would know the truth if he understood just one thing. *What is Ur?* Jessie pondered for only a moment before letting out a long, exasperated sigh. *Might be my mind is going to seed after all. Daddy always said stress ages the brain.*

Jessie put aside his questions. He dismounted and traded the rifle for the gift basket. He entered Donaciano's drugstore. The doctor hobbled from the back, parting the curtain with a clumsy wave of his good arm. When he saw Jessie, his face imploded with rage. His eyebrows melted with fury, his lips quivered with indignant words, and his nose twitched like a hunting dog mad with a scent.

"You come to gloat proper?"

"No," Jessie replied. *You dumb, insufferable…* He raised a smile along with his gift basket, placing it on the man's counter. "There's some good spirits in there. Fresh agave, some jam. Other things the twins wanted to give you."

Donaciano chewed on his lip, staring at the gift basket.

"I want it said," Jessie went on. "I do not condone violence. Even if you and I had our disagree—"

"I hope they die."

Jessie tilted his head. His nostrils flickered. His body tensed. Every muscle on his dominant side surged with heat. "What?"

"I hope," the doctor licked his lips. "That y'little boy dies." His mad eyes widened and he leaned forward. His tongue slithered from his mouth and he licked the air. "And that bitch with 'im.

The doctor continued his tirade. "I hope you ain't got the space in that grimy little cemetery a-yours. I hope you gotta dig up that whore of a wife and bury them little shits with her. Will the worms-a-started on her face? I reckon so."

Jessie let a few swears sizzle and die in his mouth. He ground his teeth.

"Personally, I'd treat them youngins like a lame horse," Marcos went on. He flicked two fingers at Jessie's face and mimed, "Poof."

Jessie smiled cordially. "Donaciano Marcos. I do believe if cruelty could be measured, you would be the standard."

"I say let them go now," the doctor went on. "Grave digging mighty hard work after they start *really* growing."

Snakes are meanest when they are scared, Jessie told his shaking fists. He forcibly relaxed his body. Then, he decided to be honest. "I am sorry for what happened, Don. But… I fear for your memory. I fear that when *you* die, you will be remembered as just another criminal."

The doctor's snarl wavered.

"I should be happy about the fact." Jessie shrugged. "But I suppose there's somethin' awful about such a human bandit as you becoming just another monster." To his surprise, the doctor had nothing unkind to say. As Jessie left, he thought he saw Donaciano Marcos bowing his head.

Or perhaps he was just blowing his snot.

Across the street, an ancient woman was loading an equally ancient wagon. Catalina Romero heaved a crate into the bed and wiped her brow. She raised her index finger and waved it like a sword. "Porfirio Pacheco, I am a woman of grace and mercy," she took a breath. "But so help me, if you ask one more question about the Lugal *myths*, I will pack you in this wagon and send y'to the Forlorn Hills myself."

Jessie listened intently. He hitched Genie to the nearby post.

"Mrs. Romero, I am a simple truthteller."

"Ms." Catalina corrected. She hopped down from the wagon. "You cannot remember I am a widow. Why should I entrust my stories with you?" She shook her head and snapped her fingers, "Find someone else to entertain your silly story. Savages murdered the boys. Mayor said so. Don't cross the mayor."

The old newspaperman scoffed, "We both know—"

With her thick accent, Catalina's words spewed in rapid succession. "I know nothing. If you are so certain, descend the bajadas, wander the playa, and if you are so lucky—you will die content with dehydrated delusions." She stormed past Pacheco, slamming her door shut.

Porfirio's arms hung defeatedly. He threw his notepad and rubbed his eyes.

Jessie approached, "What were you on about?"

Porfirio scowled at the wagon, full of crates, chests, and other miscellaneous provisions. "Catalina Romero is leaving town." He scanned the wagon madly, "Hear she stormed out the Big House, talkin' about sorcery..." He flashed a crazed, drunken smile at Jessie, "I know there is more. That's why the mayor won't let me write about it."

"Won't let you?"

"Said the town can't grieve 'properly' with me spoutin' nonsense. But there's some foulness in these murders. Course, there always is where murder's concerned. But this is..." He leaned in and whispered, "Now why would old Romero, the only woman for a hundred miles that's crossed the western slope—why is she leavin' on the eave of this mystery? Hm?"

Jessie peered into the covered bed. He wondered about the speaking stone's role in all of this. "You think witchcraft killed the miners?"

Porfirio shrugged. "I suppose so. After all, greed probably what done 'em in and greed's the worst magic of all." He licked his teeth. "Catalina may be old, but she ain't senile. She's fleeing. But what-a-from?"

Jessie's eyes darted to Catalina Romero's home. *She always said she saw the Lugal firsthand.* His heart thumped with excitement, his feet turned away from Porfirio. *I wonder if she would talk to me...* He probed for Porfirio's opinion, "Maybe the woman is tired of the West. Her son went with Collin Flowers, after all. She's got no one left."

Porfirio laughed mockingly. He drank from his flask and said, "This is why you can't seek the truth, Jessie Bingham. You," he belched. "Don' got the gumption." At that, he stomped belligerently down the road, throwing open the saloon doors with drunken strength.

"Gumption," Jessie repeated with one brow raised. He took a breath and knocked on Catalina's door.

"You are worse than a cockroach, Pacheco."

"Ms. Romero?" Jessie called. "I hear you are leavin'. I want to say goodbye."

"Why?" Catalina questioned. "I barely know you."

"What were you talking to the mayor about?"

"Wouldn't Pacheco like to know."

"I'm sure he would," Jessie replied.

"He is arrogant, drunk, and stupid. What combination are you?"

Jessie's voice cracked, "I am afraid and ashamed, mostly."

The door slowly opened. Hesitant eyes studied him. Again, Romero asked, "Why?"

Jessie glanced behind, "What do you know about Ur?"

The indignant snarl and half-smirk on Catalina's face disappeared. She whispered, "How do you know this name?"

"You recognize it, then?" Jessie's heart began to beat. His stomach turned. "You know what it is?"

Catalina pulled him inside and quietly closed the door. She brought a candle to her face. "Who," she corrected. She led him deep into the empty home. Only the useless knickknacks and trash that one accumulates over decades remained. The dust of a lifetime was in full view, like age spots on old skin. Catalina sat on a tidy bed. "*Ur* is a Lugal word."

Jessie's pride perked its head, *I knew she would have something to say.* His compassion made a point to remark, pointing at the bed, "He was a good man."

Catalina nodded, impressed that he knew the bed belonged to her boy. "Victor was greedy."

Jessie swallowed, having nothing to say to that.

Catalina, luckily, was not finished. "I blame his father. With a man in his life, Victor would not have followed Collin Flowers into oblivion." Catalina's catlike eyes peered into his own. "You know, your father almost went west with us. There's never been a luckier word said than when Laurent Bingham told me, *no.*"

"He admired you," Jessie felt the need to say. "Never thought you were..." He trailed off, not wanting to bring up old wounds.

The old woman chuckled. "Oh, I've been called mad before. It doesn't bother me now." She shook her head and folded her arms placidly.

Jessie did not know what to say. He let Catalina lead the conversation.

Catalina licked the circumference of her lips. "Do you have any idea the thrill we all felt?"

"Thrill?"

"You were born knowing the borders of the world. When I was young, maps would be outdated the moment they were printed." She painted the air around her with her memories, "A limitless ocean. The 'Final' ocean. The most beautiful lands with bounty for all. Orchards, meadows, rolling hills. And the call of gulls in the morning..." Catalina's face darkened. There may have been a lone tear, but she hid it with a well-timed bow of her head.

Jessie finally had something to contribute, "My wife was on her way to the coast when she ran out of funds."

Catalina looked up.

"She started at Rosalee's working house just to pay her way." Jessie smiled at the old woman, "Then I came along."

Catalina wiped her eyes, making it seem like she was plucking a lone lash. "Many wagoneers went destitute on their road. We thought we were smarter. My husband convinced us to take a shorter way. My oldest girl, Valentina, argued against the idea. My husband beat her for that. Over the Forlorn Hills we went."

Jessie could not imagine any scenario where he would cross those mountains willingly. He said as much to Romero, who responded,

"Yes," Catalina leaned in, contriving a smile. "But we had a guide." She stood up and began pacing, her silhouette dancing in the candlelight. "After your father refused our offer, my husband befriended a savage from the south, a nomad."

"A Lugal?" Jessie gasped.

Catalina barked a laugh. "If only. No, this was a simple savage. A Tlacon. His name was Pu'ontihotec. And he told my husband, with a bravado that should have been a warning to us all—'*The Lugal destroyed themselves. They live only in story now.*'"

Catalina chuckled, smiling ruefully at the ceiling. "Oh, it does feel good to reminisce, Bingham. Even if the remembrances all are bad." She breathed deeply, "We went west with the fullest confidence that all the world was mapped, that there was nothing more to fear from wild places."

"So we crossed the hills, hardly any care given to warnings." Catalina continued. "Pu'ontihotec assured us the Lugals were only used as legends to stop the wagons. Propaganda to keep our folk contained."

The evening air was rapidly cooling. Winds from the west flew down the Forlorn Hills. A gust swept into the room, blowing out the candles briefly. When the flames rekindled, he stared at the flame.

Catalina looked also. "Our journey before the Hills was not easy, but it was familiar. Creeks were flowing water. Woods were standing trees. Animals were mute beasts." Catalina's face morphed with fear and revolt. "The basin beyond is different, Bingham. It is like time forgot those lands."

"Our guide said the Lugals had passed into story, but he believed the legends. When we came upon a vast ruin, littered with artifacts and treasures, Pu'ontihotec warned us not to pick anything up. He said that the land was cursed. My sons did not listen, I think."

"One day, Pu'ontihotec brought us to an oasis. We were all eager to fill our skins." Catalina went silent for a moment, fidgeting with her hands. She asked, "How many children did I have, Mr. Bingham? Have the gossipers gotten me right?"

Jessie punctuated his nervous reply with a sniffle. "Five, I believe."

Catalina beamed, "Five." She glanced at him, recounting, "Two grown boys, two growing girls..." Her jaw jittered and her eyes welled. Her voice cracked, "And a baby." The old woman retook her seat on her son's bed. She cradled Victor's pillow close to her chest.

"Ms. Romero, I don't want to cause you pain."

Catalina ignored him. "We had only been stopped a few moments when strange people leapt from the trees. We knew it was a savage attack, but... I had never seen savages so armored. My husband's shots bounced off their breastplates. My sons' axes splintered on their quilted shields." Catalina's voice trembled and deepened. "Spearmen encircled my husband. They burned him alive with their spears. Burned him, Mr. Bingham."

Catalina wiped another tear, "The men all died and I never saw my girls again." The old woman stared down at the pillow, brushing her hand gently against the fabric.

Jessie watched the woman's movements. He noted how her fingers traced an invisible shape, how her hand massaged an invisible scalp. The woman's entire body was sinking into the memories of motherhood. Jessie thought about his children and looked at his lap. "How did you escape? Your son?"

"I didn't."

Jessie raised his head.

Catalina put the pillow neatly back onto the bed. The candles shivered, making a thousand silhouettes appear. Darkness danced with gangly limbs. Faceless heads stretched and contracted along shadowy lengths. "They brought me and my baby to the wreckage of the wagon. They made me look at my boys, my husband." Her throat tightened with tears, but she refused to cry. Her voice rose, "A man spoke to me. I did not understand him at first."

"At first?"

Catalina met his surprised stare. "Then, he rummaged through the wagon bed and pulled out a polished, black stone. The boys must have taken it from the ruins. It was so smooth and flat, I thought it was the devil's dinner plate."

Horror overcame him. Jessie's eyes sank deep into his skull.

Catalina smiled ruefully. "You understand, then. Collin Flowers brought the devil with his hoard. Brought the devil right to Belford." She stared at him, "And he is hungry."

So many questions came to Jessie at once, all competing for his voice, he only managed a stutter. He paused, collecting himself.

"D-did they, uh, brutalize your family, also? Like they did to Collins' outfit?"

Catalina licked her lips, "No. That was some new barbarism…" She gazed at the pillow mournfully. She swallowed, looking at her mantel. "The man brought me the stone and made me place my hand over his. Then, he spoke—"

"And you understood," Jessie interjected knowingly.

Catalina squinted. "I will never forget those words, but I did not understand. I still do not, all these years later."

"What did he say?"

Her eyes darted from the mantel to every window in the room. She leaned forward and recounted, *"We spared you and your child. This is more than your ignorance would have done. The Eyes of Ur would have destroyed you."*

"Ur…"

Catalina lifted her shoulders and shook her head. "A name, but I never learned to whom it belonged."

The two sat there for a long while in silence. Jessie's head was overflowing with questions, yet he could not voice any of them. He tapped his fingers on his thigh, thinking. *I should not keep the stone in the house. I should throw it into the river.*

Finally, after many minutes in the shared illumination, the candlelight waned. Catalina spoke. "The mayor is playing with the devil's tools. Those stones what killed my son, not any man. They'll kill her, too."

Jessie felt his heartbeat quicken. "Why don't you tell her?"

Catalina merely shrugged. "The mayor hears as well as she sees." She stood up, signaling that their meeting was over. "At any rate, I am leaving. I ain't gonna spend one more night in this land of ill omen."

Jessie rose. He spoke as the faint, flickering shadows frolicked before him. "Thank you, Catalina. You have a safe trip, wherever you're going."

The old woman saw him out. As he walked out of town and toward the eaves, Catalina called, "You as well, Mr. Bingham."

That night, while the twins slept peacefully, Jessie took the speaking stone from its lockbox and took it deep into the forest. He dug it a grave as if he were its murderer and threw it into the dirt. Once it was buried, he removed a cactus pad and planted it above the stone. With any luck, a garden of blades would soon guard the cursed relic.

Chapter 5

> *"Catalina Romero has fled town after a quarrel with the mayor. The eyes and ears of Belford report Romero had qualms about how the Big House handled the Flowers Affair. The sheriff and his faceless deputies have been extraordinarily tight-lipped about the details of the incident and this reporter has certain suspicions. For instance, why has nobody seen the strange minerals found by Collin Flowers? What treasure is the mayor hiding?*
> *The auctioning of Romero's vacant home will begin promptly at noon next."*
>
> – The Belford Inquirer

Jessie reread the front page of the newspaper. Two days had passed and Pacheco's printing press remained quiet. Normally, Jessie would not have noticed the interim, but Porfirio had been printing column after inflammatory column. He found it hard to believe the newspaperman had run out of 'gumption.' Now two days without even a pamphlet of ill-informed rumors, Jessie was starting to worry.

He went too far this time, Jessie knew. After a stretch which did nothing for his sore back, he stood up. Jessie put his hands on his hips and leaned back, trying to relieve the dullness in his spine. The hardwood floor beside the bed was not the most comfortable spot to sleep. To his left, Veola Rosalee was sleeping peacefully on *his* side of the bed. His wife's side remained perfectly unoccupied, though he had moved her pillows to the dresser to avoid getting any stench on them.

Two arms reached from the blanket; toes peeked out from the covers. Veola Rosalee rubbed her eyes, speaking groggily, "Mornin' stranger."

"Good morning," Jessie managed. He hoped the madame was too tired or distracted to hear the regret in his voice, the indecision and shame that permeated his body. His fingers twitched and curled absently.

Veola sat up, letting the blankets fall from her chest. She threw her arms high and clasped them together in an evocative stretch. She watched as Jessie hastily turned his attention to folding sheets. She declared, "Oh, don't be saintly. We had a lot of fun. Just like old times."

Jessie looked briefly at the woman. His lips jerked like a fish caught on a line. *I should never have invited her over. This was a mistake.* He secured his wedding ring, which had drifted down his finger.

"Maybe next time, you could sleep on Glendolyn's side? I'm sure she would not mind."

"Mm," Jessie hummed, sure that she would. He tried for a deep breath, wheezing slightly. A heaviness had taken residence in his lungs. The weight grew as he saw Veola in the foreground and his wife's pillows in the background. He yearned to take a full breath.

"Jessie, baby," Veola rose, bearing her body proudly. "I can' play homesteader if I'm feelin' unwanted."

Jessie turned to humor, "Last night made you feel unwanted?"

Veola's bent forward and retrieved her clothing.

Jessie felt the familiar compromise between his reason and his want. He felt his wisdom, his guilt, and his shame all drain away with the swelling below his waist. He glared at Veola, hating how she lingered in that pose to dominate his attention. His eyes were entirely on Veola's body as she began hiding it behind a summer dress.

"I can' ever know your grief, Jessie. And I don' mean to, neither. But I am a proud woman." She readjusted her brassiere, spending several seconds groping, squeezing, and teasing.

"I know," Jessie agreed impatiently. He could not bear to talk about his wife while being seduced. He changed the subject, eyes roving greedily. "You are a beautiful woman."

"Think so?" Veola asked coyly, now turning to her side. She flattened the creases in her dress, tracing the curves of her body.

"I do," Jessie approached. *And I am nothing more than a drunk.*

Veola stood tall and put a hand on her hip. She tilted her head and raised a brow, "Hm. Well, you know—I've learned to never trust a compliment from a man at half-mast."

Jessie hesitated just long enough to feel a sense of guilt. Then, he put his hands on her shoulders. Before the woman could say another word, he pushed her onto the bed.

Veola gasped as she fell. Then, she looked at him playfully. She traced a circle around her nipple, guiding Jessie's eyes to what hid beneath the fabric. She lowered her chin, eyeing the man's excitement. Her eyes flickered, waiting.

Jessie got atop her, rubbing against her dress in a rhythm to match her breathing. He kissed her neck, slowly moving to her cheeks, her forehead, and then her mouth. Veola beamed blissfully, eyes closed and mouth open. She arced her body, pressing closer to Jessie. She grabbed onto him, nails sinking into his skin. He felt her heartbeat between her interlaced legs.

Jessie lifted his body, releasing the pressure. He stared into Veola's wanting eyes, savoring her subtle squirming motions which sought to bring his body into hers.

Veola whispered, "No wonder Glendolyn fell for you so quickly..." She bit her lip to stifle a moan, "You play women like an instrument."

His eyes narrowed. *Why did you have to mention her?* Jessie felt himself rapidly softening. Wanting to salvage some of the moment, he pulled away. "That's true." Standing naked, he eyed her with a smug smile, "And sometimes, I like to finish a tune on an unresolved note."

Veola bit her lip, staring with subdued respect. The madame rose, letting her dress once again cover her. She shook her head, "I'll stay one more night, but then I have to get back to the working house." She pushed her cleavage down, "I'm not a mother, as much as some of my clients want me to be." She kissed Jessie on the cheek, collected her payment from the nightstand, and strode out of the room.

Jessie lingered for a moment, eyes fixed on his wife's pillows. He would have apologized, had he believed the dead cared to hear the babble of the living. He dressed quickly. By the time he escaped the bedroom to prepare the twins' tinctures, they were already sitting with Veola, mouths full of breakfast.

"Are you staying with us forever, now?" Elijah asked as he chewed.

"Finish your bite," Veola answered, preoccupied. "Or you'll choke."

Elijah swallowed. "Are you?"

Jessie did not want to give the children false hope. As much as he wanted his children to have a maternal figure, he was beginning to wonder about his choices. He answered, "She is just staying a little while longer."

"Why?" Ethel asked her father.

Jessie grabbed the twins' medicine and distributed it. "Because I need help," he said in a half-truth. "And because nobody has responded to our advertisement for a farmhand."

Elijah stared, puzzled. "But Ms. Rosalee ain't a farmer."

Jessie sat beside his son. At his young age, he still believed professions were born into. And as all their ancestors had farmed, the assumption was an educated one. "She will be after we are finished with her, ain't that right?"

Modest agreement from Ethel and Elijah.

Veola stood and commanded, a bit too business-like for Jessie's ears, "You two finish eating. I am going to talk with your father."

"Is that right?" Jessie frowned playfully, hoping to diffuse the annoyance in her voice. It did the opposite. He got up and pointed, "You heard her, Ethel. Stop slipping pemmican into your pockets."

Outside, Veola walked for a while before stopping. She stared at the plant mounds, where prickly pear fenced in pigweed and pole beans. "I won't play second-best to her."

"I don't ask you to," Jessie started. *Don't bring Glendolyn into this.*

"I'll watch the little devils today, but I want honesty between us."

"Devils?" Jessie stepped back.

Veola waved a hand dismissively, "Poor choice of words." She took his hand and asked, her voice soft and her eyes wide, "Why the change, Jessie? Why let me into your bed now? It has been a year since our first bout-a fun."

Jessie did not answer immediately. *Well, that's simple,* he would have liked to say. *I fear being alone because Catalina Romero preached hellfire until I was blue in the face.* He tapped his thigh, punctuating his speech, "I am worried about Porfirio."

"You haven't been to see him since I came up."

Jessie continued his half-truth, "I think the mayor locked him up."

Veola turned, "Because of his paper?"

He nodded.

"Well," Veola breathed deeply. "He shoulda known better than to mock her authority. He's lucky her brother ain't mayor still, or he'd be dead."

He may be yet, a part of Jessie dared to think. "I am going to check the stocks today."

Veola analyzed judgingly, "You're too good to that drunk."

"He's like a—" His eyes darted across the field to the family cemetery. "A mentor."

Veola raised a knowing eyebrow. She rolled her eyes, "Mhm."

Jessie changed the subject, "You think you can handle getting nopales today?"

Veola licked her lips, "You think one good lay will make me farm for you?"

"Okay, okay," Jessie glanced at the ground. He scratched his ear, "Just make sure the children gather a few for supper. I'll cook 'em up tonight."

Veola folded her arms and turned, "Go on and get saddled, you're givin' me age spots just chattin' away."

Jessie did so, glad to be relieved of Veola. He mounted Genevieve and spurred her along. However, Elijah came out from the woods and stopped him. "When you gon' be back?"

Jessie smiled, hearing the longing in his son's question. "Soon."

"Will you tell us a story tonight?"

A spasm went through his arms, shaking the reins. "Of course," he lied. "Maybe something a little happier than the last one. Oliver Pennington?"

"Yeah," Elijah agreed. He said, attempting a deeper voice, "That'd be good for Ethel."

"It'd be good for all of us," Jessie smiled. "You get on and help Veola with the nopales."

"Ethel already is."

"Ah. Good. That's a woman who has never despined a cactus pad, I'm sure of it."

Elijah sniffled and shuffled his feet anxiously. "Are you gonna marry her?"

Jessie tilted his head, "Why do you ask that?"

Elijah's voice wavered and cracked, "Because I don't want you to replace mama."

Jessie got off his horse and hugged his son. He held the boy tightly, saying, "I don't want to replace her, either." He let go of Elijah and dusted off his shirt. There was some dirt already on the boy's forehead. He licked his finger and wiped it off.

"I'm just gonna get dirty again," Elijah squirmed.

Jessie finished and promptly ruffled his son's hair. "That's why you get done with chores so quickly. Ethel and I care about proper presentation at the dinner table."

"If you ain't dirty, you ain't workin'."

Jessie interrogated playfully, "Did you think that up?"

Elijah nodded, "I been reading like you said to."

"Hm," he grunted. "Well keep reading. And watch over everyone while I am gone." Jessie vaulted atop Genevieve and departed the Bingham stead. A loitering smile lingered on his proud face for several minutes.

The elevation declined. Junipers replaced pinyons. Chokecherry replaced sagebrush stands. Then, when a large rattler was sunbathing on the road—a shrug replaced Jessie's smirk. He guided Genevieve off the trail, into a meadow of scalded, dead grass and sunbaked yucca. The fruit had just begun to ripen and many critters were busy braving the bladed leaves.

The summer monsoons had been infrequent and insufficient. Browning pine needles and sappy trunks revealed a devastated woodland. Nevertheless, the sparse torrential storms had recently saturated the ground, creating ideal tracking conditions. Not realizing how suffocated he had felt at the cabin, Jessie took his time off trail. He scanned the mud as they went, guiding Genevieve along a meandering route through the wild. Jessie saw a single bear track, but that was old. There were no traces of puma, though a handful of coyote tracks caused him to take a longer, winding way through the junipers.

Finally, after a few extra hours of travel, Jessie could smell the market in the air. That made him think about his twins' upcoming birthday. *Maybe I will get them a dog...* He entered Belford in the late afternoon. A potential buyer loitered outside Catalina's vacant home, eyeing it through the window. Jessie thought about shooing him away, but he did not want to stir up any more trouble. He rode directly to the Big House. Jessie hitched Genie beside many other beasts and apologized, knowing her penchant for solitude, "This is just for today," he told the annoyed mare. Genevieve sent a gust of air vibrating through her lips.

Jessie jogged up the pompous promenade and met with the stout servant at the door.

"No visitors," Jeremiah Horn declared. He motioned to two deputies sitting nearby in the shade. He smiled tauntingly.

"I am not here for the mayor. I wish to see a prisoner in the stocks."

"Ain't no prisoners in the stocks."

Jessie employed Mayor Thorne's own method. Using a tactic he knew to work on the servile man, he simply stared. Within seconds, the man's posture weakened. Then, his arms unfolded. As if being crushed, his palms flattened. Mr. Horn raised his hands innocently. "Ain't no prisoner."

Jessie stayed quiet, sucking in his bottom lip and glancing at the door knowingly.

Finally, the servant declared, "I ain't gotta open the door for nobody."

"That's true," Jessie finally said. "But I think as I made up fifteen percent of the mayor's storehouse last year, you should open the door. It is in your best interest. After all, who grows the agave in your spirits?"

"You ain't even had a spring harvest *this* year," Horn snarled. "She could strongarm you outta y'land whenever she fancied."

That's true, Jessie said to himself. *And she could throw you in the stocks just as quickly as Porfirio.* He changed his tone and adjusted his angle, "I want to talk with Mr. Pacheco about respect."

"Respect?" Horn snorted. "Whatchyu know about respect?"

He did not deny Porfirio is in the stocks. "I know Mr. Pacheco crossed the mayor and spoke condescendingly to her. Mary Anne and I both agree that is unwise, but I think a friend telling him so might be better than one of the mayor's—" *Minions, demons, brutes...* "Officers."

"Oh, let the bastard inside," said one of the sheriff's deputies.

Jeremiah Horn's jaw sank slightly. The pieces began to fall into place, crashing slowly into one another as the point made sense. "Think I should, Sledge?" He asked another lawman.

"I'm with Two Strings. Ain't no harm lettin' him teach the bastard some manners."

Horn ground his teeth. After an agonizing period of contemplation, the servant bobbed his head. He unlocked the Big House and led Jessie past the foyer and down a musty staircase. Horn brought him to a massive stone door and fumbled for a moment with his keys. After a delay, he managed to find the right key and opened the groaning stone entrance.

A four-armed antechamber loomed. Another guard appeared from the shadows. He was yet another deputy whose face Jessie recognized, but whose name he did not know. Jeremiah Horn took his leave and left the pair. The new deputy grabbed an oil lamp and illuminated the shadowy halls.

"What's your name, if I may ask?"

The deputy squinted at him. He lengthened his spine and broadened his shoulders, as certain men did when threatened. "Quincy Maples."

"You like being a lawman?" Jessie asked. He figured he knew the answer, but introductions were always a good time to learn about a person's character.

Quincy Maples ignored the question and said casually, "Drunks ain't proper reporters. Mr. Pacheco bein' held until he sobers up."

Jessie could smell the liquor on the man's breath. He noted the hypocrisy of the statement with a few blinks. He analyzed the antechamber, a crossroads of three separate tunnels. The oil lamps burned relentlessly in the dark, creating a humid and oppressive heat. "May I see him?"

Quincy paraded a frown. "I don' rightly know. Could be you has booze on ya. Wouldn't want the old muckraker to slip."

Jessie tried and failed to think of something witty to say.

Mr. Maples hunched his back and leaned forward, probing Jessie with an outstretched neck. Then, he recoiled like a snake and giggled. "Oh, Bingham. I only kid. You's a saint and all the world know it. Come on."

"Thank you," Jessie muttered.

"Read you still questin' for a farmhand."

"Your eyes are correct."

"More than the mayor's, I'd wager."

Jessie said nothing. He was more than shocked to find one of the mayor's men bad-mouthing her, especially in the Big House.

"If I was you, I'd sell that bit a-dust an' go to the delta. Good work down that way."

"That's good advice," Jessie lied. *And do what? Farm salt grass as an indentured servant?*

Mr. Maples guided Jessie down a lamplit hall that branched into separate jail cells. Belford was far too small and civil a town for such a stockade, but Calloway Thorne was a city dweller before claiming the mayorship. That gave him a fear of his fellow person that no honest farmer could ever have.

Further down the stockades, they encountered another of the sheriff's deputies. Jessie knew that one. He was the great beast that had beaten Donaciano. "Afternoon, Rosco."

"Yup," replied the giant. He walked away.

"Y'know," Maples clicked his tongue. "I missed havin' someone to look after. What's the use in thick stone walls and a fireproof door if we only housin' roaches?"

Porfirio rasped, "These cells should house highwaymen like yourself."

Quincy Maples simply grinned and slithered away.

Jessie approached the iron columns, peering into the cobble grotto. The shadowy outline of a slumped figure was etched into the corner. His features obscured, Porfirio looked like a toppled gargoyle. "I do believe this is the worst headache of my long life, Jessie."

Jessie joked, "Not a fan of sobriety?"

His friend groaned, "This is intolerable. I've not a clue how you do it."

Thinking of Veola Rosalee in his wife's bed this morning, he answered, "Sometimes, I don't."

Porfirio's sunken head rose. "Why'd you come?"

"There's been no paper for days. I figured the mayor had enough of you."

"I only hunt the truth," Porfirio grumbled. "Told her as much. I says: *'Ma'am, behind every social critic is a fierce patriot.'* She just gave me the dead eyes and walked away. Whore."

Jessie scratched his ear. He found himself irrationally annoyed.

Porfirio stumbled from his corner. The lamps illuminated his face, revealing a black eye and a bloodied lip. He sank back to the ground with a groan and closed his eyes. "This was the story of my career, Jessie boy." He shook his head mournfully, his words disjointed. "I wish I was like you, Jessie. If my wife woulda just died, I coulda stomached it. But to leave me." He spoke slowly, his broken words spliced together by airy pauses. "And then the kids."

"You can't replace family with work," Jessie said. "I tried, believe me."

"If I don', what-a-then am I?"

Jessie shrugged. Porfirio had every right to be sad. The mayor had taken away his source of meaning. *A man without ambition is either a happy monk or a sad degenerate.* He wagered he knew which of the two Porfirio was. "You're a good man."

Porfirio scoffed, "Being a good man is a thankless profession."

Jessie bit his tongue. He regarded the man there, slumped over with sickly eyes and limp limbs. "You were like a..." Jessie could not say what he meant without feeling disloyal. "Like a role model to me."

Porfirio strained, slowly turning his head. Though the stockades were dim, he squinted. "Role model," he mocked. "Well, ain't you stupid."

"What?"

Porfirio growled, "Why would I want someone to idolize me? I never lived up to my ideal, how could anyone else hope to?"

"Self-pity is like salt," Jessie scolded.

Porfirio glared, "Don't you dare use my words against me! That's cruel and..." He froze, clawed the floor, and crawled toward a chamber pot. He gagged for several minutes. Finally, he was relieved of his food and fluids. He curled into a fetal position.

"You won't be in here forever," Jessie hoped.

"You right," Porfirio admitted weakly. "Mayor might have me disappeared like she did her dear brother."

Jessie looked over his shoulder, not comfortable with discussing such a rumor in the Big House stockades. *He's going to get me thrown in here, too.*

"Don't you have somewhere to be? Another whore to wed?"

Jessie hated that word. His heartbeat quickened and his entire body began to sway with a quaking rage. The irritation which he had been so stoically managing burst forth. "You call Glendolyn a whore again and you lose the only friend left to you." His words flowed thoughtlessly, "You think you are some wise sage cast off by society, but you are the one shunning everyone. Have you written to your children? No. Your pride won't let you."

The contorted figure was silent for a moment. Porfirio cradled his body closer. Finally, he muttered spitefully, "Who said anything about *that* whore?"

Jessie lunged at the irons, rattling them. "Go to hell, Porfirio."

"Done."

Jessie looked disgustedly at the figure, "This cell is just what you need. You've become something, not someone."

"Clever boy. You find that in a book or fashion it by your lonesome?"

Jessie wanted to argue, but the pitiful scene steered his anger off the course. "You know, Porfirio. You're at the twilight of your life and for all your reflection, you ain't been served. I think you need a new mirror." At that, he left the muckraker to sober up.

Jessie fled the suffocating humidity, thankful for the desert air as he'd never been before. He thought of his wife, who always dreamt of the ocean. *She would have hated it there, in the end.* The thought of Glendolyn brought Jessie a sudden jolt of shame. He went through the motions of hating Porfirio, Veola, and finally—himself. Tears threatened to bar his cheeks as he fled the stockade. However, he soon collided with a figure and nearly fell back down.

The mayor snarled, "Damn it, Bingham. Watch where you are going."

As I am the only one who can, Jessie rolled his eyes. Mary Anne glared at him, her pupils somehow more drained of color than Jessie remembered. "I missed the paper," he stated.

Mary Anne lifted her brow and turned her head in a quick, knowing gesture. "Drunks make bad writers."

He immediately thought of Quincy Maples, "Do drunks also make bad deputies? Or does that enhance their function?"

"Careful, Jessie," warned the mayor. "I like you." She came down a step and tapped her cane gently against the side of his knee, "But affection is fickle."

Jessie winced away a vision of his wife.

"You knew he was in the stockades," the mayor noted.

"Mayor Thorne," he said in a dangerously lax tone. He formed a sentence, *You aren't that difficult to understand.* His mouth opened. No noise emerged from his throat.

To Jessie's immediate relief, Mary Anne laughed. She retracted her cane and leaned on it, wiping the mucus beneath her eyes and drying her hands on her dress. "Don't mistake me, I think Porfirio's paper is rather cute. Most of the time."

Jessie studied her, now suspicious of a smiling face he had not seen since the woman was a teenager and he a small child. Her curly, blonde hair had darkened since the last time he had seen her smile. He found himself enthralled and even afraid by how lightly the woman spoke. Jessie looked behind him, afraid of a trick.

Mary Anne continued, "I understand his obsessiveness with this story. Murderers, stalkers, savages—we civil folk love to fear them."

Jessie swallowed. *It is why Belford tells stories about Ghostly Mary, who killed her own brother.*

Mary Anne stared past him, "Terrors make us feel like our forefathers, make us feel like we did before civilized society." She turned, abandoning whatever errand was bringing her to the stockades, "Porfirio is using this awful tragedy to feel human, but that is a hollow approach." She looked back at Jessie, "Loitering and trespassing are so often mistaken for one another, Mr. Bingham."

Taking the warning, Jessie followed the mayor out of the stockades.

The mayor continued, her cane tapping ahead of her. "Fear is what makes us feel human." She barked a laugh, "You humble people like to tell stories about 'Ghostly Mary Anne' who made her brother disappear..." Another sigh, "We all love a good monster."

Jessie swallowed. He had perfect justification to think he was the worst husband to ever take a vow, the most absent and impoverished father, and the least loyal friend—but he never believed the worst in others. There were always too many points to the contrary. "I don't think you're a monster."

The tapping of her cane briefly stopped. Mary Anne did not say anything, but she turned her head as if she was going to. Their walk soon resumed and Mary Anne ended the conversation with a quiet, nostalgic mutter, "We love fear."

"Ma'am," Jessie overtook her at the top of the staircase. He offered his hand, but she refused his help. He swallowed, "I reckon it's the reverse."

"Indeed?" Mary Anne remarked dismissively. Her eyes darted to the side, peering at Jessie from her periphery. She whispered in a monotone alto, "Your visits to the working house have given you undue bravado, Mr. Bingham."

She gripped her cane proudly and strode down the foyer, barking at her sleeping servant, "Jeremiah Horn, you are the most useless butler I have had the displeasure of employing. You can rest when you are dead, op—"

Jessie's heart beat rapidly. The mayor was never interrupted, especially by herself. "What is it?"

The mayor put a hand on the servant's neck. After a moment, her cane began to shake. Her head moved quickly to the left and the right. Finally, she gazed at Jessie in horror. "Strangled."

Chapter 6

———◇———

"Male. Of solid build and sound mind before attempting the Forlorn Trail. Father of three children, all deceased. Resident of Greenview Sanitorium since winter of last year. Puzzle-solving abilities still rigorous, though sapience is a dubious claim. As is the case with all others, the man's memory is shattered and his human capacities withered. He does not know his name"

– Greenview Manifest

Mary Anne folded the sanitorium log. The Big House had entire shelves of reports, filled with testimonials, examinations, and experiments. All of which focused on a single type of patient: the few survivors who had dared the Forlorn Trail. Her family had always viewed them as a simple curiosity.

The Flowers Affair had changed Mary's opinion, though. *Every time someone takes the Trail, tragedy follows.* Though the sheriff could find no evidence to prove her theory, she was sure Collin had some part to play in the murders. *Why else was his body unspoiled?*

She read through another sanitorium log. *Female. Of frail disposition and fragile character. Spinster. Resident of Northridge Sanitorium as of this spring. Basic physical functions are still performed, though patient refuses to remember her past life. Instead of recalling her name, patient's mental capacities are focused on a strange fable of savage origin. Patient spends hours recounting a lost city, 'where dwells a god-king in his infinite library.' This simple sawbones has no further examinations. The woman shall live out her days in the care of the state.*

Mary paced around her office, hand to her chin. Outside, the market chatter had died away; the cricket clamor had begun. She wiped her face, removing the coagulating puss around the corners of her eyes and flicking them into the corner waste bin. She slumped into her chair with a groan and took a handheld mirror from her desk drawer. She expected to see the familiar wrinkles on her forehead, etched into a permanent scowl. She figured she would see her thinning hairline and streaks of grey. Instead, a watercolor woman stared back at her. Mary frowned. The illness was getting worse.

They will not follow me long, these dogs. A blind man could hardly hope to lead, but a blind woman? Mary replaced the mirror with a knife, brandishing it with a tight grip. She moved it to her neck and played with the idea of ending her slow descent, of terminating Thorne rule on a high note.

Mary Anne the Morose, she pictured written in bold letters. *Mary Anne the Unmade.* She threw the knife to the ground. Real tears, not sickly acidic droplets, fell down her cheeks. She savored them, just as she relished her dusty dolls rotting away in the attic.

Like sand to sandstone, her sadness hardened into a stare. She licked her finger and took to reading the day's mail. She delicately took her letter opener and angled it for the cut. She missed and cut herself.

"Shit."

Mary cleared her throat. She put on a pair of ridiculous spectacles that were supposed to help her see. She ripped open the envelope and squinted at the obnoxiously small print. A few faint lines and circles appeared. She pressed the paper closer to her face until the page wrinkled around the spectacles. *Useless,* she decided.

She lowered the letter and gazed at her reflection in the mirror. *Truly a spectacle.*

Mary glanced at the remaining correspondences and felt nauseated. She was too tired to decipher familiar symbols like they were native pictograms. She ripped up the unread letters and threw the spectacles. They shattered with a satisfying ring.

Mary wrapped her arms around her chest. Within seconds, she remembered the action was indicative of weakness and forced her arms to her side. She stood, back straight, and glared at her wall of black and white caricatures. *It will be difficult to fill in the blank parts of this wall without Mr. Pacheco.* Nevertheless, she was entering a dangerous point in her career. *Porfirio cannot go on insulting me.*

Meanwhile, the sheriff was growing too powerful. *He's got too many deputies, but what can I say without arousing suspicion?* Within a few more years, Crawford would be able to supplant her as mayor, or worse.

Mary Anne breathed deeply and listened. Crawford Biggs was tomorrow's puzzle. Outside, the crickets nearest the Big House had quieted. Her 'guards' must have actually started their patrols instead of going off and drinking. *Fuck the deputies. Fuck the sheriff.* She nodded, working herself into the necessary mindset for this evening. *Pacheco must be deterred or disposed of. He must be deterred or disposed of...* As Mary chanted her silent mantra, the jewel on her desk glinted.

The glint reflected in her eye. She approached the little stone, a jewel which seemed so different from any precious metal in her jewelry chest. For all her cousins' mines out east, she was sure she alone possessed such a mineral. She held up the artifact, analyzing the core of dancing light in the center. As always, while she held the stone—she felt her eyesight improve. The effect was subtle, but as she gripped the rock and gazed out the window, she could almost make out the moon in the sky.

For a moment, duty left her mind. She forgot all the cruel necessities forced upon her. To the great surprise of her cheekbones, she smiled. The muscles in her face strained to support the rarity. She walked to her window and stared out into the night. The stone in her hand tickled her palm, vibrating as it did when exposed to light. Mary Anne held the stone before the moon and, like she did when she was a girl, made a wish to the stars.

Mary Anne closed and opened her cursed eyes. She put the jewel down. Vile puss leaked immediately out her eyes. Mary Anne wiped it on her dress. She made a mental note to comb through her sanitorium records first thing in the morning. *I cannot accomplish much more tonight.*

Mary marched from her office, relying on the echoes of her footsteps. The reverberations changed the closer she got to the foyer. When she entered the greeting hall, she turned left without hesitation. She descended the staircase confidently. Her eyes were worst in the gloom, so her hearing excelled. Nevertheless, her thoughts soon were deafening. *That mineral must have some alchemical property, something which helps one see. I wonder if the cracked souls ever come back talking about black stones. I will have to write to the sanitoriums. Schedule a vis—*

Mary did not hear a man coming up the stairs. When his body collided with hers, she thought she was being hit by the blunt object of an assassin. Her paranoia soon lifted when she heard the beginnings of a bumbling apology. Irritated by the man's presence and annoyed she had to deal with such imbeciles instead of investigating the Flowers mystery, she muttered, "Damn it, Bingham. Watch where you are going."

Jessie Bingham was motionless, his face unreadable. "I missed the paper," he said, words full of knowing accusation.

Mary Anne did not have time to waste on simple men. "Drunks make bad writers."

The crofter's confident breaths shifted; Mary Anne heard the high-pitched tone of a tightening, nervous throat. She homed in on Bingham's timidity, glaring at him as the almost imperceivable sound gave way to an insolent comment. "Do drunks also make bad servants? Or does that enhance their function?"

Don't badger me, Jessie. "I like you," she admitted. The disarmed tone of her voice surprised her. She realized she was staring at his arms. Her wayward eyes suddenly went below his waist. *Stop that,* she commanded her girlish instincts. She swallowed and looked at him stoically. His green eyes were so warm she wanted only to speak the truth to him. *Damn this man,* she cursed. She stared past Jessie and his perfectly parted blonde hair. *He will never be your friend, or anything else.* She leaned on her cane and continued quickly, "But affection is fickle." She let her inhuman eyes dismantle Jessie's poise.

Bingham grimaced. He, like all the rest, was disturbed by her leaky pupils.

Good, Mary glared, wielding her illness as a weapon.

Then, without the slightest repulsion, he returned her silent gaze. He almost seemed undisturbed by her. Uncomfortable with the reversal, the mayor diverted, "You knew he was in the stockades."

"Mayor Thorne," Bingham said, pausing to form some sarcastic comment.

"Don't mistake me," Mary began, the moisture in her throat drying out. She may have been going blind, but she knew when someone was analyzing her. She swallowed. *He is trying to threaten me.* She lied, "I think Porfirio's paper is rather cute. Most of the time."

Jessie's eye contact remained as unbroken as hers. She hated that damnable Bingham gaze. She could feel the warmth of his stare and suddenly, she was smiling. *Stop it,* she commanded herself. *You are a Thorne. The mayor.* Mary Anne searched for something to say, something to stop herself from making another idiotic concession to the charming farmer. *He will walk all over me if I let him; that's why he is here.*

She recalled something her mother used to tell her, "His obsession with this story. I understand it. Murderers, stalkers, savages—we civil folk love to fear them."

Jessie looked away from her.

Good, she told herself. *Remember your place.* Mary Anne continued, her heartbeat returning to a regular rhythm. "Terrors make us feel like our forefathers, make us feel like we did before civilized society." She turned, leaving Pacheco to his sobriety for one more night.

"Porfirio is using this awful tragedy to feel human, but that is a hollow approach." She looked back at Jessie, whose eyes seemed to be crawling over her. She shivered, feeling uglier than ever. "Loitering and trespassing are so often mistaken for one another, Mr. Bingham."

Jessie took the hint, thankfully. Mary Anne did not know what she would have done if the man had refused to leave. Locking up an old drunk was one thing... Mary began to fidget with her cane, thinking of all the necessities she was hated for. She continued her mother's old story. "Fear is what makes us feel human." She tried her luck at humor, "You humble people like to tell stories about 'Ghostly Mary Anne' who made her own brother disappear..." She sighed, knowing she had never been very funny. "We all love a good monster."

"I don't think you're a monster."

Mary Anne realized she was tapping her cane. The fidgeting had been the only thing keeping her mind clear and when she paused, she began thinking. *I need to get him out of here. No distractions. No weakness.* Mary summarized her mother's teachings. "We love fear."

"Ma'am," Jessie stepped ahead of her. He offered to take her hand for the final step.

Mary Anne eyed the hand and wished she could take it. But she was the mayor. A mayor needed no help, especially from a poor crofter with sickly children. She could lift her shaky legs herself. She stared at the tall man, impatiently awaiting whatever rustic cliché he had prepared for her.

"I reckon it's the reverse."

"Indeed?" Mary Anne looked away. She skulked, *Conversations aren't fair when I never get to look back...* She became a statue, unreadable and imposing. She chided, speaking with the mayoral voice her mother had endowed to her. "Your visits to the working house have given you undue bravado, Mr. Bingham." She clenched her cane and led Jessie into the foyer.

She recognized the darkened outline of her servant ahead. Thankful to have another diversion, Mary charged ahead, "Jeremiah Horn, you are the most useless butler I have had the displeasure of employing." The man remained asleep, as lazy as the day she hired him. "You can rest when you are dead, op—"

Mr. Horn was always congested. Even when she found him asleep, he was always wheezing. Now, however, Mary Anne noted only silence.

Jessie whispered, "What is it?"

Mary Anne dared not trust her eyes, but her hearing was perfectly honest. Jeremiah Horn was not breathing. She brushed her hand along his neck. While she felt no pulse, she did sense a soft, gelatinous puddle where his larynx once protruded. "Strangled," she whispered. The air in her lungs left her. *This is Crawford's doing...*

"We should go," said Bingham, rushing toward her.

Mary raised her cane, "Stay back." It felt like *she* was being strangled.

"Mary Anne," Jessie raised his hands. "I'm not going to hurt you."

"Stay away," she repeated, her voice cracking in the same way it did when she was a girl. When Jessie grabbed her arm, all she could do was shake her head. For the first time in years, she was truly speechless. The farmer began leading her away from Jeremiah's body. She followed hesitantly, wondering who could have murdered her servant. Her skin crawled. *Everyone has a vendetta against me.*

Just as they started toward her office, Jessie abruptly stopped.

Mary tried to continue, but Jessie held her in place. His calloused hands squeezed her shoulders. His elbow brushed against her breast. She tensed. Had she any air in her lungs, she would have reminded the man of his manners. She could only blink at him.

He gestured at their feet.

Mary looked and saw nothing. She rolled her eyes, impatiently.

Jessie mouthed in reply, *"Muddy footprints."*

Mary swallowed. She did not struggle when Jessie tightened his grip on her. She did not fight him as he went behind her, pressing his body close to hers. She did not tense from his breath on her neck. She hesitated only when she realized they were going toward the exit. "Crawford will be waiting out there," she whispered.

A sudden clang came from Mary's office. A drawer slid open. Then, another.

Jessie bit his lip and side-eyed the corridor. "I don't think this is the sheriff's doing, ma'am."

Mary clenched her cane and looked down the hall. *Did I leave a light on in the ballroom?* Even as she asked herself, she knew that she had not. She never went into the ballroom. The floorboard above creaked. She looked up. As she did, she caught the scent of something. She sniffed.

Jessie smelled it, too. He looked at her, knowingly. Fire.

Mary never rushed to a decision, never spoke before listening. She never walked before her cane was in place, never gambled before becoming the house. But fire had a humbling quality that made sensible folk scurry. Mary turned without delay toward the exit. She gripped the door handle; it moved without her moving it.

Mary stumbled backward. Her cane fell.

The door opened slowly with a groan. The silver-laced frame glinted in the waxing moon, illuminating a silhouette with a ghostly glow. One hand clenched a spear; the other caressed his neck. His eyes were obscured by a metal helmet and yet—Mary knew he was staring at her.

She stepped back.

The man raised his chin as if concluding something. Then, he began circling her. As he moved, his armored robe clinked. The garment glimmered like metal but rustled like leaves.

Mary Anne bent her knees, wondering what strength would be required of her to leap away to freedom. She stared at the native's towering spear. *That does not look very sharp.* She did not want to find out if she was right.

The native noticed her gaze on his weapon and glanced at it. Then, he wrinkled his nose and spoke. The language was like none she had ever heard and she recognized only one word: "*Lugal.*" That was enough.

"*Lugal,*" she repeated.

The warrior breathed deeply, measuring her. He said another word but was interrupted when two Lugal appeared from the hallway. They hissed. "*Ur Igi.*"

Whatever the word meant, it widened the first man's eyes. He stared at Mary inquisitively and repeated the words. "*Ur Igi?*" He waited for her response.

Jessie Bingham did not allow her one. He rushed the Lugal, a paltry hunting knife in hand. The Lugal dodged the strike and bashed Mary Anne with his elbow. Her lungs sank beneath the strike. She plummeted to the floor. She tried to crawl away; terror kept her in place. Mary watched helplessly.

The Lugal whirled to face the farmer. He slashed the blunt spear against the stone wall. He must have hit the sconces, for a fire lit the tip of his spear and a flame licked the floor. The Lugal crouched, hissed in his ugly language, and then lunged. Mary did not see Jessie fly, but she did hear him fall. Shortly after, candle wax began melting into the carpet. Flames overtook the foyer; smoke scratched her nostrils.

Mary rolled onto her back, coughing. Embers licked her cheek and set the family portraits alight. First fell the picture of her father, Calloway the Fifth. Then went her aunt and her mother. The Thorne, one by one, toppled and shattered. Mary called out for help, but her voice was thick with fumes. She crawled.

A dozen Lugal filed past her. They walked with raised arms and flat palms, like candle-bearers in a procession. They had wrapped the polished spheres in cloth and cradled them at the breast. Mary rose and swiped at the smoke in front of her. None of the Lugal paid her any mind, save the one who had knocked her to the ground.

The tall, beastly figure turned his head in serpentine analysis. Mary met his stare as she always did. His face was deeply scarred, as if his head had been cut up and stitched back together.

Mary looked away. She took a step toward the exit; so did he. They watched one another intently. Mary peered into the smoke and felt unnerved by how reflective the man's eyes were. Mary continued her cautious encroachment, keeping both the door and the man in her sickly view. The scarred brute did the same.

Mary glanced at the door.

The man smiled at her. He threw down his spear and gestured at the door. He *wanted* her to flee.

Her chest burned in a boiling pot of primal fear. It was as if she were in one of her nightmares, cornered by a monster and unable to scream. Only, this was no dream and the monster was real. The same animal fear that kept her safe from her family surged back. She sprinted past the scarred man and escaped the Big House.

Flames were all around her. The light of the inferno cast a host of ghoulish shadows onto the eaves. The town bell tolled and the townsfolk ran. They filled their buckets at the banks of the Copper River and bailed the writhing fire. All the while, mothers and fathers called for their missing children. Not one person noticed Mary Anne. She ran for the market square, where her people were gathered to fight the flames.

The fire galloped hungrily between her and the townspeople. Cactus cackled. Embers crawled up adobe walls like flaming locusts and ignited the life within. The main street became a hall of lamps in a starless night. Even the dirt burned.

Suddenly, a cough overtook her. Within seconds, it brought Mary to her knees. The dirt seared her clothes. The ash lined her throat and sanded her speech. Mary shambled toward her people, who had formed an organized line of firefighting.

Mary waved at her folk. Her arms never made it into the air. Instead, strong hands gripped her by the shoulders and pulled her away. Mary could muster only animal shrieks. She could not tell if the town could see the abduction, or if they simply ignored her. Whatever the case, her hoarse rasps were swallowed greedily by the flames. The cracks like whips drowned out her voice, but she still screamed.

The last thing she remembered of that terrible night was the primal shrieks of a Lugal stampede. The raiders had stolen her away and the Forlorn Trail awaited her. Mary thought about Porfirio Pacheco and all the men she had destroyed for her own preservation. The people of Belford would not come after her. She was as good as dead. She drifted out of consciousness, remembering her vicious mother's own dying words: *The devil's herd has come on high to take me to hell.*

Chapter 7

"RAID on the Big House. Sheriff Biggs has taken temporary authority in the mayor's absence. All information regarding the savages shall be routed to his deputies or him directly. Willie Willows has offered his saloon to any made derelict by the inferno. Mr. Craw regrets that he is now sold out of his finest pine."

– The Belford Inquirer

Jessie held his wife so tightly that their heartbeats syncopated. He gazed at Glendolyn as a miner gazes at his gold. He swayed with her, savoring her sweet smile. He lifted a strand of her hair. She smelled as she did on the day they had met, two teenagers fumbling about in a working house neither had any business being in. He lifted her chin and smiled at her. "Hey there, chipmunk." He rubbed his nose against hers.

His wife nodded at him, but she did not speak.

"Oh," he realized. He grabbed the back of his wife's head and gently pressed her forehead to his. "Another dream, huh?"

His wife like a rug was pulled out from under him. The springtime stead became a sweaty bed. His wife became a pillow. Glendolyn's touch lingered in his mind, a cruel reminder that dreams never lasted long enough. He rolled over, trying to return to sleep.

A man sat beside the bed, legs crossed and hands folded placidly.

Jessie grumbled, "Ain't you supposed to be in the stocks?"

Porfirio offered him a glass of water, "The blaze pardoned me."

Jessie chugged the water. He analyzed his surroundings. Like every room in Porfirio's home, his bedroom was in a ruined state. He tried to look out the window, but the fire had covered it in a layer of soot. "Last I remember, a Lugal was throwing me like poplar seeds in the wind."

Porfirio leaned forward and cupped his chin thoughtfully, "Are you sure they weren't Tlacon or Kuahtec comin' back to finish their work?"

"They didn' look like Tlacon. Didn' look like any savage I ever seen, matter-a fact."

Porfirio's fingers tapped against his thigh. He glanced at his notepad and began fidgeting with splintered wood on his dresser. "The Lugal been legend since my family came north. Nobody ever seen one."

"I heard him speak the word," Jessie recalled. "He said he was a Lugal. He said it in a language I ain't heard in any trading post from here to the delta."

Porfirio swallowed and drummed on his legs, "The town's been a right mess of rumor the last few days. Ain' nobody know what's goin' on anymore, 'specially without the mayor."

Jessie blinked. "Without the mayor?" He repeated. *How long have I been out?*

Porfirio nodded, his lower lip covering his upper. "Savages took her, Jessie."

Jessie processed the information, not understanding at all where he was or what had happened. He raised a halting hand, "What happened last night?" He croaked with a dry throat, "Last I recall, I was bein' licked by a wall of fire."

A strange sadness peppered Porfirio's face, "That was two nights ago, Jessie."

"Lord almighty," Jessie stretched. *Veola is going to skin me.* Every muscle from his waist to his neck cracked like popcorn. He groaned and gazed at his palms. "The mayor," he stated his question.

Porfirio smiled, though he was mostly grinding his teeth. "Sheriff and his posse pursued them to the river. But that's where the rumors really start." He whispered, "Ole' Crawford says somethin' spooked the horses. Personally, I think it was Mary Anne's pride."

That's a tasteless joke. Jessie sucked in his bottom lip; Porfirio had no obligation to care about the mayor. She was the reason for the bruises on his face. He sighed, thinking about his children. "I need to get home. I been restin' too long."

"Sheriff wants to see you first," Porfirio said hastily.

"Sheriff can find me at home," Jessie went for a neatly folded pile of clothes. He rushed toward the pants and put them on as fast as he could. He did not bother with the last button on his shirt. "Ms. Rosalee was watchin' the twins and she wasn't happy about the fact."

Porfirio gazed at a half-empty whiskey bottle, "Ms. Rosalee was a cruel bitch and every soul from here to hell knew it, save you."

Jessie found himself frozen, analyzing why Porfirio had spoken about her in the past tense. *She must have left town after the fire.* His fear and anxiety took only a second to fester. Soon, he was immobilized and thinking, *Now I need to start back from the beginning. They need a woman in their life.* The raid on the Big House was proof that his time above the earth was limited. The twins needed safety. "I gotta go, Porfirio."

The newspaperman started after him, "Wait a moment, Jessie."

He halted mostly due to the incredible weariness in Porfirio's' voice. He turned around and was startled by how age seemed to have overwhelmed him. As the old man rolled his jaw left and right, every wrinkle caved further inward. He cleared his throat, scratched his brow, and searched the room. He found a bottle and poured himself a glass. His hand lurched toward his mouth and then, suddenly, stopped. He stared at the whiskey wistfully. Finally, his arm straightened. His wrists rotated as lifeless contraptions and poured the liquor onto his boots. After a staccato inhale, he dropped the whiskey bottle. Porfirio collapsed into his chair. He gazed mournfully past Jessie and shook his head.

"Now ain't that a sight," Jessie remarked.

Porfirio shivered, "Sheriff let me roam free, so long as I swore off the juice. Wants to do right by that whore of a mayor."

"You know I hate that word," Jessie glared.

He raised a quaking hand, "Sorry, son." He cleared his throat.

Jessie accepted the apology with a curt nod. Porfirio had every right to hate Mayor Thorne. "I *am* glad you're clean... Is that all?"

A host of hasty words spilled out of Porfirio, "The sheriff wants to see you. He's declared martial law on account of the abduction."

"That's probably wise," Jessie said. He paused for half a second before whirling around and saying, "I'll meet up with him after I check on the stead."

"I think you ought ta—"

"We can speak about this later." Jessie stormed down the stairs. He ignored Pacheco's calls and knocked the door out of his way. The hinges cried and the wooden frame thundered against the adobe.

Jessie's eyes could not see in the light. He heard wagons rolling and men moving about their business. As his eyes adjusted, he felt he had awakened in a foreign land. The street was bleached by ash. The saloon was amess in scaffolding, as were many other buildings. Luckily for the proprietors, most locales escaped with only minor damage.

The Big House, however, was not so fortunate. As Jessie went to retrieve his tethered horse, he saw the ashen foundation of the mayoral palace. A cautious pessimism formed in his throat. Jessie felt the lump grow as he came closer. Carbonized stumps and indeterminate husks were all that remained of the hitching posts and horses.

"Mr. Bingham."

Jessie turned. The saloon proprietor was dressed in black, mourning someone or something. Willie Willows took a pouch from his vest and put it in Jessie's hand. "I know you don' drink. But I want ya ta take this pipe. Had it imported from the old world. Fine piece of woodworking."

Jessie felt like there was sand in his throat. "Why?" He motioned at the saloon and the scaffolding. "I don't want anything you can't spare."

Willows turned and smiled politely. "Oh," he waved his hand. "Cosmetic damage. Besides, with the Big House burnt, my place is the unofficial town hall." He clasped Jessie's hand, patting his knuckles. Jessie did not like how much pity was in the interaction. He eyed the ashen shapes at his feet.

Oh, Genie. He knelt by a horse's remains.

Another person came forward. "I'm sorry for your loss, Mr. Bingham."

Jessie braced his knees and rose, "Yep. She was a good horse." He shook the man's hand. "How's your stead, Preston?"

The crofter dragged his fingers through his hair, breaking the immaculate part. "The grasshoppers been good to us this year." On account of having five sons, Preston McLeary was one of the few crofters still turning a profit. What was most infuriating to the rest of the farming folk was that he never turned to growin' weeds and cactus. By some deal with the devil, he was still growing alfalfa. Luckily for neighborly relations, Preston was a humble man. He shook Jessie's hand.

Jessie felt crisp, cold bills slip into his grip. "What's this, Preston?"

"For your loss," the farmer frowned and tipped his hat.

"I'm not a charity, sir." Jessie immediately remembered the mayor's recent generosity and, ashamed, followed McLeary. "Keep your money, Preston."

McLeary kept walking. "I haven't the faintest idea what you are referring to."

Jessie was befuddled. As much as he loved animals, he did not think Genie would have inspired so much generosity. *Especially with the scope of the tragedy...* Jessie eyed the main street, estimating that a walk home would take several hours.

"What are we going to do without Marcos?" worried Sean O'Siah.

"Find us a real sawbones," muttered Cornelius Craw as he hammered the last nail into a coffin.

Don Marcos is gone, too? Jessie hardly had a moment to ponder the fact when he heard a horrible shriek. He whirled around to find Kate Flowers hanging from her balcony. A rope squeezed her gurgling throat as she flailed. Folks from all corners of the road ran to help her, but to no avail. Her skin's color drained. Her arms settled at her sides.

Cornelius Craw left his storefront and inspected the dangling body. "Poor Kate... Couldn't abide by the fact her daughter was taken, too."

"Taken?" Jessie asked.

The onlookers all turned, but no one seemed able to respond. Finally, Solomon Rodgers stumbled out of the saloon, reeking of whiskey. He fell onto his knees. Hiram was close behind and held his brother's head up while he vomited.

Solomon rose without wiping his mouth. His bloodshot eyes were redder than his hair. "Ain't no god to pray to, Hiram! Just a devil. And he took my woman right from her mama's grasp."

Hiram groaned, "She weren't your woman, Solly." He pulled his brother up and dragged him out of sight.

As Solomon thrashed and sobbed, Jessie stared at Kate's hanging corpse. Then, like whiplash, he circled back. *They took Cleona and Don Marcos...* Jessie stared in the direction of home. He thought about the strange kindness of Preston McLeary and Willie Willows. He started for home, walking behind a conestoga loaded with debris. He overheard voices coming from Craw's Cradles. The undertaker, Emile Defosse was speaking with Cornelius Craw, "Preston's a good man for bringin' back the body."

"Well, he is the man's neighbor."

"Still," replied the undertaker, "Veola were a harpy. I'da left her."

Craw hammered a nail into a cheap, pinyon board. "And let Mr. Bingham come home to a dead whore in his sittin' room?"

Dread began to fester in his thumping chest. Jessie felt his body collapse inward. His senses atomized into a single fear. His breathing stopped. His eyesight became a unified blur of shapes.

Dust blew into his face, coated his gaping mouth, and produced not even a tickle in his throat. For a moment, he could hardly have been considered living.

Then, he blinked. All his thoughts turned toward home. His eyes squinted into the sun. He passed a few well-wishers without uttering a word. He focused on a herd of horses hitched outside the saloon. He evaluated the selection in the span of a step, taking the reins of a fine Saddlebred. Though the horse protested with a few snorts and neighs, Jessie mounted the beast and turned it around.

A man across the street started hollering. Jessie did not have the patience to recognize him. Even if he did, he would not have stopped. He did not give a damn about some overly fortunate man's livery. *Find another,* he glared while gunshots whistled overhead. With a kick of his spurs and a flick of his wrists, he was off. Belford washed away in blended colors.

He rode the beast bloody, without any of the regard he might have shown Genevieve. As the Saddlebred led him deep into the forest, his anticipation began to boil. He knew not what to expect when the stead came into view. He felt the weight of tears well in his eyes, but they were restrained by rage.

Just as the Saddlebred was ready to buck Jessie off, the cabin appeared on the horizon. Unlike the town, a quiet peace was upon his farm. Before the stolen mount had stopped, Jessie was sprinting toward the stead. The approach was littered with tokens of terror. Trampled earth and battered crops littered his fields.

Jessie refused to hope for smiling faces at the front door, but he had not expected the door itself to be on the ground. "Ethel!" He yelled, leaping over the irrigation ditch. He barreled through a bloodstained doorway. A bloody spear was strewn on the ground. He threw the door to his children's room open, "Elijah." The sheets were ripped and a bloody belt—his belt—was resting on the ground. Soaked sanguine garments laid on the nightstand. Jessie lifted one of the shirts. He did not know to whom it had belonged due to the repeated rips and stains. "Ethel!" He shrieked, checking under the bed. He checked under the pillows; he ripped the pillows apart.

He searched all his children's favorite spots. He lacerated his ankles against barrel cacti as he fumbled through the pinyon forest. The search was in vain. There was neither ash nor flesh to be found. Tears once again formed in his eyes. Again, they mocked him obstinately and dried in vaporous rage.

Jessie looked around the stead and realized for the first time how truly destitute he was. He had no wife, no children, and no seeds from which to sow a new crop. He walked to the family cemetery. His wife's stone was no longer a golden white; dirt obscured the precious memorial. Of all the sights, the cursed coloration of her grave put him closest to tears. But no relief.

"Son of a bitch," Jessie kicked at the dirt. He circled the cabin entrance, unwilling to abandon the search yet unable to go inside. Enraged by the immobilization, he set his sights on a stray stone in the doorway. He stormed inside, intending to cast it out. Instead, he pelted it at the medicine cupboard.

Jessie listened to the *tip-tap* of the tinctures. His arms became limp. His twins' valuable medicine drained from the cupboard onto the floor.

Once more, heavy eyes and dry cheeks. Jessie screamed for only the forest to hear. The conflicting emotions were like a disharmonious choir. His rage battled his guilt; his pride argued with his shame; all the while, his sorrow tried and failed to get a word in. Jessie stomped into the woods.

The lone cactus pad remained where he had planted it. The hole he had dug for the cursed artifact remained undisturbed. He knew not how to feel about that fact. Jessie trembled, his body unable to reconcile with his mind.

Rage overcame him. Liquid madness coursed through his veins. Jessie grabbed a fallen branch and bludgeoned whatever was nearby. He beat the pinyon trunks until the branch snapped. For a moment, his mind was still. Then, he saw the root cellar in the distance. Thunderous hate filled him as he investigated the uprooted hatch. He climbed down into the cool storehouse.

Once again, his anger was first to respond to the scene. He grabbed a nearby axe. He slashed the hog potatoes and smashed the crates of wild onion. Amidst the whirlwind, he accidentally bashed his hand. "Son of a bitch!" He swore. His finger throbbed, but Jessie savored the pain. He raised the axe and swung with as much force as he could muster. The ruined stores flew in all directions.

Finally, his savagery left Jessie breathless. He stared at his life's work and the pride of his father.

"Jessie, my boy?" Porfirio peeked in.

"You should have let me burn."

The old man joined him in the root cellar. "Self-pity is like salt. It'll ruin a good—"

Jessie's hand clenched the splintered axe. "Oh, piss on you, Pacheco."

Porfirio approached Jessie slowly, as a hunter might approach an animal. Then, he made the mistake of saying, "I am sorry, Jessie. I really am. But—"

Jessie swung the axe with all his anger, lodging it firmly onto a shelf. "If you had half a brain, you would have shut your mouth and not gotten locked up anyhow."

Porfirio swallowed. "You're right..."

Jessie threw the nearest object. A hog potato soared past Porfirio's head and smashed into the wall. "Because of you," Jessie panted. "I was not home." He threw another potato, narrowly missing Porfirio again. "My kids! The only good things left to me, are dead. They were the last bit of Glendolyn I had and you..." He shivered, unable to articulate another word. His entire body was like the fire that should have killed him.

"I know, Jessie boy."

Say 'you know' one more time and I'll bash your god-damned brains in. He licked his bottom lip, thinking of all the ways to quell his rage. Most were violent. "They're dead!"

"Look," Porfirio began, "Nobody has found any bodies. That means—"

"Don't tell me what that means," Jessie growled. "Look at their room. They were tortured, it's clear as day."

Porfirio was silent for a second. Then, he conceded, "You've got every right to blame me."

Jessie could not bring himself to agree with the bastard. "No I don't," he admitted after some time. An intolerable minute passed where neither spoke. Finally, a confession began to bubble within him. Jessie brokered a deal with his honesty and his shame, saying only, "Give me some peace, Porfirio."

Porfirio looked around the wreckage of the root cellar. "This is peace to you?"

"I'm mourning," he responded defiantly.

Porfirio came closer, shaking his head. He softened his voice, "This ain't the way."

"And you know the way?" Jessie snarled. "Hm?" He rolled his eyes, "You been a drunken mess ever since your wife left you. It's why your children left, too."

Porfirio's soft tone hardened. "I ain't denying it. That's why I'm beggin' you to listen to me. This ain't the way to mourn your kin."

"Well, I ain't gon' cry about it," Jessie argued. He was painfully aware his mind could not keep up with his heart. His words flowed out of him without a second thought. "What's that gonna do?"

Porfirio sat on one of the shelves and shrugged, "You don' think maybe you ain't able to cry?"

Jessie scoffed and glanced behind his shoulder. When the man remained silent and staring, he surged forward, anger rising. "You don' *think*. That's your problem." He pointed, "I wanted to weep for Glendolyn and I want to weep for Eli and Ethel. But then I am defeated. Done. At least with—" he rubbed his nose and licked his bottom lip. "At least with anger, I'm still fighting."

Porfirio rose, "This ain't fighting. This is self-destruction." He advanced, "You don't want to feel defeated? Good. Stop fightin' with yourself."

"Says the drunk," Jessie muttered.

"Says your friend," Porfirio rebuked. "And I ain't drinkin' anymore."

Jessie laughed. Even though it came from a place of spite, it felt good. He found himself smiling, "Now ain't that rich."

"I mean it," Porfirio smirked. He raised a hand, "How 'bout this? You promise not to steal any more horses and beat y'self bloody. And I won' start drinkin' again."

Jessie craved to feel anything other than rage, but he felt like a fool shaking hands. The last gasp of his hate came as a spiteful joke, "Will I get thrown in the stocks if I break *my* promise?"

Porfirio grinned, "More than likely. I hear that horse belonged to one of Crawford's deputies."

Jessie rubbed the back of his head. "I guess I'd better go and return that horse then."

Porfirio nodded, "I'll help ya' look." He offered his waterskin, "Drink."

Jessie took a swig gladly. Water leaked onto his chest and, as he wiped his chin—he felt renewed. He did not feel happy or whole. In fact, he felt a bodily hatred for everything in view. But at least he felt alive. Jessie followed Porfirio out of the root cellar and, with his friend's help, climbed into the light.

"Shit," Porfirio said.

"Found the horse?" Jessie covered his eyes and squinted into the sun.

"In a manner of speaking," he replied. Porfirio looked at Jessie with a mix of sadness and fear.

Jessie hated that mixture.

Soon, it was clear what Pacheco had seen. Four men on horseback descended upon them, led by the sheriff himself. They galloped toward the stead, ignoring his ransacked fields and the bloody doorway. They did not halt until they were a hair's width from trampling Jessie. He played ignorant, "Howdy, Biggs."

"Mr. Bingham," the sheriff said without inflection or emotion. "You are under arrest for disruption of the peace and theft."

Jessie stepped forward, lip furled and eyes wide. "Look, I'm sorry about the horse."

"That was a proper Saddlebred," Quincy Maples spat. He was now sitting atop the reclaimed prize. "Been with me since I were a boy."

"And you shot at it," Jessie blurted. He wanted to be jovial, as it was always best to compliment and praise an angry man. However, he was in no mood to lick boots.

Sheriff Biggs dismounted and unceremoniously unveiled a long rope. "Mr. Maples shot at *you*, Mr. Bingham. You's lucky he was drinking, as he were well within his rights."

"Well," Jessie lifted his arms in surrender. "I apologize about your horse."

"Hang him, Biggs," said another deputy. "That's how the army treats thieves anyhow."

"Who the hell are you?" Jessie raised his chin. The newest addition to Biggs' ranks had such fresh skin and such silky hair, he looked damn near childish. "Because I know you ain't old enough to sign y'name."

"Never you mind, Bingham," Biggs sighed. "Don' cause me no trouble or I'll reconsider Mr. Greenfield's suggestion."

Porfirio walked between Jessie and the men. "Now now," old Pacheco cautioned. "This is a man bewitched by grief. He ain't actin' right, we all know it. But to hang him? We all know what happened to his children, after all."

The sheriff flashed a polite frown, "I can't pardon crime at a time like this, Pacheco."

Jessie stepped forward. "Where the hell were y'all when the savages came? Busy drinking?"

"Careful, Bingham," Sheriff Biggs warned. The deputies drew their weapons.

Jessie stepped back. He raised his hands, "Man's got his horse, Sheriff."

The sheriff's cheek twitched.

Jessie pestered the sheriff. "Crawford."

The sheriff told the remaining two soldiers, "We ain't hangin' nobody." He frowned at Jessie, "But martial law gots to be respected. I can' have thievin' right now."

"Now what is justice," Porfirio blocked the men, "Without clemency?"

"I ain't a philosopher, Pacheco," replied Biggs. He took his rope and tied Jessie's arms behind his back. "Keep badgerin' me and you will join Mr. Bingham."

Chapter 8

<hr>

"Male, wanted and of ill repute before fleeing down the Forlorn Trail. Known as Dan Bandelier, Patient 1 no longer remembers his own name. Although a prime candidate for the freakshows, Patient 1 unfortunately insists on self-mutilation. We have had to restrain him. Sawbones recommended compassionate termination. Then, further patients were acquired. These specimens have also forgotten their names, though they also carry heathen jewels. These were promptly shattered, spilling luciferous flames and injuring a nurse. Under such omens, Patient 1 is to remain a ward of the state."

– Greenview Manifest

Porfirio's hands slipped through the bars. His feet pushed a bowl against the stone, toward Jessie's cell. "You have to regain your strength," he called from the other side of the block.

Jessie was not hungry.

Porfirio studied his cell, "Ole Calloway Thorne really knew a thing about sturdy stockades."

They weren't going to shut him up any other way, he smiled. Porfirio had pestered the sheriff to the point of madness, proclaiming legal statutes that, while sounding quite legitimate, were complete fabrications. The sheriff hog-tied him in a matter of minutes. Yet even stowed as baggage, Porfirio continued protesting the unjust detention of his friend.

Jessie nodded, "He sure did." He pushed the soup back to Porfirio, "You eat."

Pacheco's arms wavered, but it was only out of courtesy toward Jessie. He swiped the stew and slurped it down.

The stockade door opened with a long whine. As the basement corridors were all that was left of the Big House, bright light penetrated the dark halls. Several pairs of feet came into the hall. Jessie looked at Porfirio, now hastily wiping his mouth.

Footsteps approached. After a delay—they faded. Jessie and Porfirio shared a puzzled look.

"Get him on his feet," said the sheriff.

A cell opened and closed. The grinding metal echoed. A pained groan reverberated in the quiet caverns. The dripping of water punctuated the sheriff's interrogation:

"Speak, savage," commanded Crawford Biggs.

A deep voice spoke unfamiliar sounds. Alien words echoed in the dark halls. Among the many chilling sounds was a single word that was well-known by all. The pronunciation was spine-chilling. "Lugal."

Porfirio mouthed, "*They have a captive.*"

Jessie listened intently, adding cautiously, "*Three, if you'll remember.*"

Porfirio grinned, lifted his brow, and raised his index finger to his shut lips. They continued eavesdropping.

"Malachi, you's a savage. Can you translate?"

A scoff was heard from all ends of the stockades. A nomad's accent penetrated the cobble walls, "The Lugal were legends to the Tlacon, too. I do not know his language."

A grim chuckle. A language Jessie did not know slithered into the air.

A gasp. "He speaks the tongue of my people."

"Well translate, damn it. Ask him why he came here."

Jessie waited for the impenetrable combination of consonants and vowels to end. The man named Malachi whispered, "They came for slaves, originally. Then, he says, they realized we were cursed. His people lifted the curse."

The sheriff inquired, quite relaxedly to Jessie's hearing, "So that is why Mayor Thorne was kidnapped? To be a slave?"

The Tlacon man translated as the Lugal spoke, "She shall be a war-bride to Nerugal, warchief of the Lugal."

The sheriff grunted. "And the reason they murdered innocent children?"

Malachi was interrupted before he could finish translating the question. The Lugal may have been speaking an animal's language, but there was pride in his voice.

Malachi hesitated, "He says they did not murder any children."

"Why did I find a body with a spear in its back?"

The Lugal spoke with a booming voice.

Malachi's voice cracked and he said, breathlessly, "They had come down the slopes to the cries of children. They found a woman cruel as salted water—"

Jessie winced.

"—The children we took were innocent. They deserved a better life than wild men could provide."

Jessie's innards seemed to combine into an organ of dread, hope, and everything in between. His heart sank, his stomach rose, and his lungs contracted. He thought he might cry; he was sure he was going to vomit.

An agonizing minute followed. Finally, Jessie heard footsteps. Crawford Biggs marched up to Jessie's cell, rifle leaning against his shoulder. He unlocked the door, "Get up."

Jessie would have sprinted down the stockades; the sheriff halted him. He warned, "I don' want lawless emotion from you, y'hear."

Jessie's first instinct was indignation. His eyelids twitched nearly shut. His bottom lip rolled out of sight. He nodded and was led to the opposite wing of the stockades. The prisoner still wore his resplendent armor. Though, the metallic tunic was so muddy, it looked less like quilted feathers and more like reptilian skin. Jessie found that fitting. His legs were chained and bolted into the stone. That too seemed fitting.

"This is the father of the children," the sheriff said. Malachi translated.

The Lugal studied Jessie with a neutral expression. His skin was dark, like the other natives Jessie had met. Yet he did not share the same features. His nose was more prominent, his body was not tattooed, and his hair was not beaded. When the Lugal finally responded to Malachi, it was with an accent even Jessie perceived.

Malachi turned to Jessie, "He wonders whether... prisoners make good fathers in this wild country?"

Jessie lunged. Two deputies and the sheriff struggled to restrain him. He spat on the Lugal's face, "You murdered them. They cannot live in some hut. They need their medicine." He roared at Malachi, "Tell him!"

The Lugal heard Malachi's words and then took a deep breath. He took a step forward. His chains tightened. His eyebrows rose sympathetically.

"He is sorry for your pain," the Tlacon man translated. "He says that—" Malachi paused. "I don't know that word. I think it's a name." He asked a clarifying question. All the men stared impatiently. The nomad glanced at the sheriff and then reluctantly continued, "Mother Asura found them weeping in a cellar. The boy was bleeding. Mother Asura butchered the woman and cast away her whip. She has done you a service and has taken them as her own." Malachi swallowed, "If they perish, they will receive full funerary rites."

Veola was beating them. His spine tingled. His knuckles whitened. *She had no right. That cruel, old bitch.* His body shook so much, he could barely speak. "Tell him that—" he took a staccato breath. His windpipe narrowed, "They will die without their medicine."

The captive was pensive while Malachi translated. When he spoke, he was infuriatingly calm. "Then they will be buried as Mother Asura's kin. More than can be said for myself."

Jessie's pulse surged like a burst dam. His veins protruded and his eyesight flickered. He charged the brute only to be unceremoniously floored by the sheriff's largest deputy—Rosco Richardson.

When he came to his senses, the conversation had quite moved on. The sheriff was shaking his head. He wrinkled his nose. "Ask the warrior more about this curse. Are they related to the relics?"

The Lugal listened to the question. He analyzed the men in the room and contemplated his words as he spoke. He paused often, forcing Malachi to quickly explain, "He says an explanation would be like teaching a frog to fly. His words have no translation for such unlearned people."

"I am glad he is a humble man," Jessie seethed, rubbing the back of his bruised head. "I once fancied myself a patient man. Now, not so much."

"Silence, Bingham," Sheriff Biggs chastised. "Or it's back in the cell wit'ya."

Jessie bit his tongue, drawing blood.

The Lugal directed his attention at him and spoke a series of animalistic sounds.

Jessie shivered.

"What'd he say?" The Sheriff inquired.

"I do not know," Malachi exclaimed. "That was in *his* language."

The Lugal smiled wide and bobbed his head proudly. He spoke again in his own language. The brevity of his speech betrayed a soldier's laconic mind. The piercing stare betrayed a thinker's wit. Jessie stood up and stepped back. Strangely, he felt he *almost* understood the man's words.

Biggs beat the warrior with the butt of his rifle, "Speak proper."

The Lugal laughed. He dismissed the sheriff with a roll of his eyes and resolved back onto Jessie. Despite being of a people separated by miles and millennia, the stare kindled a certain suspicion in Jessie. It almost seemed, as they stared one another down—that they knew one another. Jessie recognized that face. *But from where?*

Suddenly, the native spoke. Yet, he neither spoke the language of the nomads nor his cryptic tongue. Rather, he spoke their very own, simple speech: "My name is Eridu, son of Usumgal, Lugal of the Erintul. I do no crime in the eyes of the gods. The water of Rosh shall not drown me. The light of Kul cannot blind me. I am a man of my people, not some animal of Umamu. Strike me down and I become one with Sunumun. You shall know only Ukum."

The Lugal had existed as fables and now, the fables spoke back at them. Every man grappled with the shock in their unique way. Malachi prayed; the sheriff grinned; Quincy Maples glared.

"Only one God," declared Deputy Maples. "Let's cut that neck and see if his fairy tales sew it back together."

"No," said the sheriff. "He is our prize. Hell, we could sell him to the freakshow and rebuild Belford twice over." He snapped his fingers and pointed at the captive, "Malachi. I want this one well-nourished and whole."

"Understood," said the deputy. "I will keep Rosco and Two Strings to guard things."

"Very good," replied the sheriff. He turned to the other deputy, the one who wanted to decapitate the captive, "Mr. Maples, you are on patrol until I say otherwise."

"Sir," muttered Quincy Maples resignedly.

Finally, the sheriff took his leave; as he did, he took also Jessie's arm. They walked back to the antechamber in silence. Crawford paused and whispered, "Everything makes more sense, now doesn't it, Mr. Bingham?"

Jessie tilted his head, not knowing the correct answer.

"I reckon Collin and his boys were murdered by this man's tribe. Reckon too they stole from the tribe. When them savages realized they was robbed, they tracked them to Belford and reclaimed their trinkets. It all seems rather perfect, don't it?"

"I suppose," Jessie replied, thinking to the contrary. *If they murdered Collin, why not take the jewels back then and there? Why wait?*

Crawford looked at Jessie knowingly. "I want an honest answer, Bingham Did those savages have any *other* reason to raid your stead?"

Jessie chose to ignore the accusation instead of lying. "What is this about a freakshow? A prize?" Jessie shook his head, "That beast is *leverage*."

Crawford accused in a gruff monotone, "Did you steal one of Flowers' stones?" The sheriff stared at Jessie as the mayor might have, with dead, unbelieving eyes.

Jessie admitted, "I took one of the rocks." Jessie tried to absolve himself. "But I threw it into the river. Figured it was bad luck to keep it."

"Mm," Crawford grunted. "Reckon they found it?"

Jessie stared at the sheriff suspiciously. He gestured down the hallway, "Reckon Mr. Pacheco should be freed?"

"Reckoning is a troublesome thing, Mr. Bingham."

Jessie clicked his tongue and shrugged, "Figure lockin' a man up for speakin' his mind is a form of lawless emotion, Mr. Biggs. Can't have that, given the circumstances."

The sheriff flashed a smirk before his entire body went into a long, calculated breath. "I'll free Mr. Pacheco soon. I just enjoy coopin' up the ole' muckraker."

Jessie's skin crawled. *What a vile creature.*

Crawford strolled toward the exit, "You's more than free to stay with the bastard." He shrugged, "Two renegade rascals sittin' in the stocks would only benefit my town."

Jessie stared at the sheriff. "*Your* town?"

"Mary Anne is as good as dead," the Crawford frowned.

Jessie had never seen such an immediate shift in a person's character. The mayor's man had no intention of rescuing the captives. "Why, Mr. Biggs, I do believe you've turned cloaks quicker than a tailor."

Biggs measured Jessie from head to foot. He let out a deep sigh. "Now that's a disrespectful opinion."

"A punishable one?"

The sheriff smirked. "Not yet." He led Jessie out of the stockades and wiped his brow, "You see, Mr. Bingham—I never make a decision without considerin' all implications." He picked up his hat hanging on the ashen remains of a guardrail.

Jessie eyed the sheriff before his gaze locked onto the western mountain range. The Forlorn Hills were an imposing row of teeth. "You sure seem ready to forsake the mayor now."

"You've got a keen eye," Crawford commented. "Keener than Mary Anne, at any rate." He stepped down the crumbling sandstone steps of the Big House. "And yet, I get the feeling—the inkling—that you want to ride west."

"The mayor ain't dead."

"And neither is your kin," the sheriff replied instantly. He shot him a stern look, "Let's not hide our intentions behind illusions. We are not speaking about the mayor."

"Aren't we?" Jessie asked. He had learned a thing or two about conniving men in his short life. *He wants to make a play.* He smiled at the sheriff, "A vacuum has been created, sir. That's true enough. But there's an opportunity you aren't seeing."

The sheriff walked to a stagecoach. "Now what opportunity is lucrative enough to follow legends into the last unknown? We ain't talkin' about a parlay. We talkin' about a people only books ever seen. Folk who ain't crossed us until we crossed them. And to follow 'em? We gotta take a road only the devil can use." A driver opened the door for Biggs.

Jessie could not abide the sight of the sheriff being pampered and chauffeured. Nevertheless, he had to try. *He's got six lawmen under him.* "Think about it, Biggs. You clearly have ambition. Why else would you abandon your boss?"

"You skippin' in quicksand, Bingham," Biggs warned.

"I'm practically swimmin' in it," Jessie said with a flared, wolfish nostril. He put a foot on the stagecoach and leaned in, "And you should be, too. What kind of legacy do you want, Mr. Biggs?"

The sheriff snorted. He was not going to answer that question. Jessie answered for him, "Seems to me that, if you follow your current play, you may get a sizable obituary in the *Inquirer*."

The sheriff nodded.

"Seems to me, though, that you want more than an obituary."

"Make your point," Crawford said impatiently. "By all rights, you ought ta still be locked up."

"My point is simple." Jessie smiled coyly, "You can be more than a short obituary if you go after the mayor. What kind of legend will Sheriff Biggs become, when he returns with Belford's lost folk?" Jessie smiled at the Forlorn Hills, "You would be a war hero, Biggs. When the West passes into myth, you will as well."

"I will die or go insane," the sheriff said, flatly. "Like the rest who tempt the Trail." He barked, "Benjie. Off we go."

Jessie let the lawman leave. He could only persuade a man so much before he felt like he was whoring his words. He reflected upon the paths before him. *If the sheriff will not go, then I will go alone.* He thought of the captive locked in the stockades.

The Lugal spoke his language.

Jessie rolled his bottom lip across his teeth. The Lugal spoke his language. He bit down his lip, realizing the opportunity. *He would be an excellent guide once we pass the Hills... Might even keep me from whatever harm always befalls the wagoneers.* His heart began to race. *If I can break him free and ride west, I might be able to trade for the twins!*

Jessie hardly took in his surroundings. His mind was becoming a cluttered maze of plans, paranoia, and palpable fears.

He perceived intermittent inputs: a dusty road, an overlook perfect for an ambush, his family rifle. The day was over before he knew it.

Jessie collapsed in his chair. *The Forlorn Trail...* He wondered what awaited him beyond the dagger peaks. He had never left home before, and though he had spent time in nature—he had never been in the wild. He blinked at the blank section of his map. *This will be the true wild, the true west.*

Fear of the unknown began to morph into excuses. *I cannot rob the sheriff. I'd never be able to return home.* He walked out of his family cabin and frowned at the desecrated crops. He dared not even approach the Bingham cemetery. *What is there to return to but painful memories?*

At once, his mind became a congress of conflicting worries. *You'd be a good-for-nothin' outlaw,* said a fear cloaked in his father's voice. *You ain't gonna chase after?* rasped the ghoulish memory of his wife. It continued, *Bein' a good man was always just a game to you.*

Jessie surrendered to the whirlwind. He could not make this decision alone, but who could he talk to? He popped his lips, "Who indeed?"

He grabbed a spade and ran into the woods. He stumbled upon the lone cactus pad just as the moon was rising. As the conflict within him came to a crescendo, he concluded his dig. He hopped into the small grave, meant to house the terrible speaking stone. He held it in his hand and swallowed. He hesitated, afraid of whatever sorcery was housed in the sphere.

The moonlight hit the center of the relic and a dozen rainbows shot forth like serpents from an egg. Suddenly, the conflict in Jessie's head died away. The many faces and voices of his anxieties disappeared and in their place, Jessie heard a regal voice:

> ***"The leaky line is one***
> ***Which too well knew the wrench***
> ***The tallest mountain tree***
> ***Is one who knows to bend"***

Chapter 9

"Stagecoach robberies were quite common in that yonder west. Robbing a sheriff, however, was practically unheard of."

– The Ballad of Jessie Bingham

Jessie loitered around Belford, gathering information about the sheriff and the captive Lugal. It was not difficult. Crawford was making a mighty fuss about his prize. His deputies were also predisposed to blabbering. The youngest one, Benjie Greenfield, looked as if he had not lived a single day. His fresh skin was accompanied by a stomach that could not hold its liquor.

"Ole' Biggs," Benjie paused to belch. He was telling Willie Willows—and most of the saloon, by extension—about the sheriff's upcoming venture. "He already secured a few buyers down Ashwood way. From there, I 'spect he'd be joinin' the freakshow circuit."

"When?" Jessie asked innocuously.

Benjie was a young man and loved to be asked questions. He stood tall and raised his whiskey glass, "Biggs and I are escortin' him in two days."

Jessie went up to Willows and bought the deputy another drink. "What time? I'd sure like to spit on the beast before you take him away."

Benjie's drunken arm smashed onto Jessie's back in a clumsy pat. "I must uphold the integrity of our plans, Mr. Bingham."

Jessie tugged at his collar. "I ain't gonna do nothing... It's for closure, y'know?"

Benjie sipped his drink and looked away. Like most young men, sadness made him uncomfortable. "Ah hell. For you, Bingham..." He leaned in and whispered, "We's leavin' at dawn. Takin' the South Road.

"Thank you," Jessie smiled. *Just the spot I had hoped for.* He gave Willows payment for Greenfield's drink and took his leave. Though, as he got up—a brawl erupted at the other end of the bar.

"Get off me!" Roared Hiram Rodgers, grappling with his younger brother. The pair were about the same size, muscular, and pale as snow. Hiram had a permanent look of contempt even when he smiled; Solomon looked perpetually surprised.

"Not 'til you take it back," Solomon sobbed. He reeked of a type of drunkenness known too well in that establishment. The young man had lost Cleona Flowers to the raids and was completely unhinged.

"No!" Hiram barked. "You can't keep dwellin' on that woman"

"That's like tellin' a fish he ain' allowed to swim," Solomon retorted. The two brothers began a wrestling match which, though entertaining for other onlookers, was not worthy of Jessie's attention.

Jessie left the saloon and made for Don Marcos' vacant pharmacy. He went around the side and tried the back door. It squeaked open, never having been closed properly after the raid. With a look to his left and right, Jessie snuck into the abandoned drugstore. He scoured the shelves for his twins' medicine. He took a fortnight's supply. Then, he grabbed some healing draughts, some antidotes for common afflictions—and departed.

"Evenin'," Porfirio greeted. He was smoking from a new pipe.

Jessie swirled around. The tinctures in his pack clanked. "Glad you can put Willows' gift to good use."

"Hm," the newspaperman replied. "Glad you can put Marcos' store to yours..." He inhaled slowly and exhaled out his nose, "What is it you are using that medicine for, Jessie?"

He scratched his brow. "Resellin' it to pay a debt."

Porfirio chuckled. He sipped smoke from his pipe.

Jessie knew his lie would not be believed. He did not care to elaborate, though. He noted a familiar stench on Porfirio's shirt, though he did not mention it. Instead, he smiled, "Glad you like the pipe. Just don' go replacin' one vice with another."

Porfirio tampered his bowl, "A man's vice can't ever be purged. It's a void that always needs filling."

Jessie managed a smirk, "How long you been sittin' on that line?"

"Oh, hell I been castin' that line like a fly fisher. I probably said that to my wife every other Sunday." Porfirio stared into the tobacco bowl and sighed. "Why were you at the saloon all day today, Jessie?"

"Men have wallowed in saloons for centuries," Jessie feigned. "Why can't I?"

"Because ya don't drink," the newspaperman responded blankly.

Jessie knew he was suspected. So, he deflected. "And you still do." He interrupted Porfirio's denial, "Don't argue the fact. I can still smell it on your shirt. The pipe smoke was a good deflection though."

Porfirio grimaced and finally, raised his hands like a culprit caught. "The poplar loses its leaves. The bear hibernates. Why can't sobriety be seasonal?"

"Because your season is incredibly short," Jessie chided.

"Don't you get sanctimonious with me," Porfirio snapped. He spoke in a hushed voice, "What the hell you think you gonna do, rob the sheriff?" He saw through the façade on Jessie's face. "I been findin' stories for over half a century, Jessie. And you've always been a bad liar."

It was no use. Jessie walked away, "Good night, Porf."

"Let me help you!"

Jessie stalled. He looked back, "Ain't nothin' you can do."

"Horse's ass," Porfirio muttered. "I could—"

"I will always love you as family," Jessie admitted quietly. He continued, before any further arguments could be made. "And that's why I can't lose you, too."

Porfirio always struggled with affection. It was one of the reasons his sons resented him and his wife left him. He fidgeted with his pocket, at last revealing the flask he had been hiding. He cleared his throat, "You at least gonna talk to Mr. Smith about gettin' a proper rifle?"

Jessie snorted, "My rifle won my grandfather half a dozen duels."

"It is positively ancient."

Jessie swallowed. "I could say the same for you."

The old man threw up his hands, "Piss on you, Jessie. You stubborn bastard."

The conversation never ended. Rather, each person walked away muttering their insults.

When Jessie returned to the stead, it was past midnight. He had no trouble going to sleep, though *staying* asleep was another matter. Not half an hour would pass before Jessie awoke in a sweat. At around two in the morning, he took a blanket and went across the hall.

The twins' bedroom was immaculate. Like a lumbering, undead mass, Jessie dragged himself onto the twins' bed. He was overwhelmed by the ghostly reminders of small, ordinary life. Little things one takes for granted, like the smell of one's child, now became the dearest thing in Jessie's world. He inhaled deeply and was brought, not to tears, but to something akin to it. He buried his mouth in Elijah's ripped pillow. He did not cry himself to sleep; he screamed.

A few hours later, Jessie woke on the living room floor. He did not know how he had gotten there. He cracked his back and forced down a bite of pemmican.

Stomach still growling, he grabbed a spade and an axe. He hiked from his property, climbed over the McLeary's fence, and crossed their orchard. By dawn, he had made it to the Southern Road. Two miles outside of town, the road circled a ridgeline. To the left was a steep ledge; to the right, a sheltered overlook with a view of the surroundings.

Jessie wasted no time finding the sickliest tree beside the road. The small pinyon was as tall as the road was wide, covered in sap, and nearly dead already. It did not take long to fell, though Jessie spent the next hour chopping at its base to make it look like a natural widowmaker. Next, he dragged it out of the road just enough to create a gap for a horse.

As Jessie prepared for the next part of his trap, he heard the approach of a rider. He hid his tools and sat on the log.

"Preston," Jessie acknowledged.

"Woah, Mr. Bingham," Preston slowed his horses. Full crates of feed bounced in his cart. "What you doin' out here by your lonesome?"

Jessie knew he was a bad liar. So, he tried to tell the truth, "I was out here huntin' a predator when I saw this tree here."

"A predator," Preston repeated. "Between the crofts and the town? You'd think it'd have the sense to stay clear."

"Guess it's a very cosmopolitan critter," Jessie shrugged. "Anyway. I should have this mess sorted out by the end of the day."

Preston eyed the tree, "Need any help?"

Again, he told his version of the truth. "I ain't got crop or kin to tend to. Toil like this keeps the grief away."

"Right," Preston cleared his throat. No man wanted to hear about another man's grief. "Well. Good luck on y'hunt."

"Thank you," Jessie waved. "And might I suggest taking the back road for the rest of the day?" He swallowed, knowing how suspicious the request was. He added, "It'd help me catch this bastard."

Preston chuckled, "Sure thing, friend. I hope you nab it."

Jessie waited until the creaking wagon wheels of Preston's cart faded. Then, he grabbed his shovel and began digging into the dirt road. The funnel he had created between the fallen tree and the road slowly became a bowl. He dug just deep enough to break a leg. Then, he hid branches and leaf clutter over the holes. By the end, the pitfalls looked like clutter from the widowmaker.

That evening, he returned home and prepared his duffel bag. A month of pemmican was squeezed in, as well as three waterskins, spare ammunition, and finally—medicine. He opened his lockbox and took out the contents. He gathered the deed to the land and put that in his pack. He did not want the sheriff to have a legal way to take the land out from under him. Though, as Jessie hid the claim deep in the duffel bag—he felt as if it was only a formality. *I doubt I'll be coming home after tomorrow...* He grabbed a few more keepsakes: a fragment of his wife's wedding dress, his father's tinderbox, and finally—Glendolyn's wedding band. He put her ring next to his and crawled into bed.

He stared at the merciless moonlight for several long minutes. Then, he decided he was not tired. *I can rest tomorrow*, Jessie told himself. It was probably a lie. He grabbed his family rifle from the mantel, his duffel bag, and then looked around the cabin one last time. On his last pass, he realized the spherical jewel had not been packed. Jessie stormed into his bedroom and found it under his pillow. He did not recall putting it there.

He set off to his ambush in silence. He thought about what his family would say if they saw him now. On the cusp of robbery and possibly murder—would his father forgive him? What would Glendolyn say?

Jessie purged all his doubt. He reached the ambush point just before dawn and hiked atop the overlook. He took out his rifle and lay prone, waiting. He stilled his breathing and peered down the barrel of the weapon.

"Well look here, boys," said a familiar, gloating voice.

Jessie jumped. "God damn it, Porfirio," he growled. The Rodgers brothers were standing beside him. He hissed, "You're going to ruin everything!"

"Oh, now," Porfirio smirked. "I think we'd be rather helpful."

"Is that right, you dr—"

Solomon Rodgers stepped forward. "Look, Mr. Bingahm. Y'ain't the only one who lost someone to those brutes. I reckon we are mourners in collective. We'd best act in collective."

Jessie glared, unconvinced, "We're goin' on the Forlorn Trail, boy. Ain't no one survived this route with their minds unscathed. Did you even prepare? Do you have rations, ammunitions?"

"Son," Porfirio said, knowingly, "You ain't even got a horse and you preachin' preparedness."

Solomon went on, "Look, we got bedrolls, cookware..."

Hiram finished the thought, "It's not a damn chuckwagon, but it'll do."

Jessie was trapped. He wanted to argue, but there seemed no argument to make. "I don't like this," he muttered. "Solomon, I understand... But you two."

"I ain't lettin' my ass of brother out of my sight," Hiram stated plainly. "He's gotten all mudbrained since fallin' in with Cleona."

Jessie glared at Porfirio, "And you?"

The newspaperman pointed at the ground, "Figure there won't be saloons so far west. Might be my best chance at gettin' sober."

"I doubt that," Jessie replied, smelling the pipe tobacco on his breath.

"Damn it, Jessie! This is the story of a lifetime, a dime novel extraordinaire!" Porfirio made a rainbow with his hands, "Think of the mysteries before us!" He folded his hands around his chin and smiled proudly. He nodded, "These city dwellers have such ordained lives, 'bout all they care to read are fantasies. And by grace! We are alive to take part in one."

"You grey-haired, infantile—" Jessie could not finish his insult. A horse's squeal and a rider's swear echoed down the ridge. He sprinted to the overlook and peered at the scene.

The sheriff had ridden into his trap, but not without an ample guard. Jessie counted three deputies riding along on horseback. One, the pasty boy named Benjie, was writhing on the ground. His horse had walked into the pitfall and was now crushing his legs. Benjie's screams echoed. That deputy would not be a problem.

Jessie aimed his weapon at another deputy. Quincy Maples had doubled back and was riding his Saddlebred bloody. Jessie prepared to fire, steadying his breath. He had never murdered a man and, when a clear shot finally came—he hesitated. He shot and missed the deputy entirely. Unfortunately, he hit the man's horse cleanly. The proud beast bucked Deputy Maples off and darted into the woods. The rider fell down the ridge, rolling out of sight.

Jessie turned his attention to the remaining deputy. Rosco had dismounted and taken cover behind the sheriff's stagecoach. He aimed at the only visible point, his ankles. However, as he was about to take the shot—Hiram and Solomon Rodgers rode into the road. A shot rang and Hiram's hat flew off his head. The brothers continued. When they rounded the stagecoach, Rosco's ankles buckled.

Jessie froze for a moment. He had planned for a robbery, but he had not come to terms with the violence. He stared at the deputy's twitching, bloody body. He gazed at the dripping puddle beneath the hollowed head of Maples' Saddlebred. *It had been with him since he was a boy,* Jessie remembered.

Suddenly, the sheriff charged out of the stagecoach. He had a pistol to the captive's head and used him as a shield. Jessie snapped out of his haze and sprinted after. He slid down the slope and cut Crawford off.

"Hold it, Biggs," he said, rifle aimed.

"Nah, you hold it, Bingham," he snarled. He pressed his pistol into the Lugal's skull, "Or I'm inclined to get nervous."

"Release the savage to me."

"Why would I do that?" the sheriff mocked. "Because you killed a few deputies? I'll hire more."

"I need him more than you."

"Sure would tickle me to kill him, then," Crawford smirked.

Jessie's eye twitched. "Then I kill you." He blinked.

"Y'ever kill a man?" The sheriff took a step closer. "Y'ever watch them think their last thought, and know it is of you?"

While Biggs was talking, Porfirio made a silent approach through the nearby pinyon stands. He halted when the sheriff stopped talking. He had his own pistol raised.

"No," Jessie admitted. He kept the conversation going as Porfirio crept toward Crawford. "But I've butchered chickens. Reckon for someone of your character and capacities, it's similar."

Crawford barked a laugh, "I just might have to call my friends from the 6th cavalry. They's so bored lately. I reckon they'd love to hunt some highwaymen. Picture it, Mr. Bingham. You hangin' from a rope, just above your bitch wife's grave... What will the fools in Belford say when they read about ole' Jessie and his ragtag outlaw—"

Porfirio buffaloed the sheriff. The blunt steel of his pistol grounded the man instantly. As he fell, the old man declared, "Ain't no newspaper to read. I'm retired."

Jessie stared at the scene in disbelief. He had not seriously considered failure, though he had not planned for success either. Now, the sheriff and his deputies were unconscious, maimed, or in Rosco's case—dead.

"You sons-a-bitches," Benjie moaned. "You'll rot in the stocks for this."

The Rodgers Brothers approached the man. Deputy Greenfield's horse was broken at the knees, legs still trapped in the pitfall. Meanwhile, its massive body rolled against the fresh-faced young man.

Hiram looked back at Jessie, shrugged, and shot the deputy's horse.

The horse's blood splattered onto Jessie's boots. He looked down in horror. He hated blood and had actively avoided seeing it for the better part of a year. He shivered, now recalling Glendolyn's face right before she died. The horror of that day came over him like a flash flood.

Jessie heard Hiram speak as if the man were underwater. "Figure this'll be pretty painless for you, Benjie."

"Don' you talk to me—" the young man winced. "Like we are friends."

"Alright," Hiram sighed. He pointed his weapon at Benjie's skull.

Jessie suddenly shouted, "Hiram, no!"

"What?" the older of the Rodgers brothers scowled. "It's only a mercy."

Jessie stormed between the two men and knelt beside Benjie. "You don't know mercy." He took a tonic from his vest, a quick fix for pain. "Here, Greenfield."

The deputy spat on Jessie's face.

"Alright then," Jessie frowned. He left the medicine beside the broken man and braced his knees. "Solomon, could you ready that black horse for me—she won't be drivin' coach any longer." He smiled at Porfirio and said, "Think you could get my duffel bag?"

The old man looked the happiest Jessie had ever seen him. He glanced at the contorted body of Crawford Biggs and kicked him. "That's for wrongful imprisonment, you swine." He tipped his hat at the unconscious sheriff and strolled up the hill. "Oh, sure. I can manage that." He whistled as he walked.

At last, Jessie turned his attention to the captive Lugal. He was still standing where the sheriff had placed him, bound at the wrists and the feet. His hair was long and proud, and his nearly naked body bore many scars. "My name is Jessie J. Bingham."

The Lugal analyzed Jessie for a long while before speaking. He then rotated his forearms, chafing his wrists against his bonds. With his palms opened toward the sun, he said, "I am Eridu, son of Lugal Usumgal."

Solomon Rodgers brought Jessie the black mare. He took the reins and said, "Well, Eridu, son of Lugal Usumgal. I have a bargain for you."

Eridu lowered his hands and straightened his posture.

"Ride with us back to your lands. Guide us as you would a friend, and in return—release our loved ones back to us."

Eridu looked down at Crawford's unconscious body. "He thought of me as a beast."

"And we will not," Jessie assured him. He waited for a moment before intuiting the man's prior gesture. He rotated his wrists and flattened his hands. "We will show you respect if you show us the same."

Eridu looked Jesse in the eye. He raised his bonds, "Will you remove these restraints, friend?"

Jessie looked at the Rodgers brothers, both of whom shook their heads. He frowned at them and swiped the sheriff's hunting knife. He cut Eridu's bonds. Once freed, Jessie feared the Lugal would dart into the trees. Instead, he raised his arm. Jessie stepped back, fearing Eridu was going to strike him. Yet the Lugal made no such move. Instead, he put his thumb on Jessie's forehead. "We are in union, Jessie Bingham. With great Parsha's aid, we shall fight together."

Porfirio returned to the group and threw Jessie his duffel bag, "Another fight? Where? I'm ready as burnt toast."

Chapter 10

"Mary Anne Thorne was lucky that there were other captives. It is doubtful anyone would have braved the Forlorn Trail for her alone."

– The Ballad of Jessie Bingham

Three days. Three days was all it took to break her. Mary felt undead, forced to live in the eerie echoes of an adolescence she strived for years to leave behind. She was haunted at every turn by ghosts of her past, reanimated now as strange and brutal slavers.

Mary had not been allowed to eat or sleep without the scarred slaver accompanying her. She could not even relieve herself without him and his friend watching her. By the third day, she had become numb to the degradation. Soaked in her own urine and crammed next to the other captives on an uncomfortable cart—she thought of her brother.

Images of locked rooms and beheaded dolls flashed through her mind. She recalled one time after her brother beat her, she hid in the cellar. Her mother had found her after a few hours. Rather than protect Mary, she punished her. Refusing to feed her for a week, her mother had said, '*The Thorne do not run from a fight. We are the fight.*' That had been Mary's education. Not a formal one by any means, but effective. She knew how to play her family's game.

But she was not in Belford anymore. She was not the mayor anymore. She was a slave. And, as she had learned while under her family's long shadow, it would be best to stay quiet.

Don Marcos, however, was anything but silent. It had taken only three days of captivity to learn much about the corrupt doctor. For one, he was clearly born with a certain arrogance. Even bound at the wrists and ankles, he spoke as if he was always above the other captives. Presently, he was demanding:

"When they come 'round with food, give me your portion."

Cleona Flowers was monotone. The young woman had no patience for the doctor, "And why would I feed wildlife?"

Don Marcos barked a laugh. "Because your damn daddy brought these beasts upon us. If you wanna do right by the Lord, you'll atone with acts of charity."

"Spare me the fuckin' sermon," Cleona growled. She had her father's high cheekbones and, from the looks of it, his temper.

Marcos licked the circumference of his lips and eyed Mary. "Give me your portion."

"Pray tell why?" Mary said in a monotone.

"Cause I'm stronger. Faster. I'm our best chance at escaping."

Mary smiled at the man's maimed hand.

The doctor glared at her, "I don' see your cane 'round anyparts. You gonna grope y'way back over them peaks?"

Mary did not respond. She hardly had the energy to respond to her thoughts, let alone the musings of a disgusting degenerate.

Don Marcos gnashed his teeth, "Thought not. As for you," he snickered at Cleona Flowers. "You lucky none of them savages bred you yet. But when they do, y'aint gonna be able to run all too quick."

Cleona bit back, "I'd reckon if the Mayor's men could beat ya so easily—you'd last about half a second with these folk."

Mary found Cleona's confidence too difficult to bear. She preferred Don Marcos' anger, as that was a better companion for her despair. She raised her knees to hide her face. She breathed the dry, naked air. They were now on the western side of the Forlorn Hills. She smelled it in the barren air. She could feel it when she licked her cracked lips. Even the skin on her hands had started to chip. She rubbed her irritated, bloody fingers. She felt as though she were a piece of ancient pottery.

Mary leaned backward, letting her face roast in the sun. She closed her eyes and tried to doze off. She had not yet escaped to her nightmares when greedy hands grabbed her waist and pulled her off the cart. Her numb legs instantly wavered, folding beneath her weight like two fleshy blades of grass.

Mary fell before the scarred one. She tried to look up at him; the ooze over her eyes had solidified. She saw only an armored silhouette, ethereal and unreal. It stared down at her against a sinking, crimson sun. He grinned at her, put a hand on her chin, and lightly slapped her cheek. Then, he grabbed her wrist and dragged her some distance to a large, white structure. The fine sand lacerated her legs, but she relished the pain. It was a welcome distraction for her mind.

Once at the structure, the scarred slaver and his fat friend tied her to a warm, white pillar. The scarred one promptly left, but the fat one lingered. He knelt before her and wiped the sickly crusts off her eyes. He frowned at the wounds on her legs. He reached into a satchel at his waist and applied a salve.

She might have thanked him, had he not looked at her with such pity. She could not abide by the look. It amplified her hopelessness more than any cruelty. She glared back, feigning strength like a rattlesnake. Before long, the fat oaf bowed his head and departed.

Within several minutes, the Lugal had erected a camp of hide tents, tethered their mounts to whatever they could find, and tied the rest of the captives up beside Mary. Don Marcos was bound beside Mary with Cleona on his left. The young girl declared as their captors departed, "Solly won' let us be for too much longer, Mayor Thorne. I'd reckon he's got the sheriff and his posse out right now lookin' for us."

Mary snorted, "Biggs ain't gonna look for none of us. He's probably campaignin' for mayor as we speak."

Marcos growled, "That's the truth, Ms. Flowers. We ain't gonna find no help out here. In fact, I'd reckon that Rodgers boy already forgot…"

Mary ignored her fellow captives. She analyzed the Lugal's strange mounts. She was certain they were some inbred monstrosity. The heads had small bumps at the top of the skull. The necks were elongated. The muscular back protruded vertically, creating a natural seat. In all, the beasts neither sounded nor seemed like horses.

So, they were fitting mounts of the Lugal. The tribe had always existed in a strange medium between fairy tale and fiction, with the only folk who seemed to know anything about them being crazed wagoneers and other, superstitious natives. Even now, with fiction made flesh, Mary had not embraced the reality of her situation. Her captors were dreamlike in their differences and Mary did her best to disregard dreams.

She sighed and looked back east at the Forlorn Hills. She snorted, *Calling these hills is like calling a wall a fence.* She tested her tethers, rolling her wrists and checking the snugness of her bonds. Strangely, she found the rope was caught on something. She turned to investigate her human hitching post.

What she saw puzzled her. The post was a rib, itself a small part of a gigantic, serpentine skeleton. She stared at the remains. Mary was certain the owner of those bones would have been the largest being on the planet. The titanic bones reminded Mary of all the religious stories she had fallen asleep to. *What other stories will seem real by the end of all this?*

Rather than think about religion (a topic that never held much weight in the Thorne household), Mary looked at the landscape. Small fissures meandered along the bony white soil, creating islands of cracked clay. The earth looked as if it were stitched together by a thousand small ravines. She swallowed the dry air and rubbed her chapped lips together. *Even if I had my vision and I did escape, this desert would destroy me.*

"What in all hell?" Don Marcos began. "They got them gangly rats, too!"

Mary turned her head and, to her surprise, saw the Bingham twins. The boy's shoulders were held by a brawny man. The other was restrained by a large woman. Both twins wore hollow, vacant expressions. Though, Elijah's face was bruised.

The Lugal brought the twins to the human hitching post. Mary noticed, however, a strange difference between the twins. Ethel was treated less harshly while Elijah was practically prodded. When they reached the other captives, she also realized that Elijah was limping. A tear trickled down his cheek as the Lugal pushed him to his knees. They then raised his arms and bound his wrists high above his chest. In every way, the little boy was treated worse than any of the other captives. This was especially true compared to his sister. Elijah was roughly restrained, but the Lugal left Ethel Bingham unbound beside her twin.

Ethel flailed her little arms, "That was stupid, Eli! You shouldn't have run!"

"She took my book!" Elijah argued.

Mary and the other two slaves looked at the pair curiously. Where had the children been the last three days? Why was Ethel not tied up? She tilted her head. At first, the twins' clothes seemed muddy or worn. Now, Mary realized they were ill-fitted, feral garments.

Mary blurted, "Why are you wearing savage clothes?"

Elijah's face twitched, saying nothing.

Ethel whispered something to her brother. The little boy looked away and ignored her. His sister tilted her head admonishingly. Then, she grabbed his Lugal-made shirt and pulled the garment up. Countless lash marks lined his back.

They've been whipping him! Mary's blood boiled. She would happily watch a grown man cry. She had made quite a few do so herself, and much worse at that. Seeing a little boy in pain though... The wordless memories of her childhood flooded back to her. She recalled all the rooms in which her brother had tormented her. She remembered the little closet which was her sole refuge in that house of horror.

An instinct Mary assumed was vestigial suddenly overwhelmed her. Without thinking of the repercussions, she tried to put a clumsy hand on the boy's shoulder. The rope at her wrists tautened. Immediately, Mary recoiled and bowed her head. *What's a hand on a shoulder?* She mocked. *That would have felt transactional. Cold. No need to commit to being sentimental.* Most kind interactions among strangers felt overly formal anyway.

It was Cleona Flowers who finally asked, "Why'd they whip you?"

"It wasn't them," Ethel chirped.

"What?" Mary gasped. "They kidnapped you."

All Ethel could manage was a quiet, "Yeah."

Mary still did not understand. She whispered to the sister, "Why is he injured?"

Ethel murmured, "Ms. Rosalee whipped him for talking back."

"Ms. Rosalee?" Mary repeated, adding the name to a list of people she would make the world forget. *That Jessie Bingham always spent too much time around the brothel.*

"She took our daddy's belt and—"

"Don't," Eli pleaded.

Ethel bit her tongue and nodded at Mary.

"No need to explain," Mary told the twins.

Elijah looked up at her, eyes welling wide with tears.

Mary looked away, leaving the boy to his vulnerable moment. *He has Jessie's green eyes, the same golden hair. He'll probably be just as handsome one day.*

Again, Cleona Flowers asked, "Is that why your face is bruised, little one?"

"I ain't little," Elijah protested.

Ethel bit her bottom lip and pulled away slightly. She looked down at her brother, "He tried to run away from her."

"Ms. Rosalee?" Mary asked.

Elijah shook his head, "The woman that took us."

Ethel confirmed with a slow nod of her head. "She was just tryna be nice to us."

"She took my book!" Elijah seethed.

Ethel stared at her twin for a long while before her eyes began to swell. She approached Mary slowly and sat on her knees. The girl croaked, "C-can you... Is the sheriff gonna come get us?"

Biggs would rather sell us than save us. Mary found it impossible to tell the truth to the frail child. Strangely, she also felt it impossible to lie. She cleared her throat and averted her eyes. "I'm sure your daddy is already coming to get you."

Ethel wiped her tears and smiled, "He can talk to birds."

"Can he really?" Mary played along, inflecting her voice excitedly as she always heard good mothers do.

"Yeah," Ethel nodded. "And he knows how to track!"

He'll die trying to save you. Mary forced a smile and a soothing voice, "I bet he's already on his way."

Elijah muttered bitterly, "Just stop."

"What?" Mary asked.

"We don't need a new mama," he mumbled.

Without thinking, Mary replied, "Neither do I." She had not intended for the remark to mean much, yet it made the twins pause. Elijah looked away, pouting; Ethel smiled again at Mary. The boy's reaction she understood—but the girl's she struggled with. It made her feel uncomfortable, almost naked. Mary could not recall a time when any child had smiled at her. Within seconds of being warmed by the gesture, Mary was hiding her face. *I wish I could wipe all this puss out of my eyes. I'm sure I am only frighten—*

Ethel threw herself onto her and wrapped her little arms around her body.

Mary stiffened, having rarely been touched kindly. Her chest tensed reactively, her legs twitched closed. It took a moment for her to steady her breathing and feel safe from the touch. *She's just a girl,* she reminded herself. *This is just a hug. Normal. Kind, even.* Finally, Mary looked down at the girl and sniffled, "I'd hug you back, but uh..."

Ethel broke down, drenching her clothes with tears and snot.

Mary panicked, thinking she had said something wrong. She looked up, "It's okay," she lied. "I, uh, I got you."

"Ethel..." Elijah complained. "She ain't mama. None of 'em is."

His sister did not listen. She tried to speak, "He w-, I ju-, they..." Her words became a mournful shriek. She clung to Mary, gripping her clothes with sweaty fists.

Mary licked her lips. She could feel her little heartbeat. She swallowed and rested her forehead on the top of Ethel's head.

In response, Ethel rubbed her head—and her snot—all over Mary's chest.

Mary quivered. She was both afraid, repulsed, and shocked. She had never felt such a warmth in her chest and, for a second, her despair left her.

The moment when Donaciano Marcos griped, "Oh shut up, girl. You'll be put out in a couple weeks without y'tonic anyhow."

Mary could not contain herself. She hissed, "I wish I could have seen Biggs break your hand."

Don Marcos' upper lip curled. He bared his yellow teeth, "Why you care 'bout these mongrels? Mammy was a whore, daddy was a beggar. Best let that illness of theirs take 'em." His face twisted into a cruel grin, "And your illness, too. Matter-o-fact. Wouldn't be surprised if them gnats as inbred as you, Thorne."

Mary had dozens of choice words for the doctor. She was given no opportunity to share them, however. Don Marcos' raised voice had attracted a great deal of attention and presently, a broad-shouldered woman was approaching. She was flanked by the scarred brute on her left. At her right was a cross-eyed hunchback.

As the three strode toward the prisoners, the rest of the camp threw themselves onto the ground. The ragged and brutal warriors waved their hands in penitent prostration. They chanted in a whisper, *"Ama. Ama. Ama."*

The trio came to Don Marcos.

This is the one the twins were referring to, Mary realized. *This is the woman who took them.*

The female warrior gazed at Elijah first with disappointment. Then, she turned her attention to Don Marcos. She said something to two men beside her. When the woman finished speaking, the cross-eyed hunchback stepped forward and put a hand on Don Marcos' forehead. The doctor's eyes lit up with animal fear.

Will they do to him what they did to Collin's men? Mary waited with bated breath. *Will they cut out his tongue, too?*

The disfigured Lugal spoke in his guttural tongue. His eyes swirled independently as he talked. Strangely, when he finished, Marcos was sweating and staring up at the man as if he had understood what was said.

The trio turned to Mary. The scarred man tapped his fingers on his thigh impatiently. Yet, for the first time in three days—he did not cast his mongering stare. He did not come and cup her ass or grab her chest. Instead, he deferred to the armored woman as she strode forward.

The woman stared down at her. Her skin was dark, like other natives Mary had seen. The Lugal's black hair was long, hanging freely below her shoulders. Though not exactly young, her breasts did not sag. If she had any greys, Mary could not see them. Nor any wrinkles. She was everything Mary was not in a woman. Mary hated her immediately.

The woman spoke a foreign language. When she concluded, the hunchback approached Mary. She saw then that his body was covered in black jewelry. *Those are the same stones Collin Flowers found.* The spheres dangled from the disfigured man's ears; they hung from a heavy pendant; they littered dozens of rings across his hands. The man's bejeweled fingers reached out. He touched her forehead. Mary's hair stood up.

"Asura will not tolerate runaway slaves." The hunchback glanced at Elijah Bingham and then stared sternly at her. "She is your matriarch and your mother."

Asura took a deep breath and then pulled Ethel away. It seemed, from Mary's point of view, she had to use some strength to pry the girl away. That must have angered the woman, for the matriarch shot a dreadful look at the little girl. She raised her hand as if to strike the child. Ethel stiffened. The matriarch arced her arm and swung her hand, stopping just before making contact. She smiled and pinched the girl's cheek.

The woman turned her attention back to Mary. After a long, curious regard, she walked over. She pushed the hunchback aside and knelt before her. She pointed at herself, "Ama Asura."

Mary blinked. *Is this an introduction?* She cleared her throat, "Mary Anne Thorne."

Ama Asura got to her feet and pointed at Ethel, "Ama?"

What does, 'Ama' mean? Mary shook her head, "Ethel and Elijah."

The woman flashed an impatient smile before repeating, "Ama?" The inflection in her voice was clear: she was asking a question.

When Mary produced no response (save a slow, confused squeak), the native touched her breast and pointed at the children.

Does Ama mean mother? Mary racked her brain for some way of confirming. A moment went by before she motioned to her belly. She folded her palms over her stomach, pointed at the children, and tilted her head.

Ama Asura nodded.

Mary saw how the matriarch's hands floated to her side, where some Lugal blade waited in its sheath. She also saw the scarred brute was sweating; the brute watched Asura intently with bent knees and a worried expression. *I cannot answer wrong,* Mary understood. She shook her head.

Ama Asura nodded and her hand left her side. She spoke to the cross-eyed man at length. Then, she grabbed Ethel's hand and departed. Mary watched the little girl go. At first, she felt nothing but pity for the child. When Ethel turned around, she suddenly felt as if she had been struck by a weapon. Mary thought to mouth a goodbye, but the hunchback moved between them.

He placed his hand back on her forehead. A surge of heat shot through her skull and down into her chest: "You are the war-bride of Nerugal, Warchief of Lugal Usumgal."

Her captor lifted his head proudly.

The hunchback continued: "You will serve him dutifully and provide supple offspring. Should you fail, or should you dare touch Ama Asura's children again—you will be buried in the great Gardens of Sunumun. Ever after, these children will know you only as nutrients in their meals."

Mary dared respond, "Her children?"

The bejeweled cretin nodded, "She has chosen them as her kin."

And at that, Mary's bonds were tightened, her mouth was gagged, and a blindfold was fastened to her face. She would not see or speak to another person for many days.

Chapter 11

The trail led them along the spine of the Hills. Up, down, up, down. Jessie passed the time imagining they were traveling on a serpent's back or a camel's hump. Eridu and Jessie dismounted and read the hoofprints before them.

Eridu mumbled, "She drives them hard. They will be on the other side now."

"She?" Porfirio inquired. He had not put his journal down since they had embarked.

Eridu nodded, "Ama Asura. My father's wife."

Jessie licked the inside of his lip as he and Porfirio glanced at one another. Porfirio probed, "And this woman is *not* your mother?"

"That is a bramblesome question," Eridu sighed. He did not elaborate.

Jessie had his own questions, chiefly concerning what type of animal Eridu's people rode. He was positive they were some new breed. They remounted and continued climbing. "What horses have two toes?"

"The prints were made by umamukin."

Hiram turned and blinked. "A what?"

Eridu dragged a hand through his black hair, "The beast has no name in your languages, for you are young. The Erintul are the last to know the name, but there was an elder time when many peoples walked. There were then a thousand names for the beast."

As was the trend, after Eridu finished, nobody knew how to respond.

Jessie fidgeted with the black stone in his pocket. It had done nothing strange or otherworldly all day. He was somewhat thankful for the fact. He had thought the wilds would be quaint, calm, or rejuvenating. Perhaps they would have been, had his children been there to warm his heart. Instead, Jessie mistrusted that feral country. His comfortable pinyons were now towering bristlecones. The lone bear track was now one of many; the pawprints were much larger. Even the water was different, clearer in some spots and metallic in others.

To stop his mind from wandering, Jessie continued the conversation, "Where did you learn our language, Eridu?"

Eridu provided a non-answer. "We are not as disparate of peoples as you would think."

"Disparate enough to not know words," Hiram grumbled.

Porfirio looked up from a piece of paper, "Only takes one enslaved wagoneer to teach 'em." He licked his lips and looked at the imposing line of mountains still between them and the Western Basin.

Eridu leaned forward and said to Jessie, "The rains will be coming soon. We should find shelter."

"Them clouds is far off," Solomon smiled naively.

"No," Jessie agreed. "Alpine thunderstorms are very punctual this time of year."

The company scanned the countryside for a suitable hollow. First, he noticed a series of boulders. They looked like the rungs of a leviathan's ladder. "There will be cavities where these rocks broke away." Jessie followed the boulders up the hillside. There, they found a suitable den with only rumors of bear. As the horses did not protest, the men made camp within.

At first, everyone busied themselves with their tasks. Porfirio stared expectantly into his empty flask. Then, he packed his pipe. Solomon insisted on doubling back to pick some wild onions he had spotted. "Make our stew tonight palatable."

"You don't know the land," Hiram protested.

"An onion is an onion," Solomon rolled his eyes. He left the cave and, reluctantly, his brother accompanied him.

Eridu sat alone, arms and legs crossed in a meditative pose.

Jessie, meanwhile, was busy arranging the pebbles around his person by size and appearance. When he had done so, he counted everyone's rations and the spare ammunition. After, he fed the horses. When he got to his stolen mare, he frowned. "The Tlacon nomads say a horse without a name is bad luck, so..." Jessie shrugged. The memory of Genevieve's ashen remains was still too fresh. "Let's not overthink things. Here you go, Girl." He fed Girl an apple and sat on the cold cavern stone.

Without a task to bail the worry from his mind, his brain began to flood. *I should never have left Veola with them. Everyone knew she was a bad woman. Everyone but me.* Jessie sat on the cold stone and buried his head in his hands. *They will be getting nauseous now.* He languished in self-loathing, as it was one of few activities available to an idle mind. *A useless husband and a useless father.*

Jessie shivered. He bent his knees and wore them like a shield. He listened to the storm. The thunder was getting louder. The brief flashes of lightning were growing brighter and more frequent. The bristlecones were groaning and swaying. The cavern was becoming a cacophony of pitter-pattering raindrops.

The Rodgers brothers returned to the cavern. Solomon dropped a heap of onions beside his bedroll. "Big fuckers out there," he panted. He took off his drenched clothing and changed into his spare clothes.

Hiram, as ever, was not amused, "Yes, and now that ya have your precious allium—can we stay dry?"

Solomon patted his brother and grinned, "Y'aint had to come." He rummaged through his rucksack and pulled out a few loose pages. He brought them to Jessie and sat beside him. He leaned forward, cleared his throat, and read the contents of the paper silently. He looked at Jessie, back at the paper, and scratched his scalp.

Jessie widened his eyes expectantly. "Go on, then."

"Well, seeing as you was married—I'm just wondering what you think about these vows?" He extended a crumpled piece of parchment.

Jessie eyed it with disgust. "Porfirio was married longer."

The old man looked at Solomon playfully. The lovestruck boy smiled, saying, "I think he approves."

"Indeed I do," Porfirio nodded.

Jessie sucked in his lip and swiped the paper, "Fine." He began reading: '*Cleona Flowers, when I first met you, my world was a selfish one. I thought love was something to be acquired, a trinket one places next to one's heart. But you are no ornament. You are ornate...*'

Jessie swallowed and gave the vows back. "They're good."

Solomon was confused, "But you barely read it!"

"Didn't need to," Jessie shrugged. "Trust me, that's a cheek-waterer."

Hiram yanked the piece of paper out of his brother's hand and read it quickly. His face was pure awe, "Where'd you learn to write like this?"

Solomon grinned at Porfirio, "I asked Mr. Pacheco if he could make my feelings into somethin' romantic."

Hiram rolled his eyes, "Well, you certainly sound educated." He got to his feet, "We should get cookin', Solly. We're fixin' to stay here all night."

"Yeah," Solomon peered outside, "That storm ain't normal."

"They won't be," Jessie told them. "The mountains block the clouds from goin' west. This is the end of the trail for the rain." As the Rodgers left, he wondered if he had sounded too arrogant. He then debated whether he had always sounded so prideful, as if everything he said had to be tinged with a tutorly tone. Would his kids develop the same trait? Would they develop at all? An intolerable forum erupted between Jessie's guilt and his anxiety. Within seconds, he was drifting off into hypothetical arguments and confrontations (mostly with himself).

Porfirio placed a hand on his shoulder, interrupting the mental mutilation.

Jessie nodded, thankful for the gesture. *I cannot help anyone if I am brittle as bone.* He fixed his posture and inquired, "Say, Eridu. How long will this journey take?"

"For your people, many cycles of the moon. For the Erintul, much less."

"That's no estimate at all," Jessie badgered. *How many days? How many miles?*

Porfirio intercepted the conversation, asking, "The Erintul?"

"The People of the Well," Eridu replied.

"Anyone for onions in their stew?" Solomon called from across the cavern. "Nobody? More for me, then."

Porfirio inhaled his pipe, "Never heard of the People of the Well... Are the Erintul related to the Lugal?"

For the first time since joining their outfit, Eridu chuckled. "Certainly."

Porfirio raised his brow and waited for clarification.

Eridu placed his hands on his lap, "There was a time, horrible and bloody, when every man fancied themselves a Lugal. Fortunately, there is only one Lugal now."

Jessie squinted, recalling Eridu's introduction. He leaned against the cavern wall and wondered about the man. Porfirio turned around, clearly coming to the same conclusion. "You are Eridu, son of *Lugal* Usumgal." He paused, "What does that word mean, exactly?"

"Many things," Eridu deflected.

Jessie and Porfirio nodded at one another. Jessie then stared at Eridu, "We promised to respect one another. That requires honesty."

Eridu folded his hands. "Lugal roughly translates to king."

"Son of Lugal Usumgal..." Hiram repeated. "So you are some kind of prince?"

A flicker of hope was shared among the men. Jessie bowed his head and smiled, *What are two children compared to a prince? This is perfect!*

"Welp," Solomon beckoned. "Supper is served for Belford's outlaws." He winked at Eridu, "We are flattered to be joined by native royalty. May he enjoy our paltry porridge."

"You've been spendin' too much time with Mr. Pacheco," Hiram grumbled.

Solomon and Porfirio chuckled.

"So, Eridu," Hiram spoke with a mouthful of food. "You seem rather well-built. A warrior type from them shoulders and such."

"All my family has served the warrior god, Parsha. It is—"

"Yes yes," Hiram swallowed. "Your *kingly* family. Which makes me wonder how you got captured. And only you. I would think a prince might be better protected." He slurped and chewed loudly, baring his full mouth, "Makes a man mighty suspicious this is all a trick."

Eridu put down his bowl. His stare was neither kind nor cruel. When he finally spoke, the words came slowly. Jessie might have thought the man was ready to turn in for the night, were it not for the subtle tremor in his voice:

"I went on that raid not for slaves, nor for Parsha's glory... I only—" Eridu interrupted himself. "I went on my own errand during the raid—"

"Which was?" Hiram probed.

"None of your concern," Eridu hissed. His shadow suddenly grew, his voice boomed, and his young face seemed to age. With a deep breath, he continued. "I left my umamukin on the outskirts of your settlement, for I knew it would be wiser to walk amongst you on foot."

"You were in Belford?" Jessie gasped.

Eridu did not respond to the question. "When I reconvened with my people, they had captured a meager number of slaves. Not enough to please the Lugal, but as we had retaken many Ur Igi, I said nothing."

"Ur Igi,"

"Priestly tools no simple folk should possess," Eridu elaborated. He quickly continued, allowing no one to ask further questions. "Your warriors were soon upon us. I rode at the rear, as any honorable combatant would in a retreat. But, as we crossed the silty stream—my mount collapsed."

"Sheriff was always a good shot," Hiram shrugged.

"My mount was not shot," Eridu asserted. "Its tongue was blue and sagged out of its mouth. Its body was shaking. Someone had poisoned it." He glared into the fire. His voice and the fire cracked in unison, "I was betrayed."

Solomon put down his bowl and wiped his mouth, "By who?"

Eridu sat up straight, "It is unwise to discuss gloomy subjects at night." He returned to his meal.

Supper concluded in silence. The men dispersed to individual nooks within the hollow. Each did their best to make bare rock comfortable. The Rodgers had no trouble sleeping, owing to their itinerant lives after losing their farm. Porfirio grumbled about his back for several minutes before deciding he would rather journal.

For his part, Jessie listened to the steady rains. The thunder had subsided, but a trickle continued rhythmically. The *tip-tap* of leaking drops had a hypnotic effect on him. He began seeing rainstorms on the cave walls, appearing as flickering shadows upon the stone. Yet, when Jessie turned to see the light source, he saw none. He pocketed his hands and stared blankly.

Eridu suddenly spoke, "An Ur Igi is not a looking glass, Jessie Bingham."

"Pardon?" Jessie turned. He had been absorbed by the crystalline raindrops that seemed to strike the dry rock. There was something behind the rains, as if they and the rock were a veil. He stood up and put his hand on the cavern wall. Immediately, the vision of raindrops faded. There was nothing to see save stone.

Eridu took a deep breath, "That jewel in your pocket. It an Eye of Ur, an Igi."

Porfirio looked up from his journalling. "You *kept* one?" He looked at Jessie proudly, "And the savages did not—" he shot an apologetic look at Eridu. "The Erintul did not take it back?"

Jessie took out the speaking stone for all to see.

"That-a kid," Porfirio beamed. His eyebrows rose like the breaching of a whale. Then, he plunged back into his papers. "Carry on, you two."

Jessie looked at the speaking stone. Streaks of blue and white rained down the glowing core, like an ethereal monsoon. He began to feel as if he could stare into the jewel for hours. He shut his eyes, stowed the stone, and sat beside Eridu. He had dozens of questions and for a while, was incapacitated by them all. He managed at last to say, "This is not the first time I have heard the name of Ur."

Eridu gazed at him with a face of mixed, unreadable emotions. "The name belongs to the God of Wisdom. His acolytes use the stones to comb the Infinite Library."

Jessie's remaining questions disintegrated in confusion and disbelief. Without anything to add, he caressed his forearms and looked away. "I am afraid I've never been much of a believer in magic."

"Knowledge of the universe is not magic," Eridu began. "It is far more dangerous."

Jessie looked back at the stern-faced man. He swallowed, "It frightened me at first and so, I buried it. Then, with my babies gone—"

"You should have left it buried," Eridu scolded. "It takes decades for one of the Ur Namen to earn the right to see with His Eyes."

Jessie repeated the stone's words, "Common eyes cannot see the vision of Ur…"

Eridu inched away and stared at Jessie frightfully, "How do you know that aphorism?"

"The stone says it… Or, uh, I suppose I say it with the stone's voice. The phrase always comes before some bit of poetry. Here," he held out the Eye.

Eridu recoiled, shivering. "It is too dangerous." He peered at Jessie, then at Porfirio. In a way, he seemed to shrink into the corner of the cavern; yet, when he spoke, his quiet voice had a disproportionate echo. "An Eye of Ur requires an unmade mind, infantile and versatile. Otherwise, the seer sees only what one *wants* to see. They get trapped in a finite section of Ur's library."

Porfirio had struck a match and lit his pipe, "You've lost me, sir."

"When used by an unworthy seer, the Eye of Ur amplifies one's spirit. They become a caricature of the self. Their preconceptions, ideals, aspirations—they implode into a singularity of the self, like one word echoing into eternity." Eridu saw that neither man understood him. He wiped his weary eyes. "Mr. Bingham should take great care to remain sane."

Abruptly, Porfirio gasped and spoke rapidly, "You reckon these stones could make a man murder his folk? His friends?"

"That is often what they do."

Porfirio nodded and flipped to a fresh page. Without looking up, he said, "We acquired these, uh, Eyes…" He scribbled a note before continuing, "From a group of miners. They went past the Hills to find them. Funny thing was, we found *them* washed up in the river. Their tongues was staked to their heads."

Eridu was silent for a long while. Embers shot up, framing his face in a flaming vignette. "Long before my city was founded, there was a great empire. Ruled by a man known now as Damu Matu, this empire was greater than any before or since. He was practically a god, for he wielded a scepter fashioned of strange ore. With it, he saw things that no one could predict, envisioned feats of engineering none could fathom. And then, one day—he perished. His scepter was broken and the fragments became the Ur Igi…" Eridu fidgeted, "My people call the period that followed, '*The Tyranny of a Thousand Prophets.*'"

Porfirio and Jessie each began a sentence. None of them were able to get a word in, however. From across the cave came a guttural shriek. The three shot to their feet.

Solomon was curled in a fetal position and cradling his stomach. His brother scrambled to his side, "What is it, Solly?"

"My stomach!" he groaned. "It's gonna burst."

Hiram pulled his brother's arm, "Not in here, it ain't. Come on, let's get you some fresh air."

Solomon clung to the ground, retching.

Jessie sprinted to the young man's stash of onions. He picked up a handful of shoots and sniffed them. They did not seem in season. He smelled the bulb; his stomach plunged with dread. "This is Dead Man's Scalp."

"He needs a healer," Eridu remarked calmly.

"No," Solomon protested. He staggered to his feet, only to sink back to the ground and gag. "Just need to show it—" a vile liquid oozed out his mouth. "The exit."

Jessie sprinted toward the horses and grabbed Girl's reins. The black mare had been stirred by the commotion and was already stomping her hooves with anticipation. "With how much was eaten, you may end up paralyzed."

Solomon blinked. "Y'all are exagger—" He screamed and clenched his stomach. Tears coated his eyes. Weary moans lumbered out of his spittle-filled mouth.

Hiram grabbed his brother and lifted him onto his saddle. "With a hard ride, we can get 'im to Silverfork."

The company charged into the thunderstorm. The horses galloped swiftly through an open meadow, guided by a hunter's moon. Paths and pitfalls were illuminated by a pale glow. A tributary stream of the Copper River glinted in the distance. "Silverfork will be situated yonder," Jessie yelled.

Towering pines swayed in the midnight breeze. Aspen shivered and quaked. Shapeless animals darted out of their way. When they finally reached Silverfork, the hunter's moon was sinking in the sky. They dismounted beside a welcome sign and walked up a small hill. Their long shadows crawled down the main street.

Hiram took his horse's reins and guided it down the road, "This is a quiet town."

Jessie stared at the saloon, *The Perennial Fountain*. The establishment looked positively dead. "What day is it?"

"No holy day I know of," Porfirio whispered.

The group continued, growing more and more wary as they went. The town was not deserted. There were clear indications of life. "Streetlamps are all lit. Doors are neatly closed. Look there! That basil is freshly potted."

Solomon whimpered, "Are we at a doctor yet?"

Eridu responded first. "Not yet, onion man."

Solomon groaned, "I can try vo—" His tongue sagged out of his mouth.

The paralysis was starting. The next body part to fail would be his neck, then his entire spine. Jessie remounted and charged down Main Street until he found the local pharmacy. Like every other building, it seemed unoccupied. Jessie knocked on the immaculately carved door. "Doctor! Doctor!"

Hiram walked past Jessie and peered through the window. Without saying a word, he walked around to the back of the pharmacy. Jessie heard a door handle groan and a chain lock rattle. Hiram reappeared, eyed the window again, and then picked up a large rock.

"What are you doing?" Jessie hissed.

"Skippin' the pleasantries," Hiram grunted.

Jessie lunged, wrestling for the rock. They grappled for a time before the elder Rodgers overcame him. Hiram pushed him away and took a step toward the window, "He needs medicine!"

"And you reckon a sawbones is going to want to help once you vandalize his business? I reckon this town's more likely to hang us than help us."

Hiram lowered his fist, but a look of indignation remained.

Jessie glared at the man. *He is abrasive, brash, and likely to get all of us killed.* As he cleared his throat to say exactly that, there was a yell from across the street:

"What in the Lord's name?"

Jessie turned to find a slouching, bespectacled man staring at him from across the road. A dingy lantern swayed in his wrinkled hand.

Hiram lowered his arm subtly to his side and gingerly dropped the stone. "Who are you?"

"I'll be asking the questions, sir," replied the stranger. He walked across the street and waved the lantern at Jessie's face. He turned to Hiram, "Whatchyu doin' in Silverfork?"

The man had not looked either of them in the eye. The mannerism made Jessie mistrustful and, despite Solomon's plight, Jessie did not answer. Instead, he looked around the seemingly deserted town, unnerved by the quiet.

Hiram lowered his chin humbly, "My brother ate Dead Man's Scalp. He needs a doctor."

Eridu and Porfirio came down the road. Eridu had put on Jessie's hat and tipped the brim to obscure his face. The stranger hardly noticed Eridu and approached Solomon with intense curiosity. The sickly man's head was slowly slumping toward his sternum.

The bespectacled stranger inspected his clothing, gliding his hand over a chevron insignia. "That's a historic stitch. The army stopped dolin' 'em out five years ago."

"Belonged to our father," Hiram responded impatiently.

"His accolades don't mean anything if he's dead," Jessie reminded the stranger.

The slouching man tutted his tongue. "A lot of people think gunfights and brawls are why the West is wild. Actually, most people die from common accidents like this. Why, I know a man who died by a kick from his horse."

"Are you going to talk him to death?" Hiram snarled. "We need the doctor."

The stranger had been halfway into another anecdote before cutting himself off. He looked at the chevron stitch again. "For the son of a serviceman, I will see what I can do."

"You are the medicine man?" Eridu questioned.

"Indeed," the stranger said. "Doctor William Kilthorpe." He walked away from the pharmacy.

"Why aren't we going to your clinic?" Jessie interrogated. He did not trust the man in the slightest.

"Because I am in my sleepwear," Kilthorpe yawned. "Now do hush up. The miners can be such an unforgiving lot when they can't sleep off their whiskey."

Solomon fell forward in the saddle. His limp, vomit-covered chin rested on his horse. The poor fellow moaned.

"Cheer up, young man," smiled the doctor. "We'll make you a right display of health by the end."

Chapter 12

———— ◦ ————

"I don't like this William Kilthorpe. A man who can't look you in the eye is a man who can't confront his own demons. What devil runs afoul in this man's soul? And where in all hell are the people?"

– Porfirio Pacheco's Journal

Jessie stared into the eyes of a brown bear. The taxidermist had done a fine job preserving the animal's features. His only criticism was they had exaggerated the bear's ferocity—setting it up on its hind legs, polishing its claws, and contorting the creature's face into a roar. Jessie walked the perimeter of the gallery, studying the strange collection of Doctor Kilthorpe.

Antlers from elk and deer adorned the doorway. Behind it, Solomon was being treated for his poisoning. He had thought there was no cure for Dead Man's Scalp, that they were only bringing Solomon to his place of final paralysis. *I suppose farmer's folklore ain't as useful as I thought.* He gazed at Kilthorpe's "Map of the West."

A cartographer had painstakingly added every settlement to the sprawling map, even overlaying which native tribe had originally settled the area. Roads were drawn, forests pictured, and even the tiniest tributary was stenciled in. The attention to detail wavered in the Western Basin, yet the map there was not blank. Instead, the cartographer had scribbled upon that sprawling desert, "Ruins."

Jessie began grinding his teeth. He analyzed the next miscellaneous item in Kilthorpe's collection: a display of mining memorabilia. From left to right, there was a chipped pickaxe, an unused stick of dynamite, a mining helmet, a tattered uniform, and a map of the local silver mine.

"These arrowheads are Kuahtec," Eridu said.

"How do you know?" Jessie asked.

"My father gathers slaves from many lands."

"Why?" Jessie asked. "What use does he have with so many slaves?"

Eridu tore his eyes from the display cases. He approached Jessie and pointed at a series of locked display cases. A rainbow assortment of precious gems glinted within. "An empire is built on the backs of its enemies."

Jessie walked to a mannequin with chains on his legs. A small sign read: *Early labor on the frontier took many forms.*

Porfirio had reclined in a comfortable green chair, framed in golden-laced wood. He curled his mustache as he spoke, "I'd like the have a chat with the Lugal, when we arrive."

"I am sure we all will have our audience with my father," Eridu swallowed. "If things go well."

The door to the gallery suddenly swung open. Doctor Kilthorpe waltzed into the room and removed his gloves, "Gentlemen."

Hiram bolted to his feet, dripping with sweat. He had not said a word since entering the doctor's home. "How is my brother?"

The doctor's gaze went everywhere but at the men in his sitting room. He looked intently at a stuffed beaver. "The fluid has been purged, but he will need some time to recover."

"Recover?" Jessie asked. "So he will not be paralyzed?" *Medicine really ain't what it used to be.*

William gave a knowing smile. "You thought there weren't no cure, ain't that right?"

Hiram choked on a deep breath and covered his mouth. He turned around and stared at the doctor's collection of mannequins. Many were dressed in archaic wagoneer fashions. "When can he ride a horse?"

Kilthorpe frowned. "Not for several weeks. The muscular tissues are badly damaged. He needs time."

"We do not have several weeks," Jessie informed him.

The doctor sighed. "I thought you would say that." He blinked a dozen times and raised a finger, "Perhaps he could meet up with your, uhm...?"

Porfirio lit his pipe, "We are surveying. But we will be needing our friend before we go." He tapped his thigh, as he always did when he told a lie. "We've got wagon space for him. It'll be no trouble."

"Gentlemen," the doctor opened his arms wide. "Your friend is in good hands. He shall be a picture of health in a few weeks."

Eridu's tongue pressed against his cheek. He closed his eyes and pointed at the collection of tribal artifacts. He feigned a frightfully convincing Kuahtec accent. "What are these? Trophies?"

The doctor's roaming eyes went above Eridu, to the display case. He approached the glass and wiped it with a handkerchief, "Do you like it?"

"No."

"Ah well," Kilthorpe shooed, "That is because it is still *real*. But this gallery—this will be history one day."

"As is the rodent's scat," Eridu grunted. "And I do not collect it."

Jessie was mortified by the man's sudden rudeness. He tried to mouth a warning to Eridu, but the prince dismissed him with a subtle wave at his side. Eridu scratched his neck, drawing Jessie's eyes. At first, he was perplexed. Then, he glanced at Doctor Kilthorpe. Dozens of chains were draped around his neck. A profusion of pendants protruded underneath his shirt.

Porfirio's pipe bobbed between his lips. "You'll have to pardon our friend. Bein' a savage, he ain't got proper manners." Upon exhaling, he scattered ashes onto the gilded armchair. "Though, your choice of décor—it ain't ordinary."

Kilthorpe's eyes wandered near to Jessie. He stared at Jessie's boots. He scratched the back of his head, "This country. This beautiful wild." He went to another display case. A tattered book rested on a folded, plaid outfit. "It ain't much longer in this world."

Porfirio humored the man. "What's the story behind that pane, doc?"

Kilthorpe beamed at the items, "You like it?"

"I don't rightly know yet," Porfirio answered.

"Come closer," Kilthorpe motioned, excitedly.

Only Jessie did so. The displayed cloth was dusty and frayed at many seams. "Seems someone outgrew their shirt."

"Not outgrew," Kilthorpe corrected. "This here was Dan Bandelier's straitjacket."

Porfirio coughed on his smoke. "How'd you come by that?"

Kilthorpe swayed like a giddy child and gazed at the ceiling with an almost cross-eyed look. His front teeth poked out as he grinned. "When they caught Bandelier, they thought he were possessed. Gave him the Lord's Word to read." He looked down at the frayed book.

Jessie saw now the Word was shredded and not from old age. *Bite marks.*

Kilthorpe folded his hands behind his back, "Y'all surveyin' for the city folk? Broadfields?"

"Mhm," Jessie and Porfirio hummed in unison.

Kilthorpe wrapped his hands around a small globe. He held it up to his eye, inspecting the old world. "Y'all gonna make this place a city, and then there won' be no West."

"Civilization comes for us all, one day," Jessie frowned. "We been up all night, doc. Know where we might find some lodging?"

"Why, you can just stay here," the doctor smiled.

"Mmm," Jessie nodded hesitantly. "Thank you for your generosity, but we already racked up a hefty sum for your services."

"No charge," the doctor declared proudly. "He was a fine patient."

Porfirio and Jessie glanced at one another. *Did he hear it, too? The tense, the tone...* Jessie was through with the doctor's eccentricity. He walked up to Kilthorpe and, with only an arm's length between them, stared him down. The doctor's eyes twitched at the ground. Something in the angle of the brow, the unsteadiness of his pupils, made Jessie uncomfortable. *He is lying.*

Jessie forced a pleasant smile. "You have an outhouse, then? I ain't about to soil a man's bed."

Kilthorpe erupted with false laughter. He said with a broad smile, "Just outside, to the left of the porch."

Jessie did not move for a second. A liar always studied his con overlong. As he predicted, the doctor leaned slightly forward with an aura of anticipation. Jessie clapped his hands and smiled, "Much obliged, sir."

Jessie followed the man's directions and went to the outhouse. He waited for a moment before slipping away. The sun was shining onto Silverfork and yet, the townsfolk all seemed to be sleeping the day away. *Where are all the people?* He walked up to the saloon and noted the eerie quiet. *Belford's wet room ain't ever asleep...* He grabbed the door. His hand sank into a layer of dust.

Jessie sucked in his left cheek and nodded. He sniffled and looked up at the sign. "The Perennial Fountain indeed."

A clang interrupted the silence. Jessie whirled around. A large, brown dog was staring him down. Mange coated its fur and its face was riddled with scars. *It may be rabid,* Jessie worried. The animal's left ear had been bitten off and its right canine was chipped. The animal took a bite from a sunflower leaf, chewed it clumsily, and trotted over to Jessie.

The stray was several strides away when it stopped, stretched its rear in the air, and lay down. It crawled over to Jessie, nibbling and biting at the air as if caught on an invisible lure. As it moved, it wiggled its tail and grumbled a series of vaguely human sounds. Upon reaching Jessie, it peeked one eye up at him.

Jessie blinked at the critter. He had never seen such behavior from an animal, especially from one so starved and skinny. He went to kneel. Just then, the dog flopped over on its side and began kicking and snorting. Jessie put a hand on its belly and said, "You belong to one of these people?"

The dog peered up with a wide, crazy eye. He opened and closed his mouth in a half-yawn. Then, he bolted upright.

"Is that a no, then?" Jessie inquired. He had always spoken to wildlife and yet, he got the feeling that he was not speaking to an animal.

The dog babbled at him.

Jessie rose. "Look, Boy. I gotta tend to some business. Was a pleasure meetin' ya and all."

The dog barked once and ran across the street. It scratched at a door madly and then looked at him.

Jessie blinked and continued his surveying of the town. He went to the next building on the main street and looked through the windows. Nobody seemed home, yet there was no evidence of an accident or hasty evacuation. He investigated the gunsmith, the butcher, and the tailor. It seemed that the entire town simply decided to lock up and leave.

Jessie studied the pharmacy across the street. Like all the other buildings, when he looked inside everything was positively tidy. *Almost like nothin' ever been used...* Jessie stepped back and gazed at Silverfork. "Like the town ain't ever been lived in." He bit his lip and just then, saw a sign behind the counter:

"Carson Bros. Pharmacy and Clinic."

"Now what in all—" Jessie whirled around, nearly jumping when he saw who had approached him from behind.

The brown stray wagged its tail. It pawed his feet and grumbled.

"I've got a liar to tend to, Boy," Jessie patted his head.

The dog took the opportunity to nip at his hand. Only, the strike was a targeted one. His blunted, black teeth skimmed Jessie's skin and pulled his wedding band clean off. With the ring dangling on his canine, he skipped away.

"Son of a—" Jessie charged after the animal, "Get back here, Boy." His pursuit led him past Kilthorpe's house, behind a derelict building (the only one on the street, in fact), and to a well-scratched door without a handle. The stray sat there, paw placed gloatingly on Jessie's ring.

"Give that to me, little one."

The dog barked once and looked up.

Had the dog been an ordinary beast, Jessie might have lunged for the ring. However, the beast's eyes had a striking quality to them. The deep brown hues reminded him of a man. When Jessie and that animal looked at one another, he felt as if he had encountered an old friend. Begrudgingly, he looked up.

Kilthorpe's Lapidarium.

Jessie stared at the sign for a long while. He gulped and looked down to thank the animal. Only, it had vanished. There was not even a pawprint. Jessie ground his teeth and retrieved his wedding band. As he put it on, he wondered if his mind had gone to seed. *Eridu said that gem made people mad...*

He had no time to contemplate *his* sanity. He returned to the horses and retrieved Porfirio's pistol. He fashioned a makeshift holster by weaving the sidearm between his pants and his belt. He untucked his shirt to hide the barrel, patted Girl, and calmly went inside.

The 'doctor' was sitting in an armchair, his legs tightly crossed. He sipped loudly from his mug and smiled, "Welcome back, sir. Would you like a—"

Jessie interrupted, "I would like to know more about the Carson brothers."

William Kilthorpe's mouth remained slightly open. After a second of deliberation, he sent a humored laugh through his liar's windpipe, "The former practitioners. Got old and reti—"

"Is that when you decided to practice medicine? What happened to your crystal shop?"

"Why, that was my brother's. He was always a crazy—"

Jessie's voice had no inflection. Ever since losing his children, he had lost his patience for sub-par people. "If you keep lyin' to me, *you* will never get the chance to retire."

Porfirio got to his feet and raised a hand, "What did you see?"

Jessie did not even allow Kilthorpe the respite of a blink. He stared down the fraud, "The entire town's deserted. Ain't nobody here but him. And he ain't even a doctor. Some other folks owned the pharmacy. He's a lapidary."

William Kilthorpe swallowed and set his cup down. He sighed and smiled. "Gentlemen."

"Careful," Hiram warned. "Jessie Bingham may be a gentleman. As for me... Where is my brother?"

"Easy," Eridu soothed, no longer feigning an accent. His voice was resolutely foreign, commanding, and deep. He eyed Kilthorpe with disgust and approached him. He raised his hand as if to strike him. He yanked his shirt and revealed a dozen, dangling pendants.

Hiram growled, "Them those speaking stones Collin found?"

"Ur Igi," Jessie whispered. The doctor carried dozens of the relics, the core in each swirling as if consumed by mist.

Porfirio dumped the ashes in his pipe onto Kilthorpe's carpet. "Tardy honesty is hardly well-received."

William Kilthorpe gazed at his glass displays with pride, "I made my fortune in this town. Owned the mine just up the road. But then the mine dried up, the businesses left... Hell, even the sanitorium was shuttered. My friends left me, one by one. And all I had was this house, and a pile o' useless money..."

He gazed into the fog of his jewels. The misty darkness was the only thing he had looked in the eye. "I thought I'd kill myself. I went over the Hills and into Lugal land. It was then that I saw a ravaged wagon... And I met Ur. He showed me a bright future, as clearly as the hawk spots the rodent. I knew I had to return and carve out that future."

The old lapidary adjusted his spectacles and paced around the room. "These beautiful treasures... They helped me realize that I was gifted a golden opportunity." Fanatic vigor took hold of his voice, "I brought the town back to its former splendor, a picture of a time now gone."

"Where is my brother," Hiram growled. He was not asking.

Kilthorpe shook his head, "The west is dying, gentlemen." He snapped his teeth and grinned wolfishly, "But in Silverfork..."

Porfirio circled the wide-eyed lunatic and put a hand on the backroom door. So caught up in his confessional, Kilthorpe did not notice. He simply continued his monologue as if suspended on stage, "I'm ahead of my time, gentlemen. How many people have walked into a myth in motion? How many had the foresight to grab the past before it was so?" He stared into Jessie's eyes with mad delight, "My friends left Silverfork, but their children will come back. And they'll be hungry for their history."

Porfirio disappeared into the back room and let the door slam behind him. The sound jolted Kilthorpe from his tirade and he lunged after.

"Hold it," Jessie revealed the pistol at his side. The man froze. His eyes were fixed on the door. Jessie aimed the pistol at the lunatic's head. "No need to rush. Let's go in together, hm?"

Kilthorpe swallowed and slowly turned the handle. The ancient man walked with lead feet down a dimly lit hall. Jessie followed behind, nauseated by a stench which permeated the corridor. The source of the smell did not remain a mystery. The hall opened into a solarium. The heat of the sun incubated the room, as well as its contents.

A wooden frame stood in the center of the room. It had three fixtures at the top, middle, and bottom of the wood. Two hinges at the side connected a long glass door. Beside the unoccupied display case was a long table cluttered with various tools and buckets. Porfirio stood at the far end of the table, his hand held to his nose. "What is it?" Jessie asked.

Porfirio slowly stepped to the side.

Jessie first saw neatly folded clothes. A chevron stitch had been methodically removed. Then, he saw the naked body of Solomon Rodgers. "My God," he gasped, his hand tensing on the pistol.

Hiram and Eridu entered the solarium. Hiram charged to his brother's side, "What did you do to him?"

The lunatic stuttered, "H-he was already numb. Doomed to be lame and subhuman. I am providing a mercy."

Solomon was entombed in his own body. His eyes swirled in their sockets. Frightened pupils screamed for help.

Jessie rushed to his aid and immediately gagged. Long tubes had been stuffed into his nostrils, connecting to a large, amber jar. "You were going to stuff him like that grizzly." He recoiled suddenly, "Those ain't mannequins out there, Kilthorpe."

"I am making him a picture of health. And such physique. I am preserving his best self for all eternity!"

Porfirio retched. Jessie's hand began to shake. He did not want to kill a man, but he felt compelled to rid the world of William Kilthorpe. "You were going to murder him!" he accused, hoping the words might make his upcoming deed acceptable.

"I am sparing him a cruel fate," Kilthorpe raised his chin. "He will be studied. Admired!"

"Stop it!" Jessie ordered. The more the fanatic talked, the easier it was becoming to hold the pistol. The ease at which his thumb now rested upon the trigger frightened him. He said, voice shaking, "You're disgusting."

Hiram appeared behind Jessie. He put a hand on his shoulder and gently took the weapon. "You ain't never killed a man, Jessie Bingham."

Jessie struggled to reply. *Not a man...* His face assumed various poses. "Never had the need."

Hiram nodded. He checked the pistol, counted the rounds, and removed all but one bullet. "Go outside."

Jessie looked away, frightened by the hatred in Hiram's eyes. It reminded Jessie of how he felt when he found out about the twins. He fled the solarium and immediately vomited. He stared into the fetid puddle and tried in vain to catch his breath.

If a man could do that to his countryman, what would Eridu's people do to his children? He felt the vibration of the speaking stone in his pocket. *And what will this Ur Igi do to me?*

A single gunshot sounded in Silverfork.

Chapter 13

∘

If only the savages could have read a few pages of the Belford Inquirer, they would have realized Mayor Thorne was more trouble than she was worth."

– The Ballad of Jessie Bingham

Despite all the senses Mary was deprived of, her sense of dread remained unrestrained. She sat in solitude as her world passed further away. She was forsaken.

The blindfold had been tied so tightly around her face, it squeezed her ears and muted her surroundings. Her mouth had been gagged with some sort of tuber—hard but gnawable. If she bit too hard and ruptured the skin—bitter, teeth-chilling fluid gushed down her throat. Then, when she gagged—the vomit had nowhere to go but her empty stomach.

She had been given no food since upsetting the matriarch. The only water she was given was at night, from the scarred brute's waterskin. As she drank, Nerugal would take the opportunity to grope her.

Three more days elapsed without hearing or seeing anything. Her stomach was a roaring void of hunger; her body ached from the constant journey and Nerugal's rough explorations. She was sure, soon, the scarred man would try thieving more of Mary's body.

One morning, Nerugal finally ripped the blindfold from her face. The blinding sun flooded into her eyes. The indeterminate rays bounced off a layer of coagulated fluid. Nerugal grabbed her chin and finally, fed her a gritty type of game. Of course, he also used the opportunity to force his fingers in her mouth. He rubbed the inside of her cheek and scratched her tongue. She thought about biting him, but it seemed useless. She finished her meal without incident.

Nerugal left her at last. She took the opportunity to observe her surroundings. Beside her, Don Marcos and Cleona Flowers were each asleep. Elijah Bingham's head was hung and his brow was furrowed. Mary contemplated saying something to the boy, though she figured he did not care for her much. She looked around for Ethel; she saw only the glare of the sun. She stared into that beating orb, letting its light bake the puss off her pupils. She blinked off the sizzled scabs and analyzed her new surroundings.

They were at the base of a deep canyon. A spear was embedded in a nearby crevice. A tattered blue ribbon dangled from the shaft. Soon, more tokens of war appeared. They passed numerous rusting sets of quilted mail armor, dozens of discarded weapons, and several sand-chewed skeletons.

She tried to get a better view of the environs; her sickly stare was a shaded curtain. The fog of her vision quickly infuriated her. So, she shut her eyes and listened to the drumming of hoofbeats. From the echoes, she inferred that the depth of the canyon was almost double the width.

Soon, Mary began to hear a change in the canyon, a new inflection point for echoes to bounce back. She closed her eyes to get a better idea of the canyon's features. *Three tall walls, forward and to the sides. Dead end?* She reopened her eyes. The canyon walls narrowed and the earth seemed to arc upward.

Suddenly, a stone rampart appeared which was as tall as the canyon was deep. A frayed banner flew at the heights; at the base, there was a crumbling breach. Around her, many wrinkled men with grey hair were kissing their index and middle fingers. Then, they pointed at the wall and bowed their heads. The hunchback was especially moved. His arms were outstretched as if holding an offering.

Mary stared at the hunchback as the slave cart rolled up and over the breach. She finally looked away and was awed by what she saw.

Towering apartments jutted up from the earth. Made of the same stone as the surrounding canyon, their rooftops were connected by ladders and bridges. The apartments were clustered so closely together, the many narrow alleys were perpetually darkened. Mary mistrusted that darkness. So did the raiders, from their sudden quiet. They rode through the watchful gloom for only a moment before they turned onto a wide thoroughfare. The road was split into two lanes by a row of trees, though these looked long dead.

The vast city seemed entirely deserted. Mary did not think it was a ruin; nor was it a ghost town. She recalled one of the books in her father's library—it was a study on an ancient culture which had died when the world was young. It had mentioned an entire city erected purely for the dead to inhabit. *That* designation seemed fitting.

Mary analyzed the concourse. *There's something large at the end of the road.* What it was, Mary could not tell. She peered at the buildings that lined the street, the alleys which disappeared in shaded darkness. *What kind of people lived here?* She squinted at a desiccated tree. Like many others in the middle of the road, the plant had grown proud and tall before dying.

Mary turned her attention to an armored skeleton slumped against the trunk. The armor had been consumed by sand and succulents. Two small cactus bulbs were now growing in the soldier's hollow eye sockets. A thread of prickly vegetation had climbed up the warrior's spear. A string of green pearls braided the arrow lodged within its skull.

When she finally looked away from the soldier, Mary's lungs emptied. They had come to the base of a massive monument, dwarfing even the nearby towers. It was not quite a pyramid, as the four gently sloping walls leveled off into terraces at several points. Relief carvings of fearsome beasts covered the slopes. Faded paint chipped off once vibrant bricks.

Ama Asura rode past on a chariot. Ethel was at her side, face pale with sickness. She, along with two mounted guards, circled the camp. They looked as if they were searching for something or someone. Whatever (or whoever) it was, they did not find it. The matriarch dismounted and began issuing brief, stern orders.

All the raiders rushed to obey. All except two. Nerugal and his fat pawn patrolled the perimeter of the camp, occasionally looking into a building or glancing at Mary. They reminded her of a cougar stalking a herd of prey. Mary pretended to be oblivious.

Soon, a makeshift camp was being constructed. Furs and hide tents were laid out upon the great concourse, fires were lit, and the raiders began to gather at the base of the pyramid. They waited for Ama Asura, who was busy kneeling before Ethel Bingham.

"Why you think we ain't in one of them big buildings?" Don Marcos asked.

Mary did not reply, distracted by the sudden sound of Ethel retching.

Don Marcos added, "That savage fuck you yet, Thorne?"

Mary had prepared a comment about breaking his other hand. Such bravado was simply exhausting now. She watched the matriarch.

Ama Asura maneuvered Ethel's body, bending her knees and laying her on her side. She fell upon Asura's lap and looked like a newborn baby at the breast. Ethel was motionless and Mary watched with a tinge of disgust. The girl was not an infant, yet she heard the matriarch's soft cooing from their cart.

"She's not her mother," Elijah muttered.

Mary stared at the pair. The matriarch had two items in her hand. She could not see what they were, only that Asura used them to wash Ethel's face off. *Is she cleaning up the girl's vomit, or is that a remedy?* Whatever the case, the girl began to cough. At that, the matriarch patted her back and wiped the child's mouth.

She's treating that child like a newborn, Mary turned away. She side-eyed Elijah, whose face was just as disgusted as her own. Though, like his sister, his cheeks were pale. Mary contemplated asking if he was sick, but it seemed out of line. Elijah was not his responsibility.

Don Marcos popped his lips proudly. "That bitch wastin' her time. But then, wouldn't be the first bitch to. Ain't that right, Elijah?"

The boy squinted at the disgusting doctor, "What d'you mean?"

Marcos craned his neck mockingly, "Y'ain't seriously think ya daddy kept y'alive all by his lonesome?" He winked at Mary, "Y'make him screw ya f'all that medicine money?"

Elijah glared at her, "My daddy wouldn't do that. He was a good man."

"Good men ain't love whoring," Don Marcos retorted.

Mary could not abide by the child's hateful look. "We did nothing of the sort, Elijah." She held her bound wrists to her chest, shielding her heart, "We only ever conducted business."

"That's what Rosalee called it, I'd wager," Marcos chuckled.

Mary looked away. The idea had never crossed her mind that she would have wanted more from Jessie. Upon hearing Marcos' cretinous words—she felt terrible. Was even her charity some corrupt game? *I deserve this fate,* she decided. She stared at her bloody, bruised legs and wondered how long someone with her condition might live. *Will they send me out to pasture when they learn about my eyes?*

"No comment, *Mayor* Thorne?"

Mary did not meet Marcos' gaze. She let the oozing puss leak down her cheek. A burning sensation reddened her face. She relished it.

"Well ain't this something," Marcos taunted. "I done went and muted the mayor!"

Mary licked her lips, taking in some of the foul liquid which had trickled down her face. She swallowed the bitter puss and ground her teeth. In that moment, Mary decided on a simple goal. She did not know how she would accomplish it, nor how it would affect her future circumstances. She did not much care about the details. All Mary knew was that Donaciano Marcos would have to die. The resolution warmed Mary's heart ever so slightly. She finally looked up at the rabid, spiteful man.

Don Marcos smiled, "Sickness is just a debt." He turned and watched Ama Asura. The matriarch had a hand on Ethel's stomach and was slowly rubbing it. Marcos continued, "And now, nature is collectin' on 'em. I always told that Jessie Bingham—best start fresh. Some seeds ain't germinate properly. I—"

"Oh shut up," Cleona Flowers finally erupted. "Ain't you ever tired of bein' repulsive?"

Don Marcos stared smugly.

"Ain't no one in Belford goin' ta miss ya none," Cleona spat.

"And the same for you two ladies. Save maybe that mule of a boy, Solomon Rodgers. I'd wager he's already on the Trail now." His lip curled up, "As buzzard meal."

Cleona laughed, "Ya think words'll break me, Marcos? I'm bound by worse things than your bad conversation." She raised her chains and her chin, saying to Elijah, "Ignore him, little one. He ain't hardly human and he certainly ain't worth none-a-our time."

Though she did not show it, Mary was impressed. She had never thought of young, giggly Cleona Flowers as particularly strong. Her sudden admiration, however, twisted into cruel guilt. From Cleona, to Elijah, to even Don Marcos—none of the other captives seemed as resigned as her. *And I was their mayor,* she told herself shamefully.

She quickly reminded herself that a good mood did not make a good outcome. Cleona's strength would wither like a great oak in drought. Don Marcos' temper would cool in the frozen chains of slavery. The twins' good nature would rot without their father's influence and for herself... *I am lucky I will be blind by the end.*

Mary looked at her captors. The raiders were hardly bothered by the conflict between the captives. The Lugal had congregated in the shadow of the pyramid. Ama Asura stood on the first step and raised her arms high in a sort of stretch. Beside her, several warriors had removed their armor and were droning a deep, resonating chant. Many overtones echoed down the concourse, deafening Mary to all else. She peered at the band of warriors. The animated figures contorted in a series of inhuman poses, bonelessly bending into animalistic shapes. *What sort of heathen ritual is this?*

Donaciano grinned wickedly at Mary, "I always thought you was like me, Thorne. Practical. Efficient." He glanced at Elijah,

"Now I see you's just a sickly spawn with a hole in ya heart. Boring."

"Careful, Marcos," Mary warned, though her voice wavered. "Or you'll end up with a hole in yours." She glared at him, but between her dread and his smirk—both knew her threats no longer carried any weight.

"Ah," Marcos looked past Mary. "I shall miss our talks, Mayor Thorne."

Mary snarled, "Y—"

A cloth flew in front of her face and covered her mouth. A hand latched around her wrists. Then, another. A terrible force pulled her away from the camp. The force lifted her body with ease and slung her atop broad shoulders.

Mary looked down at the scarred savage. Despite her bonds, she could have swatted him; despite her gag, she could have screamed. She resisted her bodily instincts to do so. She had learned torment from her brother. She knew how evil men thought. Resisting at this stage would only make it more difficult later. She had to appear weak.

It was not hard. She was weak. Nerugal and his fat friend were easily double her size, armed and armored, and had the element of surprise. Mary tried to remain calm; her breathing became erratic. Self-pity washed over her and she resigned to hoping cruel hopes. *Will they kill me after? Will I die quickly?* As the pair hauled her into a dark, derelict building, she shed a tear.

The fat one did not like that. He stared into her sickly eyes and said a word to the scarred one. The Lugal chuckled and set Mary down. Then, he took off her clothes and stared at her body. He barked at his friend, who dressed Mary in an ill-fitting skirt. Nerugal tickled his scar and smiled. Then, he grabbed Mary once again and hauled her deeper into the shadowy building.

Mary stared at the fat man trailing behind. She saw only the light from his eyes; they were sunken with shame and pity. *He does not like this. And he will do nothing to stop it. So human.*

The scarred Lugal turned into a shadowy alcove and jogged down several stairs. Light came in through a hole in the roof. The rays bounced off scattered scraps of metal, illuminating the scene with streaks of orange and brown. Fragments of pottery crunched under their feet like shells on a beach.

Nerugal threw her to the ground.

Mary's spine cracked. She instinctually skittered backward, putting her back to a wall. The scarred one growled at his friend. Mary did not need to speak their terrible tongue to know what he had ordered. First, the fat one looked at her regretfully. Then, he said a word to his friend, who quickly interrupted him. Finally, the accomplice departed.

Mary bent her knees more and more as Nerugal undressed. His scaled breastplate fell. His metallic kilt dropped. As the hungry assailant eyed her, Mary's heart began to race. She searched her surroundings. There was nothing to grab, so she held her ankles.

The savage got onto all fours and slowly crawled toward her. He relished the assault, slowly growing more erect.

Mary's arms shook with fear. Her body thumped. Her veins swelled. She could feel the temperature in her chest reach a boiling point. The past days had left her hopeless. Yet now, faced with true hopelessness, she found herself incapable of passivity. She whispered to herself, "He is not your brother."

Nerugal tilted his head at her foreign speech. He hissed in his own language.

He is not your brother, Mary reminded herself repeatedly. *Even if it happens again,* she bargained, *you've survived worse.* The rationalization only brought more burning tears to her eyes. Her body vibrated as if the entirety of her being, from her bones to her blood, were beginning to boil.

The scarred man came up to her legs and sniffed her. Then, he got to his knees and sat tall. He looked like a cobra. Then, he made his move. He took out his knife and cut the rope which bound her ankles. He stared down at her with a cruel smile. He looked at her wrists and his smile widened. He cut those bonds too.

He wants me to fight back, she swallowed. *The sick bastard wants a struggle.*

Nerugal tossed the blade and spread her legs apart.

Mary resisted, staring at the nearby knife.

The man chuckled. He spread her legs with an insurmountable force. He spat on his hand and readied himself. Without so much as a look into the woman's eyes, the rapist lowered himself onto her.

In that terrible moment, Mary's mind emptied of all thoughts. She head-butted the slaver. Even stunned, she barely managed to wrestle off his weight. In her second of freedom, she lunged for the discarded knife. She reached out; a strong hand pulled her by the foot. She curled her fingers around the blade, but it slipped from her hand. Nerugal wrangled her closer, slamming her head against the brick. He threw himself on top of her.

Mary flailed, searching for anything to protect herself with. She sank her nails into the ground and flung sand into Nerugal's eyes. He laughed and grabbed her by the hair. He slammed her head into the sand and buried her face in the dirt. He pressed his weight on her. Mary closed her eyes and—for the first time in her adult life—she prayed.

Nerugal fell upon her greedily.

Then, he paused.

His grip weakened.

Mary looked up at her aggressor.

The scarred brute was grinning down at her, but there was a change on his face. They stared at one another, two lives suspended in a timeless second. Neither knew what had happened until blood spurted onto them both. Nerugal put a hand on his chest and analyzed the pouring liquid. The gleeful smile became one of immense confusion. He stared at his erect penis and then at Mary.

She told herself to run, but her legs would not allow it. *What just happened?* She blinked at the wounded slaver. Her surprise morphed into righteous hate. She punched Nerugal squarely in the jaw. Hot breath oozed out of his mouth for the last time. With one more scar for his collection, the brute collapsed onto Mary. The blood flowed out his chest, all over Mary. With a groan, she pushed the foul man off her and stumbled to her feet.

Had she been the one to kill the man, she may have savored his death. But as she looked down at the rapist, his own dagger mysteriously plunged into his back, she wondered at her fortune. "Hello?" Her voice echoed in the vast, unnavigable darkness. *Could have been his fat friend. Finally acted on his pity...* Whatever the case, she did not like the sudden quiet of her surroundings. She felt a pair of eyes upon her. Somewhere. Mary pulled Nerugal's dagger out of his body. With the blade in hand, she went back up the stairs.

To add to her disquiet, the fat man remained resolutely at his post. He had his back turned when she came upon him. He heard her approach and turned. He looked relieved and said a word with friendly, raised eyebrows. He put a gentle hand on her shoulder.

She glanced at the man's body. There was no trace of blood on his pudgy face. His armor looked as shiny as ever. He had not a speck of dirt on him. *It was not you then...* The fat man beamed at her and rubbed her back. He began to say a few words.

Mary stabbed the spineless accomplice in his neck. With a knife lodged in his windpipe, he gurgled a word and fell down the long, dark stairs. Mary sat on the steps and listened to the pathetic man die. She waited for the gurgling wretch to be silent. After a lovely minute, the fat man gasped his last.

At that moment, the adrenaline began to wane. She stared blankly ahead, still feeling fingers crawling over her. She shivered, glancing off a ghostly advance. She felt a shadowy tendril lick her skin and, briefly, thought she was in the Big House—that perhaps this was a nightmare within a nightmare.

"Stop it!" She commanded herself. Her brother was not here. Nerugal and his friend were dead. Now, she needed to act. The matriarch and her raiders were still outside, chanting and dancing their feral ritual. *But they will not be distracted for long.*

I need to hide their bodies. At least try to hide them. A calm breeze had found its way into the ruin. All she heard at the bottom of the stairs was the gentle sifting of sand. Reluctantly, Mary crept back down the stairs. However, when she reached the bottom, she found Nerugal's body had moved further into the dark hall. Mary halted.

Just then, Mary heard a footstep. Mary turned toward the invisible sound. She swallowed. *They caught me.* Sweat dripped from her hand. She squatted beside the fat corpse and retrieved the dagger buried in his neck. She rose and blinked at the watchful dark, waiting for loud noises and marching footsteps. Yet, no such sounds ever came.

Mary swallowed. There was something else living in that city. Something in that room with her.

Mary suddenly preferred slavery in the light to freedom in the darkness. She sprinted up the stairs, nearly fleeing into the open out of fear. Luckily, the chanting Lugal reminded her to stay calm. She looked back at the stairs and waited.

No one came up. No sound came from below.

Mary retrieved her old, ragged clothes and quickly undressed. She threw her blood-stained skirt in a dusty vase and sprinkled a few handfuls of sand to cover it. Then, she dealt with the mess of blood on her breasts and belly. Mary rubbed sand between her bloody hands and applied layer after layer of dirt to her bare body. Soon, she simply looked like a ragged, dirty slave. There was no trace of blood on her foul skin.

Satisfied with her work, she donned her old clothes. She peeked out of the house and watched the warriors for a while. The Lugal were still engrossed in their ritual. She blinked at the unguarded slave cart. Ethel had escaped the matriarch's care and was holding her brother's hands. She heard Donaciano Marcos' insufferable voice.

"Why don' you go fix me a double portion, little girl. I were the only one keepin' y'all alive, after all."

A thought entered Mary's head which produced a quaint, "Hm." Her cheeks stretched. She pressed her lips. *Now that's an interesting idea,* she replied to herself. The longer she contemplated, the more and more intolerable Don Marcos' voice became. *Yes,* she decided. *That will do.*

Mary waited for the Lugal to orient their bodies away from the slave cart. When they did, bending toward their toes like wading birds, she darted into the open. Ethel was the first to see her and asked, "Ms. Thorne! Did they give you special privileges too?"

"It's not a privilege to be treated like a baby," her brother chided. "Daddy would be so mad."

"Daddy always said you shouldn't grow up too fast," his sister argued.

"You're not a baby, Ethy."

"You're not a man!"

"She's not your mama!"

The twins were prepared for a fierce argument, but Mary had no time to arbitrate it. She interrupted them. "Quiet, you two. I am not free because of 'special' privileges. Anything but." She turned her attention to Don Marcos. "I—I," she wove her lie as if she were still mayor. "We cannot live like this."

"I'm doin' just fine," Marcos snarled.

"Please, Donaciano," Mary looked left and right to sell the theatrics. She then presented him with Nerugal's dagger. "You said you would be the only one who could get help. I—" she interrupted herself for effect. "I hate it, but you are right."

The doctor's demeanor changed instantly. "I've always served our community, Mayor." He offered his bound wrists.

Mary freed the bastard's hands and climbed into the cart. Don Marcos stretched his legs and Mary began cutting those as well.

"He ain't deserve it," Elijah protested. "He deserves to be here."

"Shut up, you little shit," Marcos barked. He looked at Mary submissively, "If you please, Mayor."

Mary nodded and said to the Bingham boy, "I know it is hard to understand."

"It's downright stupid," Eli raised his voice. At that, Ethel gripped her brother's hand, "Eli. Don't. Or you'll get the mayor in trouble."

"I don't care," the twin said, louder.

"Elijah Bingham," Mary said in her most mayoral voice. "Do you recall how your father paid for your medicine this past year?"

Elijah's open mouth was quickly closed.

Mary continued, "Don Marcos may have been a mean man, but he weren't lyin'. I spent a good part of my fortune keeping you and your sister healthy."

"B-but I—"

"Do not interrupt," Mary chided. She sounded unsettlingly similar to her mother, but that was probably for the best. She cut the final knot in the doctor's bonds. "Now. Don Marcos is the only grown man among us. He has long legs and, as we all know, has a penchant for talking." She shook her head at the doctor, "I'm afraid our sawbones is the only one who might be able to get help. To get your father."

Elijah raised his nostril. After a moment, he muttered, "Fine," and bowed his head.

Mary exhaled. "Thank you, Eli. Your father would be so proud." She exhaled, "Now, Mr. Marcos. I believe you will need this." She presented him with Nerugal's dagger.

Donaciano swiped the blade and nodded, "Yes... This will do nicely." He crawled out of the cart and stared down the great concourse. The sun was setting behind the great pyramid, its shadow stabbing into the heart of the city. He turned and smiled, "I reckon we're square, Thorne."

"Only if you get help," Mary smiled.

"I'm a sawbones by trade, ma'am." He grinned toothily as he lied, "Course I'll find help."

"Then go," Mary urged. "Before they notice."

Donaciano fled down the concourse. Once out of sight, Mary took a long deep breath and groaned. She sat and closed her eyes.

"Y'ain't really think he'll send help?" Cleona whispered.

"Not a chance," Mary replied.

"Then why release him?!" Elijah badgered.

At last, it was Mary's turn to grin. "Because I was tired of the way he talked to all of us. And I needed his tethers."

"But he don't deserve to be free!" Elijah argued.

Mary smiled at the child, "And he won't be. Trust me." She wiggled her toes, pointing attention to her legs, "Now," she looked at Ethel. "Did your daddy teach you your knots, sweet one?"

Ethel nodded hesitantly.

Mary gestured at her legs and her wrists, "Think you could tie me up with Don's old rope?"

Ethel clearly did not understand why she wanted to be rebound, but luckily she did not have the same knack for arguing as her brother. When the last knot was secured and Mary's body happily immobilized, Ethel climbed down the cart and frowned at her brother, "I don't hear them singing. I should go back to Ama Asura. She don't like it when I visit."

"I think that's a good idea," Mary smiled at the girl. So stirred by her help, she almost said, *'It is no wonder your father worked so hard for you two. Thank you.'* She managed to open her mouth, but the words felt too sentimental. Instead, she stated without looking at either twin, "I am so glad I helped your father this past year." And at that, Ethel returned to the matriarch.

Mary closed her eyes. Just as she was about to finally get some rest, however, Cleona whispered, "What happened to you?"

She recounted the day in her head. She felt the frayed edges of her dirty dress and replied, airily. "Nothing."

"Well, uh," Cleona cleared her throat. "If you ever want to talk about, uh, *nothing*. We women know a thing or two about the topic."

"Mhm," Mary replied.

Chapter 14

"There are worse tragedies to live than one's own."

– Porfirio Pacheco's Journal

Twinkling eyes sparkled from within the encapsulated mist. The Ur Igi watched Jessie as he watched it. The ethereal fog within the jewel expanded and shrank, syncopating with his breathing. He felt as if he were watching an animal dream, but that the animal was the cosmos itself. The allure of understanding tempted him to probe deeper. Fear restrained him.

I cannot end up like Kilthorpe, Jessie told himself. He stared sadly at the headwaters of the Copper River—a small alpine lake surrounded by sheer peaks. At the water's edge was Greenview Sanitorium. Like Silverfork, the halls of the insane were freshly abandoned.

Jessie thought about all those folks who were thrown into those cells. *If the stones could make Dan Bandelier forget his name, what will they do to me?* Jessie shuddered and waded into the water. The dagger peaks had shed their winter coats, but the lake was still frigid. He lifted his heavy arm and steadied his mind. He had to get rid of the jewel. *All those folk in the sanitoriums. Collin and his doomed men. They must have looked with Eyes of Ur.*

Jessie could not go mad. His children needed him sane, or at least in the state they had left him. He uncurled his fingers.

"Whatya doin' out here?"

At hearing Porfirio's voice, Jessie floundered. He pocketed the speaking stone and turned. "Bein' a fool, truth be told."

The newspaperman gave him a mistrustful look. "Let's clothe ya in somethin' dry."

They walked back to their unfortunate campsite. Jessie had protested the location to no avail. Better, they thought, to lodge in the abandoned sanitorium than to let Solomon be exposed to the elements.

The forest was dense, full of watchful eyes and unfriendly jaws. The rustling of leaves and the cracking of sticks were as common as cricket chatter. Jessie would have preferred the noises to the quiet which awaited them in the sanitorium. They approached the red-brick façade. Jessie did not like that building and its mementos. Greenview had for the most part remained intact since being abandoned. All the rooms were sterile and yet so devoid of comfort, hardly livable. That was, except for the cellar. Jessie disliked that room.

"We'll have ta let him pass," Porfirio murmured.

"Try and tell Hiram that," Jessie whispered, climbing up the stairs. He pushed the heavy doors open; the madhouse groaned.

Hiram was tending to his brother in the main hall. It was the only room in the building with any windows and despite being abandoned, none were broken. The light illuminated the dirt on their bedrolls. Porfirio had hoped to snag a proper bed, but the beds in that place were hardly up to his standards. They were more like stone altars.

Solomon was laid out on his bedroll. He had not moved all day. Everyone knew what needed to happen. Even the young man understood, from the tears in his rooted eyes.

Hiram took a spoonful of soup and opened his brother's mouth. He croaked through a tightened throat. "I'm goin' ta find

Cleona, Solly." His voice was high-pitched and cracked like an instrument out of tune. "And I'll take care-a her until the end of my days. For you."

Hiram closed his brother's eyelids and stood up. He spoke after a moment, "I, I need to be alone for this."

"If you want to talk. I uh, I know—" Jessie interrupted himself.

Hiram snapped. "You have no idea, Mr. Bingham. How could you?"

Jessie stared emptily at the paralyzed man. His voice failed him. He began to pick at his cuticles (a bad habit he had learned from his wife). "When Gl—"

Porfirio grabbed Jessie's arm. "There's a time for talking and a time for listening." He gave him a sad sort of smile, with his mouth raised and his eyes downcast. "Come on, son. Let's the three of us give him some space."

Eridu, Porfirio, and Jessie left the main hall. Leaks in the ceiling created trickling, ephemeral streams. Their wandering took them up and down the three stories of the sanitorium. Contrary to what Jessie had pictured, the building seemed quite comfortable. The rooms were spacious and bright. There was even a library on the second floor. Their exploration inevitably brought them to the cellar. Unlike the rest of the sanitorium, that room was dark and claustrophobic.

Porfirio lit the nearby lantern and placed it on a sooty furnace. The smell of coal mingled with a distinctly human stench. Unlike the rest of the sanitorium, which looked as if a maid had come to clean it only yesterday, the cellar was riddled with fishbones, refuse, and ornaments. A dress was pinned to a mirror, though that was shattered and the powders, ointments, and other cosmetics had spilled onto the floor. A silver locket was tarnished and the portrait within too worn to discern.

Eridu put a hand on the mirror, "Frail are the works of great folk."

"As our mayor must now be learning," Porfirio muttered.

"A valuable lesson for the Thorne," Eridu commented.

Porfirio's eyes darted toward his forehead and landed upon the Erintul suspiciously. He squinted. "How'd you know the mayor was a Thorne?"

Eridu's cheek twitched. He massaged his brow before turning toward them. Performing his peculiar sign of respect, he rotated his wrists and showed his palms. "My father married the high priestess of Sunumun, as was tradition. Every augur bode well for the union."

Porfirio snorted, "You'da been a great politician out east. I ask ya a question and ya turn around with a story 'bout your daddy."

"I am explaining myself," Eridu answered, a subtle shaking in his voice.

Porfirio pocketed his hands and raised his bushy brows. "You'll have to slow down, then. I ain't have my journal with me, nor do I have the faintest regardin' this *Sunumun*."

Jessie glanced to his left and right. He wished they would quiet down. *Something else is in here.* He looked behind at the staircase, fully expecting to see a pair of eyes. *Calm down,* he told himself. *This place is a ruin, same as Silverfork.*

The prince nodded. "Sunumun is one of our Great Lugals, a god."

"And why was it a good omen, your daddy marryin' one of her priests?" Porfirio inquired. "I assume that's what ya meant by an *augur.*" He took a pen from his pocket and scribbled a few words on his arm, "Give me a cursory description, if ya please."

"Sunumun is the Goddess of Life. Her highest adherent is entitled *'Ama.'* It translates to 'Mother' in your language... Every Lugal in Sand's Rest had taken an Ama for a partner and had many children. But Ama Asura was different. She was as barren as our desert. She provided my father no heirs and, after much trying—he took a slave to bed."

"When the slave became pregnant, my father gave her the name *Ama Inanna.* Ama Asura never forgave him for that. Nor was she kind to me when I was born. But then again, the people were never kind to her for being infertile. She was mocked often at the ziggurat for that."

Jessie studied Eridu's face. Again, it seemed eerily familiar.

The Erintul's hands became fists and his body shook. He raised his foot to kick the tarnished locket, though he restrained himself at the last moment and took a deep breath. "I should have known when Asura came on this raid that she would try to send me to Namsammun."

Porfirio cleared his throat, reminding Eridu to explain strange names.

"The city of the dead," Jessie blurted.

Eridu whispered, "How did you know that?"

Jessie blinked. The knowledge had been in his mind as if it had *always* been there. It had not even occurred to him that the knowledge was new, or particularly uncommon. He blinked at Porfirio.

The old man clicked his tongue. He folded his hands, "One question at a time. This *Ama Asura* character." He scribbled a few notes, "She is your, uh, stepmother?"

Eridu nodded, still looking at Jessie.

"And she came on your tribe's raiding party?"

"Ostensibly," Eridu finally looked at Porfirio, "to study the wildlife introduced by the barbarians. As chief gardener, none questioned her."

Porfirio pointed his hands at his face and snorted, "Barbarians. Now ain't that a turn of phrase…" He scribbled a comment onto his bicep. "So this unkindly stepmother comes to Belford with a host of equally unkindly raiders… And you reckon she is responsible for your current predicament?" He curled his mustache.

Eridu massaged his chin and stared into the glass. "I may never have known I was betrayed, were it not for the onion man." He looked at his reflection with fire in his eyes, "His symptoms mirrored my animal's." He stared at Jessie's reflection in the mirror. "She gave me a tonic to drink before the raid. And a good beast died because of it."

"*She* gave you a tonic?" Jessie asked. "Just you?"

"Of course not. Everyone drinks a strengthening brew before a battle. It is tradition. But I did not want to—" he cut himself off. "I did not want to feel strong that day. So I gave the, uh—" he looked at Jessie for the name.

"Dead Man's Scalp," he replied. "The sheep over at the O'Siah stead ate some last season. All but two died."

"I gave it to my mount. And when we retreated—with just enough slaves to appease my father but not enough to be a burden—my animal floundered." He chuckled ruefully, "We have no such herb in my homeland." His eyes had grown fanatical and his voice was both exhausted and fervent. "Who else would know of such a plant? Who else but Sunumun's chosen? The, the—" he paused to think of the word and glared at the ground, "The bitch whose shadow has always darkened my life."

"Easy, son," Porfirio soothed. "Ain't no reason to lose your religion. We believe you, now. Don' we?"

Jessie said nothing. *If a sheep could eat Dead Man's Scalp, so could his two-toed creature. Especially if they have never encountered the weed.*

Eridu bit his cheek. "We should leave soon. We lost much time staying in this... What is this place to you?"

"A sanitorium," Porfirio answered. "Where we keep those folks who ain't got proper minds."

"Hm," Eridu hummed. He made for the exit.

Porfirio raised his voice, "I believe this Asura woman is a mean one."

"She is," Eridu turned, frowning. "And likely plotting against my father as we speak." He stepped again toward the exit.

Porfirio would not let him leave, "And as we are on the subject of leaders with a tyrannical nature—you've still not explained how you knew Belford's mayor was a Thorne."

Eridu sighed. He elongated his spine, showing that he was much, much taller than them. He could probably make quick work of both in a brawl. His broad shoulders were well-worn and his hands quite calloused. After a delay, he turned. He said, a nostalgic smile on his face, "Because my mother told me."

"We ain't been raided by your kind before," Porfirio inquired. He adjusted his hat, "How'd she know about us?"

Jessie caught onto the fact just as Eridu explained. *Because she was a slave...* He peered at Eridu's facial features closely. Once again, he got the sense he had seen that nose and those eyes on some other face.

Eridu relaxed and looked up at the rising moon. He smiled and, as he spoke, it was as if the rage from earlier was washed away. "My mother remembered Belford fondly. She told me it was a charming place for a slow life, that one day we would see it."

Jessie gasped, "She was one of Catalina's daughters! You are a Romero."

The hunter's moon and Eridu's smile began to wane. "Perhaps in another life, I might have been." He looked down at his feet and did not speak for some time. "Imagine my sorrow then, when I learned that my grandmother had left your village just days before I was to meet her."

"You wasn't lyin' then," Porfirio whispered. "You ain't come for slaves."

"Slaves are my father's obsession. And his people's." Eridu bit back. "I only wanted to learn more about my mother."

Jessie approached the Erintul carefully. "What happened to your mother?"

Eridu flinched at the question. His hands twitched across his face in a chaotic display of pained emotion. "She died when I was young."

A gunshot abruptly ended the conversation. The clamor reverberated in the pipes and echoed in the cellar. Dust rained on their heads. The three men looked at one another with trepidation. It was done, then. Jessie picked at his cuticles. Only once Eridu and Porfirio began to walk could Jessie bring himself to return. They walked back to the main hall as pallbearers, stepping carefully and somberly.

They heard a commotion as they neared. "Get back!" Hiram shrieked. He was sprawled atop his brother's body with a pistol pointed down a gloomy corridor.

Jessie raised his hands, "Hiram! It's us!"

"Get on, quick!" he commanded.

They did as he bid. Jessie sprinted to his bedroll and grabbed his rifle. "What is it?"

"A goddamn dog!" Hiram flailed. He fired another shot at the hallway. A four-legged whirlwind leapt into an adjacent dormitory.

Jessie approached the corridor curiously.

"I'd stay back, Mr. Bingham. It looked mighty feral. Probably rabid."

"Was it brown?" Jessie called. "With human eyes?"

"What the hell do we care what color it is? It's tryin' to take Solly!"

Jessie laid his rifle on the ground and turned. "Hiram," he said, calmly. "Put down your weapon."

"No!" Hiram shrieked. "I—I won't let him become some beast's meal."

Jessie sat beside Hiram and put a gentle hand on his shoulder. In the span of a second, Hiram went from slapping away the embrace to seizing up. His lips quivered. The revolver slipped from his sweaty hands. The elder Rodgers began to sob. He hid his head in Jessie's arm, "I couldn't do it. I can't."

"I don't think I could, either." Jessie lied. He patted the man's back. "And we won't let anything get to Solly, alright?" Hiram pulled away and looked for his revolver. Jessie kicked it away. "I know this dog, Hiram. Trust me."

His face wrinkled in confusion. "You *know* it?"

"I found it in Silverfork," Jessie explained. "Or rather, I think it found me. It led me to Kilthorpe's old gem store."

Hiram dragged his fingers through his scalp, "I can't. I can't let Solly—"

"A wandering dog is a good omen to my people," came Eridu's soft yet commanding voice. "Especially in this beastly place... Trust Mr. Bingham."

Hiram shook his head even as he agreed, "Alright. Alright." The elder brother stood up. Porfirio and Eridu took him back to the other side of the hall.

Jessie, meanwhile, walked toward the corridor. He whistled and waited. A four-legged shadow poked its head out of the dormitory. It peered up at him, panting. "It's okay, Boy. Ain't nobody gonna shoot at ya."

The stray from Silverfork retreated into the dormitory only to return with something in its mouth. It brushed past Jessie, periodically checking to see where Hiram was.

Porfirio coughed.

The stray leapt back.

"It's alright, Boy," Jessie encouraged. The dog looked back at him with its knowing eyes.

The stray continued its approach. Paw after wary paw, the stray neared Solomon. Once beside the paralyzed figure, it dropped something into the enstoned hand. Then, it skittered out the door and into the forest.

Jessie bit his bottom lip and walked toward the paralyzed figure. He knelt beside Solomon and found a dozen mysterious berries.

"What is it?" Hiram whispered.

"Berries," Jessie replied. *Ones which I have never seen before.* All his conventional wisdom told him to discard the fruit. Plenty of people had stuffed their starving mouths with unknown fruits. A good majority were soon interred. He glanced at the exit of the sanitorium. As aspens quaked in the wind, he debated. *It could be a remedy...*

He glanced at Hiram and gulped. *If I am wrong, he might well shoot me.* Jessie took a deep breath and cleared his mind. He grabbed the tiny berries and opened Solomon's mouth. Jessie slipped the fruits in and made sure they fell into his throat. The man made a choking sound. A foul fluid foamed around his mouth.

Hiram screamed and pulled Jessie away. "You son of a bitch! You murdered him!"

Jessie fell onto his back. He tried to scramble away; Hiram was too quick. The older brother tackled him. He pinned Jessie's hands to the ground and glared down vengefully. Jessie did not resist. He closed his eyes and prayed.

Hiram roared, "You killed my brother, you son of a bitch!"

"No," Eridu remarked. "He did not."

Hiram turned, stupefied. Jessie pushed the man off and jumped to his feet. Hiram walked toward his brother; Jessie watched from a safe distance.

The prince knelt beside Solomon's body and held up the limp arm for all to see. Like a blade of grass blowing in a faint breeze, Solomon's fingers twitched.

Chapter 15

◊

"I cannot tell whether Jessie is so different because of his grief, or because of that damned relic he keeps staring into. What does he see in that dull rock? I am sure I do not want to know."

– Porfirio Pacheco's Journal

It was as if the farther he traveled from home, the more his mind was led astray by doubt and despair. The pair made for the worst type of nightmares. Long after the rest of the men had turned in, Jessie lay awake. What awaited him beyond the veil tonight? When he blinked, he saw Elijah's corpse. In the silence, he heard Ethel's screams. When he slept...

Jessie clenched the Ur Igi tighter and pulled it to his chest. The faint hum was keeping his chaotic thoughts at bay. Something about the Forlorn Trail was making his dreams feel more real. Jessie sighed, preferring exhaustion to nightmares. He looked at the night sky. The celestial canopy twinkled with reds and greens as if in bloom. The rhythm of his heartbeat steadied as he watched the glittering, cosmic boughs. Jessie had always marveled at the corsage of stars which wrapped around the world. The Kuahtec called it 'The Place of Spirits.' The speaking stone's faint hum added credence to the name.

Eventually, Jessie found enough peace to finally risk sleeping. The humming subsided. The lights dimmed. He slipped away into whatever dreamscape awaited him...

A child's cry woke him immediately.

"Are you well, Kisima?"

Jessie tried to speak. When he tried, his mouth was not his own. He wanted to turn and see who addressed him, but his body failed him. He was gripped by an immobilizing depression akin to what he felt after Glendolyn's passing. He simply stared into the darkness, waiting. After some delay, a voice came from him, "Just another bad dream, Galamah."

A woman approached. She wore a long, white dress and held a glowing orb. It illuminated Jessie's view. Suddenly, his neck muscles twisted and he looked down. What he saw amazed him, but he could not gasp as he wanted. As if through a window, he was staring down upon a feminine body—his body. The woman named Kisima stared at her hands, which were deeply scarred. "I gave him the sickness. I killed him. My son. Our Lugal!"

Galamah took Kisima's hands. Jessie felt every sensation as if the hands were his own. "The web of blame is not woven by one."

Kisima tore her hands away and ripped a pendant from her neck. She threw it to the ground, shattering the black stone. "I saw with Eyes of Ur and he still died. What high priestess am I, Galamah?"

The robed woman pulled away, "Wh-what are you saying?"

"I wandered His halls. I combed the library and failed to find a cure for the plague." Kisima stood up and paced around the room. Only now did Jessie realize how elegantly the woman lived. He stared at her gilded wardrobe, her many jeweled artifacts. She grabbed a vessel shaped in the form of an ox. "But someone may yet find a cure." Wine poured out its horns into a white cup painted with red spirals.

"Kisima," the woman hurried to her side. "This is the path of madness."

"It is the path of life," Kisima declared. Jessie felt the woman's fiery resolve in his own heart. He saw visions of a son who was not his. Kisima's emotions felt akin to his own when he decided to go after the twins.

"Common eyes cannot see the vision of Ur," Galamah pleaded. "They will all be destroyed!"

"Karakul will be destroyed if we do nothing," Kisima responded. Jessie could feel her boiling resolve as if it were his own. The high priestess walked out of her room and into the night. She stared down the steps of a great pyramid, at a lamp-lit city of many towers. "Maybe one of them will find a cure."

Jessie's body jolted left and right in sudden, mechanical movements. His vision narrowed into a single, bright slit as Kisima's voice faded into the void. As Jessie and the odd woman diverged, he felt nauseated and weak, like one who drank too much the night before. He stumbled through the darkness, attempting to feel his way. Only, there was nothing to feel. He walked in a perfect emptiness.

Is this what Eridu meant? Is this the Infinite Library? Jessie found it hard to believe he was in some repository of knowledge, as there was not a book to be seen. He was more inclined to believe he was in some twisted dream all his own. *Then if this is my dream... Where are my children? Where is Glendolyn?*

The black walls suddenly crumbled around him, revealing a small hole from which to crawl through. Jessie ran to the opening and peered inside. Children coughed and women wept. Jessie wasted no time. He crawled into the opening and was greeted by many happy children.

"Kisima!" The children screamed, hugging Jessie's waist.

Again with this woman, he thought.

A crippled man approached. His face was lacerated with ugly, purple scars. A stutter nearly prevented him from speaking, "I t-t-told them y-you w-were coming." He grimaced, "Th-they were s-so excited!"

Kisima beamed down at them, "I was once an orphan, too." She knelt, "We cannot forget our roots, can we?"

The orphans shook their heads. An older boy coughed. Kisima's attention shot to that child. "You've gotten tall, Sagastu." She put her hand in a woven basket and retrieved a ring. The swirling starlight emanating outward enamored the smaller children. "I've something for you all."

The oldest protested, confusion in his voice. "But we cannot use them."

"By whose authority, Sagastu?"

The tall orphan was stupefied. "Y-yours... The Ur Namen?"

Kisima looked at the cripple and then at the older child. "I will share with you an aphorism, created long ago by Namgalanzu himself. It is taught to all acolytes at our temple. I even taught it to my son before we knew he would become the Lugal." She smiled and Jessie felt a terrible sadness. He pictured a man he had never seen and nearly wept.

> *"Dichotomy holds answers*
> *Like boxes within boxes*
> *None have the time to tell the truth*
> *Yet none tell a lie"*

Jessie felt a hand on his shoulder. His eyesight shimmered as Kisima once again faded into a singularity. His surroundings darkened, but he was not in the void. *Why am I standing?* Jessie peered at his surroundings. He stared up at a waning moon and realized he was reaching for it. The speaking stone was in hand.

"Son?"

Jessie let his arm fall and with it, the Ur Igi he had been holding. He put the stone back into his pocket. "Hey, Porf."

Porfirio questioned, "What you doin' up?"

Jessie spoke neither truth nor lie. "Nightmares."

Porfirio cocked an eye, "I never took ya for a sleepwalker."

Their campsite was situated past the tree line, on a vast fell. Such little grew on the high slopes of the Forlorn Hills that Jessie could see their fire even from a great distance. Indeed, he worried they were too exposed. He said nothing to Porfirio about the matter. The old man was still giving him strange looks. Jessie admitted silently, *I did wander far.*

The Rodgers brothers were sitting by the fire when they returned. Hiram interrupted himself to say, "Thought you was fixin' to fly away."

"Had to stretch," Jessie stated.

Porfirio opened his tinderbox and lit his pipe. "What you two doin' up?"

Solomon spoke quietly. His voice was an airy whisper and demanded complete quiet to be heard. "J-just tellin' lies."

Hiram turned to his brother. "What really chaps my ass 'bout that doctor was how self-righteous he was."

"I don' remember," said Solomon. He wrapped a blanket tighter around his body.

"Mmmhm," Hiram nodded. "Bunch-a horse shit, of course. He was goin' on and on 'bout the end of the West. Wanted to preserve it by preserving people. Sick bastard."

Solomon shivered and at that, his brother let the topic die.

Porfirio inhaled his pipe. To preserve his tobacco rations, he had begun to dilute his stores. When he spoke, a trace of wild mugwort mingled with the smell of tobacco. "What was *your* nightmare, Hiram?"

The man said nothing and glanced at his brother. Solomon shrugged and whispered, "I reckon my nightmares are pretty obvious."

Porfirio glanced at Jessie, contemplated asking the same question, and took a deep drag from his pipe.

Solomon warmed his hands by the fire, "And you, Mr. Pacheco? Why can't you sleep?"

"Well," Porfirio tampered his bowl and relit it. He stared into the campfire, "I can't stop thinkin' bout that animal, the dog. I open my journal to write about it, but I can't seem to describe what I saw. It just don't make a lick-a-sense."

"It was a Shepherd of Umamu," said Eridu.

"So he ain't asleep, after all," Hiram said, knowingly.

"I was," Eridu rose. "But it is hard to rest among restless men." He joined the others around the fire. "In wild days before cities, the great beast ruled. Umamu we named him and we feared him. For it was he, in the form of a great cat or mighty eagle, that would steal our babies from their cradles. But it was also he that kept the world of beast and man separate."

Eridu's eyes twinkled with firelight, "Even now, there is a temple in Sand's Rest devoted to Umamu. But it is not revered like the Singing Spire of Ur, the Gardens of Sunumun, or the Reservoir of Rosh. Only wild dogs inhabit the sanctuary now, and that is good."

"Seems a waste of a temple," Hiram interjected.

Eridu nodded, "So it would seem—but men fear that temple and are glad that it is occupied by good beasts. For it is said that in those dark halls walks every creature that has ever lived."

Jessie looked up and gazed into the fire. The entire company's vision now intersected in the flames. Between gentle gusts, they looked at one another. "And the dog we saw, you think it came from your temple?"

"Perhaps. Perhaps not. The Shepherds of Umamu are born wanderers. They search the wild places their entire lives."

"Search for what?" Jessie asked. "It seems too starved to be looking for food."

"The Steward of Umamu is not a simple dog," Eridu said. He recalled, "I said that every beast which has ever lived walks within Umamu's temple—and this is true. But not all beasts are animals. A man can be feral, too."

Jessie caught the Erintul's eye. "Like Kilthorpe."

"Yes," Eridu agreed. "A Shepherd, however, is meant to bring a wild man back to his humanity. We are fortunate to have met one."

Jessie fidgeted nervously. He went to his pockets. He felt guilty at the action and so picked at his chapped lips. He peeled the dry skin and tried not to think about the Erintul's words. *It was just a dog,* he knew. He stated simply, "Dogs are always the kindest-hearted."

Hiram snorted, "Well you did it. You done went and made me tired." He stretched, "We might need more of these little fairy stories, Eridu."

The native fired a flickering glare through the blaze. Then, he bowed his head, "I am glad. Perhaps now *I* can get some rest."

Jessie scratched his face, "Uh. Before you do, I uh... I had a dream. Well, I was wonderin' if..." Jessie exhaled and asked bluntly, "Do you know who Kisima is?"

Eridu's eye twitched. "How do you know this name?"

Jessie was silent. Porfirio lied on his behalf, "She came up in an old book I had in my library."

Eridu crossed his legs and folded his hands. "*Your* library?"

Hiram yawned, "Man's practically an encyclopedia. Gots more books than a McLeary's got sons."

Eridu grunted. Nobody spoke. When Hiram's quips became loud snores and the campfire was mostly embers, the prince threw on another log. The fire blossomed in a vibrant display of orange buds before settling again. "I know of Kisima." Embers flew into the air, "But how do you? Be truthful."

Jessie shrugged, "I could not sleep. And the, uh, the speakin' stone, it makes this little drone at night. I thought it might keep the nightmares away. But when I went to sleep, it was like I was living another's. I *was* Kisima."

Eridu stared gravely into the fire. "It is said the Eyes of Ur produce a great echo."

"Perhaps it does," Jessie conceded. "Who was she, though?"

"Kisima was a high priestess of Ur and mother to the Lugal of Karakul. She and her son were the chief enemies of my grandfather. We warred often, trading lives and slaves for centuries until—one year—a sickness came from the east. All the Erintul were affected, but Karakul was the most populous city and it was devastated. Kisima's son, the great Lugal, was taken by the sickness."

Jessie found himself nodding. "I felt her pain. I moved with her legs... She gave Ur Igi to a group of children. Orphans."

Eridu moved closer to the fire and watched the surroundings suspiciously. "When my grandfather learned the Lugal had perished, he sent my father to conquer Karakul. But when Usumgal arrived, it was as if the city had sacked itself." He shivered, "They entered the city through a breach and found the

213

feasting halls full of corpses. They had drunk a concoction of foul liquids. At first, my father thought they had committed suicide. They happily looted the city until they stumbled upon the craftsmen's quarter."

"They found, sitting in the road, a young child with sunken eye sockets. He was chewing an Eye of Ur when they found him. At first, the warriors thought to slay him—but my father wanted answers. He feared the sickness might lead to madness, that perhaps Sand's Rest would be next. He asked the child what had happened."

"*My name Is,* said the child. *What is your name?*"

"*Usumgal, son of Ulanammu,* answered my father. The boy laughed at him and said:

> *"Names are imperfect*
> *Definitions incomplete*
> *Request to be called by your real name*
> *I will call you a frog"*

"The boy swallowed the Eye of Ur and jumped to his feet. He pointed at the bodies littering the street. The child giggled and sped down the street. *Wait!* My father shouted. He and his warriors chased the maddened boy to the steps of the great ziggurat."

"The boy delighted in the chase, giggling and singing as the men tried to catch him. He posed questions as he evaded them. Insane little quips like, *What is Is?* Then, just as my father was ready to put a dart in him—he was captured."

"It took many hours and riddle-sifting to discern the truth. From his crazed commentary, we finally learned that Kisima had sought to make every child in Karakul a seer. She had hoped that, by swelling the ranks of the Ur Namen, a cure might be found. And so began the Tragedy of a Thousand Healers—when every man, woman, and child claimed to have a cure for the sickness.

The many faces of truth looked upon one another and became a singular blindness."

The fire crackled and embers flew past Eridu's burning gaze. "My father named that feral boy Namru and took him as his slave. Then, he ascended the great ziggurat. After all, he had come to conquer Karakul. He was determined to look upon it as a ruler. But when he reached the pinnacle..." Eridu shuddered, "My father never spoke about what he saw as he looked upon his ruined prize. Whatever the case, my uncles say he was never the same after that. They left Karakul to rot."

Many minutes passed in silence. Jessie had seen the high priestess. He had *been* her. She had gone to the orphanage and doled out gifts with the finest intentions. "She only wanted to save her people."

"Salvation is not our gift to give." His weary stare lingered on Jessie's pocket.

Jessie looked away from the flames and stood up. He grabbed the Ur Igi and tossed it lightly in the air. When he caught it, the jewel seemed strangely heavy, like a cloth swollen with water. "I am not a conqueror. I am not a priestess. I just want to see my children again."

"As did Kisima." Eridu rose. "Beware of want, Jessie Bingham. For it is want, and not eyes or ears, which combs the Library."

Porfirio adjusted his tall hat. The gleaming white was now a dirty, soot-stained brown. Still, it added a few inches to his frame. "Thank ya for the story, Eridu. I confess I had a dam in the ole lexical flow. Reckon I'll need a new journal now." He began a sentence but was interrupted by a whooshing sound.

Jessie did not see what happened. First, Porfirio's hat flew off his head. Then, an object ricocheted off a nearby rock. Hiram had been lying down when the commotion began. The mysterious item landed by his eye. He pushed himself up and raised the item for all to see.

"A dart," Jessie breathed. Just then, another projectile zipped past his ear. It might have hit him, but Eridu threw himself through the flames and tackled Jessie. They rolled together down a small knoll which had neither rock nor shrub to hide behind. Eridu flung himself up and stared into the darkness.

Jessie staggered to his feet, "What is it?"

Eridu said nothing, for a galloping tide answered. Mounted silhouettes sifted through the darkness, descending upon them from three sides.

Jessie made for the camp. Eridu stopped him, "No. It is too far to run. Stand with me."

"Against horsemen? I need my rifle!"

"These are neither horses nor men."

Jessie made sure his and his wife's wedding rings were fixed on his fingers. Then, he turned to face the riders. The first assailant rode down a rocky slope, spearpoint glimmering. Jessie pivoted, fighting the urge to flee.

Meanwhile, Eridu also adjusted his stance. He bent his knees and raised his hands in a flimsy posture. Yet, when the rider was only a stride away—he suddenly whirled to the side. Hands like whips snatched the spear from the rider's hands. He slashed the spearpoint against the stone and sparks flew.

The first assailant wavered and fell from the mount. Eridu leapt onto the warrior and plunged the barb through the quilted scale. The spear did not puncture the assassin's armor; instead, the force rippled down, immobilizing the warrior. Eridu leapt back and let the warrior reclaim the weapon.

The assassin reached for the spear, but just then—an inferno expanded from the barb. A wreath of liquid flame engulfed the warrior's head. The assailant shrieked as the unrelenting blaze swirled around, baking the attacker's body from head to foot. The inferno quelled as quickly as it began. When its life was extinguished, so too was the assassin's.

The warrior's helmet rolled off, revealing a woman's carbonized face. Jessie gazed at her, the explosive weapon, and then at Eridu. Jessie had so many questions but now was not the time. Thundering hooves were approaching from behind. Jessie turned around and, just as he saw his attacker—he was launched into the air.

His back slammed down. A sharp pain shot from his spine to his ears. He heard Hiram shout and Porfirio shoot. Jessie tried to get up, but the pain in his back was too great. The attacker turned for another advance. Jessie fought the pain in his neck. He rolled, grinding his body upon the rocky floor of the moors. A glancing blow sliced into his arm.

He had to get up. He pressed his hands into the gravelly soil and pushed himself afoot. Blood gushed from his biceps. He clenched his arm and searched the fells for his attacker. He spotted her quickly, galloping at great speed toward Eridu. The Erintul had planted his feet and waited.

Just before being assailed, Eridu kicked up the discarded, charred spear. The explosive point was blacker than the night sky. He lunged at the attacker.

The assassin let her mount be skewered. She then used the sudden stop to fling herself behind Eridu. She landed gracefully and swept her weapon in an arc. Eridu jumped over the blade but was knocked off balance. The assassin seized the moment. Her spear became a blur of motion. Rapid strikes withered Eridu's defenses, forcing him to retreat up the knoll.

The third woman rode down the hill, spear held aloft by a strange contraption. She would have sent the spear flying, were it not for a lucky shot from Porfirio Pacheco. A single shot of lead entered and left the woman's unarmored head. She fell forward and was trampled by her mount.

Jessie watched Eridu for a time, afraid of doing more harm than good. The prince held his own against the assassin, dodging every strike and even landing a few of his own. Yet, the last woman was not so easily bested. As Eridu parried and countered, she reached out and grabbed his blackened spear. Eridu's weapon snapped in half.

A flurry followed. Eridu deflected a myriad of murderous blows with nothing but an oversized stick. Then, that too shattered. Eridu was left with nothing but his hands.

Jessie finally mastered himself. He grabbed a rock and charged the warrior. She heard his approach and turned. Jessie threw the rock, hitting her squarely in the chest. She slid on the gravel and missed a strike meant for his throat.

Eridu saw the opportunity and grabbed the woman from behind. He grappled her to the ground and wrapped his brawny arms around her neck. He yelled, "*Su Taka-i-Mannu?*" He shouted again, "*Su Taka-I-Mannu?*"

The warrior rasped, "*Ama Asura.*"

Eridu's eyes filled with fiery hate. "*Anas?*"

The warrior said nothing.

A vein in his forehead began to throb. Eridu tightened his vise. "*Anas?*"

The woman let out a satisfied, raspy hiss. "*Zi sag gal dari... Lugal Asura.*"

All emotion left Eridu's face. His knuckles cracked as less of the woman's neck became visible. The assassin began to kick. Eridu's cheek pressed into the writhing warrior. As she kicked more and more viciously, the anger left his eyes. As her breathing failed her, his grew meditative and slow. He closed his eyes as he closed her windpipe. Following a loud crunch, Eridu exhaled and released the warrior. Her twitching legs resembled those of an insect.

"I—" Jessie had no words. He had never seen such a brutal killing, nor such an effective fighter as Eridu. He looked away from the scene, nauseated by the woman's corpse.

Porfirio and Hiram sped down the knoll. "What was that?"

"Now I am beyond certain," Eridu got up and gazed at the high fells. "Ama Asura is planning to overthrow my father."

Hiram raised his gun, "Then you're worth less as a guide than as a prisoner."

"What in all hell, Hiram?" Porfirio growled.

Hiram's finger tensed on the trigger, "Think about it. This woman clearly don' have a liking for him. If we trade him, we get our kin quick and clean."

"And if she loses her coup," Eridu dared to step forward. "You will have assaulted the Lugal's only legitimate heir." He dared another step, staring down the barrel of Hiram's revolver. "How easily he would condemn your kin. He would likely make you watch their fates." He continued his approach.

"Don't you take another step," Hiram growled. "I ain't gonna be murdered by savage whores on account of some princeling."

Solomon ran down the hill and, seeing his brother, exclaimed, "Hiram, what are y'doing?"

"Savin' Cleona," Hiram hissed.

"We'd have all been murdered just now were it not for him," Jessie argued.

"Were it not for him," Hiram turned to his brother, "They'd not give two shits about us."

Eridu surged for Hiram's revolver. In the span of a second, he had disarmed the man and thrown the weapon to the wayside. Within another, he had Hiram pinned to the ground. "You are correct. Ama Asura would care little for you."

Hiram squirmed.

Eridu pressed his face into the mud, "In private, she might reward you—but in public, she would play the game of public appeal. Especially if your plans align and she has deposed my father. Lugal Asura will not reward barbarians. It would threaten her legitimacy." He stood up and walked to the slain assassin.

Hiram groaned and sat upright, "Say you's right. How the hell are we goin' ta contend with an army of savages?"

Eridu picked up Hiram's revolver and tossed it back to him, "By avoiding fights one cannot win."

Hiram took the double meaning and stormed off. Solomon trailed after, begging his brother to calm down.

"How did these women find us?" Porfirio asked. "We're two miles north of nowhere." There was now a noticeable hole in his hat.

Eridu coursed his fingers through his hair, "Asura is leaving guards behind to watch the passes." He shivered and gazed at the rocky crags still before them. "We will have to find another way over those peaks."

"Ain't no horse can climb much higher than this," Jessie shrugged. "And I doubt the Forlorn Trail is very comfortable on foot."

"It is not," Eridu replied. "But it may be our only choice."

Chapter 16

◇

"What Don Marcos failed to understand was that the harshest cuts make the deepest callouses. Mary Anne Thorne had spent years within the wicked halls of the Big House. In many ways, she had already lived a slave's life, escaped her shackles, and risen to prominence. The doom of Don Marcos was merely the start of a new cycle."

– The Ballad of Jessie Bingham

I overstepped, Mary feared. *When dawn comes and Don returns, he need only point a finger in my direction.* She had made a terrible plan, thought nothing of the repercussions, and was doomed to await the results of her fatal miscalculation.

Even a savage can riddle this murder. Warchief missing. Warbride suspiciously dirtier than any recalled seeing her. She argued with her despair, *How many of these slavers would have remembered how dirty you were?* Mary nodded, *I am an insect to them.*

Still, hounded her anxiety, *They may not speak Marcos' language, but he only needs to gesture at me. That matriarch will put it together. Of all the stupid folk in this world,* Mary swallowed, *she is not one.* She was a lot like Mary. *If I led this investigation, I know what conclusion I would come to. Nerugal was killed by his slave.*

Mary squirmed with regret. She winced, *I planned Montgomery for a year, leaving no detail unaccounted for. And now, to lose it all on a hasty, unnecessary plot.*

But was it unnecessary? After a moment, Mary decided it was not. She needed tethers. Don Marcos provided them. She needed a deflection. Marcos provided one. Nerugal seemed a prominent man. His disappearance had to be explained.

Mary ground her teeth, quite weary of the constant back and forth. She wished she could drift off into her dreams, to mute her many misgivings for just a night. She would rather preside over her paranoid delusions than concede to her nightmares. So, Mary focused on whatever might silence her disquieted mind. Most of the slavers had retreated into their tents, but one among them was restless.

The hunchback paced around the camp, probing the shadows of the city. Mary had watched him for much of the long night. *Namru,* she recalled his name. *What keeps this nightmare awake?* She figured the disfigured man feared Nerugal's *true* murderer—the faceless shadow. Mary shivered, hearing the sifting of sand over and over. She had heard his body being dragged.

Across the camp, beneath the sleeping pyramid—Asura and Ethel were sprawled out on a comfortable pile of furs. Ethel had not left her side all evening. The girl was held so tightly at Asura's breast that Mary wondered if she could even get a proper breath.

The child's brain was clearly addled by losing her mother. *And now without Jessie...* Mary wondered what insecurities that little girl must have. What fears had the matriarch played upon to make the girl her puppet? What trauma could make a child so receptive to a cruel, merciless woman?

Mary blinked at Elijah. He was the opposite of his sister. He despised Mary, Cleona—everyone. He insisted on isolation in his corner of the cart. If either Cleona or her so much as bumped against him, he would kick them.

Mary yawned. She closed her eyes for only a moment. When the heaviness behind her eyes began to take her away, she jolted awake. *No nightmares. Not tonight.* She was used to nightmares, of course. On ordinary nights, she even preferred them. Good dreams always set the standard for a day too high, ruining hers in the process.

She pried her eyelids open and fought the urge. Second by second, they slowly shut. When they had finally closed, she told herself to open them after a moment. After a moment, her sleepiness argued for a minute. After a minute, she was asleep.

Her dreams took her to the halls of the Big House. Her brother, Montgomery, chased her. Inevitably, their mother caught them and—seeing Mary weep—locked the two in a room together. Trapped with her brother, she tried to scream. He washed over her as a literal wave—drowning her in briny, groping water. Two catlike eyes stared at her beneath the water, waiting for her to finally suffocate.

When at last she awoke—she was drenched in putrid sweat. The night was still young—and the hunchback continued his vigil.

Mary spied on him. Namru, like Mary, was anxious to see the dawn. She heard it in his wary steps, his sporadic stops, and his muffled whispers to the darkness. His knuckles popped at the slightest sound, clenching a weapon at his side. Every time his hand went to his weapon, Mary heard a scuttling sound.

When the sun finally rose, the city did not brighten. The canyon's shadow stretched into the city, cloaking them all in a relentless gloom. The raiders hurried to disembark. Hasty bites were swallowed and provisions were placed atop their camel creatures.

Mary's chest thumped with anticipation. *They realize he is gone,* Mary knew. The suspicions started first as worried faces. Then, one among them passed by the slave cart. The warrior, a skinny woman with a blowgun strapped to her back, immediately sprinted to Asura. The matriarch charged the slave cart.

Mary looked away. She waited, listening to the matriarch's angry breaths. Asura stepped onto the cart and, slowly, approached Mary. She knelt beside her and looked a long while at her clothes. Asura put a finger on the fabric and traced a line through the layer of dirt. She removed her hand and inspected her fingertip. The matriarch grunted and leaned forward. She sniffed Mary's neck.

She knows, Mary blinked.

Asura met her gaze. Her eyelids narrowed. Her nose and left cheek rose. The expression resembled either a snarl or a grin. Mary was not sure what it meant. *She is a Lugal. Even a grin might mean something different.*

Asura's face snapped. Her brow leveled into a flat, empty stare. Her nostrils flared. Her mouth opened slightly. That expression was singularly defined. Rage. She licked the tops of her teeth, cleaning her last meal. She glanced to the periphery, where Don Marcos had sat.

She whispered, "*Sukur-i-Parsha Su Sansasa-min.*"

The hunchback muttered something in reply.

That infuriated her more. She stood and shouted, "*Sukur-Parsha Su Sansasa-min!*"

The slavers all froze. Then, within seconds, they divided into two groups. Mary counted fifteen in each band. *Search parties.* One group rode down the concourse, the other began systematically entering each nearby dwelling.

Mary swallowed. She looked up at Asura, who stared down the causeway with a murderous scowl. Mary glanced at Elijah and Cleona; both were fidgeting.

They'll find that dress he put on me. Damn me! I should have hidden it better.

A few minutes elapsed before, inevitably, the band entered the place of Mary's assault. Agonizing seconds passed before they all hurried out.

Mary did not breathe. She eyed their silhouettes, wondering if they had found the bodies. She picked at her cuticles. The Lugal moved toward her. She shut her eyes. Their footsteps neared. Thunderous boots came to the slave cart and, remarkably, they passed.

Mary turned her head and watched as the search party investigated a litany of other dwellings. Less time was spent with each successive inspection until, at last, the raiders gathered before Asura. They bombarded her with shaking voices. Mary needed no grasp of the language to suspect what was being said.

They've found no bodies, Mary dared to smile.

She may as well have spoken aloud, for Ama Asura quieted the crowd with a booming command. *"Namru!"* she beckoned. Asura and the matriarch approached the slave cart; the other warriors dispersed.

Elijah and Cleona scooted to the far end of the cart, avoiding all eye contact with the disfigured man. He squatted, analyzing Mary while he listened to Asura. His face was unreadable, uncaring. *No, that's not it,* Mary studied. *Emotionless.* He listened as the matriarch spoke at length. He offered few words, yet when he did—the tone of the matriarch would change. *They are deciding what to do with me.*

Asura barked a command at Namru. Finality was in her tone. The hunchback's vagrant eyes swiveled onto Mary. His bejeweled hands rose. She prepared for the tingling force of the hunchback's hand.

Namru's voice was quiet and stern. "Nerugal was a powerful man. A hardened warrior. The Lugal loved him."

So this is the end, Mary realized. She eyed Namru's blade, a curved dagger fashioned of obsidian. Mary was too petrified to move. Every word bludgeoned her brain with weariness. It was as if she had to absorb a library's worth of books to comprehend his speech.

Namru grabbed her chin and squeezed. "But Ama Asura did not."

Mary swallowed. She waited for the rest of the hunchback's words. That could not be all, could it? Yet, as time wore on, Namru's hand fell and he relinquished her from his spell. He glided away like the wraith he was, becoming absorbed in Asura's long shadow.

Mary suddenly felt feverish. Weariness overwhelmed her. Visions of symbols she had never seen flashed through her head. Sounds she could not pronounce echoed in newly excavated caverns of her mind. She fell forward, finally forced into a deep and terrible sleep.

Her dreams took her again to the haunted corridors of her family's home. The walls were enlarged, and the furniture was massive. In the darkness, she waited. On queue came the *boom doom* of her nightmare's approach. Mary jumped up, barely gripping the door handle. She slipped out of the corridor and into her mother's dressing room. She hid there until, like always, the stomping caught up to her. She darted to the adjacent gallery, but the *boom doom* kept following her. Mary darted into the hallway. *The closet,* she knew. It was like her family did not know the room existed, as only the servants ever used it.

When she reached the end of the hall, though, her closet had disappeared. Trapped, she waited for the pursuer to catch up. *Boom doom, boom doom.* Mary turned to see her monster. Oddly, it was not her brother chasing her. Mary did not know what it was. She stared into the thousand eyes of a many-faced goliath.

Mary forced herself awake. Little Elijah Bingham was looking at her with a mix of fear and disgust. When he realized she was looking at him, he turned his head dismissively.

Mary swallowed. It felt like someone was standing on her chest. She wiped the puss off her eyes. Ethel Bingham sat beside her, giving her brother a cold look. She scooted closer to Mary and touched her forearm. "Ms. Thorne, why are you shaking?"

The girl's touch sent a ripple through Mary's body. She felt the sudden instinct to hit the child. Her back straightened. "Because I'm cold," she said through gritted teeth.

Ethel said to her twin, who had somehow acquired a fur blanket. "Eli. Give Ms. Thorne the blanket."

Elijah said and did nothing.

"Eli! What would daddy say?"

"He'd tell you to sleep in your own bed and not be a baby."

Ethel's face scrunched up. "I'm doin' the smart thing! Ama is nice if you let her be nice!"

Elijah licked his top lip in the exact manner of his father and rolled his eyes. He stood up, bracing his rocking body on the side of the cart. He extended the fur blanket to Mary.

"No, thank you," Mary shook her head. "You are a child. I'll be—"

Elijah threw the blanket onto her body.

Mary's spine snapped to attention and her hands covered her breasts. She felt a sting in her belly. *Just a blanket*, she told her reflexes. She closed her eyes and exhaled.

"Better?"

"Mm," Mary grunted. *Why do they insist on this kindness?* Mary had never felt such unabashed care and, in a way, she felt disgusted by it. It evoked a similar repulsion as the thought of incest.

Elijah sat and said, quite reservedly, "You can put your head under the blanket for a bit. That makes it warmer."

A sudden gust of wind slithered into her ears. It coiled around her neck and sliced her skin. The gentle caresses made her want to curl up in a dark hole and cry. She ground her teeth and tensed her body.

"Do you, uh," Elijah started hesitantly. "Want another blanket?"

Mary grimaced, letting the gentle breeze glide off her face. *Do not give that man any more power*, she commanded. *It is just the wind.* Every time a wisp of air would glide into her ears, she struggled to breathe. Even knowing her imagination was running rampant, she could not help but feel human fingers on her skin.

"Ms. Thorne," Ethel whispered in a high-pitched tone. "Are you crying?"

She's talking to me like a child, Mary heard. *That little bitch is talking to me like a child.* She clenched her jaw and stifled a few swears. "Just my disease. You know about that, don't ya?"

"It's okay to cry," Ethel persisted. "My daddy says it's a great thing to be able to cry."

"Your daddy is a..." Mary could not continue her insult with two wide-eyed children hanging on her every word. "A good man."

Elijah looked up. The glare in his eyes washed away. He bounced his little legs and rubbed his palms together. He sniffled up a great glob of snot and swallowed it. "When my mama got sick, he made her favorite food every day."

"Okay," Mary answered, not knowing why the comment was particularly pertinent or helpful.

Elijah scratched his hair.

Mary rubbed her eyes with her forearms and quickly changed the subject. Cleona Flowers had not said a word. The young woman was fixated on the grand pyramid. She asked, "What, uh— where are they?"

"They found him," Cleona replied. Her foot tapped anxiously.

"What? When... How?" Mary turned around and saw the full band of raiders gathered at the steps of the central pyramid. The throng of slavers shuffled anxiously. Their glossy silhouettes all looked toward the sky. Mary tried to peer up at the pinnacle, but her eyes failed her.

She whispered, "See anything?"

"The cross-eyed hunchback is climbing down now," Cleona whispered. "The rest are making room for him... He's coming this way!"

Mary fumbled with her blanket, wiggled free, and kicked it back toward Elijah. She sat down just as Namru reached the slave cart.

The hunchback eyed them menacingly. He put his ringed hand on the back of the cart and unlatched it. The wooden gate fell parallel to the bed of the cart. Namru slid it to the right, removing it entirely. He then leaned it against the cart as a makeshift ramp. Finally, Namru cupped his hands and, like a dog swimming, he beckoned them to descend.

Nobody moved.

Namru sighed. He spoke rapidly. Mary felt she *almost* understood what he was trying to say. She stared at him, waiting for some sign as to what he wanted. The man's eyes roamed independently of one another, probing. Without words, it was clear what he was asking. The left eye glared at Mary, the right at Elijah. He beckoned them again.

Reluctantly, Mary got up. A short while later, Elijah did the same. They walked down the ramp, initially joined by Cleona and Ethel. However, the hunchback halted those two before they went down.

"He's my brother," Ethel protested. Her upper lip nearly touched her nose. She folded her arms as she thought of her argument, "You don't get to—"

"Alright, little one," Cleona put her hands on her shoulders. "Let's watch from here, okay?"

Ethel licked her lips and nodded wordlessly.

Did Marcos talk? Was Ama Asura lying? Mary stumbled nauseously toward the pyramid steps. The slavers who looked at her only added to the anxieties. They looked at her like someone looks at a cockroach. *They know,* Mary understood. *I played my hand and lost.*

She began climbing up the pyramid. A hand reached out, startling her. She gasped and looked back. The hunchback pulled her back to the concourse.

Why am I here, then?

Suddenly, Asura's voice rang out from the heights. It carried down with ease and reverberated through the city. Whatever she had said was met with jeering and cruel words by the raiders at the base of the pyramid.

Asura's speech boomed through the ruins, echoing until all her words seemed to combine into one deafening din. Just as her voice began to fade, the Lugal began to chant:

"Parsha. Parsha. Parsha."

Namru alone was silent. Mary traced his stare and looked to the pinnacle. She saw nothing at first. Suddenly, the chanting grew louder and Mary thought she saw a wisp of movement at the top of the stairs. Soon, it was speeding down the great man-made mountain, leaving a trail in its wake. Mary thought she knew what was thundering down, but waited with bated breath nonetheless. Soon, there was no doubt. Donaciano's broken body plummeted down the pyramid, smearing the long climb with his blood.

Mary looked away and thought to shield Elijah's eyes. Yet, the boy did not look afraid or disgusted. Instead, he stared at the steps with a strange immersion. His gaze was awe, almost reverence. As the body broke against the stone steps, Mary thought she saw a smile on the child's face.

The vessel of crushed bones rolled off the last steps and skidded to rest at their feet.

Mary trembled as Ama Asura's voice echoed once more. Namru put his ringed hands upon them both. His voice joined Asura's in translation:

"I am Ama Asura, high priestess of Sunumun and nurturer of the Great Garden. I have taken you all into this garden and bid you remember: I take no issue with pulling weeds."

Namru held them in his grip after Asura finished. He forced them to watch as the Lugal gathered around Donaciano's body and, one by one, kicked and maimed it. Blood squirted onto their toes. Bones popped and cracked.

Once the carnage was complete, Namru spoke. "Those who run from a mother's love will starve. Those who undermine a mother's family will be destroyed."

Mary was disturbed, though not by the mutilated corpse or the violent slavers. She was not even that perturbed by Asura's blatant threat, having been on the instructing side of such violent statements herself. Ending the day with nothing more than a warning was the best outcome she could have hoped for.

No, Mary was disturbed by how utterly enchanted Elijah was. His jaw was open and his eyes were wide. The boy did not even blink. And yet, his stare was not on the corpse at his feet, nor on the woman who had just threatened him. No, the little boy was fixated on *her*.

What should have been a source of pride, a sense of victory, became little more than shame. *What am I to this child, now?* Mary shut her eyes.

Chapter 17

⸻⸻⸻◦⸻⸻⸻

"Educated folk have no business in this land of myth and murder."

– Porfirio Pacheco's Journal

The next morning was spent in debate. All agreed they could not follow the raider's trail any longer. Presently, Eridu was explaining their options. It seemed the Erintul knew more of the Hills than any settler, learned or otherwise.

"We were following Asura's band to the Maw of Damu Matu. It is the least treacherous way across the divide, but her warriors will wait to waylay us." He pointed south, "A little over two day's march that way will take us to the Pass of Kul. That crossing will be safer, I think."

Porfirio twirled his mustache, "How-d'ya-know that ain't guarded, too?"

Jessie exhaled sharply. His mind wandered far from the forum. *We are five men against a host of vicious warriors.* He watched Eridu and registered not a single word. *What use is a prince with a bounty on his head?* He glanced at Hiram, fearful the elder Rodgers was becoming too reckless. *If he can pull a gun on Eridu, what else might he do?* He rubbed his eyes, failing to scratch the infernal itch beneath his indigo eyelids. *The twins won't be able to keep any food down. Poor Elijah is going to—*

Porfirio had appeared in front of him. He questioned as if repeating himself, "Jessie?"

"Hm?"

233

"Your thoughts?" Pacheco asked. "An extra day bothers me none, but as your—" he let the silence euphemize any mention of the twins.

"I don't want to waste any time debating."

"We will waste time if the northern pass is guarded," Eridu insisted. "Then, we will be forced to go south regardless."

"You managed just fine last night," Hiram pointed out, cleaning his revolver.

"The Maw of Damu Matu will be well guarded," Eridu reiterated. "And I am just one man."

"How far are we to the northern pass?" Porfirio asked.

Eridu paused then spoke with reluctance, "The sun will still be rising when we reach it."

Porfirio clapped, "There ya have it. We'll go on ahead, scout a bit, and if we find to our chagrin a guarded pass—then we tail it south. Only an extra few hours of delay!"

The matter was settled for the moment. The company departed north. They made good time, mostly owing to Eridu no longer having to share someone's saddle. The Erintul had found one of the assailant's mounts last night and took it as his own. The camel seemed soothed by the Erintul's presence, though it cared little for horses.

Gradually, a ridge began to rise from the ground, growing ever higher. By noon, the sheer rocks dwarfed the travelers and looked like a wall of broken parapets. "We will keep this mountain to our right until we reach the pass," Eridu told Jessie.

"Least we'll have some protection from that flank," Jessie replied, looking left at the fells.

Eridu sighed, cracking the muscles in his neck. "I would not trust the Backbone of Damu Matu. This is a dangerous land."

"You've mentioned that name twice now," Porfirio began. "Is it another of your gods?"

The question was not an easy one for Eridu to answer. He stopped himself just as he began and waited several seconds before, quietly, he stated, "Damu Matu was a man."

Porfirio stared blankly. "With a mountain for a spine."

"He did not remain a man," Eridu continued, speaking barely louder than a whisper. "For he was the greatest Lugal and Namsammun the greatest city. So great was he and so bright his scepter, that his people began to *think* him a god. And how could they not? He starved out Hunger. He had quenched Thirst."

Jessie added, speaking in an unusual cadence, "Soon, he too was convinced he was a god."

"How?" Eridu awed. "How do you know this?"

Jessie started to explain, yet found himself lying, "The Tlacon nomads have a similar story."

"Hmm," Eridu hummed. "Perhaps the horsemen describe also the *Fall* of Damu Matu?"

"I do not know," Jessie responded casually, finding it odd that he did recollect, vaguely, such a story. He found it even odder than he had just lied. What had possessed him to do so?

Eridu paused, only speaking once Porfirio pressed him. He cleared his throat, "Damu Matu angered the gods and so, Ukum salted his fields. Rosh flooded his valleys. Kul hid the sun. When at last Damu Matu admitted defeat, great Parsha himself thrust a spear at Namsammun. The palace sank into the ground, burying Damu Matu beneath the Earth. But the gods were cruel. Damu Matu was not allowed to die. They granted him his godhood. But it was a cursed divinity. Thereafter, he became the god of the dead. Namsammun became a city of the—"

A groan from the deep silenced Eridu. The ridgeline rippled. Rocks tumbled down and, briefly, the earth quaked. Jessie struggled to calm Girl. The horse reared and readied to bolt. She may well have, had the quakes not quickly subsided.

A sudden calm came over the fells. None moved nor dared to even breathe. Long after the quakes subsided, Eridu finally shuddered. He glanced up at the citadel of stone. "What you call the *"Forlorn Hills"* is but the roof of Damu Matu's dead city. Every year the citadel grows, swelling with more and more souls."

The conversation died. Only Porfirio's scribbling carried any echoes of the Erintul's words. They rode in silence for many miles, each man staring long at the granite peaks. Jessie felt there was more to the story of the fallen Lugal, but he could not find any words that told the tale.

Just before noon, the parapets of stone began to shrink. The high granite walls began to slip into the earth. The company slowed and Eridu dismounted. "I will go ahead."

"No," Jessie disagreed. "You are known. If there is a presence there, I am just a humble barbarian."

"With an antique for a weapon," Porfirio muttered.

Jessie shot him a silencing look, "They will respond less aggressively if I am all they see."

Eridu scowled, "Mr. Pacheco, do you have a looking glass that Mr. Bingham can borrow?"

"Sure do," he answered with a gravelly throat. Porfirio rummaged in his pack to such a degree it seemed he was intentionally delaying them all. He finally handed Jessie a pair of binoculars and, without looking at him, muttered, "Be safe."

Jessie nodded, "I'll be back soon." He lowered the brim of his hat and walked along the ridgeline. He had never crossed a mountain before and assumed, naively, that the pass would be narrow, jagged, and almost artificial in design. Yet there was no grand natural gate, no port of entry to the Western Basin. Instead, titanic shadows of snow-capped peaks began to stretch out across the moorland.

On either side of Jessie were rows of toothy peaks. *The Maw of Damu Matu indeed,* he thought. *Aptly named.* The slopes were draped in crumbling shale. The bright tops glimmered with the last remnants of spring snow. Jessie scanned the sprawling valley, seeing only the mountain's black, scaly hide. *Shale will be hard for the horses to walk on at this grade. Could be slow going.* He lay prone and looked through Porfirio's binoculars.

A game trail meandered along the northern flank of the valley. The path led for about a mile to an outcropping of tan rocks. It was the only flat land on the horizon, but it was shielded on one side by mountains. *If there are raiders encamped, that is where they'd be.*

Jessie kept his head low and jogged southeast until he got a better view of the outcropping. He peered through the binoculars. A strange assortment of shapes appeared in the distance. Strangeness gave way to familiarity. Familiarity became fear. At first, he was distraught. Then, as more nuances filled his vision, he became bewildered. He removed the binoculars, suspecting some trick; then, he looked through them again. "Host on High," he whispered.

Jessie sprinted back to the other men. They were all mounted and, when they saw him coming down the fells, rode out to meet him. Porfirio threw him Girl's reins, "How many?"

"I do not know. Dozens?"

"Dozens?!" Porfirio's voice shook.

"It is as I feared," Eridu turned his mount. "They will send scouts after y—"

"No," Jessie interjected, panting. "They will not."

"They are a full warband," Eridu yelled. "Sukurru, that smart bastard. He must have—"

"They *were* a full warband," Jessie elaborated. He met all their confused stares with one of his own, "I—I do not know what happened... They are dead."

Eridu's stare hollowed into a look of disbelief. "Dead?"

None could believe they had been that fortunate and all were silent as they rode into the Maw of Damu Matu. Jessie gave Porfirio his binoculars. He promptly passed them on. "I can't see a damn thing at my age. Wanna take a gander, Hiram?"

Hiram gazed through the looking glass, grunted, and handed the binoculars to Solomon. The brothers nodded at one another and each pulled out their weapons.

The eerie calm of the valley unnerved them all. Porfirio's hand tremored. Solomon's breathing was erratic and Hiram was jittery. Eridu was the worst of them all and as they neared the sandstone outcrop, he whispered, "This is a trap."

They rounded the mountain and, at last, came upon what Jessie had seen from afar: a ransacked camp littered with corpses. The carnage was utterly complete. The tents were frayed. Blood soaked the earth. Yet, there was only one corpse among that devastation. In the middle of the camp, lying naked with limbs spread open, was one of the Erintul's warriors.

Eridu galloped up to the corpse and frowned, "One of Asura's acolytes. These were deadly foes."

"I see only one foe," Porfirio dismounted. He looked around the camp and traded his pistol for a pipe. "Where are the rest?"

"Down there," Solomon pointed.

Jessie trotted to the edge of the overlook. Surely enough, a pile of corpses was heaped on the valley floor. Mounts and men intermingled in broken poses. Blood coated the tawny rocks. Jessie turned away, disgusted by the sight.

"Like stampeding game off a cliff," Jessie remarked. He returned to the lone corpse in the center of the camp. A bullet had entered her through the chin and exited without obstruction, leaving the back of her head wallowing in a crimson mire. *Whoever did this made a point of her death.*

Jessie stared at the corpse, trying in vain to turn away, or at least view it as an anatomical lesson. A purely educational visit between living and dead. But he could not do it. He stared at the woman's face. *The eyes always take the longest to die.* The bloody skull contrasted with those beautiful eyes in ways Jessie had never wanted to recall. He stared into the amber pupils and heard his wife's laugh. Only the weapon at her side kept his cheeks dry. *She would have tried to kill you. She is not Glendolyn.*

He could not help observing aloud, "She's not that old."

"What was that?" Porfirio asked.

"N-nothing," Jessie walked away. He had hardly taken a step when he grimaced, paused, and approached a ruined tent. He tore a tattered strip of fabric from the splintered post. Then, he returned to the slain woman and draped her body in the cloth.

"Who you think coulda done this?" Hiram asked Eridu.

Jessie did not listen. He felt so bad for the woman. He wished he could have saved her, or that she could have died just days before, quietly in her sleep. He shuddered at how horrible her last thoughts must have been. *Had she been prepared to die? Did she leave a lover or a child?*

"Son," Porfirio offered a hand. "We can't linger here."

Jessie woke from his thoughts. He looked around groggily. He nodded and cleared his throat. "Right."

They left the camp in pursuit of an ever-setting sun. The light blinded their eyes and Jessie thought that was well. For in shadows, he continued to see that woman's corpse. A year of forced forgetfulness became like a swollen levy.

Porfirio rode beside him, "There weren't nothing you could do."

Hiram overheard the comment and naturally did not understand. "Why should he care about some savage bitch?"

Jessie's jaw stretched to the side. His bottom lip folded inward. He tried and failed to explain why he was so shaken. But even the thought of explaining his sudden sorrow was unbearable. He nodded at Hiram, "You're right."

Porfirio's gaze lingered on him for a time. The toothy mountaintops began to flatten. Soon, the Maw of Damu Matu was filled with molars instead of canines. The granite spires were replaced by sandstone bluffs. The slippery shale slopes and lichenous boulders were replaced by small shrubs with bony branches.

Jessie pretended to be fixated on the changing scenery, saying as if he cared, "Those trees down in the canyon are pinyon."

"I am unfamiliar with that word," Eridu commented.

"Hm," Jessie hummed. He did not have the energy for much more than the smallest of talk. He glanced at Porfirio, who was still looking at him with immense pity. He mouthed, *"I'm fine."*

The old man frowned and let Jessie ride ahead.

The pass widened even further. The road sank deeper into the earth. As dusk approached, they entered a deep gorge. Flowing between the canyon walls was a small stream. It flowed softly and quietly, gathering only trickles of snowmelt from the Forlorn Hills.

Jessie veered toward the stream and followed it for a time. He heard Solomon ask, "Is Mr. Bingham okay?"

Before anyone could answer, Jessie exclaimed, "These *are* pinyon." He reached out and pulled a cone. "And the pine nuts are ready for harvesting already!"

"Yes," Eridu said, suspicious of the man's excited tone. He noted, "The seasons come sooner in the west."

"Seems like it," Porfirio agreed. "Hardly summer and this stream ain't more than an arroyo now."

"The river will not make it out of this canyon," Eridu remarked.

"Let's hope we do," Hiram said, dismounting. "All in accord ta stay here an' let the horses drink?"

Solomon followed his older brother's lead and retrieved his waterskin. His bodily twitches had improved, but his stutter was stubborn. "A-and the r-riders, too."

The men all dismounted and brought their horses to the water's edge. All save Jessie. He could not bring himself to move, nor tell Girl which way to trot. He felt drained of energy, as if a tumbleweed that had finally found a fence, or a rock which had rolled down a hill only to putter out upon the plains. He stared at the ephemeral stream.

Porfirio approached again. "Here, son. Drink."

"I'm not thirsty."

"Girl is," Porfirio smiled at Jessie's mare. "Why don't you leave her with me and you go for a walk?"

It was in those moments when Jessie could hardly mouth a simple, *'thank you,'* that he wanted to hug and thank the man the most. He managed only, "She'd like that."

"Go on then," Porfirio gestured at the pinyons. "Get some pine nuts to go with the pemmican. I reckon we'll be goin' without a fire tonight."

Eridu seemed to think they should keep moving, but Jessie did not linger for the debate. He wandered into the pinyon woodland and, for a while, was distracted by how similar the western slope was to the eastern. Twisting pines curved in dramatic fashions. Curling junipers wore white, bark robes upon their swirling trunks. It was as if a great dance was slowly taking place over centuries, with pinyon mingling with juniper in a sandstone ballroom.

Jessie's thoughts turned toward home. His own woodland was probably up for auction. His family cemetery would be buried by new tenants. All his father's work was now in the hands of the sheriff and the bank.

Jessie evaded his sorrows by focusing on a task. He collected pinyon cones with trembling hands. He gathered as many as he could carry. Reluctantly, he returned to the stream. As he approached, he heard muffled voices. He lingered at the eaves, making no sound. Porfirio was presently whispering and it was clear he did not want to be overheard. Nevertheless, the irritation in his words made them carry.

"It ain't none of your concern how a man is actin', ya hear?"

Hiram whispered something. Solomon nodded. Eridu cupped his chin.

Porfirio looked at the three and leaned forward. "That woman we saw today, hardly older than a child with a bullet in her brain..."

"You said he has never killed anyone," Eridu remarked. "I have seen warriors react to their kills in similar ways."

"Mm," Porfirio grunted.

Hiram cocked his head, "What you mean, *Mm*?"

A long debate must have begun in the old man's mind. He was silent for a while before he sighed. He lit his pipe and tampered the bowl. He rested the stem between his lips and said, "Y'all ain't know Glendolyn Bingham too well, did ya?"

"Saw her at the workin' house once," Hiram answered. He quickly added, "Ain't never, uh, *worked* with her, though."

"You wouldn'a had the opportunity. Jessie was her first and only client. He fell for her faster than a day-old heifer." Porfirio inhaled. When he spoke, the embers in his pipe gave his face an orange glow. "They ain't had the happiest marriage, but they was a kindly pair and was workin' through their, uh, dilemmas."

Hiram commented, "Weren't he unfaithful toward her? Slept with that Rosalee?"

Jessie fidgeted with his ring.

"Like I said, they was workin' through things..." Porfirio relit his pipe. "And Glendolyn wasn't under no illusion about Jessie's coarser nature." He chuckled, "Gave him hell when she found out, though. Threatened to leave him." He coughed, "I thought I'd help smooth things over. Invited them over for supper, y'know?"

"They seemed cordial enough. Not happy, but not angry. So, eventually, I brought out the food. Glen—" Porfirio's voice cracked. "She couldn' swallow her meal. I thought I'd cooked it too tough, y'know?" He took several rapid puffs from his pipe. "But it weren't the food. It was her. She had a, uh, a tumor."

"Don't none-a-ya repeat this," Porfirio said, looking in Jessie's direction with haunted eyes. "But I reckon Glenny gettin' sick was what saved their marriage..."

"How?" Solomon asked, enchanted as all folk were by another's misfortune.

Porfirio took a hearty drag from his pipe and let the smoke ooze out his nostrils. "Ain't nothing sweeter to a guilty man than carin' for a sick woman... Anyway, poor Glenny could hardly eat by the end. Jessie had to feed her liquids and then, one day—" Porfirio looked around. "I don' want none-a-ya speakin' a syllable about this to Jessie. Ain't no man wants belated pity."

Porfirio waited for them all to agree. He sniffled and rearranged. He relit his pipe and started, "One day, Glenny seemed to deteriorate. Both she and Jessie had an idea of what to do, so they dropped the twins off with me for the weekend."

Jessie stared into Porfirio's eyes. He had never realized how hard Glendolyn's passing was on him until today.

"He took her outside that night to look at the stars. Glenny always loved the stars, y'see? She was fascinated by 'em. Always wanted to see what they looked like in the south..." Porfirio's voice quivered. "That night, they slept under the drape of heaven and Glendolyn—" the old man's voice snapped like a twig.

Jessie shuddered. He had never wept over that night. In fact, he could not remember the last time he had cried at all. The idea that another person could weep over his wife added to his shame. He picked at his cuticles, a tick he had acquired from his wife.

"Glendolyn begged the boy to put her out. Begged him!" Porfirio wiped his eyes and again spoke in a hushed voice, "She did not want to be in pain anymore, y'see... And so, well—it were the merciful thing to do, and Jessie's always had a compassionate soul."

"He killed her?" Hiram gasped. "And I said he did not understand, that day in the sanitorium..." He looked at his brother. "I can' believe he had the strength to do it."

"Mm," Porfirio grunted. "So when he saw that woman today, bullet in her—"

Jessie could not hear another word. The deed was done and they knew now why he could not leave that woman naked in the cold. That would have to be enough for them. He had worked too hard for the better part of a year, making amends for his behavior and being a good widower. If he were to break down now, it would be a disservice to his children. He had to stay strong. He deliberately stepped on the first branch he could find and cleared his throat. "Got some good pine nuts. Not much, but hearty."

Rearranged bodies and scuffled conversation precipitated his arrival. He lay the harvest out at his feet and sat with the men. He smiled at them.

"How was your walk?" Porfirio asked, his eyes scouring Jessie for some clue as to whether he had overheard them.

Jessie could not look the man in the eye. He broke one of the cones apart and chewed one of the pine nuts. He lied, "I feel much better now."

Chapter 18

<hr>

"I must be the air in the lungs that keeps one afloat. I must be the lift that keeps a wing aloft. If I succumb to the men's despair, we are as good as dead. Truth is, there is some misfortune brewing. One which I fear we shall soon be entangled in."

– Porfirio Pacheco's Journal

The sun rose; the waning moon lingered. They ate hurried bites of pemmican before moving on. They followed the wandering brook through the woodland. Temperatures soared as the elevation plummeted.

Jessie spent the time listening to birdsongs. They were strikingly familiar to him, with the Forlorn Hills presenting no barrier to birds. Meadowlarks fluted beside whistling honeyguides. The woodland was a woodwind which Jessie had heard many times. It almost felt like home.

Out of his periphery, he caught Solomon staring at him. The young man rubbed his wrists.

"Yes?" Jessie asked.

"I w-was just wonderin' if ya'd s-still be interested in a f-f—" He winced, "Son of a bitch." He cleared his throat, "If ya'd be interested in a farmhand once this is all done?"

Porfirio growled, "Y'ain't think to respond to his ads?"

Solomon stuttered. "I just w-wanted." He massaged his forearms, "See, I come from a prideful fam—"

His brother cut him off. Hiram could not bear to hear his brother's new speech impediment for very long. "Don' listen to him, Mr. Bingham." He put a hand on his brother's back and patted him forcefully, "Ain't no home in Belford for any of us."

Solomon's tongue slipped through his lips. It did not move when he next spoke, "B-bu-wha-bout ather we, uh—" He grimaced and sucked his tongue back in. The effects of his paralysis seemed to only return when he was under pressure. He voiced carefully and slowly, "Maybe the mayor will pardon us?"

Hiram snorted, "Never known a Thorne to pardon anyone."

Jessie shrugged, "Mary Anne is different."

Everyone but Eridu recoiled. Porfirio choked on his pipe smoke and spilled ash on his lap, "What?"

Jessie crossed his arms. He was not about to explain that, without Mary's pity, he would have lost his farm and maybe even his children. "She's got a good heart."

"Horseshit," Hiram spat. "She robbed our daddy blind and when he couldn't pay her, she had the sheriff beat him. Took our farm and took his life."

Solomon bit down and, with great effort, managed to say, "B-b-booze took daddy."

Hiram began scratching his face. The mannerism had become more frequent since Solomon's poisoning. Now, he would spend most conversations looking away from others and picking at his face. He analyzed a piece of his skin, "You was too young to remember right."

Jessie shrugged. Perhaps the mayor did abuse the Rodgers clan. From his perspective and the perspective of most folks in Belford, Branton Rodgers was an arrogant steader with too much stake in peach orchards.

Porfirio put away his pipe. "Ain't no use in arguin' with him, Hiram. Even when they's as rotten as beetle kill, Jessie's always had a softness for the sickly."

"More should," Jessie muttered.

Porfirio suddenly realized the double meaning of his words and tried to rescind them. "I, I didn' mean that, Jessie. We all—"

"Glendolyn's dead," he resolved. Spite bubbled up his throat. Before he could think about it, he alluded, "Ain't no need to speak about her *today.*"

The other men knew they had been overheard. Hiram started picking his nose. Eridu folded his hands. Solomon tried to apologize only to give up when he found no words. Only Porfirio dared speak. "They was just—"

Jessie cut him off, unable to bear the man's explanation. He would rather let the topic die. "It's fine. But, so much as frown at me today... Ya hear?"

Porfirio exhaled and nodded. He lit a match only to extinguish it on his jacket. He sighed and the company quieted. Even the birds were silent. At first, Jessie thought he had startled the canopy itself. Soon, they noticed strange tidings at the water's edge.

Hiram muttered, "Chokecherries is trampled here."

Solomon glanced at Jessie and added, "Earth is flattened."

Eridu rubbed his mount's neck. The camel's head lowered and its ears drooped. "This could have been the other warbands."

"*Other* warbands?" Jessie snapped. "How many slaves does your father need?"

The prince ignored the question. "Yes..." He sounded almost excited, hopeful. "The other two warchiefs. They are loyal men, Sukurru especially." He smiled at them, "I do not think we should worry."

Solomon cocked his head. Hiram shrugged. Porfirio fidgeted with his mustache. Jessie dismounted and crept to the water's edge. Many prints mingled along the bony stream. Coyotes, cougars, crawdads... "And horses."

"What did you say?" Eridu questioned.

"Hoofprints all along the water's edge. And these ain't two-toed like your camel. These belong to a horse."

Eridu licked his lips as he tried to process. His face folded in on itself. He rubbed his palms together and rested his fingertips on his nose. "It could still be Warchief Sukurru or Kabahum. Mud can be deformed."

Jessie doubted that and rode warily. The stream began to thin. It threaded around the legs of a mesa, becoming only a gossamer spindle.

Solomon cleared his throat. Everyone turned. He bit his bottom lip and stated very slowly. "Why ain't none of us seen the Lugal before now? Ya seem plenty plentiful."

"The *Erintul* say that the Backbone of Damu Matu, the Forlorn Hills, is cursed." He glanced at the muddy tracks. "Many Lugals have ruled under its shadow and those who stayed to the west lived to be old and wise. Those that did not, or went south to conquer... Many tribes have myths of terrible empires, ungodly men, bloody wars." Eridu added, quietly, "And in the end, divine retribution."

"But why now?" Solomon pressed.

Color faded from Eridu's face. His bravado drained away as he opened his mouth. Only a breathy whistle came out until he said, "The great sickness." He glanced at Jessie, "The one I spoke to you of, Mr. Bingham. The city of Karakul was destroyed. Gud-Sukud and Alallion were depopulated. Now, only Sand's Rest remains."

Eridu looked ahead, "But we are too few to carry on as we once did. Our loyal warriors, fertile mothers, and hardy workers were all killed by the disease. The life that we had enjoyed for millennia was shattered. Even with the Ur Namen's vast wisdom..." He croaked, "We needed more people."

Eridu looked behind. The prince seemed to age within the span of a blink. The light hit his downcast face, revealing wrinkles Jessie had never seen. The prince spoke with gravel in his throat, "But in crossing the Forlorn Hills, we broke the taboo of Damu Matu. My father is now the wayward Lugal, our city the terrible empire." He stared at a horse's hoofprint. "And some barbarian horde is riding for my home."

Jessie noted the irony of the prince's lament. "Could be your folk stole some horses."

"And the stolen horses must also have butchered Asura's garrison," Eridu sniggered.

Hiram flicked a scab, "None of it makes any sense. Nobody cares 'bout the frontier back east. Took the 6th cavalry two years to muster. It'd take 'em at least a season to retaliate against a raid. Especially one orchestrated by uh... Well, uh, myths."

"Look," Porfirio spoke up. "It ain't any use debatin' when we ain't got all the facts. Probably won't serve us any good, neither. Why, before long we'll have our dearest Binghams and lovely Lady Flowers back to us. And without a bloody war to boot, I'll wager!"

Eridu curled his lip as he studied Porfirio. "You were either quite the charmer in your youth—or you weren't born with that crooked of a nose."

The newspaperman chuckled and pointed at his jaw, "It ain't pay to have so many opinions when you have a fondness for the juice."

Jessie turned his growing irritation into a joke, "Yes, you're a regular o-pinyon pine."

The old man grinned as he rolled his eyes, "There's a special layer in Hell for punsters."

Solomon was the first to chuckle, which made his brother snort. The two began to *hee* and *haw*, causing even Eridu to giggle. Jessie thought they all sounded stupid. He grew increasingly agitated as their stupid laughter echoed against rocks. He clenched his fist and chided, "Y'all are m—"

Abruptly, Eridu's mount stopped moving. The camel let out a concerned roar and kicked its legs. Jessie looked at the Erintul and his strange beast. Eridu dismounted and inspected his animal. He pried open the camel's jaw and looked at his tongue. He sighed with relief. Pondering for a period, the prince pointed past the mesa. He pinched his thumb and index finger together. Then, he cupped his other hand around his ear.

They all intuited that meant '*Be quiet.*' The prince continued on foot, guiding his camel with a firm grip on his lead. The animal followed, ears hanging limply.

The men took queue. Jessie retrieved his rifle. Porfirio pulled out his pistol. The Rodgers went for their revolvers. They rounded the mesa and the stream severed itself upon the riverbed. A hundred silver hairs combed the pebbles before disappearing beneath wet sand. The surrounding space widened as the river-carved rocks and gorges retreated. Great bluffs became mounds of red rock. What had been a continuous bulwark of stone was now just a few scattered forts along the horizon. They entered a vast plain of parched grasses.

Eridu's mount began tugging its lead. It reared and snorted, only going a few strides before they realized what it was so disturbed by. Laying in the plain was a headless camel calf. Despite the clean cut and no signs of predation, Eridu blamed coyotes. He urged them and his mount to continue. Yet, they soon found more slain camels. The fields were littered with their corpses. After a mile's trek, they came upon an ashen compound of several buildings. Hot embers still hopped from charred wood. Carbonized bodies sizzled beneath a ruined roof.

"These were good people," Eridu finally said. He rummaged through the debris, heaving off a fallen beam. He knelt by a faceless body, "They were herders of umamukin. Honest, kind."

Jessie scowled, *They earned their fate when you came east.* His hypocrisy was immediately apparent to him. When there was no face to look at, he was more than fine to see Eridu's people dead. Without a face, they were only savages.

Porfirio had something in his hands. "Look here, y'all."

"What'ya got, there?" Hiram said, never taking his eyes off the horizon. He listened for the slightest disturbance.

Porfirio raised the tiny object for all to see: a small, lead ball. He flicked it, leaving residue on his fingertips. "Paper cartridges everywhere. Long rifles, I'm guessing."

Jessie began noticing the clues, too. The grasses at the edge of the compound were stained black like a row of dirty paintbrushes. "I reckon that's black powder."

Hiram smiled, "That's great!" He punched his brother squarely in the shoulder. Solomon winced and looked away.

"What is great, exactly, about murder?" Eridu demanded. He tossed the burned beam to the ground. It collapsed into a cloud of dust.

"You fuckin' hypocrite," Solomon snarled. "You c-came to rape and raid, same as whoever did this!"

"I only wanted to see my..." Eridu bit his bottom lip and said a word in his language, a swear of some kind.

Hiram, however, was strangely quite happy. "The army is out here," he looked at Jessie and Porfirio excitedly. "That's 6th cavalry or you can put me in a sanitorium!" He glanced at Solomon, who was shaking his head morosely. "Come on, ya sons-a-bitches. We got reinforcements now!"

Jessie stared at the environs even more suspiciously. "No, we don't." He frowned at Hiram, "It's like y'said to Solomon." He strapped his rifle across his back and rolled his shoulders. The muscles popped as he talked, "We assaulted a sheriff, murdered his deputies, and robbed a stagecoach." He spat, "We're outlaws."

Hiram glared at them all, but he knew Jessie was right. "Then what?"

Jessie stared at the beaten plains, the broken plants, and the bruised earth. "We ain't gonna find Ama Asura's tracks now, but I reckon the cavalry'll be tailin' them anyhow."

A wry look came upon Hiram, "If they manage any successes, we will be right behind for the spoils."

Solomon nodded, "Follow 'em like buzzards."

Porfirio lowered the brim of his hat. "Well, that sounds like a fine course. Shall we?"

Jessie caught Eridu's eye. The man's face was taut with worry, his wrinkles deeply etched upon his sunken brow. *Any success by the army is a tragedy for his people.* He exhaled, tried to be empathetic, and gave up on it. He rode past the prince and stared at the plains.

The 6th cavalry, Jessie marveled as they followed the new tracks. That army had been tasked with quelling the Tlacon and Kuahtec uprisings. With those tribes gone, perhaps the army was finally taking notice of the Forlorn Trail. He surveyed the cavalry's wake; it had rampaged through the shortgrass, plowing through it like a razor to a head of hair. *How'd they get wind of everything up at Belford? How'd they make such good time?*

"Solly?" said the man's older brother. The youngest of the company had a tear in his eye. "Solly, hey," Hiram said again. "What's got ya in a knot?"

Solomon swallowed and put his hands behind his head, in a defeated sort of stretch. "We really is just a bunch of varmint." He scoffed, "Don't matter th-that he's a prince." He scowled at Jessie, "Or you and I been wronged. We just some no-good varmint."

"Well to the law," Hiram smiled. "And they the ones who is least concerned with lawfulness."

"Hear hear," Porfirio added heartily. "And our fine country was founded by outlaws, Solomon."

"Outlaws with prospects," Solomon pointed out. "Ole' Kate Flowers would just turn in her grave if I marry Cleona now. Ain't got nothin' to give her but a life on the run."

"Oh, piss on Kate," Porfirio growled. "She married Collin Flowers and that man was the biggest con since Calloway Thorne himself." He talked rapidly, waving a finger, "Now if you think Cleona'll be content bein' saved by some jackass, thunder-skull soldier with a comfortable pension—you'd best eat lead now."

"A soldier with a salary," Solomon echoed. He nodded solemnly, "I suppose even if we fail, the army'll save her soon..."

Jessie had heard enough. "God damn it!" The others all looked at him. "We ain't gonna fail. If you don' have the goddamn gumption to continue forward, go the hell on back!"

Porfirio whispered, "Son, lower your voice."

"Don' you dare patronize me," Jessie whipped. "We're outlaws," he raised his hands. He could not tolerate another fretful phrase. The more that those around him doubted, the less he believed he would see his children. "So the hell was the devil and he got a nice plot in the end!"

Jessie's chest heaved. Solomon bowed his head. Porfirio massaged his temple. Eridu stared ahead, deep in thought. The combination of responses made Jessie immediately embarrassed by his outburst. The feeling instantly morphed into intense irritation.

The day went on like poured molasses. Jessie idled in his saddle, doing his best to contain himself. His first challenge was Porfirio's chewing. The man's teeth were not what they once were, and as much as Jessie wanted to point out the fact, he restrained himself. With his jaw clenched, Jessie listened to the relentless *slp-tlk-slp-tlk* of the man's chewing.

Soon, Jessie's mind began badgering him with its own, incessant variety of mental digestion. *Would the kids fare better if the army takes them in? Would some kindly marshal adopt them and give them an easy life?* The hopeful thought soured Jessie's mood further. *More than likely they'd be sent to some orphanage and grow up mean.*

Jessie's mind turned upon itself cannibalistically. It lashed out against its hypocrisy and declared, *You're growin' up mean from this excursion. Why, you robbed a lawman, after all. You were an accessory to one and possibly more murders. You are not the father they remember. You are not what they need.*

"Son of a bitch," Jessie muttered. He did not look up, though he knew he had attracted the others' attention. He added, "Bit my tongue."

They let him be. Initially fine with no one asking what was wrong, Jessie was soon fuming over the lack of respect and care the men showed toward him. *They are more than fine with gossiping about me and my wife, but when I am around, they're*

mutes. Useless friends of convenience. Bunch of belly-aching sons o—
"

Jessie's mind once again remarked upon its hypocrisy. He scoured his immediate surroundings for a distraction. Unfortunately, he was soon fixated by Hiram's tick of picking at his face. Jessie was shocked he had never noticed it before. The disgusting mannerism turned Jessie into a boiling tea kettle. Rather than comment on the uncivilized habit, he stared at Hiram's dirty revolver.

"Stop!" Jessie ordered. "Stop it, damn it. Hiram, what the hell?"

Hiram's head bobbed like a buoy. He stared disinterestedly, "Pray tell, Mr. Bingham?"

Jessie marched up to him and grabbed the man's revolver. "What you think you're gonna do with this?"

"Shoot someone."

Jessie shook his head, "Look at this wear!" He craned his neck, looking for Hiram's maintenance kit, "Where's ya gun oil?"

"That shit ain't necessary."

Jessie closed his eyes and when he looked at the man again, he admonished, "What kinda man ain't got a..." He went back to his horse. He caught Solomon staring worriedly at Porfirio, but he did not care. He retrieved his gun oil and his cleaning rod. "Didn' your father ever teach you that a tool needed as much care as a limb?"

Porfirio said, a tone of warning in his voice, "Not everyone's father was yours, Mr. Bingham. And that ain't such a bad thing."

Jessie flashed a look at him. *What the hell is that supposed to mean?* He ignored the comment and put the wire brush through the barrel of the revolver. He cleaned it vigorously and pulled it out expecting a fine assemblage of gunk and grime. He saw nothing and cleaned harder. "Son of a.." he said, arms tensing. "This is why you need to abide by a strict—" he gritted his teeth, "regime—" he growled— "Of cleaning!"

Jessie unsheathed the wire brush and, to his immediate fury— the cleaning rod was snapped in half. He shut his mouth and licked the bottom of his lip. He sighed and threw the cleaning rod away. "You owe me, Hiram."

"I don't owe you shit," the man replied. "And y'best rein in that temper of yours."

Jessie glared at him for a time, chewed on a litany of phrases, and decided to remain quiet. *He* would have to be the bigger man. He gave Hiram the revolver. Jessie took a deep breath and got back on his horse.

A thank you, kindly, would have sufficed, he thought. He glanced to his side, ignoring the admonishing looks from the other men. He gazed to his left, acting as if he were more interested in the surroundings than any of them. He pocketed his hands and furrowed his brow as if something on the horizon had caused sudden contemplation.

After a few minutes, Jessie tired of the façade. *You just need a bite and you will calm down.* He groped his pockets for some pemmican. As he searched for the stray strip of jerky he *knew* he had left, he was reminded of Ethel's habit of hiding her pemmican. For the first time that day, his chest lightened.

He finally found a handful. Instead of taking a bite of leathery fruit and meat, however, the contents of his pocket bit *him.* A jolt surged up his arm and into his head. His eyesight shimmered and his sinuses swelled. The hum of the speaking stone echoed in his body. He tilted his head as one does when water clogs the ear. A thousand nibbling fish bit his heart. A thousand voices clamored to be heard.

Chapter 19

◇

"At the end of this journey, I reckon this might be an eventful read. I have my share of villains, but only after today did I remember who my hero was. I wish I had been more like him. Maybe then my daughter would write to me."

– Porfirio Pacheco's Journal

When his eyes opened, the Ur Igi had taken over his senses. Jessie peered through the eyes of another. Despite feeling overwhelmed and afraid, his heart rate did not accelerate. He tried to no avail to look around. He waited, trapped in whatever prison the speaking stone saw fit to fashion. Like dirt washing off during a rain, his vision slowly attuned to his surroundings. He rode a camel creature, an umamukin. He was staring down a dark canyon. So deeply had the gorge been carved, the drag was permanently shaded.

"Lugal Ulanammu will attack any day. By now, he knows my son is dead."

Kisima again, Jessie realized.

"What can we do with so few?" fretted a woman. She tugged on an Ur Igi pendant.

"They will not have gone unpunished, Galamah. Damu Matu's plague surely spread to Sand's Rest."

Galamah peered into the canyon. Kisima traced the woman's stare to their guards. The loyal soldiers were below, plucking wayward citizens from holes in the rock and ferrying them back to the city. Some clawed at the rocks and wept, others resigned to

258

their fates. "Our people flee the city, Kisima. And those that do not..." Galamah shuddered. "Our people are—"

"Our people are trying!" Kisima shouted. "Even now, there might be one who has combed the Library. One who is on the cusp of a cure! Even now, little Sagastu and the orphans are hard at work!"

Galamah despaired, "They've found only death and madness! It is the Tyranny born anew."

Jessie's face warped as he felt Kisima's rage. He felt the need to strike Galamah down. He hated her as he had never hated anyone. The feeling was surreal, like a fish might feel if it suddenly had grown wings. Every fiber of his body yearned to murder the wailing woman. Various methods of torture crossed Jessie's mind; some were so cruel, he knew he could never have thought of them himself. A subdued hatred washed over him as Kisima's voice trembled, "Who is the high priestess of Ur? Is it Kisima or Galamah?"

The other priestess was silent. Then, she ripped the pendant from her chest and threw it to the ground. "I do not know anymore."

Jessie felt the quaking of Kisima's body. "Do not bother attending the feast tonight. If Parsha is to bless us, the warrior god cannot see such cowardice." Kisima swallowed, "In fact, do not bother returning to Karakul at all."

Galamah's eyes shimmered. She lifted her chin and declared, "With pleasure." She rode a few paces before turning, "What would your son think of you? Ruling over this fallen city?"

Jessie felt Kisima's fingers twitch toward her weapon. It took the wretched woman leaving Kisima's sight to finally give Jessie some sense of serenity. The high priestess barked at her guards. "Let the cowards flee. Sand's Rest will send them to the slave auctions soon enough." She snarled at a soldier, "Take me back to my temple."

Kisima's sensations and emotions crashed like a wave into Jessie's consciousness. He wanted to cough as if *his* vocal cords were becoming strained. Kisima's thoughts became his own, *I cannot cough. I cannot show weakness.*

They walked down the dim road until they came upon a mighty, decorative rampart. The wall was made of painted blue bricks. Interspersed were golden animals which Jessie had no names for—but Kisima did. He looked up and recognized: *Anzu, Labu, Mushussu.* Kisima marveled at the wall. The tallest ladders would struggle to scale the heights. The strongest engines could not break the gate. Kisima swallowed and turned her attention to the right of the great gate. Her stomach plummeted. No army need lay siege now. A group of dissenters had broken the wall and tried to flee the conscription. Her own people had broken her defenses.

Kisima crossed the crumbled threshold. "We will use this as a funnel. Usumgal's warriors will be slaughtered." Even as she said it, Kisima wondered if she would be ravaged during the sacking.

The Way of Parsha was alight with activity. The orphanages had spilled out onto the street and all Kisima's new acolytes were busy learning the Library of Ur. Quite a few had taken happily to Kisima's task of finding a cure for the plague. The little orphans, so unburdened by a long life, were all busy testing a variety of possible antidotes. *They are so imaginative. Pure,* Kisima told herself. She hailed a group of orphans, no older than five years.

"What have we here, little neophytes?"

They looked up at her. To her horror, it seemed their eyes had spread across their faces. When they looked at her, it was with crooked, crossed vision. A small girl tossed something into a bubbling cauldron. Kisima thought the object looked vaguely like a hand. The girl spoke happily, though not in the common parlance.

"I see," Kisima nodded as if she understood. She smiled at them and quickly continued down the concourse. She bowed her head and ignored the rest of the children.

Her thoughts became Jessie's: *They've created their own languages, too. I doomed them. They're little monsters, all of them. I should have listened. The common eye cannot see His vision. I've given them infinity only for their minds to fracture into infinitesimals.*

The Way of Parsha was the largest road in the world. The trees in the middle of the concourse lit the street with orange and red fruit, their canopies shadowing only a fraction of the way. Hanging vines coursed down the balconies like waterfalls. Kisima tried to find beauty in the sight. She saw only ruin. When passersby looked at her, she did not see faces—only skulls wrapped in flesh.

At her temple, Kisima dismissed the guards. "Attend the feast in my name," she commanded them.

"You will not be going?"

"I must see my son." She scaled the high steps and entered her chambers. She entered a small closet, enclosed in gilded bars. Jessie did not know what he was staring at, but he felt a pinprick of Kisima's pride. Suddenly, the closet began to descend a vertical shaft. Jessie wanted to look around, yearned to be afraid. All Kisima felt was cold dread and hatred.

The gilded bars opened. They were in the heart of the mountainous monument. Kisima stared at the floating lamps of liquid light; Jessie felt an upwelling of shame. The high priestess wandered the dim halls for ages. Jessie might have marveled at what Kisima passed, but the priestess did not linger. She ignored magnifying glasses built on iron pedestals. She walked past giant aquariums of strange fishes. She entered a hall of masks, each vividly painted and each wearing decorative Ur Igi for eyes. Even those haunting masks were hardly looked at. Kisima walked with singular purpose.

Finally, the narrow corridors widened. Statues adorned the room, each holding a glowing orb lit by unknown sources. Kisima passed many stone likenesses, each guarding a gilded sarcophagus. Armor and facial features were elaborately painted upon the coffins. Kisima came to the final statue and turned. The last sarcophagus was unadorned and plain. She approached.

Suddenly, a hidden figure appeared from the shadows. It was a child.

"Sagastu," Kisima smiled. *What is he doing down here?* Jessie heard the woman's thoughts. "You will miss the feast!"

The boy was visibly shaking. He blinked several times as if something was irritating his eyes. Like the other orphans, his eye sockets seemed to have deepened. He stared at her with crossed eyes. "You cursed us."

"I gave you a gift I could not even give to my son."

"And look at him," Sagastu snapped. "He rests while we..." He swallowed and his voice cracked. He turned and yelled, "QUIET!"

Nobody is there, Kisima thought. *He's lost control of the Library.* She took a step back.

The child growled, in a voice far deeper than belonged to him. "I do not intend to live with a thousand minds in mine!" He placed a hand in his tunic and retrieved a butcher's carver. The rusted blade would not cut cleanly. Sagastu began breathing erratically. "Run."

"I am the high priestess of Ur." Her voice hardly carried as she stated, weakly, "You will do nothing to harm me."

"You will run," Sagastu commanded. He lifted his leg and placed his grimy, peasant foot upon her son's sarcophagus. "Or I will deface him. Damu Matu will not recognize him when his soul comes to Namsammun."

Kisima trembled. She gazed at her bejeweled hands. Tears trickled down her face. One by one, she took off her rings. Steadily, Jessie felt his own senses returning to him. He felt as though he were between two worlds, like he was swimming with his eyes halfway in the water and in the air. He saw Porfirio and yet heard Kisima as she said, staring at her son's sarcophagus, "My poor boy." The woman began to weep, though she now had Hiram's face. She took off her last ring and Jessie heard an echo, "The failures of our forebears echo longer than the triumphs."

And all was silent.

Jessie blinked at the company. As he looked around, a ghostly butcher's carver seemed to manifest in the air. He wiped his eyes and found, to his great surprise, they were coated with tears. He almost thought he was still dreaming (or hallucinating, whatever the case). *When was the last time you cried?* He asked himself. He glanced at the men.

They hardly noticed him or his wettened cheeks. They were all staring down a vast and wrinkled cliff-face. Resembling chapped, earthen lips was a vast bajada. At its base, the plains faded into a flat and desolate desert. Islands of cracked claystone stitched the land together. Together, the chiseled horizon looked like the scales of a great lizard.

Jessie rode up to the others and asked, "How long have we been riding?"

The men turned and looked at him worriedly.

Jessie recoiled. "What?"

Eridu inhaled sharply and looked at Porfirio. "It is as I said." The Erintul descended the bajada. Hiram and Solomon each gave Jessie a fearful look before following the prince down. Once the others were out of earshot, Porfirio whispered, "You ain't right, Jessie."

"I'm fine," he argued. "I was asleep."

"You were asleep?" He seemed more perturbed than before. Porfirio glanced at the other men before riding close to Jessie. "Son, your eyes were wide open the whole ride."

Jessie wiped his eyes. He felt no need to carry on lying and said, "Must have been the speaking stone."

Porfirio stared at him, contemplated some reproach, and thought better of it. "Let's clear off this bajada. I don' like how watched I feel."

Jessie pondered the intent of Porfirio's words as Girl carefully trotted down the sandy slope. They reunited with the three others and continued west, chasing the setting sun. Each man contemplated the vastness in their own fashion. Hiram held his revolver close to his chest, wary of the howls coming from behind them.

Solomon asked Porfirio about his vows. He no longer thought they were sufficient and they were presently occupied with the finer details of the afterlife. "I gotta have a piece in there 'bout that," Solomon insisted.

Meanwhile, Eridu had become even more stoic. He seemed to be actively avoiding any eye contact with Jessie.

Jessie, for his part, was dreadfully tired. Looking into the Eye of Ur made him beyond weary. He felt like his children did after a long day. So much information bombarded his brain, the only way to process it all was to sleep. Yet, another part of him forbade any rest. They had tarried too long already. *We need to make good progress tonight. We need to...* Jessie repeated his mantra until it twisted into another form of counting sheep. *We need to...* He rested his eyes.

"What in all creation..." Hiram muttered.

Jessie awoke to his surroundings. A great skeleton was subsumed in the sand before them. The skull was flat, long, and toothless. The vertebrae were as tall as Jessie and wove through the sandy embankment where the animal had died. It was larger than the Big House by far. He blinked at Eridu. "What is this leviathan?"

The Erintul stared at the massive remains. When the prince spoke, it was with reverence. "Long ago this basin belonged to Rosh, Great Lugal of Water. This was his pool and that was his son. Then, Ukum—Great Lugal of the Desert—challenged Rosh to a drinking contest. They drank for three months, but Ukum could not be sated. The Desert won the basin for himself and killed all of Rosh's children."

Eridu studied the mighty skeleton. He dismounted and circled the remains. He peered down at a pile of desiccated scat. "Asura camped here." He looked around and shrugged. After a delay, he squinted at something in the distance. The Erintul broke into a brisk walk. He bent forward, poking his head into the creature's cavernous jaw.

"What is it?" Porfirio called.

The prince said nothing. He sifted sand and charcoal until he pulled out a dusty item. None of them quite knew what it was. Eridu thumped it against the bones, shedding a layer of ash. Jessie immediately recognized the title and vaulted off his horse. He snatched the book and gazed at it mournfully.

"Oliver Pennington!" exclaimed Solomon. "I always loved those stories."

"Mama always read you the one with the dragon," Hiram reminisced. His nostalgia was reflected in a warm smile, "Belong to one of yours, Mr. Bingham?"

Jessie brushed his fingers along the ashen title, *The Many Mysteries of Oliver Pennington*. He recalled his last day with the twins. He had been in a hurry to find Porfirio and left the twins with Veola. *And Elijah ran after me.*

'When you gon' be back?' His son had frowned.

Jessie had heard the disappointment in his son's question. *'Soon.'*

"Will you tell us a story tonight?"

'Of course. Maybe something a little happier than the last one. Oliver Pennington?'

Jessie exhaled a staccato series of breaths. Elijah had been waiting for him. *And I broke my promise.* Jessie looked up and away from the frayed reminder of his failing fatherhood. The others were looking at him with damnable pity. He cleared his throat, "We went a long way today. This is a good place to make camp."

The others were eager to rest. They laid their bedrolls within the leviathan's maw. Solomon fixed supper and doled out portions. When it came time to dish Jessie's meal, he added an extra ladle's worth.

Jessie could not stomach the sentiment, let alone the food. He excused himself and got some fresh air. It was becoming impossible to move, as if the quagmire of his memories was becoming a hardening clay. He remembered his good memories with the children, of Ethel composing her first poem and Elijah catching his first fish. Oh, how he had hugged them. He closed his eyes and remembered their little idiosyncrasies. Elijah had started giving him a half hug, as he was already beginning to develop an

I-am-a-man complex. Ethel, meanwhile, was still in the throes of loving her father as if he were faultless. Her mother's passing had made her cling to childhood. She yearned to be his baby girl forever. He could still feel her little hands on his back, clinging to him as she always had.

Jessie took out the frayed copy of Oliver Pennington. He flipped through the pages. Sad thoughts coalesced into a weak smile. *She's starting to annotate,* he saw. He had told her to do that, but he never thought Ethel would listen. He read and reread his daughter's comments.

'*Funny,*' he read, hearing Ethel as an echo of the past. '*Cute,*' rang her sweet voice. Jessie marveled at the power of his daughter's pen. *I'd almost forgotten what she sounded like.* The smile on his face soured. *What else will I forget?* A frown formed, *What will they forget?* The gluttonous sorrow in his mind latched onto the sentiment. *Will we just become strangers? Will I find them only to be like an old friend from a past life?*

He had to say aloud, "That could never happen."

And yet it had, with his wife. *I can only hear her voice in my dreams, and who knows if that is truly what she sounded like?* How could he be sure he would not forget his children if he had forgotten their mother?

Jessie winced. He could not go through this right now. He had not forgotten Glendolyn. *A year is a long time,* he pardoned his memory. His irritation like a boomerang came surging back. *And so what if you forgot her voice? She left you to raise them alone. On a dead farm, no less... Son of a bitch, I ca*—he interrupted himself. He had been on the cusp of decrying his wife for dying. Jessie took a deep breath and rejoined the company.

The men had finished their supper. Jessie's uneaten portion was placed on his bedroll. He brought the bowl to Porfirio. The old man was outside, scraping the contents of his bowl and cleaning as best he could with minimal water. He tried to scrape the hardened gunk on the sides of the bowl. His hands began to tremble. The bowl fell.

"Let me," Jessie lunged.

"Y'aint needa do that," Porfirio said. "I can handle it."

Clearly not, Jessie nearly said. "These stains here need a certain strength," Jessie said, scrubbing a dirty bowl madly. When the smudges would not come out, he asked, "Any-a-ya got steel wool?"

"Nope," Hiram replied.

Jessie scrubbed rapidly with a mostly dry washcloth. "Ya can't eat from a dirty bowl," he explained. When he was satisfied with his work, he inspected it thoroughly. The stain remained. Jessie channeled all his strength into scrubbing. Every oscillation of the washcloth made him angrier and, in a moment of clarity, he thought to himself, *Everything is going wrong.*

The simple thought drowned all others. His anger dissipated, the washcloth fell to his feet. Jessie Bingham broke down. Tears flowed down his cheeks and coated his dry lips like floodwaters through an arroyo. A small whimper escaped him which all the men heard. Jessie paid none of their reactions any mind. He could not. He was immobilized by his weeping and the more his sadness overwhelmed him, the more he reveled in it. He did not feel happy as he wept. Rather, *not* feeling angry gave him a lightness to his breaths.

Hiram chuckled and said, "Ole' Bingham's lost his nerve."

"Eat shit," Porfirio growled, wrapping his arm around Jessie ushering him away from camp. Jessie obliged, unable to fight anymore. Porfirio sat him down far from the others and let him cry for a minute.

Jessie wiped his eyes, exhaled, and said, "I've gotta finish those dishes."

Porfirio put a forceful hand on his shoulder, keeping him sitting. "It's okay to grieve."

Only a second went by before Jessie's eyes filled with tears again. He admitted, ashamedly, "I thought I'd moved on from Glendolyn's death. Then all this happened and..." He sobbed, "I h-haven't ever cried for her. What kind of man ain't cry for his wife?"

"One who feels guilty," Porfirio replied instantly. "Trust me. We all have our ways of grieving. It's not unnatural to be angry." He took out his pipe.

Jessie took the pipe and tossed it into the sand. "If I don't see my children again, I don't know if I can live. Especially not if I have to live with this... This angry shell I've become."

"Grief's got a way of turnin' us into caricatures of ourselves," Porfirio said. He rubbed Jessie's back and sighed, "I remember reading dime novels as a boy. There was always a character with that trait. Couldn't say 'death' or some trauma-related word. I never-not-once thought it seemed realistic. Then my wife left me and I couldn't say 'divorce' unless I were drunk."

Jessie wiped his eyes. "When I learned about Glendolyn's sickness, I became delusional with hope. Suddenly, I lived in a world where nothing could go wrong. She was going to be fine, the children weren't sick, and the farm wasn't dryin' up." He chuckled, "All the while, yep, I couldn't say certain words. I still find it hard to say—" a mass formed in his throat. "Tumor."

"You've always been a kind, hopeful fool." Porfirio beamed, "It's why even the mayor liked ya." He got to his feet and offered Jessie his hand. "Let's get some shut-eye."

Jessie swallowed. He did not feel happy, but it felt good not to be angry. "Thanks, Porf." He took his friend's hand and returned to camp. He went to fidget with his ring, though it now seemed to better fit his finger. He looked up at the starry sky and, for the first time since the twins' capture, he did not feel ashamed.

Chapter 20

"Mary Anne Thorne has assumed the duties of her brother as interim mayor. Her first act is to conclude the search for her missing brother. Sheriff Clydesforth was also dismissed. Rumor has it he disagreed with the new mayor's decision. Whatever the case, he has left town for good. An army man by the name of Crawford Biggs will take his place as Belford's new lawman."

– The Belford Inquirer

Mary wished she could go numb to the monsters in her dreams. The sleepless nights had become routine and her eyes carried great bags under them. The voices around her filtered through her ears as if she were underwater.

"Ms. Thorne?"

Mary blinked slowly and turned to Elijah. "Hm?"

"Who is Monty?"

"A man. Why?"

Elijah said, as only a child could without sounding ridiculous, "He can't get you in your dreams. Those are yours."

I must have been talking in my sleep. Mary smelled the vomit on the child's breath and muttered, "As is your nausea. Keep it in, next time."

Cleona snapped, "He's a child, you cruel woman."

"So are you," Mary reminded the girl.

"It's not his fault," Cleona glared.

Mary met her stare as she would have as mayor. The entire endeavor soon exhausted her. She exhaled and addressed the sickly child, whose head was bowed in shame. "Sorry, Eli. I have not slept very well."

Elijah Bingham shrugged. "Worse women have said nicer things to me. It's okay." He scratched his ears as much as his bonds allowed and sniffled. "How did you know the mean woman would capture Doctor Marcos?"

Mary had not known. She frowned and stared into the vast desert. The monotonous browns and tans were beginning to wear on her. "I figured he was not much of a runner."

"But he could have hid. Or stolen a horse." Elijah spoke with fascination and wonder oozing out of every word. "How did you get him?"

He sounds like a fisherman awing a catch. Mary almost smiled. She yawned, "The thing about any good con is—"

"A good *child* don't need ta hear this," Cleona interrupted. "Elijah, little one. Drink some of that water."

"I don't want it," Eli mumbled stubbornly.

"Your sister gave you that waterskin," Cleona reminded. "And she's doin' better than you."

"That mean *bitch* did," the little boy argued.

Cleona looked at Mary for support.

"I'm not his mother." She grinned at the boy, "She *is* a bitch, ain't she?"

Eli grinned back, but the gesture morphed into gagging. His stubbornness lasted all of ten seconds before he dry-heaved bile off the side of their cart. Weak and trembling hands clenched the waterskin and doused his face. That seemed to help the nausea.

The day ended uneventfully. Ethel tried to break away and see them, but the matriarch did not allow it. Ama Asura took to braiding the girl's hair all evening. She even hand-fed the girl her dinner. Meanwhile, Elijah curled up in a spiteful ball and scowled himself to sleep.

Mary was not so fortunate. She tossed and turned as her fears churned. She watched the waning moon as it fled the sun's whip. Her only rest was found in long blinks and enveloping yawns. As the beating bright orb rose over the Forlorn Peaks, she finally fell asleep.

As ever, her dreams took her to the Big House. She immediately fled to the broom closet. There, she waited for her nightmare to manifest. She crawled between the crates and knelt behind them. For a moment, all was quiet. Then, boots began to thump down the hallway. They approached slowly, reveling in Mary's terror. They halted at the entrance to the closet. A grim chuckle escaped her monster. The door squealed ajar and long, serpentine fingers coiled into view. *Tap, tap, tap.*

Mary was bound by her terror. Yet, another monster had come up from behind. It said with a nauseating stench, "Ms. Thorne?"

She woke immediately to a body next to hers. She choked on her breath and skittered to the other end of the cart. Only after some time did she realize that the body belonged to Elijah. She cleared her throat and rubbed her eyelids. She caught Cleona's weary gaze and immediately looked away. Elijah, however, was not so easily ignored. He crawled over to her and asked, barely audibly, "Do you like nopales, Ms. Thorne?"

"I do," Mary lied.

"I'll get you some," the boy promised.

"Alright." She looked to her side and contemplated what else to say. She struggled with any nice word, though. Sentimentality seemed like such a risk in their situation, a tumorous weakness that might spread to other aspects of her character. She decided on a smile, yet when she looked up, Asura's head was turned toward her. Head cocked, it seemed the matriarch was glaring at Mary.

Suddenly, she remembered Asura's warning beside the bones of the leviathan: *"Should you dare to touch Ama Asura's children again—you will be buried in the great gardens of Sunumun. Ever after, the children will know you only as the nutrients in their meals."*

Elijah did not notice and so, crawled even closer to Mary. He looked at her expectantly.

"Wh-what?" Mary asked.

Elijah slid his jaw as he chewed on a remark. His eyebrows scrunched together, deep in thought. "How do you make bad people go away?"

Mary caught Cleona's judgmental stare. *She'd have the little one enter this new world without a sense for truth.* She looked at Elijah. *Your father's kindness will get you killed out here.* "Bad people tend to make themselves go away."

"But how did you know Don Marcos would get caught? How did you make your brother disappear?"

"Eli!" Cleona hissed.

Mary sucked in her bottom lip. Never had anyone so bluntly remarked on her brother's disappearance. She evaded his question, "Planning something for Ethel?"

Elijah shook his head emphatically, "N-no. Just... I heard my daddy talk about it once. That the last mayor went missing and that—"

"That his sister made him disappear," Mary finished. She nodded, "Yes, that is the story."

"Did you?" Cleona Flowers questioned.

Mary sighed, wishing she had her cane to lean on and a bottle of whiskey to sip. She tapped her fingertips together. She glanced at the sweltering wasteland. The desert was nothing more than a great brown streak. It was as if a sloppy paintbrush had been dragged across a rough canvas. "After Montgomery left Belford—" she took a breath and thought of what to say. She exhaled slowly and licked the inside of her bottom lip.

Elijah grew impatient, "But *how* did you do it?"

"Why do you care so much?" Mary asked, a tinge of defensiveness in her tone.

Elijah looked at his lap and mumbled, "I don't wanna be whipped again..." He started to speak, but the memory of Madame Rosalee's abuse made him falter. After clearing his throat, he muttered, "I can't be."

There were certain experiences and sensations which Mary regarded as clichés. Among these had always been the idea of motherly love. She never understood why other girls would swoon over babies and froth at the mouth when thinking about having their own, glorified parasites. For years, she had assumed they were liars, fools, or a mixture of both.

Yet now, Mary stared at the dejected boy and saw herself. Suddenly, her wrists chafed against her bonds. The urge to hold Elijah overwhelmed her. "I—"

Cleona Flowers interrupted her, "All you need-a know is after Montgomery Thorne went missing, the *new* mayor started goin' blind." She glanced at Mary, "No need for the specifics, I'd reckon. Not a story meant for children."

Mary was shocked at her boldness. *Montgomery has nothing to do with the disease,* she tried to say. A clog in her windpipe let only air out. She frowned at Elijah.

The boy glared at Cleona. "I am not a child. Not anymore."

"He's right," Mary agreed. "And this is not a civilized country."

Cleona blinked a dozen times. Finally, she scoffed, "Corrupt him. Fine. Ain't my kid."

Mary ignored her and addressed Elijah. The answer to his question came to her quickly. It was as if she had stowed it away long ago. "People do bad things 'cause of some weakness they ain't conquered in themselves. They take this weakness out on others."

Elijah was now fixated on her. Mary had never had someone (that she had not threatened) listen so attentively to her. She continued, "Marcos was a garden variety villain. Do you know much about him, Eli?"

"Only that he kept raisin' the price of our medicine," Elijah responded.

"He came from the delta," Mary informed him. "And he was poorer than a tithe bowl in hell. And that humble beginning led him to a prideful end."

"Because he was insecure?" Elijah cocked his head.

"Exactly," Mary smiled. "He yearned so much for status and acceptance, the poor bastard ain't seen that I was only lettin' him free to distract the slavers."

"From what?" Elijah asked. Cleona turned.

Mary forced out a breath. "Donaciano was not the only bad man who disappeared that day."

"The scarred one," Elijah realized. He gazed at her like a holy man at an idol.

Mary smiled weakly. "Yes." She nodded and began to caress her forearms. She intended to let the conversation fizzle, and while it did—the interaction was not over. Elijah scooted up to her and, without so much as a word or a look, laid on her lap.

Mary's arms levitated above the boy's head. Unsure of what to do, she acted as if the uncomfortable pose was intentional. Over the next minute, she slowly moved her hands to her belly. Yet, that posture was even more unpleasant. At last, she surrendered and rested her hands on the boy's back. She took small breaths, feeling embarrassed suddenly by how much her chest moved. She rearranged her hands a dozen times before, finally, she had to say something. Luckily, the monotonous desert finally changed scenery.

Cleona squinted and proclaimed, "Is that a lake?"

Mary turned her head and Elijah sat up. Mary saw nothing but a sliver of blue on an already cloudless horizon. "The Final Ocean?" She wondered.

"I hope not," Cleona declared. "Else all them wagoneers who took the safe way west ain't never made it, neither."

That's true, Mary realized. *What if the Final Ocean was Lugal land all this time? How many people died to come here, or worse?"* The caravan continued to the water's edge. The salty smell hit Mary immediately. As they traveled along the shore, Elijah whispered, "That's saltgrass, Ms. Thorne."

"Is it really?" Mary pretended to be impressed. Saltgrass farmers were as common as mosquitos on the Copper River delta.

Elijah bobbed his head excitedly and took her enthusiasm as a license to elaborate. He had hardly taken a breath before a look of worry bubbled up his face. His cheeks swelled. Before Mary knew it, her chest was covered in vomit.

Cleona looked at Mary fearfully. Elijah moaned and tried to apologize, only gagging more. He managed to keep the next bit down, swallowing it with a wince. He stared at Mary ashamedly and began scooting away.

She should have been mad. Even as she stood up, Mary wondered at her sudden change. Yet, instead of scolding the boy, she shouted at the slavers, "Someone help this boy!"

The caravan stopped. A few warriors laughed at her, others ignored her. Rage filled her and drained all rational thought. She eyed the nearest warrior and spat on him. The glob landed directly on his cheek.

"Medicine," she demanded.

The disrespected warrior dismounted, but a lone command halted him. The matriarch and the hunchback had come from the head of the column, Ethel in tow. The little girl's hair was in a vibrant braid that matched the matriarch's. Asura climbed into the slave cart and, without any emotion in her eyes, backhanded Mary. She fell upon her bound arms, crushing her hands. Her cheek slid along the wooden cart. A dozen splinters penetrated her skin.

Ama Asura stepped over her and knelt before Elijah.

Mary tried to get to her feet but could not manage it. She heard Ethel tell her brother, "Let her help, Eli. She's nice."

"I don't want her help." He struggled audibly, "Stop! No, st—" he dry-heaved.

"It really helps, Eli! I had some, too."

Cleona helped Mary sit up.

Elijah was kicking and wailing, "I don't care." He winced as Asura forcibly applied a shining, white ointment to his neck. The boy cried and thrashed. Eventually, Asura muttered a word and shot to her feet. She looked at the child and scoffed. She said something to Namru, who shrugged. The matriarch turned and grabbed Ethel's hand.

Ethel tried to smile, "It's going to help, I promise."

Elijah wiped his tears. He glared at his sister, "She's just Ms. Rosalee in savage clothes."

Ethel broke from Asura who said, "You're bein' stupid. You got yourself chained up because you can't be respectful or kind." She concluded, "Daddy would be so sad at you."

Elijah pointed at his cheek. The bruise was only now beginning to fade. "You'll see."

Asura took the child back to the front of the column. The day ended and Mary paid the price for her outburst. The Lugal made camp at the water's edge. Fish was caught and cooked; spices filled the air, but the three slaves did not eat. The three went to bed with grumbling bellies.

Yet, in the morning, Ethel woke early and made her way to their cart. She carried a few leftover scraps of meat and a handful of dried fruits. She handed them out, saying sorry to Cleona and Mary.

"What about me?" her brother asked.

Ethel shook her head, "Daddy taught you to be smarter. We gotta look after ourselves and all you wanna do is act up."

Elijah fumed, "And you just wanna be her slave. You look just like her!"

Mary whispered, "Eli. Keep your voice down or we'll get hurt again."

Elijah paused, saying nothing until his sister tried to offer a bit of fruit. He swatted her hand, "I don't want some bitch's food."

Ethel looked as if she would start crying again. "Daddy told us to accept kindness wherever it's found."

"Daddy ain't here," Elijah grunted.

The tears his sister had restrained flowed silently down her cheek.

"You be kind and make gift baskets," said her brother. "But I ain't gonna be weak. I ain't gonna be wronged."

"Daddy did his best," Ethel whimpered.

"Daddy only scraped by because Ms. Thorne pitied him," Elijah growled. "And if he were still around..." he chewed on his remark before lashing out for a final time, "He'd just leave us with some bitch anyhow."

Ethel shook her head and looked over at Ama Asura. The matriarch was nearby, staring at the slave cart with doom in her eyes. Reluctantly, the little girl hopped off the cart and walked slowly back to Asura. The matriarch cloaked her in an embrace and brought her out of view.

The rest of the morning, Mary wondered what to say to the skulking child. Finally, she said, "Ethel was just trying to help us, Eli."

Elijah said nothing.

"You're her brother," Cleona stated.

Mary pictured a shallow grave no one would ever visit. *As if that means anything,* she remarked to herself.

Chapter 21

"Karakul was never truly abandoned. Pockets of madness lingered in the deep city. Kisima had released something far worse than the plague. It infested the streets and left the entire city a place of dreams. Even after a generation, some aura continues to bring the crazed down that ruined concourse."

— The Codex of Kul

After his breakdown, everyone started to treat Jessie with a greater deal of kindness. Almost on the hour, Porfirio would ask him if he was doing well. Jessie would respond with the same few words every time. He did not mind the attention, as it was a good thing to be looked after. Still, he wondered if he had been too eager to show his emotions. He hoped they would still respect him.

Jessie focused on his tangible problems. Their stores of pemmican were beginning to dwindle and what little cactus fruit was found grew atop great prickly spires. All agreed that, for the time being, they would not risk climbing those barbed pinnacles. Soon, however, they might need to.

What most bothered Jessie, however, was not the possibility of starvation. Rather, it was Eridu's growing dread. It was as if Jessie's demons had consumed the nearest host and were now plaguing the prince. Every night while dreaming, he muttered frightened words. Every morning, his eyes reddened more and more. This alone would have bothered Jessie, but he refused to speak about why he was suddenly so jittery.

Jessie thought he knew. The speaking stone had become unnervingly active. Even quarantined in his pocket, the jewel was no longer simply humming. The further they trekked through the desert, the more it began talking. For two days, it had badgered him with aphorisms and riddles. For two days, Jessie had ignored it and tried to separate the stone's world from reality. It was growing more difficult.

> *"A hard nut is nutritious only*
> *With the strength to crack it*
> *A hard truth is only helpful*
> *To one with ample humility"*

Jessie tried to ignore the voice. Like the heat of the desert, the Ur Igi was inescapable. The longer he went without acknowledging the Eye, the louder it became. It was like jumping in quicksand. On the third day since passing the leviathan's bones, Jessie became desperate. He hid the Eye at the bottom of his bag, stowed the bag on Girl, and listened to the wind.

The stone grew more relentless. The voice branched into many and seemed to ride the wind. Like a distant choir, they chanted aphorism after ominous aphorism. The words were hardly human, as if articulated by the sifting of sand, the crumpling of leaves, and the lapping of waves.

> *"Well-used pens lose their ink*
> *Well-used coil gets a kink*
> *The most impressive thoughts*
> *Come from brains yet unwrought"*

"Enough!" Jessie hissed.

The men looked at him worriedly. Eridu especially gave him a grave look.

Jessie swallowed, "Nightmare."

No one believed him; none said a word.

At noon, they were sitting atop the eroded banks of an arroyo. Eridu was pacing, hand placed thoughtfully at his chin. Occasionally, he would look at the cavalry's tracks, mutter something to himself, and shake his head. Meanwhile, the Rodgers and Porfirio played cards and did their best to write Solomon's vows. They all thought they were close, but Solomon was not happy with a few lines.

"What about one of them metaphors? Y'know, comparin' Cleona…"

Jessie's speaking stone tuned out the conversation. The din was becoming deafening, as if an ambient song was playing both within his pocket and far to the north. Whispers unlike anything he had heard from the stone were buried in the song, like water in a humid wind. *That orphan said he was cursed, that thousands of voices were making him go mad.* Once again, Jessie played with the idea of discarding the Ur Igi.

Eridu blurted, "They are going toward the Chasm of Rosh."

They all looked at the Erintul, whose brow dripped sweat.

Eridu cleared his throat and explained, "This arroyo is the beginning of a vast ravine, where all the water from the mountains once flowed."

"A proper barranca, then!" Porfirio declared adventurously.

"Do not be so eager." Eridu peered mistrustfully down the arroyo. "At the end of the Chasm is the city of Karakul."

A flash of light caught Jessie's eye. It looked like a lone rider coming toward them. Old words uttered by dead strangers filled his mind. He stifled the urge to repeat them even as he stepped toward the rider. The noisy wind was picking up. "Karakul fell," he muttered at last.

Nobody replied.

Jessie wiped his eyes. They were feeling heavier than usual, as if his eyelids were slowly being stretched to the side. He looked back at the rider and saw only a mesquite tree. He turned to the others and saw that they were looking at him fearfully. He raised his shoulders and shielded his chest defensively, "What? Why are you lookin' at me like that?"

Eridu dragged his hand over his forehead and through his hair. He muttered some proverb, "The sightless man is one whose eyes are opened too wide." He scooped up a handful of hot sand and let it fall through his fingers, "Yes, Jessie Bingham. Karakul is destroyed. But even in ruins, my people would never willingly enter that city. It is a Kisutag, a place of cultic ritual."

Hiram glanced at the hoofprints of the 6th cavalry. "Them hoofprints don' follow the arroyo. They veer south."

"Yes," Eridu acknowledged. "Your army must have great scouts, for they do not follow the path of Asura."

Hiram walked toward the arroyo and squinted at the dried riverbed. "Is them horse prints, Mr. Bingham?" He did not wait for an answer and began climbing into the trench. "I don't think they is."

"I wouldn't go down there," Jessie warned. "Rattlers love arroyos."

Hiram immediately stood up. He took a wide step away from the edge and dusted off his pants. "Then we follow the 6th cavalry?"

Eridu blurted, "Yes," as Jessie declared, "No." They each stared at one another. Eridu pointed at the eroded riverbed, "It is dangerous, you just agreed."

"I said there are rattlers in there, yes." Jessie shrugged, "But how do we know the army will lead us to our kin?"

Eridu chose to ignore the question. "It is madness following that route."

"The army ain't been out this far west," Porfirio added. "How'd they know to fear this ruined city?"

Again, Eridu ignored the question. "We are too few to venture that way!"

"What if Cleona is still down there?" Solomon gasped. He stood and got onto his horse. "Damn the snakes!"

Eridu flailed. The prince could barely find his words. "You cannot help them."

"We ain't just strollin' the Forlorn Trail to make a memory," Jessie reminded. "This is why we are out here."

"This is stupidity!"

Just as Jessie started to argue and chastise Eridu as a coward, the speaking stone spoke for him:

"Those who hear
Without listening
Speak
And do nothing"

It was as if the jewel had taken a side in the argument, though whose side remained unclear. They all stared at one another. Only the wind dared utter a word, and upon its howling whispers was an ethereal song. Jessie tried to speak but was afraid of whose voice would come out.

"Jessie, son," Porfirio finally said, voice trembling. "I think you'd best skip that stone."

Jessie reached into the bag. The Ur Igi was glowing. Jessie retrieved the jewel and shivered. He suddenly felt feverish. Voices on the wind began saying words in foreign languages. Jessie shuddered, for they were no longer foreign to *him*.

"I thought I was different," Jessie admitted. "When you spoke of common eyes, Eridu..." He took a deep breath. "I suppose it was arrogant to think mine weren't common."

"And uncommon to admit it," Eridu replied.

"I just fancied I had a higher affinity for the jewels, perhaps a cleaner conscience..." He snorted, realizing after all his childish tantrums the last year—how delusional that opinion was.

Porfirio managed a weak smile, "People don' like ya 'cause your perfect, Jessie. Folks take to ya because y'admit when you're wrong."

Jessie smiled. "I appreciate that..." It took a minute to find his words, but nobody pressed him. At last, he stated, "I feel I am like tryin' to breathe underwater with a reed that can't reach the top."

Eridu approached. "I do not want to overstep. But when I saw that relic in your possession... I knew soon it would be the Eye that was in possession of you."

Jessie nodded. "Well. It was kind of you to let a man make his own mistakes." He took a deep breath, not just for himself but also for the spirits in his soul. "Nevertheless, I do not think I should be done with the stone. Not yet."

"Jessie Bingham," Eridu began, voice ringing with fearful overtones. "You are making mistakes thousands have made before you. Mistakes that ended them. Your head is overfull with the thoughts of ghosts."

"These ghosts are still useful," Jessie responded frankly. He did not expect the group to understand him, let alone condone him. Wisdom and lunacy are synonyms to the common. At least, that was what the voices were presently telling him.

"You know what happened in Karakul," Eridu warned.

"I do." He recalled Karakul as if it had been a second home. It fluttered in his memories with nostalgia more than dread. He *wanted* to see what had happened to the city. More importantly, he feared what had become of those cross-eyed children. "You gotta trust me. All of ya. I know I sound crazy. I know I act crazy. I probably am crazy at this point. But there's crazier out here that we don't want to meet naked."

Hiram and Solomon glanced at each other and then at Porfirio. "Naked?" Hiram questioned.

"This Eye gives me premonitions. I know the streets of Karakul better than any scout. If anyone can find Cleona, Solly—it is me."

That convinced Solomon and by extension, Hiram. Porfirio and Eridu remained deeply disturbed, however. The two convened, whispering in hushed, short sentences for several minutes. As they argued, Porfirio began shaking his head more and more. Finally, he swore, "God damn it, fine!" He pointed at Jessie, "That thing ain't nothin' but vine weed climbin' up your soul!"

Eridu mounted his camel and clicked his tongue. "I do not know what the Eye will do to you when we enter Karakul. That place is a focal point of darkness." He shook his head, "But I cannot deny the merits of your argument." He steadied his breathing and sat kingly upon his steed. The fear on his face washed away in stoic resolve. "My father came to this city as its conqueror. I will see it once, too."

And that was how the decision was made, not by consensus but with deep apprehension. Nobody liked the Eye of Ur, and none so much as Jessie. Yet they tolerated the madness out of hope of saving their loved ones. As many thousands had done before.

Porfirio sulked. Jessie tried to cheer him up with some casual talk about Solomon's vows, but the old man interrupted him. "I'm choosin' to trust ya, Jessie. But you gotta promise me something."

"Of course," Jessie said.

"Don't agree to a proposal y'ain't heard yet," the old man scolded. "Y'got to promise me that when you're at the precipice, you'll know to step back."

Jessie pretended at first not to know what he meant. Porfirio was too cunning for that, though. He bowed his head and nodded. "I promise, Porf."

"Appreciate that."

"Mhm," Jessie replied. He had not realized how stifled his breathing had become. His muscles ached as if they had been under strain for weeks.. "I know it's strange, Porf. Insane, really. I just feel like the stone, or something in it, *wants* me to find the children. Is that ridiculous?"

Porfirio rummaged for his pipe. A half-smoked bowl waited for him. He lodged the stem in his mouth, "Not any more ridiculous than a tribe outta legend comin' down the Hills. Or this old skeleton ridin' out with y'all to exact justice upon them."

Jessie smirked, "I suppose not." He peered at the surrounding gorge. The sheer sandstone was unlike others he had seen. As common as grass on the prairie, shells were cemented within the rockface. He was sure his wife knew all the names of the different shells. Jessie smiled and said, wanting to change the subject, "Glendolyn would have loved this."

Porfirio paused, tinderbox in hand. After a second, he snorted and smiled at him.

"What?" Jessie asked. "She always wanted to see—"

"I know, son." He put away the unlit pipe. "It's been a season and some since Glenny made you smile."

"Hm," Jessie grunted. *That's true.* He pointed at the stony shells. "Make sure you put those in your account. There's a little girl out east somewhere who loves the sea. She'll want to know about this."

Porfirio turned away. He lowered the brim of his hat and subtly wiped his face. "I can do that."

Jessie exhaled. It felt like he had held his breath for a year. He patted Girl's neck and said, "We done alright, so far—haven't we?"

Girl snorted.

"Laconic as ever."

"That's good," stated Porfirio. "If the horse started talking, I'd know we were fucked."

The seashell street sank into the shadow of the sandstone canyon. Eridu rode ahead. He no longer seemed jittery, though he often looked up at the top of the gorge. Pebbles occasionally rolled down the sheer slopes, worrying them all. After several instances of falling debris, Eridu had enough. "I am going to scout ahead."

"Think that's a good idea?" Jessie called. "This is a—" It was no use. The prince had already galloped out of view.

Without Eridu, the pebbles no longer fell into the canyon. After an hour of calm, the men could not help feeling hopeful. They wove through the foundations of the desert. The horses' hooves echoed like drums upon the earth. Jessie bobbed his head to the rhythm of the ride. Hiram began to hum. Solomon tapped his thigh. They listened to Hiram's melody for a time and knew the tune. His wife sang it often to him, and then eventually to his children. When Hiram had finished the first verse, fully intending to be done, Jessie continued quietly:

There's a rose that grows
Along the shores of Red Port
There's a rose who strolls
Along the rows of Red Port

> *I'll meet her tonight*
> *A gift at her door*
> *For the rose of Red Port*
> *I'll brave any thorn*
>
> *There's a ship that sails*
> *Across the seas of Blue Grass*
> *There's a—*

The winding chasm suddenly widened, revealing an awe-inspiring sight. Faded blue and gold stones jutted up from the rocks, forming a crenelated fortification. The wall would have been impassible, were it not for a ruined section at the right. Porfirio rode his horse to the base of the bulwark and peered up at the decorative rampart. "Bas-relief lions, elephants, and other beasts..."

I have seen this place before, Jessie recalled. He studied the area. *This is where Kisima exiled her advisor, Galamah.*

"Looks like the city's been raided," Hiram said, riding his horse gingerly across the breach.

Not quite, Jessie remembered. He now regretted singing. He rode toward the breach and asked, "Where is Eridu?"

They had forgotten about the prince. They searched near the ramparts, calling his name in as loud of voices as they dared. Yet, to no avail. The Erintul was nowhere to be found.

Hiram peered into the gloomy city. "Maybe he's past the threshold?"

Jessie tried to quell his nerves. "He'll be waiting on the concourse," he declared. Then, he ventured into the morose metropolis. Fragments of everyday life were strewn beneath his feet. Though he did not remember seeing them, the painted jars and decorative drinking vessels reminded him of a life he had never lived. He shivered with ghostly nostalgia and looked back.

The men had not moved. He shrugged and told the truth, "Trust me. The speaking stone showed me this place, once."

"Oh right, obviously." Porfirio grunted, "Because a prophetic vision is just so commonplace. Really calms the nerves of us common folk." He added as vast, ancient towers rose on either side of them. "I saw it in a hallucination!"

Jessie turned, "Quiet, Porf. This place is—" He shook his head and veered left, away from the thicket of apartments. They crossed onto the wide concourse. *The Way of Parsha*. The men gasped and reveled in the massive walkway. Jessie shivered, for it was like looking upon a corpse. *There was so much life on this street.* As they rode down the road, he saw fragments of memories he had not made himself. Cauldrons, discarded tools, and shattered black metal littered the massive street. The trees that Kisima had once gazed up at were now brown and bony.

The hooves of their horses echoed against the towering apartments. Whatever was in that city would know they were coming. Jessie peered to his right, down an alley shaded by tattered awnings. A skeleton tilted its head at him; its body was strewn up high, the limbs pinned by four separate spears. An assemblage of metal items rusted beneath the bones. Jessie patted Girl's neck. "Easy," he said, mostly for his own sake. He took out his rifle and peered down the promenade. The pyramid's peak pierced the stone canopy.

"My God," Porfirio gaped. He crossed his heart and said a prayer. "That's more a mountain than a temple." His fingers fidgeted at his holster.

Jessie said nothing. *If only they could have seen it before the sickness.* Knowing what Karakul had been made the ruin more haunting to traverse.

"I don't like this," Hiram whispered. "You think maybe Eridu meant to leave us?"

None replied. Though Jessie mistrusted the prince at first, he did not think the man would have willingly deserted them in the city. Jessie gazed at the growing menace of the massive pyramid. *Perhaps his fear overpowered his will, though.*

"Wait..." Hiram peered. "Is that—is that Eridu?"

Surely enough, at the base of the pyramid, they saw a man's broken body. They dismounted and rushed the corpse, dispersing a flock of feasting buzzards. They were heartened at what they saw—if heartened one could be from seeing a dead man.

"Don Marcos," Jessie whispered.

Porfirio spat, "Serves the fucker right."

Jessie looked at his friend sternly. "Don't say that." He frowned at the man's body and followed the clues of his death. He craned his neck and saw a trail of blood leading up the pyramid steps. "Seems like a ritualistic murder..." His stomach churned. *What if they did this to the twins?* He broke into a brisk walk. He searched the pyramid, dripping in sweat. His eyes twitched as he found it impossible to even blink.

"Jessie!" Porfirio called. "They aren't here!"

"But why is *he* dead, then?" Jessie growled. "What are those savages doing to them?"

"Jessie..." A warning was in the old man's voice. "This ain't the time."

He ignored him, charging down an alley in pursuit of what he believed to be footprints. He saw that they led into a darkened building. He darted into the dwelling and combed the dimly lit room until, to his great surprise, he stumbled upon a vase. It was dusty but for a lone streak. At its base, the layer of sand looked slightly compacted. Jessie leaned in to inspect the contents. However, the men's chatter finally got to him.

"We should not have come here," Hiram's voice shook with fear, "We should not have come here."

"He was right," Solomon stated.

"That weapon's not army-issued," Porfirio remarked grimly.

Jessie peered at the vase. Though he suspected some mischief in that room, it would have to wait. He left the building and squinted down the concourse. He did not need to ask what they were referring to. The answer walked toward them.

Eridu's mount stumbled down the wide road. The setting sun cast a long shadow behind the creature. The camel was soaked in blood. A shattered spear was embedded in its hindleg. It let out a mournful wail and collapsed, becoming another corpse upon the concourse.

Jessie jogged to his horse. He patted Girl's head and led her to a dark cleft between two large towers. He patted her mane and said, "Stay here, Girl. I'll be back soon."

The horse protested with a stomp of its hooves. It was smart enough to know it was being left behind.

"Sshh," Jessie patted her mane, calming her slightly. He whispered, for just the horse to hear, "If I don't come back, you get out of here."

"Where you think you runnin' off to?" Porfirio called.

"I found Eridu's trail," he replied. He gave Girl a final goodbye pet and walked toward the suspicious ruin. After hearing only *his* footsteps, he turned and gestured at their horses, "Get them out of sight." He had no time to persuade. "We're huntin' now."

Slower than Jessie would have liked, the trio gave in. They hid their horses and provisioned themselves with meager rations and ample ammunition. Porfirio took no food, but he had plenty of tobacco.

"Good," Jessie exhaled. He led them into the abandoned dwelling. "I think they took him in here." He darted to the suspicious vase and rummaged inside. He pulled out a bloody shirt and for a second, believed it belonged to Eridu. His heart sank and then rose when he realized it was a skirt. He sighed. Whoever had left the clothing was not who he was searching for.

"So he could be anywhere," Hiram groaned. "Fantastic. We should have listened to the son of a bitch and gone 'round."

Jessie discarded the skirt. "Let's not water before the planting. There's still something strange about this place." He did not wait for or even hear Hiram's quip. He crept further into the ruin.

Winding stairs led them into a roofless room. The sheen of the dappled light made the air around them glitter with dust. The floor was coated in a thick layer of sand and littered with odd artifacts. Porfirio knelt to examine one and gasped.

"What is it?" Jessie inquired, staring at the last bit of paint that still adorned the room. A myriad of colors dotted the walls, hinting at the remnants of a mosaic.

"Either the rattlers here is larger," Hiram answered for Porfirio. "Or that's from a man."

Jessie turned and sure enough, the sand had been parted with the width of a man. "Someone's been dragged. Recently, too."

Solomon went prone, "L-look here, Mr. Bingham."

Jessie did so, squatting beside the man and peering at the red, speckled sand. "I reckon that's blood." He got up and began tracing the trail. It was not hard, for the body must have recently been moved. They reached the far side of the roofless room just as the sun began to fall behind the pyramid. Darkness saturated the city as the company halted.

An inconspicuous cavity was carved into the rock. Though thin and jagged, the gap was large enough for a man.

"I'm not g-goin' in there," Solomon muttered. His eyes were fixed on the blood-stained rocks on either side of the cavity.

His older brother was less blunt about his trepidation. Hiram took a step back, "If he's dead—and by rights there's blood to prove it—why should we risk our skin for him?"

Porfirio stayed silent and deferred to the group.

Jessie did not care to be the group's arbiter. Nor did he wish to explore whatever lay within. Nevertheless, he could not stomach leaving Eridu behind. He looked at Solomon, "It would be bad luck to abandon someone to save another." He turned to Hiram, "He's their prince, too. Without him, we sure as hell are doomed." Finally, he met Porfirio's eyes.

The newspaperman took out a handkerchief and wiped the dirt off his pistol. "Hell, haunted caverns, ruined cities. More fodder for the masses when I publish this journal."

"And one day," Jessie faced the darkness, "I hope I can read it." He held his rifle close to his chest and squeezed through the gap. He led them into the abyssal tunnel. The foul darkness was impenetrable. He said and the cavern echoed, "Keep your sidearms ready. Ain't no tellin' what lurks down here."

Chapter 22

<hr>

"Seventy-seven men of the horse folk captured by Warchief Kabahum. Attrition culled the weak. Twenty-six sent to Taruk. Thirty-eight river folk brought by Warchief Sukurru; ten females to be sent to the harem. The rest go to Taruk. The late Warchief Nerugal brought only two slaves, none of tomb-building caliber. One female to be sent to the harem; the other not of breeding quality. She will not last long."

– Foreman Wardu's Ledger

Waves lapped against the shoreline. Saltwater wafted in the air. Elijah stared into the mist. He whispered, "There's a sea dragon out there, Ms. Thorne."

"Is there really?" Mary muttered. *I do not know how he can see anything in this fog.* Even if she could see more than a foot ahead of her, the water was not her immediate concern. Dawn had come and it had brought ominous sounds. Elijah could not hear it yet and that was good. But she could.

A baby cried.

A whip cracked.

A long chain rattled at dozens of points.

After a quiet second, the cycle continued. The infant bawled, now further away. The whip cracked. Dozens of souls stepped in unison. Metal clanked.

"What was that?" Cleona muttered.

They hear it too, now. Mary did not respond. They had been found, and not by friends. The whip gave way to the rattle. The metal clanged. The chain gang grew louder. The baby's bawling grew quieter. Mary rolled her fingers along her knuckles, skipping one at a time. The pattern and the physical touch distracted her brain from using its imagination. Soon, she no longer heard the crying baby.

Suddenly their cart began to roll gently. The wheels quieted. Cleona stared at Mary, who noticed the change too. "Ain't been a road since Belford," the young woman remarked. She gathered the frayed ends of her dirty dress and rolled them into balls.

Elijah's crossed legs vibrated. He inflated his cheeks. As the chain gang came closer, his body bounced faster. His cheeks deflated. The child craned his neck. His eyes went wide and he lowered his head below the side of the cart, "There's another monster."

Two of Asura's female guards rode past. "Many of them," Mary replied.

Cleona shuddered. "What could that be?"

Mary looked ahead. Unsurprised at seeing nothing, she dismissed their comments. Just then, the ground quivered; ripples went through their cart. Mary homed in on the source and heard a resonating hiss. A great shadow loomed. *Useless little orbs.* "Elijah, what am I looking at?"

The boy shook his head. "I don' got a clue. It's, It's big."

Mary could have inferred that from the damnable silhouette *it* made. "Well describe *it*, da—"

Like curtains, the fog abruptly parted. Even Mary could see what loomed before them: a steaming field of geysers. The earthen pustules hissed and popped, cloaking the adjacent shoreline in mist. Yet, that was not what had startled Elijah and Cleona. Mary shivered as a grand copper archway took a slow, unliving breath. The fog around the geysers briefly cleared. The metal arch groaned. Valves turned and hissed hot vapor. The steam floated toward the top of the arch, where a drape of red, vining plants basked in the humidity. Mary thought it looked like a serpent halfway submerged in the sand, draped in the devil's saddle.

The caravan passed directly under the arch. Mary swatted the fiery leaves out of her way; twisted fruit made her nose tingle. The bright light behind and before her was muted by a dark, red tint. She would have thought she were in a cave, were it not for the hissing valves and glinting copper. She gazed up at the construct's underbelly, wondering what technology (or religion) could have made the arch possible.

They emerged from the gloom. She was befuddled by the single serpentine pipe. So, when she heard the din of many more venting valves ahead and saw the faint outlines of additional arches lining the road—she gasped. She absorbed her surroundings. The shoreline was peppered with tidal pools, each containing a gasping geyser. Within every one of these pools, a grand archway rose. What was more, the archways were not isolated pieces of architecture.

To her right, Mary thought she espied great towers. She could not see much else, but she could hear the fountaining of water from their coppery heads. She could smell the produce at its base. The glint of green around each tower betrayed their function. The Lugal were farming. Here it seemed, the desert did not reign. *What deal did these savages make with the devil?*

"That's corn growin' there," Elijah commented. "And squash." He stared at the islands of greenery before turning back at the steaming arches. He sniffed the air and pointed toward the misty shoreline. "How are they waterin' crops with saltwater?"

Mary had no answer for the child. After a while, she grew accustomed enough to the din of the geyser fields to home in on the chain gang again. *They altered their course.* They were now moving parallel to Asura's band. The gang's march parted the tall grasses like a snake in water. When that dreadful chain rattled, crows cawed. One flew past Mary's head. It had something fleshy in its beak.

They came into a rolling meadow. Bees buzzed between artificial mounds of earth, atop which grew islands of corn. Squash sprawled out in the understory, cloaking the soil. Despite the verdancy of the meadow, Mary did not see any farmers. For all that bounty, not a soul sowed or reaped. The only building she saw was a large corn crib. The four pillars that kept the corn away from vermin were carved in the shape of a hoofed beast. The ramp leading to storage was shaped like an elephant's trunk.

The whipping sounded like popcorn now. The chain gang began to overtake them. Before long, the sounds of their march began to shift, growing lower in pitch as they passed Mary's band. She looked around at *her* slavers. They rode slowly, as if they would prefer to linger. *Or they do not want to reach their destination.* Mary recalled what the hunchback had said, *'The Lugal loved Nerugal. But Asura did not.'*

Whatever he had meant by that, it was clear that Mary found herself amidst a plot. She looked ahead at Ethel. She could not make out the particulars but she was sure her hair was still braided in imitation of the matriarch's. *She has not left the woman's side. I wonder if she's been told anything? Doubtful...* Mary snorted a chuckle. Even on a march to damnation, she was planning a con.

She stared at the Lugal lands, wiped her eyes, and craned her neck. The rumors of a town were manifesting. The road widened. Mudbrick homes with flat roofs appeared. Their cart rolled steadily along. One of the slavers yelled something. A voice replied from above. Mary looked up.

Standing on those rooftops were many people, all clothed in vibrant hues. Their dark eyes looked down on them with curiosity. Children pointed at them and spoke excitedly. *'The freakshow has come to town,'* she imagined they were saying. She bowed her head.

It was strange to hear the Lugal language spoken by children. The guttural consonants and throaty vowels had been solely the language of her captors. Now, little girls giggled and goggled in the same gross speech. Mary could feel juvenile laughs directed at her. She peered out her periphery.

A line of Lugal had gathered outside the houses. Elegant skirts were worn by men and women alike. Precious gems lined their bodies and adorned their fingers, though none of the stones were black. Mary glanced at her frayed and muddy outfit. *These peasants are better dressed than you've ever been...*

The cart rolled to a stop.

Was their march finally over? Were they at the end of the Forlorn Trail? Mary listened. She heard the Lugal speaking quickly. She heard Ethel and Asura exchange a few words. A gruff man growled. A few fearful words replied. *That is not a slaver's language.* Mary looked up. Her jaw dropped. Joined at the feet by a weighty chain were at least a hundred slaves. Their hands were bound and their ankles were chained one after the other. All waited in a queue as, one by one, they were judged by a burly Lugal.

Cleona whispered, "Those are Tlacon. And Kuahtec"

Mary was dumbstruck. For months, all the frontier had wondered where the nomadic natives had gone. The Tlacon and Kuahtec had been the greatest threat to Belford and the western towns. They even bested the 6th cavalry (giving Biggs even more reason to hire more deputies). Then, as all the frontier feared the worst—the tribes had vanished.

Elijah whispered, "They got captured, too?"

Mary swallowed. *So this is where they went. Enslaved just like us.* She lied to Elijah, "It will be okay."

The burly man growled and the chain gang took a step forward. He inspected a young girl, a Tlacon no older than Cleona. He barked another word and two slavers removed the chains from her ankles, separated her from the others, and ushered her out of view. The burly man ordered the line to advance. The next to be inspected was a strong-looking Kuahtec. He exuded an aura of power.

The burly Lugal kicked him in the groin. The Kuahtec fell to his knees. Two other slavers rushed over and unshackled his feet. Then, they removed him from the line and ferried him to a wharf at the water's edge. Moored at one of the docks, though, was no boat Mary had ever seen. For one, it was so massive Mary could reliably make out its features. There were no men on the deck, for it was convex like a turtle's shell and lined with deadly spikes. At the bow of the ship, Mary espied a snake's head made of iron.

Elijah swallowed, "I guess it weren't a sea dragon."

All her experiences up to that point had yet to change Mary's worldview. What she believed to be true was still true, despite being a captive. She had been the mayor of a frontier town. The world was mapped, and a few native tribes still vied for the least populated parts. Now, she felt like a child just born into the world. She stared at the ship which had no oarsmen, nor any sails, and decided, *the frontier is a lie.* She whispered to Elijah, "Stay close to me."

One by one, the slaves were dispersed to their respective destinations. After the queue of Tlacon and Kuahtec was dispersed, Ama Asura met with the burly man. She spoke with her head raised. The taskmaster nodded, saying nothing while the matriarch led. Then, he uttered a single word. *"Nerugal?"*

He wants to know where he is. How will she explain that rapist's demise? Mary listened anxiously. Whatever Asura said, she did so with ease. Even a deaf man could have detected the deceit in her tone.

The taskmaster was silent for a moment. He replied with a word Mary did not recognize. From his inflection, she surmised he was asking another question. *"Air-eee-doo?"*

Asura stuttered. Mary squinted, noting the matriarch had shifted and was now pointing her body away from the taskmaster. Asura then bowed her head. Mary did not need to know the language to know the matriarch told another lie. She wiped her eyes and pointed at the slave cart.

The taskmaster froze. After a moment, he began whispering. Whatever he was saying, Asura grew increasingly frustrated. Just as Mary was beginning to hear his voice clearly, the burly man cut himself off and glanced at the slaves. He eyed Mary and cocked his head at Asura.

The matriarch called for Namru. The hunchback brought out Ethel Bingham. The taskmaster smiled mischievously at the girl. He nodded as he planned some devilry. He raised his eyebrow as well as four fingers.

Asura swatted his hand away. The taskmaster looked insulted and yet, it seemed the power dynamic favored the matriarch. The Lugal looked at his long parchment. He pointed at the dozen of slaves waiting at the wharf and then flashed three fingers in Asura's face.

He is not happy with her haul, Mary guessed.

Asura again denied him, raising two fingers.

The taskmaster snarled and gestured at the cart. Mary's heart plummeted into her stomach. *She still wants Elijah.*

Namru came to the cart. He plucked Elijah's hand from Mary's as one does fruit off the vine. Only Elijah's eyes said anything, and they practically shrieked. Mary wanted to lunge after. All she could do was pick at her cuticles. She felt like a cow in a slaughterhouse. Finally, Elijah called out for her, "Ms. Thorne!"

Mary wished her hearing was not so good. She bowed her head and focused on the burly taskmaster. The man gnashed his teeth and growled at Asura. The matriarch ignored him, instead kneeling before Elijah.

"Ama Asura," she re-introduced.

The boy looked at his feet.

"Elijah Bingham," Ethel replied, smiling at Asura.

The matriarch did not move. After another wait, she said, emphatically, "Ama. Asura."

The boy raised his head defiantly. His voice cracked. "I don't need a new mama."

Ethel was mortified, but the matriarch did not know any better. She smiled at the boy and pinched his cheek. Her nails left a mark. Then, she undid his bindings and patted his arm. She stood up and flashed a smile at Mary.

Worse things had been said to her; worse still had been done. Never had Mary felt so angry. She wanted to snap the conniving crone's neck. Better yet, she wanted to break her legs and lather her in her own blood. *I would savor the coyote's howls as they homed in on you.* Her neck cracked from the building tension as she watched Asura ruffle Elijah's hair. She took their arms and brought them to the wharf.

But instead of going to the beastly, iron ship—they joined a line of women boarding several canoes. The minuscule vessels looked like minnows beside a giant, basking turtle. As the men were prodded into the dark confines of the spiked ship, Asura leisurely led the twins toward a canoe. Mary lost them in the crowd of well-dressed Lugal.

Suddenly, the taskmaster exhaled and his eyes narrowed on Cleona. His orders were swift. Two slavers came into the cart and took her by each arm. "Where are you leading me?" she dared ask.

One of the foul men grinned; the other frowned. She was dragged toward the canoes.

Mary thought she understood. The men would be taken to the armored vessel; the women would go with the well-dressed Lugals. Mary picked at her cuticles. She tensed her thighs and narrowed any gap between her legs. She raised her chin and awaited the taskmaster's inspection.

The brute looked at her for barely a second. A disgusted look permeated his face. He rubbed a fat finger across her cheek and over her eyes. He gazed at his moist fingertip and grunted. He said a few words which made the other slavers laugh.

He turned his back on Mary and gave his command. The slavers took her out of the cart, but neither smiled at her. They looked away with immense repulsion. They cut Don Marcos' old bindings off her ankles and still she struggled to walk. Rather than take her to Cleona and the other women—they took her to the men. Had Mary any remnant of her pride, she might have been offended.

Instead, she gazed across the wharf at the twins. Ethel was being lifted onto a canoe and obscured from view. Elijah, however, craned his neck and watched Mary go. Their gazes met and Mary welled with tears. Her knees buckled and she halted. She felt weak for admitting it, even in her thoughts, but the child had given her so much strength. The slavers tugged at her to continue walking.

"Ms. Thorne!" he called for her.

Mary had to look away. For her sake, she had to forget the child. Like most of her friends, the child had been in her life just long enough for his leaving to hurt.

The iron ship awaited her. Man-sized spikes jutted out of the hull. Steam burst from the snakelike prow. The ship was terrifying. Mary guessed that was the point. She joined the other slaves in a line. Step by step, she crossed under the metal threshold and went below deck.

The first level of the hull stunk of sulfur. Lugal warriors walked briskly to various locations, ignoring (or enjoying) the arrival of new slaves. Mary kept her face hidden and was left alone. She walked down a flight of echoing stairs. Once on the second level, her nose was assaulted. Sweat and fouler stenches permeated the air.

Mary was prodded to continue. She rubbed shoulders and other body parts with dripping, stinking slaves who could not make way for her arrival. An iron door shut behind her, enclosing them all in darkness. The warped wooden floor above provided only slivers of orange illumination.

Mary stared into the gloom. Dozens of eyes, some curious and others hateful, looked back at her.

Mary stood with her back to the door and looked at her feet. Some slaves spoke their native languages. She could not tell which were Kuahtec or Tlacon. They sounded the same to her. There were others, though, who spoke *her* language.

"A woman," said a slave.

"What an insult."

The ship unmoored. Rhythmic splashes heralded a new chapter of her enslavement. The salty air infiltrated the ship, infesting the already rancid air with a fishy smell. Soon, she grew quite nauseous. Mary had never been on a ship before. The only thing keeping her from vomiting was the constant ridicule.

"Look at her eyes. She'll be dead before the end of the week."

"I can see why the Lugal did not want to breed her."

"I'll take her."

Mary focused on her breathing. If she was going to survive, she had to show stoic resolve. She could not vomit. She dared not weep. She took a long breath and tried to find strength in past experiences. Although, when she went to tell herself she had been through worse—she decided that was—at last—a lie.

What is the use? She asked herself. *Why stay strong? To be a more lucrative slave?* She swallowed and thought the terrible truth: *It would be best to die quickly.* The muscles in her cheeks surrendered. Her lips quivered. Tears flowed silently. She ignored the other slaves. She heard only the thumping of her forlorn heart.

That was until a commotion came from the deck. A Lugal let out a surprised shout. This was followed by many other voices. She heard splashing. Footsteps stomped across the ship. All the slaves held their breath, wondering what new development now took place. *They are coming below,* she heard.

Suddenly the iron door opened. The slavers prodded a little boy with the hilts of their savage blades. A whimper escaped him. The child waddled into the enclosure. The irons at his heels dragged behind his tiny feet. The slavers shut them in again.

Mary gasped. She knelt before the child, barely able to form a whisper from the shock in her voice. "Elijah... What did she do to you?"

The child looked up and flashed a weak smile. "I couldn't let you be alone."

Mary choked. She turned away in disbelief. Alone was all she had ever been. A dozen times she tried to speak. A dozen times the truth proved too difficult to describe. The only words she could say were the ones she knew Elijah did not want to hear. "What about Ethel?"

The boy did not reply and Mary began to fear she had upset him, that he would ask to be taken back to Asura and she would be alone forever. She stuttered, trying to find anything at all to say, "Your hair is wet."

Elijah scratched his scalp, "You already left the dock."

Her voice cracked, "You jumped in?" She felt she was in some dream which soon would become a nightmare. She shook her head in disbelief and asked, "Why?"

"My daddy once said," Elijah began, "that you wasn't a bad person. You just had to play a bad part in lots of people's stories."

"Your father said that a-about me?"

Elijah came up to her and leaned on her.

She wanted to hold his head at her breast. Due to the shackles on her wrists, all she could do was push him away. "You said you did not need another, uh..."

Elijah stared at her, his eyes wet with his own tears. "I thought nobody was like my mama. I thought they was all mean, like Ms. Rosalee or Ama Asura."

Mary snorted a self-deprecating laugh, "And I am not mean?" Her voice quieted to only a whimper, "What lies did Jessie tell you to believe the best in me?" Again, she turned away.

And again, Elijah Bingham went to her side. "My daddy told me once, that you shouldn't get mad at the stepping stone for bein' wet. Just move to the next stone."

There are no stones left to step to, little one.

"Do you like fish, Ms. Thorne?"

Mary's chest convulsed as if from a hiccup. "I do," she whispered.

Elijah looked toward the walls of their rocking enclosure. "I bet there's some out there."

Mary nodded. She replied weakly, "I bet there is." She yearned for him to lean on her. She craved the feeling of his affection but dared not ask for it with so many people listening.

"W-want me to catch you some?"

Mary said nothing. How could she? The truth was they would never see water as a fisher. They would see it as livestock saw water. Mary flashed a smile at Elijah. She could not lie. It did not behoove the child to fantasize about a life that was no longer for them.

"Mam—" Elijah caught himself and went silent; Mary heard that first syllable well enough. Her heartbeat increased. She had been called so many things in her life, but never that. She yearned to hear that word just as she also craved for the child to hate her. Elijah turned to his side. Mary thought he might leave her alone. She braced for the fact and resolved to not care. She sat down and put her back to the wall.

Elijah sat as well, leaving some space between them. Eventually, he leaned on his hands. Over the course of the next minute, he inched toward her clumsily, dragging his irons on the ground. Finally, the boy curled his body into a ball and rested his head on her lap. Despite his shackles, his little hands tried to hold onto her.

The walls she had carefully constructed since childhood crumbled. Mary Anne Thorne sobbed as she never had before. She tried to compose herself but the floodgates would not close. The tears flowed until the reservoir emptied. Only when she had no more tears to spare, when her cheeks were as salty as the water surrounding them, could she calm herself.

For the first time since going blind, the act of wiping her eyes did not coat her hands in puss. Her tears had washed the filth away. She looked down at Elijah and began to speak. Only, the little boy was now asleep, drooling on her leg. Mary chuckled and swept her hand along the boy's back, tickling him slightly.

A native behind asked Mary, "Are you that boy's mother?"

Mary turned her head. Though she had suspected eavesdroppers, she had not expected to see the entire congregation of slaves looking at her. Strangely, she saw them a deal clearer than before Elijah had joined her. Their eyes were not suspicious, nor were their faces cold or cruel. A few looked at her with tears of their own.

Mary flashed a faint smile and looked down at Elijah. "I am now."

Chapter 23

—————————◆—————————

"When the eyes act as the feet, the legs become deformed. When ego reigns, the neck becomes crooked. When the mind conquers the body but not itself, both wither."

— The Codex of Kul

At the start, the darkness was impossible to navigate. They felt their way like blind men, all the while speaking to one another out of fear of getting lost.

"Where's this lead, ya think?" Hiram whispered.

Jessie did not answer. Strangely, he was beginning to feel as if he knew his way through the crumbling cavern. He blindly dragged his hands across reliefs he knew adorned the walls. Kisima's flight into the catacombs had imprinted memories he had never made. It was as if he navigated as Kisima and not Jessie.

After an unnerving silence, Solomon gasped, "What was that?"

Jessie turned and said, as calmly as he could, "Relax. This passage leads beneath the central pyramid."

Porfirio muttered. "Saw it in that devil stone, eh?"

Jessie ignored him, deciding to answer by elaborating. "There's a mention of this place in the Infinite Library, yes."

"So you know where we are going?" Hiram whispered in awe. He was practically standing on Jessie's heels.

"Not quite," he replied, wiping Hiram's vaporous breath off the back of his neck.

"S-so," Solomon stuttered, trying not to let the quiet overtake the company. His voice trembled, "W-what d-do you think happened to this, uh, city?"

A moist breath wet Jessie's neck. *Son of a bitch,* he thought, *give me some room, Hiram.* He wiped his neck and muttered, "You remember Eridu saying his people were struck by a deadly sickness?"

"It wiped these folk out, too?" Hiram intuited. His voice had come from further back, this time.

Still, a hot breath blew on his neck. *Must be Solomon,* Jessie decided. He scratched his head and stated, "Not entirely. One of the priestesses gave Eyes of Ur to the orphans in the city. She hoped that one of them might, uh..." he paused, not sure how to articulate an idea he did not understand. "She hoped one of them might have a vision. And then, find a cure."

"That must-a been like givin' a loaded revolver to a toddler," Hiram whispered.

"Mm," Jessie hummed.

"What exactly do them, uh, Eyes of Ur..." Solomon started. "What they do, exactly?"

Jessie tried to speak, but the hot breath distracted him. "Damn it, Porf. Give me some room."

Porfirio whispered, "Any more room and I'll lose ya." True enough, it seemed the old man was far behind Jessie.

Jessie halted and told them all to do the same.

One pair of footsteps quieted. Another two pattered to a halt. Jessie listened, breathless. Hearing nothing, he exhaled. He continued walking and whispered his response to Solomon's question. "The Eyes don't do anything *exactly.* It's all relative." Jessie sighed. *I only saw Kisima because... Because her anguish mirrored mine. The Eye only knows like for like, perhaps.* He frowned. If he could not understand the Library, how could those three? "It's like Eridu said, all them days ago—explaining it would be like teaching a frog to fly."

"I-is it like reading a book?" Solomon inquired.

"No, not, n-not quite," Jessie mulled over the thought in his head. "At times, the Eye is mostly an ambiance, like a soft breeze. A song you ain't realize you listenin' to 'til you hummin' day and night. But sometimes, it seems to come alive—as if something awakes."

"What was that?" Porfirio shivered.

They all stopped. Footsteps continued before fading.

"I think it was me," Solomon admitted. "I keep steppin' on someone."

"Ah, well," Porfirio started walking only to stop once again. His pace quickened, "Let's keep goin' before somethin' down *here* awakes." His body brushed past Jessie's, though there was hardly any weight to the man. *He's got to eat more and smoke less*, Jessie thought.

"Is it like bein' drunk?" Solomon pestered.

This is like explaining mathematics to Ethel. They just are not ready, yet. He sighed, "It is more of a... hallucination. A dream particular to the dreamer, though linked to those who've gone to sleep before."

Hiram asked, "Think them stones were the cause of all them cracked wagoneers?"

"I reckon so. Remember old Dan Bandelier?"

Hiram snorted, "I do. And I don't fancy rememberin' his fate, or that bastard Kilthorpe."

Solomon stopped his teeth from clattering long enough to ask, "What about Kilthorpe?"

"He had the man's straitjacket displayed in a cabinet," His brother explained. "Imagine that. The quickest draw reduced to a bumbling mess that can't even say his name. All for goin' down the Forlorn Trail."

"The man's cupidity what done him in," Porfirio whispered. "We ain't destined for the same comeuppances."

Jessie halted. Despite shoving past Jessie, Porfirio's voice was still coming from the back. *Unless that shove wasn't Porfirio.* He listened to the trio's conversation, noting the placement of each man.

Solomon's teeth clattered. "What could make a man forget his name?"

Behind, Jessie noted. He did not answer.

"Mr. Bingham?" Hiram called, fearful they had lost him in the dark.

Behind, Jessie heard. He addressed the question, keeping an ear all the while for any sound coming from in front of the company. "The Eye of Ur seems keen on riddles. Aphorisms. Like it is testin' you. It has a way of makin' a man feel small and big at the same time."

"You're startin' to sound as cryptic as Eridu," Porfirio noted.

Behind, Jessie gulped. He gripped his rifle and said, "I want everyone to listen very carefully."

"What is it?" Hiram scrambled for his revolver, audibly.

"Now don' get jumpy on me," Jessie warned. "I don't want to get my head blown off because one of y'all shoots into the dark, but..."

Someone coughed. Jessie could not tell who. He found the echo so distorted, it seemed as if it came from ahead.

"But what?"

"I think we're bein' followed."

Solomon stuttered, "S-should we turn around, then?"

"I doubt we'll lose our trail if we turn," Porfirio whispered.

"Stay alert," Jessie ordered. "We cannot go back."

Time passed as shades of grey in the darksome catacombs. A quiet hour could have been a minute; a startling sound could spawn a ceaseless second. Fear ebbed and flowed. Temperatures rose as they descended and the harsh, dry air became humid and sticky. A stench permeated the dark corridor, growing as a faint light began to glow.

None dared remark about the light, the widening of the cavern, nor the loud echoes of their approach. Jessie kept a firm grip on his rifle, listening for any sign of movement. As the illumination increased, he began to see familiar carvings on the wall. The sense of déjà vu was like nothing he had ever experienced.

To his left, he saw a bas-relief carving depicting a robed man wearing a plumed crown. As they progressed, the man took off his clothes, his jewels, and finally—his crown. The man was shown walking for a time until, as the tunnel opened into a vast antechamber, the man began to crawl.

Jessie might have followed the man on his journey, were it not for a red script scribbled over the remainder of the relief.

"I wonder what it says?" Solomon whispered.

"Nothing good," Porfirio guessed.

Jessie had never seen the symbols with his own eyes, never written them nor spoken the words they represented. All the same, he knew what was written. He had heard those words spoken, seen the man who had spoken them. "The failures of our forebears echo longer than the triumphs."

Jessie walked ahead, knowing now exactly where in the catacombs they had come. He exited the antechamber and entered the main mausoleum of Karakul's Lugals. Orange orbs held by statues lit his way. Jessie turned, expecting to see an ornate sarcophagus. What he remembered was not what appeared before him.

Each coffin was unceremoniously defaced. The painted faces were broken, the lids opened, and the remains scattered. The mausoleum was a carpet of bone fragments mixed interchangeably with precious jewels. *This was no tomb raiding,* Jessie knew. He stepped carefully over a withered heap of glittering bone dust.

"Stop that breathin' on my neck," Hiram suddenly hissed.

"You was breathin' on mine," his brother snarled.

Porfirio growled, "Well one of y'all best stop steppin' on my boots."

"You was steppin' on mine!" Solomon argued.

"You dumb bastard," Hiram hissed. "He's behind you."

"Wait," Solomon's voice shook with a sudden realization. "I'm in the back."

"Y'all," Jessie stopped. The others did so as well. A strange pattering faded into quiet.

Porfirio whispered, "Y'hear that echo?"

"There weren't an echo," Solomon knew.

Suddenly, Jessie saw a shadow slip between the pillared hall. He raised his rifle and signaled to Porfirio. The man nodded and crept forward, taking cover behind a headless statue. The orb it held caused Porfirio's pistol to cast a twisted shadow.

Jessie stared down the barrel of his rifle. He followed a flash of movement to his left. By the time he had a clear shot, the veiled figure had skittered behind a shattered sarcophagus.

It is coming closer, Jessie knew. He cleared his throat, "Show yourself!"

Only labored breathing replied. A second later, the shadow glided forward, hiding now behind a pile of desecrated remains.

"It don't move like a man," Porfirio whispered. The figure came closer, zigzagging behind the debris of a shattered tomb. As it ran, Jessie saw what he meant. The shadow's head was disproportionately larger than the rest of its body. When it ran, the head hung low on a hunched back. The legs were bent even in motion and the feet were small.

Again, the figure moved. Just as Jessie got a clear shot, it evaded him. The shadow skulked out of sight; its breathing almost sounded like laughing.

Suddenly, they heard a soft footfall behind them. Jessie did not immediately turn, though he should have. Hiram roared, "Solly! Look out!"

Before Jessie could turn, Solomon crashed into him. He fell face-first upon the skull of an old king.

"Holy hell," Porfirio gasped, firing a shot.

Jessie staggered to his feet and fired a shot into the darkness.

A high-pitched, animalistic laugh mocked him in reply.

Jessie put his back against the wall. He aimed his rifle haphazardly, searching for the specter in the shadows. Only now, he saw two figures darting through the dark. He glanced at Hiram and Solomon, who were still on the ground. "Get up, quick! There's more than one!"

Solomon crawled from under his brother and pushed him, "Hiram. Get up! Get yo—" Like a thread being snipped, his words were cut off. "Hiram?"

Jessie diverted his attention. A bolt was lodged in Hiram's back, though it looked like no normal dart or arrow. *It looks like a scorpion.* Six metal legs gripped Hiram's crimson clothes. A bronze tail pierced his skin.

Hiram lifted his head. "Sss—" his mouth frothed. He tried to reach for his brother. He collapsed, twitching.

"Good God," Jessie gasped. He gripped his rifle. When the shadows moved, he fired another shot. Not only did the specter evade him, but three new figures now skittered toward them, giggling as they came.

"Hiram!" Solomon shrieked, pushing the now motionless body.

"Solomon," Porfirio yelled, firing his pistol. "We need ya!"

"He's dead," the man's brother wept. He shrieked, "Hiram!"

"Sounded like he saved your life," Porfirio spoke rapidly. He fired another shot; a guttural cry came from one of the figures. "Don't let that be for nothing!"

Solomon could not. He began to hyperventilate, pushing his brother's corpse. "Get up! Don't leave me out here!" He plucked the metal scorpion from his back and cradled Hiram's head.

"God damn it!" Jessie fired his rifle; the round ricocheted off the rocks. "It's just us, Porf."

A shadow launched itself from cover. More a creature than a man, the thing leapt at them with thin, emaciated legs. Its gigantic head was terrible to behold, for bored into its eye sockets were two, onyx gems. Jessie could see the scars where he had surgically carved out his eyeballs. He fired at the figure. Chunks of skull and brain rained onto the ground. The creature landed at Jessie's feet.

Its legs were so bowed, its feet so shrunken, it was as if the entire lower half was vestigial. The steaming stone eyes were drowned in a puddle of blood.

All was suddenly very quiet.

"Leave us!" Jessie commanded. "Or you will end up like him!"

The shadows hissed in reply. One by one, the evasive figures revealed themselves. No longer did they skitter or sprint. A dozen disfigured souls lumbered toward them. Porfirio fired a shot at one; when it fell—another took its place.

Jessie did not know what to do. He fired shot after shot, but it deterred the lumbering men little. Indeed, killing them only seemed to add more to their ranks. After seven shots, Jessie's rifle let out a dull crack. He would have to reload.

The hunched beasts were encircling them. Their bejeweled eyes stared at them with cruel curiosity.

Jessie looked around. Past the tombs, at the other side of the hall, was a dark passageway. He knew not where it led. "We need to run," he decided. "Forward, through that tunnel."

Porfirio took a step toward the exit, "Solomon, son. If you are goin' to sacrifice yourself, do give me your brother's weapon."

Solomon's hand lingered on his brother's shoulder for a moment longer. He equipped Hiram's revolver and stood up. His entire body quaked. He pointed the dual revolvers at the throng, "If I don't make it out of here, Mr. Pacheco. You'll bring Cleona my vows?"

Porfirio lowered his chin, "I can do that."

Jessie gripped his rifle like a staff, "Alright. On three."

Porfirio methodically reloaded his pistol.

"One."

The creatures hissed, the gems in their divergent eye sockets swirled with liquid color. Their long fingernails scraped the surface of sarcophagi. The gangrel people had them encircled.

"Two."

Porfirio took out his handkerchief and wiped the dirt off his cheek.

"Three."

They charged forward. The only figure blocking the exit was short and shriveled. He looked almost like Jessie, aside from the atrophied legs and self-mutilated face. Jessie took no pity on him for the similarities; he swung his grandfather's rifle. He knocked the beastly man to the ground, forcing a way through.

They sprinted until the corridor abruptly ended. "Feel for the way," Jessie called. He patted the stone hastily until he cried out, "Here!"

"Right be—" Solomon was cut off. A thumping sound was heard, followed by a terrible shriek, "Jessie!" Twin revolvers reverberated.

Jessie whirled around just in time to see Solomon sliding into the darkness. Twin slugs shot into the darkness, ricocheting against the stone. Jessie leaped after Solomon's hand. "Hold on," he yelled as his own body began to slide. Whatever had grabbed the young man was far stronger than Jessie had realized. He screamed, "Porf!"

Porfirio barely aimed his pistol. He inhaled, cocked his brow, and fired. A single shot zipped past Jessie's ear. A shriek was followed by a hiss. Light feet skittered into the void.

Jessie helped Solomon up. The young man looked as if he were about to vomit. He accused, "Y-you could have shot me, old man!"

"And I might still if you get nabbed again." He broke into a sprint, "Come on!"

The labyrinth echoed with the howls of their pursuers. Rabid footsteps followed them through the darkness. Darts soared past their ears. Little, metal scorpions latched onto the rocks and stabbed the stones with their venom. Eventually, they came to a narrow bridge. The blackness below was greater than anything before. It was a void.

"You two first," Jessie yelled.

Porfirio swayed as he went, almost falling were it not for Solomon's hand on his shoulder. For his part, Jessie seemed to know the bridge. He suspected Kisima had come to this point in her flight.

Suddenly, gangrel appendages reached up from below. Howling creatures nipped at their heels. A hand with monstrous fingernails reached out from beneath the bridge and latched onto Jessie's ankle. He shrieked and hit the hand with the butt of his rifle. The hand tightened its grip and pulled Jessie toward the darkness. He slipped toward the abyss.

Solomon grabbed Jessie just in time. With his free hand, he fired his pistol. The beast shrieked and released its hold. The long nails sliced into Jessie's flesh.

Solomon heaved him up and panted, "If I don't get to die today, neither do you."

Jessie smiled weakly. He looked back at the narrow walkway. "They're closing the gap."

The catacombs clanged. Past footsteps echoed beside the present, creating a crackling din. The hissing laughter grew quiet, but it never faded entirely. They came upon crossroad after crossroad. Every time, Jessie felt he knew the way. "Right," he panted. "Left." The labyrinth walls widened as they went. Their steps echoed like thunder in the cavern. Hails of darts flew past them, slamming into the stone. Jessie and Solomon could have easily outrun their pursuers, but they dogged Porfirio's weary stride.

Luckily, a faint glow was coming from the far end of the hall. He felt the memory of Kisima in that terrible pit. Every turn brought him closer. Jessie's déjà vu assured him they would soon be safe. There *was* a light at the end of the tunnel. He knew it. There had to be. *For Porfirio's sake.*

The old man rasped, "I ain't got much left in me." He pulled the journal from his back pocket. "If you would be so kind as to see this to a publication house."

Jessie handed the journal back, "You see it yourself. We ain't dyin' here."

But Porfirio could not keep up any longer. Jessie towed him behind, tripping on the now sandy stone. His slipping feet heartened him and soon, he saw it: a thin fissure in the rock. Crimson light slashed into the cave.

Jessie turned, "We've made it, Porf!"

"That crack is thinner than the one that brought us into this hellhole!"

Jessie went to the exit and oriented his body parallel to the fissure, "It's the only—" A figure obstructed the way. Still in her regal garments and garbed in fine jewelry, the skeleton of Kisima was lodged in the crevice. A dismembered arm lay beside a butcher's carver at the fissure's mouth.

The hissing now grew louder. Gemstone eyes peered out at them from all corners of the hall.

Jessie pulled Kisima's skeleton out of the way. "You first, Porf."

Porfirio swatted at his lower back. His face suddenly changed. His hand lingered. His face folded into a pained expression. He ground his teeth and yanked. "Son of a—oh. Oh dear." A scorpion dart was in his hand. A green poison still coated the metallic tail. His hands shook even more than usual. His face went pale. Porfirio dropped the dart, wheezing.

"Porf!" Jessie tried pulling him toward the fissure.

"I already been go—" he paused to wheeze. Porfirio leaned forward, bracing his body on his knees. His windpipe was narrowing with every breath. He looked up and grinned solemnly, "I ain't goin' no farther."

"Porf," Jessie began. His voice broke, "I can't do this alone."

"Might be you can't," Porfirio took a deep breath and peered into the catacombs. "But we can't go together."

Jessie choked on his words, "Don't leave me out here."

"This adventure has been great fun, Jessie. The finest retirement I could have hoped for." Porfirio turned his back on Jessie. "But a gentleman," he paused to catch his breath, "knows when to say farewell to a good thing."

Jessie could say and do nothing. He glanced out at the encroaching wall of soulless, gemstone eyes.

Porfirio looked at the mob and then back at Jessie. His voice splintered into two pitches—one low and weary, the other high and strained. "Who knows, maybe *I* will finally get to be in the paper."

"Ain't nobody want to read about you," Solomon declared, pulling Porfirio by his dirty collar. He barked at Jessie, "Keep it moving. I'll get him through with nothin' but a shaved mustache."

Jessie nodded and squeezed through the fissure. When he looked back, Solomon and Porfirio were still lodged in the rocks.

He clamored back to the pair, but Solomon swatted him away. "I got 'im, you make way for us."

The cruel cackling of the cavernous horde grew to a crescendo, but it was joined by Porfirio's hearty laughter. The creatures hissed and Porfirio hissed back. "What a way to die!" he laughed. He pointed his pistol.

Jessie struggled, squeezing himself through ever tighter gaps in the rocks. He could smell the desert, he could feel the heat. The sunlight finally struck his skin. Five shots rang out from the depths.

Chapter 24

<hr>

"Taruk was the second mightiest city-state, after Namsammun itself. When the shoreline receded, however, the city was abandoned. Ever after, the sprawling ruins became the playground of Lugals. There, in the vast nothingness, they contemplate their mortality and build monuments to spite it."

– The Codex of Kul

They sailed for perhaps a day until disembarking. The Lugal freed their wrists and let them walk of their own volition. Still, many slaves including Mary struggled to find their footing. Most had cramps, aching joints, and numb limbs. So, when they were not ushered into the same dingy carts Mary was used to, she relished the opportunity to walk. Even after hours under the hot sun, she still appreciated the simple freedom to move her legs.

The slavers rode on either side. They made it very clear that the slaves were not on a stroll. If anyone strayed from the march, they were whipped back into formation. This was enough of a warning for some. However, one young man dared to escape. At noon, when the slavers were all taking a quick drink beneath the shade of a mesquite tree, he bolted.

The slavers let him get a head start. They laughed as he ran and jeered when he looked back at them. Finally, two men sluggishly mounted and rode off to capture him. They dragged him back with his hands bound. His left eye was purple when he was shoved back into formation.

"That was unwise, Kuruk," admonished a tall man. Mary assumed he was a Kuahtec from the beads in his hair.

The one named Kuruk grinned, "Now we know they are arrogant. It will benefit us to know their hearts." Mary figured he was a Tlacon from the horse tattoos on his forearms. Each horse symbolized one mustang he had broken.

"They enslave men," said the Kuahtec. The green and blue beads in his long hair rattled. "Of course they are arrogant. And now they will know you are brash."

"Better to be foolish than to be a coward," replied the Tlacon named Kuruk.

The Kuahtec raised his brow.

Kuruk grinned.

The Kuahtec gave the slightest smirk.

Kuruk patted the man's back, "If only they had captured your brother."

"Hotah is a fine chief," replied the one named Tahatan.

"For all his fierceness, he has no voice," Kuruk grunted. "He dared not argue with Chief Hotah about his vision. Now look at us!"

Mary listened attentively. She recalled a time that seemed so far gone, when the strangest thing that had happened on the frontier was the disappearance of the two tribes. The Kuahtec had lived in Belford before settlers pushed them out; the Tlacon had wandered up and down the Copper River before the ranchers chased them away. The two tribes had joined together to make war against the frontier. Ashwood was raided, Belford was threatened, and the army was called on.

It had seemed that a terrible war was brewing. Then, just after winning a battle against the 6th cavalry—both tribes vanished without a trace.

A man ahead of Mary spat, "Hotah be damned. Without his vision, we would have stayed on the plains."

Another native eyed Mary and Elijah, "Look at them. Weak. Sickly. They would have been trampled under our horses."

Mary held Elijah's hand and ignored them. She could feel the little boy's pulse. She tried to distract him by pointing, "What is that, Eli?" She could see only a faint outline of something large coming over the horizon.

The child squinted. "It looks like a boat. Not like the one we was on. This one looks like an old wooden boat. It gots holes for oars."

They got closer and Mary saw the vessel for herself. It was larger than the boat they were ferried in, with two splintered masts and a rusted, iron cap at the prow of the vessel. Half the ship was submerged in the ground. She wiped the puss off her eyes.

Kuruk abruptly asked her, "Were you born blind?"

Mary looked to her left. She stuttered, "I can still see, somewhat. And uh, no. I was not."

The Tlacon inspected her closely. He popped his lips. "I did not think so." He looked away with no explanation as to why he had asked the question.

Mary was acutely conscious of how damp her cheeks were. With no bonds around her wrists, it seemed her itchy eyes were all she could focus on.

Kuruk frowned smugly, "Your mother did not expose you when you were young."

"To blindness?"

Kuruk grinned and said to Tahatan, "The wagon folk claim to be civilized, they do not even have healers."

Tahatan did not laugh. He analyzed Mary stoically before grunting, "We expose infants to your affliction to harden them up. Your mother failed you."

I knew that already, Mary thought. Suddenly, she comprehended his words. "You know what is happening to my eyes?"

Tahatan frowned, "Every Kuahtec knows of your affliction."

Mary blinked at him to elaborate.

The Kuahtec obliged. "We are taught that one day, Carefree Child walked the Great Field. They did not notice the other beings trying to take a share of the harvest. As they tromped through the rows of corn, they stepped on Caterpillar. Angry that they could not see him, he cursed the Carefree Child. Their eyes would pupate, just as Caterpillar would—until at last they could see him."

Kuruk shrugged, "A bit of mushroom powder will cure that up." He looked around, "Though I doubt it will rain enough to find one of those out here."

Mary blinked. She was already resigned to going blind. The fact that there *was* a cure and that it would elude her forever made her eyelid twitch. She shivered in the heat. She gulped and feigned strength, "Caterpillar has not taken my ears."

"You have a brave's spirit," Tahatan smiled. "Was your husband a soldier?"

Kuruk regarded her curiously. Other natives also turned to see her answer. *They would have lost many friends to a soldier.* "I am unmarried." She swallowed and looked straight ahead. She could feel the natives analyzing her.

Kuruk narrowed his gaze. "What is your name, leaky eyes?"

She had to lie. Few folks had favorable things to say about the Thorne and fewer still among the natives. Her father had conned the Kuahtec out of their homes, dammed the river, and let his son scalp Tlacon braves for sport. She concocted a fake name and back story. She would not need it.

Eli declared proudly, "This is Mary Anne Thorne."

Son of a bitch, Elijah Bingham.

Every native within earshot suddenly turned. Glares, grins, and unsavory looks settled upon Mary. Kuruk spat at her, turned, and muttered, "Great Mother is kind to punish your lot."

Mary wiped the spit off her chin. In truth, her family probably deserved that. Besides, there was no dignity in defending the deeds of dead sinners. She resigned to a penitent silence. She had to make friends, as uncouth as these ones might be.

"Y'all best keep walking!" snarled little Elijah. "Unless you want them riders to beat ya!"

"Eli!" Mary hissed. *There is a time for teeth and a time for tea,* came her mother's adage. "They already hate the name of Thorne. Don't make them hate the Bingham name, too."

Tahatan looked up. "Bingham? As in Laurent Bingham?"

"That's my grandaddy."

The Kuahtec's face brightened. "How is that old fool? Did he ever take my advice and plant pigweed?"

The child stared up at him suspiciously. "He died before I was born... But my daddy and I grow lots of pigweed. Hog potatoes, too."

Tahatan arced his head and cocked his brow, "That so?" He smiled. "I was the one that told your grandfather to switch his crops, you know?"

Elijah's jawbone swiveled back and forth. He sucked in his right cheek and chewed on it. He asked, warily, "Do you know my daddy?"

Tahatan put a hand to his chin, "Jamie, right?"

"Jessie."

"That's right..." Tahatan nodded. "He must have been around fifteen when I saw him last. How is h—" He frowned. "That was a thoughtless question, I am sorry."

Elijah declared, "He's on the trail right now. Probably only a day behind."

Tahatan smiled in the way adults do when a child says something blatantly false.

Kuruk snarled, "That's more than can be said for our chiefs."

Tahatan sighed. A weariness was in his voice as if words could rust. "Ignore him. He would have had us slaughtered by the army and our families penned in like cattle."

"And where are we going now?" Kuruk muttered. "To a slave pen."

The tension was palpable for only a minute. Then, with a bluntness only a fool or a child could possess—Elijah asked, "Why are you all here?"

Nobody answered. A few turned toward the Kuahtec named Tahatan. He coursed his fingers down his long, beaded hair.

Ever the impatient one, Elijah pressed, "You beat the 6th cavalry and disappeared without a trace!"

Tahatan nodded, "After fighting your army, the chief of the Tlacon had a vision of doom. Great Mother came to them and said that if our people stayed, the wagon folk would be feeding us scraps through iron bars."

Kuruk growled, "And so we fled! Even after our victory! To the edge of the Forlorn Hills. He thought it would be a safe refuge, that the wagon folk would never come in great number to harass us there."

"And they did not," Tahatan argued.

Two Lugal slavers barked at them. Nobody needed their words to be translated. Tahatan whispered, "How could the chiefs know the Lugal had awakened?"

"Awakened?" Mary asked. *The natives were always a superstitious people.*

Kuruk eyed the pair of slavers. When they rode out of earshot, he muttered, "The Lugal are an ancient tribe, more related to demons than to people. Their seers speak to gods through vile stones..."

The same stones that Collin found, Mary understood. *That the hunchback, Namru, wears as jewels.*

"The rocks induce madness in all who stare into their glittering depths," Tahatan said. He met Kuruk's oppressive glare, "They rarely leave their holdfast beyond the Mountains."

"But they do leave," Kuruk argued. He turned to Mary with a flared nostril and a crazed look. "When the spirits are angry, the Lugal march down the Forlorn Hills."

"Why have none of my people seen them?" Mary asked. "Why do only drunks and half-mad historians ever mention them?"

"They are a slumbering horde," said a native Mary had not noticed. His hair was whiter than snow and his face was as wrinkled as the cracked clay around them. "When my great, great grandfather was a boy, the Tlacon rode as far south as Snake Lake. Then, the Lugal came."

"They enslaved the valley and sacrificed its population to their gods."

"I've never heard of that," Elijah commented.

The elder eyed the cloudless sky, "The conquests of the Lugal are as ephemeral as a desert stream. They are locusts and when they are finished with a field—they retreat to their homeland. They have not been seen in the south or east in generations.

The white-haired native nodded. "We should never have made camp in the Hills. We woke the Lugal from their slumber. They fell upon us before we could get to our hors—" the elder began coughing.

"Peace, elder," Tahatan soothed. He looked at Mary sternly, "I only hope our people have gone back east. Better to war with greedy men than evil spirits."

Mary recalled a fat Lugal with a dagger in his neck. She pictured the blade plunged through Nerugal's heart. "They are no spirits," she glanced at a column of riders. "They bleed as easily as any man."

Kuruk and Tahatan both laughed.

Elijah snarled, "She killed two of them. With just a knife!"

Just one, Mary admitted to herself.

Tahatan's laughter ceased. "The Lugal fight with the swiftness of the pronghorn and the strength of a buffalo." He blinked at her, unconvinced.

Mary stared at him, eroding his self-assurance with as much ease as with any man.

Tahatan finally broke. He massaged his neck. "You are not joking?"

Elijah again spoke for Mary. "Mayor Thorne does not joke."

Kuruk and Tahatan glanced at one another. Kuruk rolled his eyes. Tahatan frowned at the numerous captors, "You will need more than a knife, now. Their bolts find us without aiming. Their spears are bottled hellfire waiting to lick your face."

Mary said nothing. She had no plans of murdering anyone. *I don't need to start a revolt. Not yet anyhow.*

They walked a mile or so more, though distance was difficult to discern. They used sunken vessels like signposts on a trail. They must have passed a dozen ships before the sand began to shimmer. Mary squinted. All the others seemed to shuffle and look up, but it took her longer to see. She almost asked Elijah to describe the object to her. *Best not look weak,* she decided.

So, she waited as the shimmer of light turned into a sliver of brown. Then, the details began to fill in. Two great walls on either side rose from the earth. At first, Mary thought they were entering another canyon. As they approached, however, a large hill appeared behind the walls. The sun was falling behind the top of that hill, casting a great shadow that engulfed the slaves.

To their right, another gang of slaves was marching toward the hill. They walked slower, were fewer in number, and were soon to intersect with her group. Mary stared at the pair of walls. They ran parallel to their approach and were not joined by a gate. About a third of the way up from the ground, a platform of solid rock branched off into separate, square rises. A ship was moored in the sand beside one of the platforms.

This was a harbor, Mary realized.

The fresh line of slaves intersected with the weary. One of the slaves stumbled, tripping the man in front of him. A Lugal rode toward them and whipped each of them severely. After ten lashes, the two men were kicked back into formation.

Like tributaries funneled into a river, their group merged with the other. They passed the slave who stumbled and Tahatan whispered, "Where did you come from?"

"The tomb."

"What is that?"

The slave did not look up. His voice did not inflect. "You will soon find out."

They crossed the threshold. She stared up at the docks as a fish once might have. She looked down. Innumerable shells were cemented into the ground. Mary felt small beside the massive piers. Though no ships were moored, a shanty of tents and awnings littered the harbor. Bits of mudbrick were plastered onto the finer, artisanal walls. The decorative reliefs were covered by haphazard clay dwellings. Within those dwellings, shriveled and grim figures watched them pass.

The walls around them eventually widened. They left the long harbor for a circular amphitheater. Mary glanced at her feet. The seashell sandstone remained. *This was once a harbor, too.* She glanced at the center of the amphitheater, where six piers jutted out in a symmetrical symbol. Three figures stood at the end of three piers.

The slavers dismounted. Tahatan was moved, along with all the Kuahtec. They were ushered to the right pier; a plump slave awaited them. Kuruk and the other Tlacon were sent to the central pier. The slave atop that pier looked as well-fed as any Lugal.

Meanwhile, Elijah and Mary were sent to the left pier. The figure that stood above them was a woman. A grey streak ran down her hair. Other than that fact, she seemed about Mary's age.

A great man ascended the central rise. He spoke something in the Lugal's language. It was the burly taskmaster who had sorted them all. He stared at them with proud contempt. He reveled in his own voice, holding one arm at his side and keeping the other aloft. He strode across the pier like it was a stage. When he finished, the taskmaster displayed his palms for all to see and took his leave.

When he had gone, the three figures began speaking. The right figurehead spoke in Kuahtec, the slave in the center spoke the Tlacon language. The woman above them, however, did not speak immediately. She stared at Mary strangely, searchingly.

Mary bowed her head. *Did I do something wrong?* Why was the woman so fixated on her?

333

The sun disappeared behind the hillside city, cloaking them in shade. The woman finally spoke, "You have come to the ancient city of Taruk. You shall be grateful to die in its bones. Today, you will be given a jug from which you will wash yourself and transport your water."

The woman paused. A slaver came and handed Elijah a massive jug which he could barely carry. He handed Mary a similar vessel. It was made of plain clay, ugly to look at, and had a chip on the lip.

"Do not lose your jug," continued the woman. "Do not break your jug. If you do, you will die and Foreman Wardu's lions will devour you."

"Tomorrow, you will be assigned a job. This will be your job until you perish. Do it well and be rewarded with food and rest. Perform your work poorly—or try to escape—and you will be fed to Foreman Wardu's..."

I know that voice. Mary gasped.

"What is it?" Elijah whispered.

"...These are the words of Foreman Wardu. Be dismissed." The speaker stared down at them for a second. She might have frowned, but she was too far away for Mary to tell. She pivoted as if to approach them. Then, she went rigid and hastily departed.

"Are you okay, Ms. Thorne?"

Mary tried to shake her head; she was too stunned to move. *How? How could she still be alive?* When she finally found her voice, it was airy and weak, "I know her. I know that woman."

Chapter 25

◇

"Prior historians were quick to judge Bingham for his poor judgment in leading his men into that tunnel. Contemporary analysis is somewhat more forgiving of him. The Prithewood Historical Society has even gone so far as to argue the Forlorn Trail was never going to lead Bingham to his children. In their view, his prior tragedies were necessary trials that would eventually mold Bingham into the figure we all know."

– The Ballad of Jessie Bingham, 3rd edition

They ran as far as they could. Though the three of them had made it out of the catacombs, Porfirio was barely clinging on. The poisonous dart had left a green bruise on his spine and the desert heat did them no favors. Before long, Jessie and Solomon had to take turns keeping him upright. At dusk, they came upon a parched grove.

They collapsed into the cool sand. Jessie met Porfirio's listless stare. Drool pooled below the man's mangled mustache.

"You tried to die on me," Jessie muttered.

"Might still," Porfirio whispered.

Jessie was too fatigued to scold him. He did not recall falling asleep. When he awoke, it was to a blissful forgetfulness. In that momentary amnesia, there was nothing wrong in the world. Indeed, he thought of nothing but the simple fact that he was now awake. Then, he made the mistake of looking up at the stars. The weight on his chest returned. His difficulty breathing resumed.

Jessie rolled onto his side, "Porf?" He stared at his friend's belly, waiting and hoping to see it rise. "Porf?" He began to panic.

Porfirio took a deep, gravelly breath. He smiled weakly, "Still here."

"Good." Jessie felt wedged between the terrible past and the uncertain future. He felt so immobilized, he knew he had to get up now or risk wasting away. He pushed himself up, groaning. A coat of sand slid off his sunburnt arms. He looked at his surroundings.

He figured the place was once an oasis. The only plants which grew now were a carpet of cacti. The new growth crawled among the bones of bare mesquite. Jessie patrolled the parched grove. He found Solomon sitting alone beside a whitened tree trunk.

"Solly," he acknowledged, not knowing what to say or how to say it.

"You ever wonder if you love someone enough?"

Jessie's first thought was of Porfirio, then his wife, and then himself. "I reckon so... Hiram?"

The younger brother nodded. "I always felt like I never loved him like other folks loved their brothers. When I said, *'Love ya,'* it were just words. I ain't felt that bond. At least, I thought I didn't. Now that he's gone though, I'm sure I did..." Solomon buried his face between his legs.

Jessie had no consoling words. He walked back to the center of the barren oasis and knelt by Porfirio. "Think you can walk?"

"Doubt it."

"Stand?"

Porfirio licked his chapped lips. "Unlikely."

Jessie sighed and sat beside him, "Porf, you son of a bitch. Why are you so insistent on dying?"

Porfirio coughed, "I been living so long for all the wrong reasons, Jessie." He looked up knowingly, shook his head, and closed his eyes. He took a deep breath. "Guess I'm giddy to die for the right."

Jessie had nothing to respond with. He tried to find something hopeful to say, but what use was it? Hope would not cure Porfirio's poisoned wound. Hope would not bring back the dead. Jessie stared at the old man's stomach, measuring the time between breaths.

Jessie's own body went into a wretched stasis. Hopeless thoughts churned in his mind like a water wheel of doom. Jessie fidgeted with his rifle. He wondered how long his body would take to decay, who or what might find his bones, and whether dehydration *needed* to be the way he died.

Jessie swallowed. He felt his organs clamoring for fuel, but he had nothing left to give. *Just as I have no medicine left to give the twins. Even if we find them, it would be a short reunion.* That realization gave him a brief catharsis. He turned his rifle and positioned the barrel under his chin. When the cold weapon touched his skin, he saw his wife.

She was hopeless, he recalled. *She had no other options.* He shivered, remembering how he held Glendolyn's hand at that moment. He had purged the visuals from his memory, but he still remembered how—after the deed—her fingers twitched.

Jessie burst into tears. He let out a mournful wail and dragged his nails through the sand. The harshest realization was not that he had failed, but that could not give up. He cursed himself softly, "God damn you..." He slammed his fist repeatedly in the sand. "Fuck, fuck, fuck!"

Something rustled behind a bony bush.

Jessie froze. The creatures from the catacombs had caught up to them at last. Solomon rose, patted his side, and swallowed. He had misplaced his revolver. Jessie nodded, blinking toward his discarded rifle.

Heavy breathing came from the shadows.

Jessie lunged for his rifle. He aimed at the sound. "I ain't in a mood to play games, creature."

A stick broke.

Jessie fired his weapon.

An animal yelped and jumped up. The figure was unmistakable. Four bony legs sprinted into view. With its ribs visible and its ears flopping, Jessie recognized the stray at once. He took a step toward it. That only made the animal flee faster. It darted into the desert.

"Mr. Bingham," Solomon craned his neck. "I reckon that was the same dog that saved my life, back in Silverfork."

How? Jessie asked himself. *It can't be the same animal.* He glanced at Porfirio and had a thought. It was a foolish thought, founded on fantasy more than rationale. And yet, he had to heed it. "Shit," he grunted. He began to nod, slowly at first and then rapidly. "Shit," he groaned. He broke into a sprint.

"Where are you going?" Solomon retrieved his revolver.

"Stay with Porfirio!" Jessie called back. "This ain't no happenstance."

"What if them things come back!"

Jessie did not respond. He had no plan. Just a lunatic's fancy and a hunch. He pursued the feral dog into the sprawling expanse.

Though both were malnourished, the dog was far faster. It ascended a tall dune just as Jessie had reached the bottom. He called out, "Hey, Boy. It's me. I was just startled, is all!" As if it understood, the dog was waiting at the top of the hill. Its tail was straight and its ears attentive. There was no doubt it was studying Jessie.

He studied it in turn, remembering Eridu's belief about stray dogs. He recalled the prince's words, *"A Shepherd of Umamu is meant to bring a wild man back to his humanity."*

Jessie toyed with his wedding ring. "I admit I were a bit unhinged, Boy."

The dog barked at him.

Jessie could not tell if the dog was being playful. He approached.

The stray tilted its head inquisitively. It retracted its back paw.

Knowing the dog could spring away at any second, Jessie stopped moving and crouched. "I'm sorry I shot at you, Boy. Ya heard me shoutin' earlier, right?" Its unique form of grumbling was a clearer 'yes' than he sometimes received from his children.

"I been tryin' to work on my anger. But, if I'm honest—I think there is a time and a place to feel it and if it ain't now—then you may as well call me savage." He blinked at the stray and snorted, "Funny. I used to have to justify myself to my children. Now I'm doin' it for a stray."

The dog grumbled at him and sharply exhaled. It turned its head in admonishment.

"Might be I'm a stray too," Jessie acknowledged. He sat on the sand. The pair watched one another before it was clear the animal was more patient than he was. Jessie patted his legs. "Come here, Boy."

The stray raised its butt into the air and stretched its forelimbs toward Jessie, pawing the sand as if it were swimming. It cooed cutely before suddenly slumping over.

"Playin' opossum, fella?" Jessie smiled. "Come here, Boy."

The dog blinked at him, tongue slipping slightly out its mouth. Then, it jumped up, barked, and trotted further into the desert.

He's toyin' with me. Jessie clicked his tongue. His knees cracked when he stood. His legs wobbled as he went down after the dog. A part of him thought it was a waste of energy to pursue the pup. Another part craved the creature's company. "Oye, Boy." He recalled his horse whom he had never properly named. Though his voice cracked, he offered, "You got a name? Rex? Rufus? Ruben? Oh, come here you little rascal!"

The dog turned and replied with a taunting bark. It skipped into a stand of organ pipe cactus.

Jessie awed the thick wall of spines. *The little fella led me right to food.* At his feet, prickly pears grew like weeds. On either side, except for a small opening in the stand, columnar cacti grew over twelve feet tall. Jessie wished he had gloves, tongs, and a fire. While the prickly pears would do nicely, it was the pitahayas growing atop the organ pipe that made him salivate. They were larger than any back home, bright red, and perfectly ripe.

Jessie's stomach roared. He rotated ninety degrees and sucked in his (admittedly shrunken) gut. He side-stepped the sharpened spines and entered a sprawling maze of cacti. He saw the dog's wagging tail before anything else. He stepped into the open. Suddenly, he could not catch his breath. His heart plummeted. Jessie could not move.

A man on a horse stared down at him. Beside him was the stray, looking happily at the rider.

Jessie blinked at the man. Dozens of men stood behind him. Dozens of hands drifted toward weapons. Jessie's legs shook. His hands trembled. Sweat leaked down his head. Encamped in that clearing were perhaps a hundred natives. However, these were not the Lugal Jessie had grown used to. No, these were a type of native he had seen before—though not for a long, long while.

Tlacon, he gulped.

The rider dismounted and measured Jessie up. He was just as tall, but his armor made him seem like a giant. His helmet was made from a bison's skull. The horns made him resemble a satyr. A great pack jostled behind him, decorated with many great eagle feathers. To Jessie, he looked like a harpy. The man's face was tattooed extensively; his eyes were obscured.

The Tlacon stared at him, unmoving.

Jessie contemplated running. By that point, however, it was too late. A man had silently come up from the side. Jessie had only enough time to see that he was Kuahtec. The beads in his hair whipped his lip as a fist floored him. Before Jessie knew it, his hands were behind his back and he was being brought to the center of the clearing.

Jessie's captors kicked his back and pushed him to the ground. "Crawl," said the Kuahtec which had punched him. He did so, moving slowly toward a tall teepee. He paused at the entrance. Feeling the Kuahtec's moccasin behind him, he hurried into the dwelling.

The Tlacon warrior was within. He removed his bison helmet and placed it on a deerskin rug. He crossed his legs and sat beside his helmet. The stray dog lay beside him, panting happily. Jessie took slow, quiet breaths. *Those hooves we followed were not the 6ᵗʰ cavalry.* At the far end of the teepee, sitting aloof, was a woman. She quietly knitted, apathetic to the proceedings.

"Crawl," said the Kuahtec again.

Jessie thought the native meant for him to crawl, but the Tlacon raised a hand, halting him. From behind came a scoff, a kick, and a groan. A man fell into the teepee, barely able to catch himself before he hit his head. He wheezed and rose beside Jessie.

"Eridu!" Jessie gasped.

"So you know this blood-thief," the Tlacon spoke. No question was in his voice.

Jessie eyed the prince of the Erintul. His face was bloodied and his body was bruised. Eridu had not been taken as quickly or as painlessly as he had. "I do."

The Kuahtec took a seat beside the other native. "Our enemies in the east conspire with those in the west. We should pin them to the cacti and let the coyotes eat them."

The Tlacon folded his bottom lip over his upper and contemplated. He rolled his right fingers over his left knuckles. "Perhaps." He leaned forward. "But not until we introduce ourselves." He raised his brow and waited for Jessie.

"My name is, uh, Jessie Bingham."

The Kuahtec made a face and almost started to speak. His face wrinkled with even more contempt. He deferred to the other man.

"I am Chief Hotah, Jessie Bingham." The Tlacon gestured to his compatriot, "This is Chief Tacano of the Kuahtec." The Tlacon took a deep breath and his voice lowered. "I hope it is self-evident that it does not behoove you to lie to us."

"I try not to lie as a general principle, Chief."

"Good," the Tlacon replied. "If you would be so kind as to prove that to us." He straightened his posture and nodded at Eridu. "This one will not respond to us. Does the Lugal know your language?"

Jessie frowned at the prince. *It is best to tell the truth, right now.* He nodded at the chiefs.

Tacano the Kuahtec hissed, "I knew the blood-thief was a liar."

Hotah calmed his friend with a wave of his hand. With his other, he began petting the dog. "One truth does not make trust, Mr. Bingham. Now, tell me: what is one of the wagon folk doing with this..." Hotah's face wrinkled in contempt.

Jessie was quiet. Though the man wanted to hear the truth, some forms of honesty were harsher to hear than others. He started from the beginning, hoping to gain their trust by fostering some sympathy. "It seems so long ago, but it was only a few weeks. This man was among a band of warriors that raided my town."

"What town is that?" Hotah interrupted.

"Belford."

Tacano grunted.

Jessie continued, "They burned the Big House to the ground. They took the mayor and several others captive. Among them were my children."

"You look like a child yourself," remarked Chief Hotah. "They must be young."

"Eight years old," Jessie answered.

Hotah leaned back and inhaled. He looked with a raised brow at Chief Tacano. "Two truths?"

"Two truths," replied the Kuahtec Chief.

"Now for three," Hotah glanced at Eridu. "Why do you show happiness at seeing a Lugal?"

Jessie need not lie. "He is my guide."

Hotah's stare grew stern and unwavering.

Jessie glanced at Eridu, whose own, bruised voice practically screamed, *Be careful.* Jessie eyed the beaten man as he recounted, "This one was captured by our sheriff."

"Crawford Biggs?" Hotah inquired, astutely.

"Unfortunately, yes," Jessie explained. "He wanted to sell him, Eridu, to a freakshow."

Tacano noted, "It is not like your sheriff to be merciful. Or kind. Too cruel for even your army."

"That is true," Jessie acknowledged. *The sheriff's infamy is greater than I guessed.* "Biggs refused to go after our captives. He only wanted to enri—"

Hotah interrupted to infer the rest of the story, "And so you were dishonest in your actions."

Jessie figured it would benefit him to be frank. "I robbed the sheriff's stagecoach, yes."

Tacano continued smirking as he turned slyly toward his fellow chief. After a long moment of stoic silence, the chief of the Tlacon grunted. "That must have been quite the sight." He asked, "Three truths, Tacano?"

"Three truths," the Chief of the Kuahtec agreed.

"And yet," Hotah stood up. He walked toward them. "Three truths does not an honest *pair* make. We have heard one lie out of you, blood-thief." Hotah knelt before the prince of the Erintul and looked down upon him. "Do not add another."

At that, the chief walked to the other side of the teepee. "Why did we find only you, blood-thief? Why did we not find your friend in that canyon?"

Eridu took his time answering. Whether out of contempt or a brave resolve bordering stupidity, he simply said, "You did not look hard enough."

Tacano shot to his feet, but Hotah laughed. "I deem that was a truth, my friend."

"An arrogant one," growled the Kuahtec.

"Yet no harm done to humble men." He peered at the man. "Why did you cross the Hills?"

"For slaves," Eridu answered quickly.

Hotah took a deep, loud breath. "Is that entirely true, blood-thief? Is that why *you* raid the lands of free people?"

Eridu waited almost overlong. The teepee grew hot with suspense. The tension was heard as subdued breathing, as a faint breeze. The dog beside Hotah whined.

"He is false," Tacano snarled. "He deserves t—"

"I came to see my grandmother."

Tacano chortled as one does when hearing something one does not want to believe. "A Lugal grandmother in Belford?" He shook his head, "Not only a liar, but a bad one, too."

"It is not a lie," Eridu glared.

Hotah was looking at Jessie and not the prince when he deemed, "Two truths, Tacano. Two truths."

The Kuahtec chief glared at the Erintul. He spat at his feet and sat back down. "One lie remains."

"So it does," Hotah acknowledged. "Eridu the Lugal. How many men do you lead from Belford?"

"Four."

Tacano snorted, bemused. "We only sought to farm and fish and the wagon folk rode against us with an army. A clear lie."

"That is not yet clear to me," Hotah stated. "For I remember Crawford Biggs as a scheming, mean sort of lawman. If the mayor *was* taken, as they claim, I would think he'd sooner abandon his folk than free them." He looked at Jessie, "Are there *truly* only five in your band?"

"No," he answered reluctantly.

Their eyes narrowed in judgment. The muscles in Tacano's neck cracked.

"But Eridu would not know this," Jessie elaborated. His body grew cold recounting the tale, "We were five only a day ago. When we saw he was missing, we searched the ruined city."

The person at the end of the teepee looked up from their knitting. They turned and Jessie realized that the person belonged—at least at one time— to the so-called wagon folk. Their face was pale, their hair was thin. And despite the dress, their face was markedly masculine. They looked to be the oldest person in the teepee, and perhaps the camp.

Hotah lowered his voice. Footsteps shuffled outside the teepee as a growing audience tried to eavesdrop. "That ravine seemed the perfect spawning ground for bad energy. Our two-spirit bid us go around." He looked over at the person knitting. "They said a watchful plague seeped from that deep city."

Jessie admitted, "Eridu warned us against that route, too. But we did not listen. Then, when he went missing..." Jessie's voice cracked as he recounted his failure, "I—I saw a trail of blood. A body was dragged. I thought he was taken into this, this tunnel. Beneath the temple."

Eridu's eyes widened with amazement; his voice trembled with dread. "You went into the temple catacombs... and lived?"

"*I* lived, yes. But we were ambushed in the darkness." Jessie's throat narrowed, allowing only a whisper, "They were—" He shuddered.

The two-spirit raised their head, nodding slowly to themselves.

"Lugal?" Hotah inquired.

"No," Jessie knew. "The Lugal are strange, but they are men. These were like men with animal minds. They were shadows."

None spoke until Eridu, in a deep and gravelly voice, explained, "They are the Kisutag, Jessie. After the city's fall, they lingered and infested the dark places of that ravine. It is why I argued against going that way."

"And I should have listened," Jessie bit back, suddenly quite angry. "I did not." He threw up his hands while his head bobbed as if from nausea. "We lost one in the catacombs. Another is dying at this moment! Please, if you would go with me. That dog, he—" Jessie cut himself off, feeling they would certainly call him a liar if he told the truth. "Please, help me save my friend. He has been poisoned."

An owl hooted. An eavesdropping native coughed. Tacano glared at them both; Hotah leaned forward and rested his chin on his hands.

"I have heard enough," Tacano stood. "Honest or not, it is a risk to keep them alive."

Hotah nodded. He did not get up. He glanced at the dog beside him; his lip stretched toward his cheek in contemplation.

Tacano grew impatient. "We cannot spare them, Hotah. The wagon folk drove us from the plains. If it weren't for—" He clearly had something to say, though only an exasperated groan escaped him. Tacano ground his teeth. He pivoted, with one foot toward the other chief and one at Eridu. His hand was on a hatchet. "The blood thieves took our families. They are our enemies."

Jessie suppressed the instinct to run. He glanced at Eridu. The prince stared pensively at Tacano, awaiting his hatchet with calm indifference.

Chief Hotah petted the dog as he rebuked, "The Tlacon and Kuahtec were once enemies. Now, our confederation rides as one."

Chief Tacano lowered his proud head and let his hands fall to his side, "A meager band of exiles in a cursed land."

Hotah clasped his knees and rose. The eavesdroppers on the other side of the teepee scattered. Hotah stood a head taller than Tacano. Jessie quickly counted the visible horse tattoos. They were arranged like a chain around his neck. *He has broken thirteen horses.*

"Sunka likes this one."

Tacano rolled his eyes at the dog, "Sunka likes everyone."

"True," Hotah grinned at the animal. "But something was strange about this night." Hotah rubbed his chin. "You have met Sunka before."

"Twice. He saved a man's life." *And might again, if they do not kill me first.* He looked at the emaciated animal and stated, "He belongs to you?" *We must have been trailing them all this time.*

Tacano muttered, "Nothing *belongs* to anyone. Though your people fail to see that."

"Enough, Tacano!" Hotah ordered. He shot a weary look at his fellow chief before agreeing, "Sunka roams like any Tlacon. He is a free animal that chooses his companions." He stepped forward.

"Hotah…" The Kuahtec chief seethed. "If you are acting off another vision, I beg you to listen to reason instead."

The Tlacon chief ignored his compatriot, "Rise, Jessie Bingham."

He did as he was told and bowed his head.

"Look me in the eye."

Jessie looked.

"You have suffered and lost much. But it seems the spirits are not done with you." Sunka trotted toward them, licked Jessie's leg, and trotted out of the teepee.

Hotah opened his arms like a bear and clasped Jessie's shoulders, "And the spirits are not done with our people, either."

"Hotah!" Tacano whispered. "This is unwise."

"He is an honest man committing violence for honest reasons. Same as us. And we have so few braves as it is." Hotah raised his brow as one might raise a shield, waiting for Tacano's arguments. The Kuahtec provided none and so, the Tlacon turned to Jessie. "Ride with us and one day soon, you may see your children again."

Jessie glanced at Eridu, "And my friends? My guide?"

"*He* is an odd case," Hotah strode toward the prince and stared down at him. "I think, in another life, we might have been friends."

Tacano fidgeted at his side. The hatchet swayed, tapping against his thigh.

"But *he* has no common goal I can see. That makes him a danger to us all."

Tacano took out his hatchet and strode toward the Erintul.

Hotah extended an arm, blocking the chief's advance. "We only know this land from legend, Tacano. His information will be useful for us."

Eridu and Jessie glanced at one another. The prince nodded slightly and cleared his throat. He extended his open palms, "Thank you, Chief."

Hotah lowered his chin in a curt nod. "Tacano, send a healer out with your braves. Follow Sunka and bring their wounded to camp."

Tacano ground his teeth, "Whatever you say, Hotah." He stormed out of the teepee.

"Will my friends be, uh—" Jessie did not want to finish his question.

Hotah sighed. "Do not worry. He will treat your wounded honorably," he knelt and pulled Eridu up. "He is right to be wary. His brother, Tahatan, was taken in one of your raids."

"I will do what I can to make things right," Eridu promised.

"I want to believe you," Hotah replied. He lowered his voice, "But as your early lie weighs heavy against your later truths... Tell me, Eridu of the Lugal, would your people trust you if you let an enemy captive walk freely?"

Eridu glanced behind, "Such a decision would endanger you. Betrayal would be a constant worry, Chief."

Hotah smiled, "*That* is the truth." He stepped toward the exit, "I think we will all feel much safer once you are tied up."

Jessie had been waiting to ask a simple question. He caught up to Hotah, "Chief, wait."

Both Eridu and Hotah stopped and looked back at him. The Tlacon folded his hands in front of his waist and stood tall. "Speak, Jessie Bingham."

"You got the truth from me. From Eridu."

Hotah raised his brow, "You will not be getting three truths from me."

"That's fine," Jessie acknowledged. "I need only one."

Hotah's stare was piercing. "One truth."

Jessie took a deep breath. "Where are we going?"

Hotah frowned. "Is it not obvious?" He ducked through the exit of the teepee and held the flap for Eridu and Jessie. The bright night was still young and many folk moved about the camp. Some natives gathered around campfires. Others rode through the cactus thicket, rifles in their hands. A handful of older boys worked together at a grindstone, sharpening their hatchets. A woman slept with a baby at one breast and a pistol at the other.

Hotah whistled and a massive steed came to his side. He climbed atop the saddle and retrieved his rifle. The firearm was bedecked with feathers. At the butt of the rifle dangled the fleshy remains of an enemy's trigger finger. The chief of the Tlacon eyed the west. "We are going to war."